continued on next page . . .

THE BRIDE TRILOGY

THE SHERBROOKE BRIDE • THE HELLION BRIDE • THE HEIRESS BRIDE

"Coulter is excellent at portraying the romantic tension between her heroes and heroines, and she manages to write explicitly, but beautifully, about sex as well as love."

—*Milwaukee Journal*

THE VIKING TRILOGY

LORD OF HAWKFELL ISLAND • LORD OF RAVEN'S PEAK • LORD OF FALCON RIDGE

"Coulter's characters quickly come alive and draw the reader into the story. You root for the good guys and hiss for the bad guys. When you have to put the book down for a while, you can hardly wait to get back and see what's going on."

—*The Sunday Oklahoman*

THE LEGACY TRILOGY

THE WYNDHAM LEGACY • THE NIGHTINGALE LEGACY • THE VALENTINE LEGACY

"Delightful . . . brimming with drama, sex, and colorful characters. . . . Her witty dialogue and bawdy, eccentric characters add up to an engaging, fan-pleasing story."

—*Publishers Weekly*

The
SCOTTISH
BRIDE

CATHERINE COULTER

JOVE BOOKS, NEW YORK

This is a work of fiction. Names, characters, places, and incidents are
either the product of the author's imagination or are used fictitiously,
and any resemblance to actual persons, living or dead, business
establishments, events, or locales is entirely coincidental.

THE SCOTTISH BRIDE

A Jove Book / published by arrangement with
the author

PRINTING HISTORY
Jove edition / January 2001

The Penguin Putnam Inc. World Wide Web site address is
http://www.penguinputnam.com

ISBN: 0-515-12993-3

A JOVE BOOK®
Jove Books are published by The Berkley Publishing Group,
a division of Penguin Putnam Inc.,
375 Hudson Street, New York, New York 10014.
JOVE and the "J" design
are trademarks belonging to Penguin Putnam Inc.

PRINTED IN THE UNITED STATES OF AMERICA

10 9 8 7 6 5 4 3 2 1

To Anton,
who's a cracker.

—C. C.

1

Northcliffe Hall
August 15, 1815

TYSEN SHERBROOKE GAZED out the wide windows onto the east lawn of Northcliffe, his brow furrowed thoughtfully. "As a matter of fact," he said, "I did know that I was in line for the title, Douglas, but I was so far down on the list of rightful heirs that I never imagined it could actually happen. Indeed, I haven't even thought of it for a good decade. The last grandson, Ian, he's really dead?"

"Yes, just six months before the old man died. It seems he fell off a cliff into the North Sea. The solicitor seems to think Ian's death is what shoved Old Tyronne into the grave. Of course, he was eighty-seven, so he probably didn't need much of a push. That means that you, Tysen, are now Baron Barthwick. It's an old barony, dating back to the early fifteenth century, when men of importance were barons. Earls were later additions, upstarts for a very long time."

"I remember Kildrummy Castle, of course," Tysen said.

"It's right on the coast, below Stonehaven, overlooking the North Sea. It's a beautiful place, Douglas, not immensely tall with no windows like the old medieval Scottish castles, but newer, built in the late seventeenth century, I believe. I remember being told that the original castle was destroyed in one of their interminable clan fights. The new one, it's got gables and chimney stacks— a good dozen of them—and four round angle-turrets. The lower floor of the castle is closed off by the building itself and attached to a curtain wall that encloses a very large inner courtyard." Tysen paused a moment, seeing everything from a younger perspective, and his eyes glistened a bit as he said, "Ah, but the countryside, Douglas, it is untamed and wild, as if God gazed down upon it, decided against our modern buildings and roads, and left it untouched. There are more crags than you can begin to count, and deep-rutted paths, just one narrow, winding road, really, that leads to the castle. There's a steep, rocky hill that goes down to a beach, and wildflowers, Douglas, wildflowers everywhere."

This was quite a poetic outpouring from his staid, very serious and literal brother. Douglas was pleased that Tysen not only remembered Barthwick so well but also appeared to admire it immensely. He said, "I remember your going there with Father when you were—what? About ten years old?"

"That's right. It was one of the best times of my life."

Douglas wasn't at all surprised. It was unusual that any of them had ever had their father completely to themselves. Whenever Douglas had his father's full attention, he'd felt blessed by the Almighty. He still missed the former earl, an honorable man who had loved his children and managed to tolerate his difficult wife with a wry smile and a shrug of his shoulders. Douglas sighed. So much change. "Since you are now the holder of an ancient medieval barony, I suppose I shall have to let you sit above the salt."

Tysen didn't laugh, but perhaps he did smile, just a bit. He hadn't laughed much since he'd decided to become a man of God when he was seventeen. Douglas remembered their brother Ryder telling Tysen that of all the men placed on this benighted earth, it was a vicar who should have the greatest sense of humor, since God obviously did. Just look at all the absurdities that surrounded us. Hadn't Tysen ever observed the mating ritual of peacocks, for example? And just look at their buffoon of a prince regent, who was so fat he had to be hoisted in and out of his bathtub? Ah, but Tysen was serious, his sermons high-minded, stark in their message that God was a stern taskmaster and not apt to easily overlook a man's lapses. Tysen was now thirty-one years old. He certainly had the look of the Sherbrookes—tall, well built, brown hair streaked with blond, and Sherbrooke eyes the color of a summer sky. Douglas was the changeling, with his jet-black hair and dark eyes.

But Tysen didn't have his siblings' love of life, their seemingly inborn boundless joy, their belief that the world was a very fine place indeed.

"Sitting above the salt—I haven't heard that phrase in a very long time," Tysen said. "I suppose I must travel to Scotland and see what's what." He sighed. "There is always so much that demands my time here, but Great Uncle Tyronne deserves an heir who will at least see that the estate is run properly—not that I have much experience in that area."

"You know I will assist you, Tysen. You need but ask. Would you like me to accompany you to Barthwick?"

Tysen shook his head. "No, Douglas, but I thank you. It is something that is my responsibility. I have an efficient curate who can assume my duties for a while. You remember Samuel Pritchert, don't you?"

Oh, yes, no way to forget that dour prig. Douglas merely nodded.

"No, I will go by myself. All the heirs dead. Douglas, I remember all the cousins. So many boys. All of them are really dead?"

"Yes, a great shame. Disease, accidents, duels, a case of too much revelry. As I said, the last heir, Ian Barthwick, evidently fell off a cliff into the North Sea. The solicitor wasn't specific about exactly how it happened."

"There must have been six boys to inherit, all of them before me. And that's why, as I remember, Great Uncle Tyronne set me up as an heir. It amused him to see it done legally—to place an English boy in line for an ancient Scottish barony. Naturally he never expected that it would come about."

"And now it's yours, Tysen. His jest came back to hit him in the face. The castle, the rich grazing lands, more sheep than you can count even when you're trying to fall asleep—all of it belongs to an Englishman. And many of the crofters and tenants are fishermen, so that means that even during bad times, no one starves. It isn't a wealthy holding, but it is substantial. I understand that Great Uncle Tyronne didn't believe in clearances. None of that has ever been done on Barthwick land."

"Good for him," Tysen said. "It's a pernicious practice, Douglas, dragging people off land that they've farmed or raised sheep on for hundreds of years." He paused a moment, then said, "I suppose that my son Max is now the heir to the Barony of Barthwick. I do wonder what he will have to say to that."

He would probably quote some Latin, Douglas thought. His brother's elder boy was very intelligent, quiet, a scholar, perhaps even more serious than his father had been at his age. He had been named after their grandfather, the only scholar in the entire line of Sherbrookes, so far as Douglas knew.

"When you leave, Tysen, bring the children here, and Alex and I will look after them. Your Meggie can whip not only her brothers into shape but her cousins as well. Heathens, the both of them."

Tysen did smile then, a slow, calm smile. "She is amazing, isn't she, Douglas?"

"Just like Sinjun at her age. Meggie will rule your household, Tysen, if you're not careful."

Tysen looked appalled. "No, really, not at all like Sinjun, Douglas. Perhaps she looks like Sinjun, but a hoyden like Sinjun? Oh, no. I remember Sinjun could drive you to Bedlam with her antics. Oh, no, Meggie is much more restrained, much more a little lady than Sinjun ever was."

Douglas said, "Do you remember how Father threw up his hands when Sinjun kicked Tommy Maitland in his backside and he went flying off a cliff? Thank God he didn't break his neck."

Tysen said, "And that time she sewed all your trouser legs together? I can still hear you yelling, Douglas. No, Meggie isn't like Sinjun was. She's very obedient. I've never had a day's worry with her." Suddenly a slight furrow appeared between his brows. "Well, perhaps she does have our two servants at her beck and call. Perhaps also the boys do obey her quickly, usually without fuss. Then there's Cook, who actually bakes dishes just for Meggie. But it is her sweetness, her patience, that gains her the love and obedience of all those at the vicarage, even her brothers."

It was difficult to restrain himself, but Douglas didn't roll his eyes. Was his brother completely blind? Evidently so. Meggie was careful around her father, the chit was that smart. He said, "I remember I boxed Sinjun's ears so many times I lost count."

Tysen said, "I did that once. As I remember, I was thirteen and she was nine and she had tied the tail of my favorite kite around Corkscrew's neck—you remember Corkscrew, don't you, Douglas? What a dog! He was the very best. In any case, then Sinjun throws a stick and off goes Corkscrew, and believe it or not, that kite lifted off the ground, before it got tangled up in one of Mother's rosebushes and got ruined. I smacked her before she managed to run and hide from me." Then, very suddenly, Tysen managed a very big smile. "I hadn't realized—I will see Sinjun and Colin. It's been too long." He rose and stretched. "Well, I suppose there is no time like the present. Samuel Pritchert will take good care of all our people. Thank you for taking the children, Douglas. I believe I will leave on Wednesday. I daresay I can write a good dozen sermons in my head, it will take so long to get there."

Meggie quickly ran down the long hallway when she heard her father moving toward the door of Uncle Douglas's estate room. She ran right into her aunt Alex. "Goodness, Meggie, are you all right?" Alex grasped her niece's arms and eyed her closely. "You were listening, weren't you? Oh dear, I did too at your age. Your aunt Sinjun still does. What is going on, Meggie?"

"Father is going to Scotland on Wednesday. He's leaving the boys here."

Alex raised a brow. "Oh, yes, the new title. It's right that he should go. And what about you?"

"Oh," Meggie said, giving her aunt a very wicked smile. "I'm going with him. He needs me, you know."

"You think he will take you?"

"Oh, yes," Meggie said. "Is there anything I can do for you, Aunt Alex?"

Alex Sherbrooke just stared down at her niece and lightly touched her fingertips to her lovely hair. Tysen didn't have a chance, she thought. She sent Meggie up to the schoolroom to have luncheon with her brothers and cousins. They were evidently holding special races, using the tables and desks for obstacles, their tutor, Mr. Murphy, had told her as he'd mopped the sweat off his brow. Alex knew that Meggie could bring them back to order. She was still smiling when Tysen and Douglas came out of the library.

"Hollis just told me that luncheon is served," she said.

"Indeed, my lord," Hollis said, giving Tysen a rare smile. "The title and dignities will suit you well."

"Thank you, Hollis."

Alex said, "Is the new and very worthy Baron Barthwick ready for some of Cook's thin-sliced ham?"

"How very odd that sounds," Tysen said thoughtfully, then he added in a very serious voice, "And be sure that I am seated above the salt cellars, Alex. I am now that important."

She laughed, as did Douglas, but Tysen didn't. He merely acknowledged with a slight smile that he'd said something that could be construed as moderately witty, then asked about his nephews' health.

"Their health is splendid," Douglas said. "It's their damned good looks that are driving me to the brink of madness. Both James and Jason will slay the women, Tysen. By God, they are only ten years old—the same age as little Meggie—and already all the local girls are showing up on our doorstep at all hours, presenting colorful bouquets of flowers wrapped up in pink ribbons for Alex, presenting me with homemade slippers, even plates of tarts that they claim they baked with their own small hands—anything to bring themselves to the twins' attention. Most of the time, they have no idea which twin is which, so you can imagine how many pranks the boys play on them." Douglas shook his head, then added, "Thank God, so far the boys take it in stride, but it's nonetheless nauseating and portends bad things for the future."

Tysen said as he seated himself at the small dining table, "I suppose they do greatly resemble your sister, Alex." He added matter-of-factly, "It's true that she is the most beautiful woman I have ever seen. Isn't it strange that the twins should look so much like her and not like you or Douglas?"

"Tony, damn his eyes, just laughs and laughs whenever that is pointed out," Douglas said and handed Tysen a plate of Cook's famous thin-sliced ham, sprinkled with her renowned Secret Recipe that always had badly crushed basil leaves in it. "At least Tony and Melissande's children look like we could be their parents, so that's something. Now, Tysen, let me tell you the rest of what Great Uncle Tyronne's solicitor wrote."

2

Eden Hill House, the Vicarage
Glenclose-on-Rowan
August 16, 1815

"No, MEGGIE, AND that's an end to it."

But it wasn't, of course. He realized suddenly that he was now seeing Meggie with Douglas's eyes. Another Sinjun? Sinjun had driven him beyond sanity when he'd been young, and then he'd tried to ignore her because life had become serious for him and Sinjun was always mocking and teasing him. She laughed a lot, and she'd called him a prig when she was thirteen, which was probably true. He sighed and looked down at his daughter, waiting, but not for long.

"Please, Papa, it's more than necessary."

Ah, that serious little face, that intense voice. He felt himself weakening and stiffened his back.

"You need me. You know what a help I can be to you, truly. You won't even know I am there. I'll just help you all the time and then disappear."

Reverend Tysen Sherbrooke, a devout man of God, a man who loved his children, who seldom ever had a cross word no matter how far off the path of righteousness a member of his congregation had strayed, said yet again, "Please, no more, Meggie. I will not tell you again. You will not come with me. You will go to Northcliffe Hall with your brothers. Don't you understand? I'm going to Scotland. I do not know what to expect. I was there years ago and all I remember is rutted paths, sheep everywhere, and barren stretches that went on and on until you wanted to collapse. It is probably still barbaric, with outlaws littering the roads—if there even are roads. I don't remember any. I truly have no idea what I will find. I want you here, safe with your aunt and uncle."

Meggie, as reasoned and calm as Sister Mary MacRae, the only Catholic nun in the area, said, "Aunt Sinjun lives in Scotland. It can't be savage, Papa. If there weren't any roads when you were there, there will be now. Aunt Sinjun would have had them built. We don't need roads, anyway. We will ride. It will be wonderful. You need me."

Tysen stared down at this child of his loins, at this wondrous creature who was, for the very first time, bringing back more memories of Sinjun, memories that he now realized had made him many times want to strangle her. Ah, when Sinjun had tied the tail of his kite around Corkscrew's neck. He realized now as he looked down at his daughter that he'd rather exaggerated a bit to Douglas about Meggie's placid self. Had he truly said she was obedient, gentle? Maybe not. If he'd ever really believed that, he'd been blind. He'd been a doting papa, not recognizing what was right under his nose. Actually, he realized in that instant that Meggie could be gentle and obedient or she could be utterly outrageous, like Sinjun.

He just didn't want her to be like her mother, Melinda

Beatrice. He immediately closed his eyes against such a wicked, disloyal thought. No, Melinda Beatrice had been a sainted woman, perhaps just a bit on the unctuous side, but that wasn't something to bring despair, perhaps just an occasional sigh when a parishioner's face tightened after she'd offered well-meant advice. He shook his head and looked down into his own Sherbrooke blue eyes, Sinjun's Sherbrooke blue eyes as well, and touched his fingers gently to Meggie's soft, Sherbrooke light hair. "Why, Meggie, do you believe I need you?"

She looked at him straight on and said, "You are far too nice, Papa. You are too good. You don't see the wickedness in people. Sometimes you don't really see people at all. Your thoughts are too elevated, perhaps too refined and aloof. You need me because I will keep bad people away from you. I will keep females away from you who would try to make you love them and marry them. I will—"

He laid his finger on her lips. He didn't see wickedness? His thoughts were too elevated? Too refined? Was that truly what she believed? He supposed that when he'd asked her why he needed her he'd expected her to fold her tent somewhat, at least retreat to embrace another argument. He shook his head at her, bemused. He didn't recognize wickedness? He was too nice? Blessed heaven, he was easy prey to females who would try to trap him into marriage? He said, with just a touch of irony in his voice, "I appreciate your belief in me, Meggie, although I do not know what I have done to make you believe me such a weakling. As for the ladies, I promise you that I am always on my guard."

"But Miss Strapthorpe nearly nabbed you, I heard her talking of it to one of her friends. She said she was this close to having you. Just one kiss, she said, and you would feel bound to marry her. Then there was that time she trapped you in the vestry."

"But I didn't kiss Miss Strapthorpe, and I managed to escape the vestry with my clerical collar still around my neck."

"Papa, was that a jest?"

"Certainly not, Meggie."

"I didn't think it could be, since you don't waste your time in anything frivolous. Now, Papa, I know you didn't kiss Miss Strapthorpe—if you had, she would be my stepmother now, and let me tell you, Papa, that would have made even Max turn green around his collar. As for Leo, I'll wager he would have run away from home."

"Enough about Miss Strapthorpe. I am a grown man, Meggie. I can see to myself. I promise not to bring back a stepmama to you and the boys."

"But—"

He touched his finger to her mouth again. "Now, sweetheart, for the last time, you will not accompany me. You will remain here. I swear to you that I will be on the alert for wicked men and for females out to nab me. No, don't say anything more. You will not strain my patience. It is not appropriate for a man of God to yell at his child. It would cause consternation if it got out."

Meggie grabbed his hand. "Papa, take me with you, please. Wicked people do abound. One man alone cannot see all of them or hear them creeping up on him. And ladies in particular know how to creep, I—"

He marveled at her determination, her seemingly endless string of arguments.

Her small hand was now on his sleeve, tugging. A beautiful hand, he thought inconsequentially, long fingers, graceful. Sinjun's hands, not her mother's. "I haven't seen Aunt Sinjun and Uncle Colin for three years, not since they came to London and we traveled there to visit them.

I want to see Phillip and Dahling. I don't really care about Jocelyn and Fletcher. They're still just babies."

Tysen just shook his head again, seamed his mouth tight so he wouldn't say something that could hurt her feelings, and made for the door. He said over his shoulder, "Mrs. Priddie will help you and your brothers pack. You will leave in two days. I am leaving tomorrow morning, very early. Obey me, Meggie."

He heard some grumbling as he closed the door behind him, but he couldn't make out the words. Meggie was ten years old, perhaps on the verge of turning thirty. No, older than that. He was thirty-one, and surely she had passed that ripe age. He realized now that his brother Douglas was right. Meggie was just like Sinjun had been at her age—intense and carefree by turns, always smiling, always giving orders to her brothers, wanting to take care of everyone. And stubborn—so stubborn that she made up her mind and simply plowed ahead. And she could be demanding and unreasonable, and if she continued with this, then he would perhaps have to discipline her, but he didn't want to.

He'd spanked her just once, last year, something he doubted he would ever forget, but Mrs. Priddie had told him that what Meggie had done deserved for her to be locked in her room on bread and water for a year. He'd been afraid to ask her, but Mrs. Priddie rolled it right out of her mouth without hesitation. "She tied the sexton's bell rope to Molly the goat, Reverend Sherbrooke. Then she carefully placed half a dozen old boots all around that dratted goat—who wanted all of them, naturally, since she had also poured some porridge in each boot. The bell rang and rang because Molly had to have all that porridge. Oddly enough, it nearly made a melody. Sexton Peters nearly croaked of apoplexy on the spot." Then Mrs. Priddie had lowered her voice. "I heard him, Reverend Sherbrooke. I heard him, and he cursed a blue streak. You must speak to him. It was not at all what a sexton should be saying."

But Tysen imagined that his sexton's ire had reached such heights that the bad words had erupted out of his mouth without his consent. Tysen had spanked his daughter, and she hadn't cried, not a single tear. However, his guilt, when she had just looked up at him, her blue eyes shining with tears that wouldn't ever overflow, had made him want to beg her forgiveness. He'd managed to get out of the room before he committed that act of folly, but it had been very close.

He walked now to his bedchamber and began to methodically pack his clothes in a valise. His valet, Throckmorton, had died the previous winter of just plain old age, a smile on his toothless mouth because the very young and pretty tweeny Marigold was stroking his gnarled old hand. Tysen hadn't seen fit as yet to hire another man. He was a clergyman. It seemed rather ridiculous for a clergyman to have a valet. Mrs. Priddie did quite well with his clothes.

He was also a rich clergyman, but he usually didn't pay much attention to that. Douglas dealt with most of the details, knowing Tysen had no interest in it. Now Tysen was a Scottish baron in addition to being a rich clergyman. He was now Baron Barthwick. It was enough to make him briefly question God's mysterious ways.

He ate dinner alone in the small breakfast parlor that evening, spoke to his sexton who had cursed a blue streak, Mr. Peters, spent more hours than he cared to with Mr. Samuel Pritchert, his curate, a man with a long, thin nose and a dour disposition who could have a recluse talking to him within three minutes. It was amazing how people would almost instantly spill their innards to Samuel. He was competent, his sermons of the basic sin-and-punishment variety, and he would keep Tysen's flock intact in his absence.

Then he went to his sons' bedchamber. There was a light coming from beneath the door. He knocked lightly, then entered.

Max, nearly nine years old now, was reading—no surprise there—his long legs stretched out in front of him, his arms cradling a huge book, a candle burning right over his left shoulder. He was, Tysen thought, looking with pride at his elder son, more of a scholar than he himself had ever been. Max spoke Latin, read Latin, even cursed in Latin when his younger brother annoyed him, which was fairly often, when he didn't think his papa was listening. Tysen didn't understand a great deal of what he said, which was probably for the best.

Leo, named for Leopold Foxworth Sherbrooke, the third earl of Northcliffe and a gentleman who'd held honor above all else, even when it meant having his head severed from his body, was standing on his head, his stockinged feet against the wall. He looked like he was sleeping, his eyes closed, perfectly at his ease. He was probably thinking about his uncle Douglas's horses, which he was allowed to ride at Northcliffe Hall. Tysen shook his head and cleared his throat. "Boys, I came to say good-bye to you. I am leaving very early in the morning."

Max immediately lifted the great tome from his lap and laid it reverently on the carpet. Tysen saw that it was in Latin. As for Leo, he simply dropped his legs over his head and came up in a single graceful roll, grinning. "I want to ride Garth, Papa. He's a mean brute."

Tysen knew that Douglas would never allow Leo even to sit on that vicious stallion's back, thank the good Lord.

"We know that we're to go to Uncle Douglas," Max said. "I have been wondering, Papa, if Leo and I will have a title now that you do. You know, James is Lord Hammersmith and Jason is an honorable. Perhaps as the elder son, I will now be Sir Something?"

"I'm sorry, Max, but you and Leo are still just the same. I suppose you will be able to say that you are Lord Barthwick's very honorable sons, though."

"We are already honorable, Papa," Max said. "Uncle Ryder is always saying that honor is what men must embrace," he paused, then added, "if you're not embracing a woman that is. Er, that's what Uncle Ryder says, Papa."

"Yes," Tysen said. "I am not surprised."

"Besides," Max said, shrugging, "who wants to be a Hammersmith? Silly name, doesn't mean anything. James likes it, though."

"Speak for yourself," said Leo, who was straightening his trousers and pulling his socks in order. "I'm not even eight years old and I'm already a rat-faced little idiot."

"Blessed Lord above," Tysen said, startled. "Where did you ever hear such a thing, Leo? Rat-faced? That's quite offensive; contrive to forget it immediately. The little idiot part as well."

"That's difficult to do, Papa, since Meggie called him that when she was angry with him. It was just yesterday that—"

Tysen closed his eyes. "Your sister called you a rat-faced little idiot?"

"Yes," Leo said, then dropped his chin to his chest. "Perhaps I deserved it, Papa. Meggie's face was very red, and for the longest time she couldn't think of anything to say to me, and then that just popped out of her mouth. Then she shook her fist at me. But at least she didn't smack me in the head or throw me in the bushes like she usually does. She just walked away and slammed a door."

"May I inquire what you said to your sister to deserve such an epithet?"

Max said, "Leo cut a wide strip out of the back of her skirt and her petticoat. When she walked, you could see her drawers. Marigold finally realized what everyone was staring at and ran screaming after her before she could get too far outside the vicarage gate."

Tysen thought, You are indeed a rat-faced little idiot, Leo, but naturally he didn't say that. He said very quietly, "I am vastly disappointed in you, Leo. The good Lord can only imagine what your mother would have said."

Max said matter-of-factly, "Mother would have shrieked, pounded the wall with her fists, and had hysterics for at least two hours. Leo prefers Meggie's punishments. Why, just two days ago, she took Leo's neck between her hands and nearly squeezed the life out of him." Max was silent for a moment, then said, "About Mother and hysterics, that's what Mrs. Priddie said Mother would do whenever one of us didn't mind. I don't remember, myself."

Tysen didn't remember the pounding fists, but he did remember the hysterics. He said, "I will not be here to enforce your punishment, Leo, but here it is. You will not stand on your head for six days. You will not do any flips down the corridors of Northcliffe Hall. You will not cut anything at all with your scissors. You will treat your sister like a royal princess. Do you understand me?"

Leo bowed his head. "Yes, Papa. I understand."

Max looked perplexed for a moment, but the look was gone so quickly that Tysen wasn't at all sure he'd even seen it. "You boys will obey your aunt and uncle. You will enjoy yourselves when it is allowed. You will not accept any gifts from young ladies who come to North-cliffe Hall to bestow them on your cousins or your aunt and uncle." Then he hugged both of them and even patted Leo's head.

He heard Leo say to Max as he closed the bedchamber door, "Papa didn't say anything about me not standing on my head at night—he just said six days."

"Leo," Max said, "you will surely go to hell."

"No, Papa wouldn't allow that," Leo said. "Why couldn't Papa at least inherit a title that would make us lords? Surely there must be a dukedom lying about not being used. We'll be just the same. Maybe Uncle Douglas has an extra title or two hidden away in some old book that he doesn't need."

"Uncle Douglas," Max said in his lecturer's voice that drove both Leo and Meggie right over the brink, "has only one extra title, and James has it. You know that. He's a viscount—Lord Hammersmith—because Uncle Douglas is an earl and he doesn't need it anymore. Well, no, ac-tually, he's also a baron of some sort. I don't remember the name."

Leo said, "Poor Jason. He's nothing at all. He's as bad off as we are."

Tysen was smiling, he couldn't help it, even though he knew he should give a token frown. He didn't sleep well that night. He'd looked briefly into Meggie's bedchamber, but all the lights were off and she was obviously asleep. He hated to disappoint her, but there wasn't a place for a little girl on this trip. The good Lord only knew what awaited him in Scotland. He looked forward to seeing Sinjun and Colin and their children.

He left the following morning at dawn, his driver Rufus and a stable lad tiger as his to ride behind the carriage and pay all the tolls, both provided by his brother and both sharp at their positions. His own gelding, Big Blue, was tied to the back of the carriage under the watchful eye of the tiger, whose unlikely name, Rufus had told him, was Pride.

He didn't realize that his tiger wasn't really one of Douglas's stable lads until they were in Edinburgh five and a half days later.

3

Taurum per cornua prehende.
Take the bull by the horns.

August 22, 1815

IT HAD BEEN a long journey. Tysen was riding Big Blue
when at last they entered Edinburgh. He had written nine
sermons in his head during those five and a half days, and
he had to admit, in his more objective moments, that none
of them was presentable enough for God's hearing. They
were, he thought, looking at the mighty castle soaring
upward from its craggy ridge in the center of the city,
rather—no, he didn't want to say it. Oh, very well. Truth
be told, they were boring. They nearly made him nod off
to sleep. Talk of hell's fires kept the congregation alert,
but it never made him feel exalted when he was done,
and thus he rarely threatened his flock with brimstone.
But these nine sermons, they'd been bland, touching on
this or that without much rhyme or reason to any of them.
One of them did dwell perhaps overly much on the ne-
cessity for a woman's obedience. He thought of Meggie
and shook his head at that. Then he thought of Melinda
Beatrice and felt guilty.

They had both been so very young, so very much in love with each other, and they saw only a life that was narrow, yet filled with hope and goodness and an endless desire to be of service to God. At least that was what he had wanted. He sighed.

Tysen heard a boy whistle and waved to him. He remembered Edinburgh, but now he saw it through a man's eyes, not a child's. The Castle, he thought, oh, how Meggie would have enjoyed the Castle. No, what he'd done was correct. For heaven's sake, it had rained a full four days on the journey up here. Today, at least, it had ceased raining early in the morning. The sun now glistened overhead, and it was so clear he knew he would be able to see the smudged mountains on the horizon beyond the Lothian plain and the Firth of Forth if he were standing on the Castle ramparts. He clicked Big Blue around a crowd of people who looked to be surly for some reason, and waved his carriage behind him toward the road to New Town, north of the castle. Literally dredged from a malodorous swamp, New Town was a masterpiece, with all the magnificent gardens and squares surrounded by splendid Georgian buildings. He had no idea if Sinjun would be at their residence here in the city. Regardless, he knew Old Angus would let him spend the night. At the west end of George Street, they finally reached Charlotte Square. Another left turn, and they were in Abbotsford Crescent. Kinross House was located directly in the middle, opposite a small, very green park. It was a tall, skinny house, older than its neighbors, but it looked immaculate, flowers planted everywhere, the paint fresh, the shutters hanging straight and proud. There was a new slate roof, if he wasn't mistaken. The rectangular lawn was freshly scythed, the walkway swept clean. Tysen was tired, but the sight of his sister's lovely house made him smile.

Tysen remembered Meggie saying that her aunt Sinjun would have had roads built if needed. Well, she'd certainly made the Kinross town house a work of art. Its newer neighbors were lovely as well, but Kinross House had style—old style—and it was better. It was unique.

He hoped Old Angus was still in full possession of his wits and thus would recognize him and not shoot him with his blunderbuss—a very valuable weapon, Sinjun had said to him once, and laughed. To his utter surprise, he looked up at a shout from an upper window. Then Sinjun was sticking her head out and yelling down at him. "Tysen! Is it really you? Bloody hell, we just arrived yesterday. Dahling wanted to stroll down the Royal Mile and, well, I wanted to as well. Colin is up at the Castle, speaking to Lord Stallings. Dahling and Phillip are with him, doubtless roaming through all those drafty hallways, asking endless questions of all the poor soldiers. Oh, it is so wonderful to see you. Come in, oh, yes, do come in!"

Old Angus came out of the house, looking older than the Castle, his homespuns bagging at his knees, his white hair blown all over his head, and a big smile on his seamed face. "Och, ye be Master Tysen, her ladyship's brother, nae doubt."

"Aye," Tysen said, savoring that lilting word on his tongue, and dismounted from Big Blue's back.

"Well, now, ye hae yer man just come wi' me and we'll see to them nice horses ye got. Aye, who's the little pullet riding up behind?"

"My tiger. His name is Pride."

"Aye?"

Then Sinjun was there, throwing her arms around him, hugging him until he was kissing her hair and hugging her back, and then holding her loosely in his arms, he said, "You are looking quite fit, Sinjun. And it isn't raining, thank the good Lord."

"And you, Tysen, are as handsome as ever. Oh, goodness, I had no idea you were coming. And just look—why ever would you do this? It is surely the most unexpected thing you've ever done. But why is she riding on the back of your carriage? She looks fit to drop. What have you done? Oh, I see, she demanded to do it, and you allowed it. You spoil her, Tysen."

It took Tysen only a moment of sorting his way through his sister's words before he had the most awful foreboding. He turned slowly to stare at his tiger, Pride.

"Well, Meggie," Sinjun said, "come down from there and give me a hug. I'm sure I will come to understand why you've become your father's tiger. Was it a wager? No, naturally, your father never wagers. I'm not certain if that is because he believes wagering to be a sin or whether he believes he doesn't have the Sherbrooke luck and doesn't want to lose his fortune."

Tysen looked at his daughter, who had just pulled off her disreputable woolen hat. Her once beautiful hair was matted and oily.

He closed his eyes, looked heavenward, and without another word, turned on his heel and walked into Sinjun's house. Luckily, the front door was wide open. Standing right inside was Agnes, Old Angus's wife, and she was wearing a huge apron wrapped around her large middle.

"And jest who be ye?" she demanded and crossed her massive arms over her equally massive bosom.

"I," Tysen said, "am a man of God who is desperately trying to keep firm control of himself."

"That's right. Ye're the reverend," Agnes said and gave him a big smile from a mouth that held only three teeth.

There was no yelling to the ceiling, no foul curses, no bodily threats. No, Tysen merely regarded his filthy daughter, standing very close to her aunt Sinjun in the drawing room, and said finally, his voice low, controlled, very cold, "I am severely disappointed in you, Meggie." Without pause he turned to his sister. "I have inherited the Barony of Barthwick from Great Uncle Tyronne and am now Baron Barthwick of Kildrummy Castle. My new castle and holding lie some seven miles south of Stonehaven. I am here in Scotland to see to my lands, determine what it is I will do, and spend some time with you and Colin. Also, I believe the Barthwick solicitor, a Mr. MacCray, is here in Edinburgh. I will need to speak with him."

"Yes, Donald MacCray is here. He is very popular, particularly with the ladies." Sinjun then just gave her head a slight shake and went down on her knees in front of Meggie. "You are a mess, dear heart. Why don't you come with me upstairs and we will get you bathed and changed. Did you manage to bring clothes? No? It isn't a problem. Dahling is quite the young lady now—all of fourteen—but surely she must have some older clothes still in her drawers."

Meggie, looking over her shoulder at her father, who hadn't moved from the same spot and who was giving her a very stern, emotionless look, dropped her shoulders and said just above a whisper, "I'm sorry, Papa, truly. But I had to come with you, to protect you, to take care of you."

"Go with your aunt, Meggie," Tysen said, and walked over to one of the lovely bow windows in the drawing room. He heard a sniffle, heard her leave the room with Sinjun. He closed his eyes, appalled at what she had done. For five and a half days, his little girl had ridden on the back of his carriage. Where had she slept at night? In the stables of the inns, naturally. He started shaking, just thinking of what could have happened to her. He prayed now, thanking God for keeping her safe, since he, her father, hadn't done so. All that blasted rain—what if she became ill? What if she died in Scotland because he never gave his borrowed tiger a second glance? Sinjun had known it was her immediately. He was her father, and he was blind.

It was devastating.

Tysen was still utterly white when Sinjun came back into the drawing room. It had been on the tip of her tongue to remonstrate with him for his coldness, despite the fact that Meggie's outrageous deception had nearly curled her own toes, but at the sight of him, all white about the gills, all she could think of doing was hugging him until he regained some of his color, which is what she did. "It's all right, Tysen," she said over and over against his cheek, holding him tightly against her. "It's all right. Meggie is fine. Mary is with her, helping her bathe. She is all right, no bad aftereffects. Stop worrying."

He heaved a very big breath, then slowly pulled away from her. "I never even noticed her, Sinjun, yet you knew it was her right away. So did Old Angus. But not her father. Bloody hell, what kind of a man am I?"

He'd said "bloody hell," the favorite Sherbrooke curse. Sinjun just couldn't believe it. She gave her brother a dazzling smile. "Parents see what they expect to see, it's that simple. Stop feeling guilty. It doesn't become you. Yes, that's better, you've finally got some color. Now, what are you going to do?"

Tysen said slowly, "I would like to thrash my daughter for her appalling behavior, but I don't think I'll be able to bring myself to do it. I spanked her once last year, and the guilt nearly laid me low for a week. What do you suggest, Sinjun?"

"It's difficult," she said at last, after worrying her lower lip. "Let's ask Colin, all right? He and Dahling and Phillip should be back shortly for luncheon."

Tysen nodded. "May we stay with you for a couple of

days, Sinjun? Then we will go to Kildrummy Castle and see what's what."

"I think that is a lovely idea. I could have Old Angus ride to Kinross and fetch Fletcher or Jocelyn. Would you like to see them?"

At the mention of his young niece and nephew, Tysen said, "Meggie said they were just babies and didn't have much interest, but I disagree. I should like that, Sinjun."

"Well, Jocelyn is only a little mite, just turned a year old. However, little Fletcher is three and won't shut his mouth. Do you know he talks to horses? He listens to horses, and I swear to you that they communicate. He even changed two of their names, claimed they weren't happy with the ones they had."

"What were the names?"

"They were named Olmar and Grindel. Fletcher listened to them, nodded, and then changed them to Fireball and Thor. I swear to you their steps are higher now, they fling their manes and flick their tails just like they're colts again, and they stamp their hooves whenever someone calls them by their new names. It's amazing."

Tysen gave her a small smile, but it still showed his very white Sherbrooke teeth. "I should like to introduce Fletcher to my horse. I wish him to see if Big Blue is satisfied with his name."

Sinjun laughed merrily and took his hand. "Come and tell me all about this inheritance of yours. I remember about Great Uncle Tyronne, but goodness, weren't there a good dozen boys to inherit before you?"

"Very nearly," Tysen said. "It's sad. They're all dead. Ian, the last of the heirs and Old Tyronne's last grandson, fell off a cliff into the North Sea not above six months ago. Then, I suppose, Great Uncle Tyronne just gave up. Although, as Douglas pointed out, the old man was eighty-seven years old. That left only the Englishman—namely, me. I doubt anyone is very happy about that."

"But who is there to be unhappy?"

Tysen just shook his head. "Actually, I have no idea who is living at Kildrummy at the present time or if there are any relatives remaining. I will see Donald MacCray on the morrow. He will provide me with all the information I need. Now, Sinjun, before I face my daughter I should like to fortify myself with a cup of tea."

4

THREE-YEAR-OLD FLETCHER KINROSS told his uncle Tysen that Big Blue was displeased with his name.

Tysen stared at the precocious little boy in his father's arms and asked, "What is the name he would prefer, Fletcher?"

Fletcher put his thumb in his mouth, leaned toward Big Blue, who was looking back intently—actually looking at the little boy—Tysen was sure of it. "Papa, you must let me down," Fletcher said. When released, he walked right up to the big gelding, and to Tysen's surprise but no one else's, the soon-to-be–former Big Blue lowered his head and lipped Fletcher's hand, blew on it, and stomped his left front hoof several times.

"Don't worry," Sinjun said. "No animal would ever hurt him. Isn't it amazing? Ah, yes, I believe Big Blue has spoken."

Fletcher patted the horse's neck, then turned back to his uncle Tysen and said in his clear child's voice, "He tells me he is not blue. He tells me he doesn't even like colors. He wants to be named Big Fellow." The thumb went back in the mouth, then his small arms went up for his father to pick him up again, which he did. Colin Kinross said, "Well, Tysen, what do you think—can you bring yourself to call him Big Fellow?"

Meggie started laughing. "Oh, Aunt Sinjun, it is marvelous. Big Fellow—I like it."

"If that's what he wants," Tysen said, and he sounded utterly bewildered.

Phillip Kinross, sixteen and quite a handsome young man with his father's dark hair and wicked smile, just shook his head and said, "It isn't bad, Uncle Tysen. Fletcher was mad at me when he renamed my horse. I can tell you I was worried with what he could come up with, but his name is now Edwin, which, actually, suits him just fine, and me as well."

"What was his name before?"

Fletcher grinned at his very serious uncle, who'd always been very kind to him.

"It was Claymore," Phillip said. "Fletcher said my horse was peace-loving and thus the name Claymore made him very nervous."

And so the following morning, Big Fellow, with Tysen astride, rode beside the carriage that held one lone passenger—his ten-year-old daughter, who had been wise enough not to argue with her father about her displacement as his tiger. It was a beautiful day. Fleecy white clouds in wondrous shapes filled the sky, a slight breeze moved in from the sea to dry the sweat on Tysen's brow, and the scent of wildflowers filled his nostrils. He saw clumps of heather ranging from deepest purple to snowy white, in the most unlikely places—poking out of crevices in black rocks, pushing through low-lying stone fences.

A day and a half of beautiful summer weather brought

them to Kildrummy Castle. Tysen saw the ten or so chimney stacks rising high into the air, the round turrets curving outward on each corner of the huge square manor. It wasn't at all like the older castles he'd seen—soaring stone buildings with slitted windows high above the ground, cold and stark against the Scottish skies. No, Kildrummy was newer, with its slate roof and light gray stone walls.

"What do you think, Meggie?" he asked, pulling Big Fellow next to where she was leaning out the carriage window to see.

"It's sitting up on that barren stretch right over the sea like a big bird of prey," Meggie said. "There's that huge forest just off there to the left, but nothing close to the castle. Goodness, it's all bare land and it looks like there are deep ditches all through it. We should fill in all those ditches. We should plant trees. It is too stark, too forbidding." She licked her lips and frowned just a bit. "It's scary," she added. "And lonely. But the forest just beyond is lovely."

Tysen, whose memory of Kildrummy was that of a ten-year-old boy, had agreed with Meggie. That stretch from the castle to the forest was an ugly piece of land. It was stark, and barren, what with all those strewn rocks and boulders. Those jagged ditches, or whatever they were, were dangerous. Walking or riding through that land would require a good deal of attention.

Now, as a man, however, he believed it magnificent. He wouldn't have changed a thing. He would have made his way carefully through all the boulders and crevices and admired it. But if Meggie wanted trees, she would have them. If she wanted all those crevices filled in, so be it. He said, "I will inquire what trees would best survive here. We'll have to examine all those ditches and see where we would get enough dirt to fill them. You, my girl, can find out about the flowers outside the castle walls."

She beamed at him and he frowned. Oh, dear, she saw that he was still upset with her. She said in a very small voice, "I wonder if any of the round turrets are bedchambers. I would really like that."

"We will see," Tysen said, realizing he shouldn't say yes to her immediately. He was still infinitely upset with her. He still awoke in the middle of the night, his belly cramping at the thought of his ten-year-old daughter hugging the back of the carriage, splattered with mud and rain, sleeping in the stables. He drew a deep breath. Had Douglas or Ryder been her father, he didn't doubt for a moment that they would have thrashed her.

Sinjun had come up with no proper punishment by the time they'd left, and Tysen was still stymied.

Kildrummy Castle. It was his now. He was Lord Barthwick.

Late that night after the sun had finally dropped behind the hillocks in the west and the air was clear with just a touch of light left, Meggie sat on her narrow bed in the south turret that looked over the barren stretch to the forest—lush and green and covered with pine trees and the occasional sheep. She mentally began her planting, staring at the closed-in inner courtyard of the castle. But every time she thought of something colorful to plant she thought also of her father's anger at her. Not that he ever acted angry. No, he acted disappointed, just looking at her, all aloof, with distress in his eyes, and that was much worse. Meggie sighed and slid deeper under the fat quilt that was older than her father, maybe even her grandfather.

At dinner her father had been polite, just as he'd been since Edinburgh, nothing more—surely no outward show

of anger. She remembered the one time he'd actually
raised his voice and spanked her. That had been when
she'd tied the bells to the goat and he'd played a rather
clever tune, if one attended to it carefully.

She wished he would yell again, maybe even thrash her.
At least it might make him forgive her more quickly. She
remembered once when Uncle Douglas had yelled at one
of the twins—Jason—and smacked his bottom three
times. Then Uncle Douglas had picked him up, scoured
his head with his knuckles, told him he was an idiot,
tucked him under his arm, and carried him to the stables.
Uncle Douglas had probably let Jason be his tiger that
day.

She had disobeyed her father, who was closer to God
than anyone. Regardless, she had not been wrong to come.
She knew, knew all the way to her bones, that her father
would need her.

Mrs. MacFardle, in Meggie's immediate estimation,
hadn't appeared at all pleased to have the new English
lord here at Kildrummy Castle. Dark looks, she'd given
Papa, beetled black eyebrows drawn nearly together over
her forehead every time she had looked at Meggie.

Finally, she'd shown them about and reluctantly served
them dinner. Meggie wished Mrs. MacFardle were more
like that ancient old woman at the inn where they'd
stopped for lunch in Clackmanshire, who'd patted Meggie
on the head, her voice singsong and very soft, murmuring
Scottish words that Meggie thought were endearments,
like "a wee *gowan*," which she was told later by dear
Pouder meant "a little daisy." As for her father, he was
braw, and that, Pouder said, meant he was a handsome
fellow. Meggie didn't think that Mrs. MacFardle thought
her papa was *braw* at all, not even after he'd said a very
eloquent grace over their dinner, which, Meggie believed
with all her heart, didn't deserve any grace at all. The pile

in the middle of her plate was called haggis, Mrs. MacFardle told them, a sneer in her voice. Every Scot, she said, ate haggis and thanked the good Lord for providing such a splendid edible. Meggie took one look at that sheep's stomach with its runny brown ingredients stuffed inside, fastened her eyes on the dark blue carpet that covered the dining room floor, and ate four slices of rich rye bread smeared with thick yellow butter.

Her father took one bite, spoke quickly to Mrs. MacFardle of the huge luncheon he and Meggie had eaten at the Wild Goose Inn, then took one more small taste which meant that as an adult, it was his duty to be polite. There was no one more polite than her father. Even surrounded by sinners, he was polite. Even driven from his own parlor by ladies who pursued him shamelessly, he was polite. He needed her, badly, particularly here in this foreign land, and he would realize it, sooner or later.

It was at dinner that they learned that Mrs. MacFardle was also the cook. Just thinking about it made Meggie hungry. And now her stomach was growling, but she had no idea where to find the kitchen in this huge, rambling place that seemed older than Northcliffe Hall, even though it wasn't.

She snuggled down, aware that the stone walls of her bedchamber were thicker than her leg. That was comforting, because a storm was blowing in off the sea. It wasn't too long before she heard the wind, swirling off the water, battering against the windowpanes. Then the rain came, hard and fast, striking the glass with a great deal of force. She wished she wasn't alone. She wished she wasn't so cold deep down inside where the thick warm quilt couldn't reach. At three o'clock in the morning—she knew it was that late because a tremendous slash of white lightning lit up her turret bedchamber and she could read the old clock that leaned against the mantelpiece—she just couldn't stand it. She was so cold and so scared that she knew her heart was going to burst out of her chest. She grabbed a blanket off the bed, wrapped it around herself, and left the bedchamber. She began the trek to the laird's massive bedchamber that overlooked the angry sea.

She didn't knock on the closed door, just slipped inside. Another bright streak of lightning and she saw her father's outline in the middle of the massive bed. She eased next to him and wrapped her blanket around her. She was safe now. She could feel his warmth even through all the covers. She snuggled even closer to his back. Nothing could hurt her now. Meggie sighed and went immediately to sleep.

Early the next morning, Tysen awoke slowly, instantly aware that he was in Scotland, sleeping in the huge laird's bed, and felt his child pressed against his back. He smiled. When the children had occasionally began to come into his bed, he'd learned soon enough to wear a nightshirt. He remembered that Melinda Beatrice had been relieved when he'd donned the nightshirts she'd made quickly for him, a good half dozen. She'd never said anything about his sleeping unclothed, since that was how he'd been raised, but Tysen had known that she was embarrassed when she sometimes saw him naked. He supposed that he too was relieved once he started wearing the nightshirts. He'd matched his wife, both of them covered from tip to toe with white batiste. He also knew that she hadn't liked performing her marital obligations, for he'd once overheard her saying so to her mother. It had never occurred to him that she wouldn't want him once they were married, since he'd been desperate to touch her, to kiss her, to come inside her. He'd always believed her reticence, her shyness, were fitting and proper but that she would change once it was deemed by God and the Church to be the thing to do. But no, she'd suffered him. That was the way he thought of it each time he needed a man's relief. She'd suffered him. She was a lady. He supposed that was simply the way it was. But then he would think of his brothers and their wives and how they were always touching and laughing and kissing behind the door. No, he turned off those thoughts. They were worthless. They were probably ungodly as well, but he didn't want to examine them closely enough to determine that. Life was life, and he was a very lucky man.

He saw the bright sunlight pouring through the series of eight narrow windows that gave onto the sea. The water was blue and calm. He heard seagulls shrieking as they dove for their breakfast. After the violent storm of the night before, even the air in his huge bedchamber seemed fresher, brighter, drawing in the sunlight. The beauty of it touched him. It was God's gift after the violence of the night.

He gently moved himself away from Meggie, saw her curl up into a little ball, her sleep unbroken. He eased her under the covers and lightly kissed her forehead. The storm must have frightened her, and the strangeness. The lightning tearing into that turret room must have been a sight. He lightly touched his fingertips to her cheek. So soft she was, and she was his. Even when she disobeyed him he loved her, loved her and her brothers so much that it humbled him, the completeness of it, the infinite richness of it.

He straightened. Kildrummy Castle. It was now his. He was now the laird. He said the words aloud, feeling them roll on his tongue, sing their magic into his mind. "Kildrummy Castle." It was his responsibility, no one else's. It hadn't really sunk in until this very moment, as he stood there looking out over the North Sea. This would be his home until he died, and then it would pass to Max. He wondered if the harsh beauty of the place would move

Max to his soul, or if his scholarly son would just return to Euripides without a second thought and perhaps quote some offhand Latin.

Tysen bathed and dressed behind a screen in case Meggie woke up, then took himself downstairs. The wide front doors were flung open to the enclosed inner courtyard. The morning sun burst through into the castle, filling the vast entryway. Tysen could see dancing motes of dust in that brilliant sunlight.

Pouder, so very ancient that he seemed propped up, was seated in the old high-backed chair right by the large front doors. The old man blinked, scratched his hand, and Tysen wondered if he ever left that chair, even to sleep. He bade him good morning. Pouder gave him a nearly toothless smile that was singularly sweet and said, "Och, my lord, it's good to have ye here. No valet, I see. I always wanted to be a gentleman's valet, but Lord Barthwick said I was too old to learn."

Tysen, who wasn't stupid, and thought the old man was grand, said quickly, "If you would like to see to the placement of my clothes in the laird's bedchamber, I would be very appreciative."

"May I even fold yer cravats, my lord?"

"My cravats need to be arranged as well, Pouder. I thank you."

"Ah, at last I will be a valet-in-training," Pouder said, sighed softly, and let his head fall forward to his chest. His white hair settled gently onto his shoulders. He was asleep.

"Aye, a valet-in-training," Tysen said quietly, savoring the taste and feel of that strange term on his tongue. He went quietly out the front doors, careful not to disturb Kildrummy's butler.

He stepped outside to see MacNee, a handsome young man who looked after the stables. Rufus was with him, ready, Tysen thought, for his breakfast. But MacNee wanted to chat a bit. "Big Fellow is happy," MacNee said. "All settled in, ate his oats, drank all his water. Aye, ye slept well in the laird's bed, my lord?"

"Aye," Tysen said. He was a "my lord" now. It felt very odd.

"Aye, that bed draws a body down and soothes his brow. Och, me brain's not pulling its weight, my lord. Mrs. MacFardle has asked me to take all the eggs she collected to Barthwick Village, just down a ways from here, and sell them to the local folks. Too many eggs we have now, ye see, since the chickens squawk and twitter during storms and jest lay and lay. Ye need to go back inside, my lord, and have yer breakfast."

Tysen was smiling as he went once again into the grand entrance hall, dominated by Pouder, sleeping quietly in his chair. MacNee and Rufus went to the kitchen and Tysen went into the small breakfast room with its impossibly old dark paneling and ancient portraits of dead animals strung up on lines in sixteenth-century kitchens. He would remove all the painted gore from the walls and make them white. The dark old carpet would come up and he'd have the lovely wood floor polished until it sparkled. He blinked at himself. It was the first time he had ever thought like this. He'd always, he supposed, simply accepted his surroundings as they were. Besides, Melinda Beatrice had seen to the vicarage. He didn't recall if he'd even been asked if he liked this carpet or that piece of furniture. But now, here at Kildrummy Castle—it was all his. Yes, those floors would be polished until he could see his reflection in the wide, thick boards. He also wanted to meet everyone, hire every worker available to clean his house. He wanted to tour his lands, count the sheep, learn what kind of fish the men caught. He rubbed his hands together. England was a long way from Kildrummy Castle. He felt light and happy.

He felt infinitely blessed.

He ate porridge that Mrs. MacFardle begrudgingly served him, found it excellent, and decided his first visit would be to Barthwick Village.

[You are] the veriest varlet that ever chewed with a tooth.
—Shakespeare, *King Henry IV*

Mary Rose stood in the shadow of the thick pine trees and watched the new Baron Barthwick stride out through the gate of Kildrummy Castle, wearing buff riding britches and a dark brown jacket. He looked very fine, very much an English gentleman, not that she was all that certain, for she'd only seen a few in her twenty-four years. He was young, but that wasn't a surprise. She'd overheard Uncle Lyon telling about the Fall of Barthwick, now in the hands of a demned Englishman, one too young to know what he was about. Then he cursed Tyronne Barthwick for not ensuring an heir—half a dozen boys weren't enough and then the old coot had the gall to die when he'd only reached his eighty-seventh year. And then her cousin, Donnatella, had laughed at her father and told him not to worry, she would see to things. Mary Rose knew what that meant: if the English baron was at all to her liking, Donnatella would marry him. At least that was possible. The Edinburgh solicitor Donald MacCray had told them that the new baron was a widower. How sad, she thought, that such a young man had already lost his wife.

The baron appeared tall and lean from Mary Rose's vantage point, and he had light, thick hair that a slight morning breeze was ruffling on his brow. He was leading a big bay gelding. She watched him swing ever so gracefully onto his horse's back, straighten in the saddle, and look around him. Then he threw back his head and breathed in very deeply. She heard him say something to his horse, like "Big Fellow," which was surely an odd name.

She wished she could see him up close, but of course she couldn't. Nor would he wish to see her anywhere near him, since she was the Local Embarrassment. She watched him ride toward Barthwick Village, just to the south, watched him until he rounded Bleaker's Bluff, which rose up a good fifty feet, and was lost to her sight.

She turned and began her trek through the pine forest back toward Vallance Manor. She had just cleared the trees when she heard horse's hooves coming toward her. She ducked behind a particularly fat pine tree.

But she wasn't fast enough. The horse stopped close by. She heard it blowing, heard a man say, "Easy now, Barker." There was no help for it. She wasn't a coward. She wasn't about to race back into the forest and hide among the trees.

Mary Rose straightened her skirts and came out from behind the pine tree. The sun was bright overhead, everything shone, the greens were utterly green, the wild grass lush, thick, vivid. The storm from the previous night had washed everything to a high shine.

"Ah," he said, striding toward her, "I thought I saw you come this way, Mary Rose. You always liked watching from the forest, hiding away so you could see but not be seen."

"Hello, Erickson," she said, fear and dislike blending to make her voice very cold. "I just saw the new Baron Barthwick ride from the manor."

"Of course he didn't see you, did he?"

"I can't imagine that he would be interested in seeing me," she said, and took a step sideways.

He frowned down at her, tapping his riding crop against his boot, and patted Barker's neck when he shied a bit. "No, don't try to run away from me, Mary Rose. Don't be afraid. I just want to talk to you."

"How is your mother?" Mary Rose asked.

He frowned, hit his riding crop again against his boot. "She is as she always is. I don't want to talk about my mother, Mary Rose."

"Do you think the new baron will have a party?"

"I don't care about the bloody new baron. I want to talk to you." But he only looked at her, didn't say a thing. Before she could draw another breath, he'd grabbed her, pulled her tightly against him, and kissed her—her ear, her cheek, then grabbed a fistful of her hair and pulled her head back so he could have her mouth. She struggled, but it didn't matter. Erickson was much larger than she, and he was holding her much too tightly. She finally managed to stomp hard on his right foot. She felt his jerk of pain, but then his mouth was on hers again, and he was trying to thrust his tongue between her lips. "No," she said, and then his tongue was inside. She bit him hard.

His head jerked up and he cursed, then shook her. "Why did you do that? Damn you, why?"

His hold loosened, and she managed to jerk free of him. She didn't pause an instant, just raised her skirts above her knees and ran as fast as she could. She heard him mount his horse, knew he could ride her down in just seconds. No choice. She ran back into the forest, deeper and deeper, zigzagging left to right, then into the heaviest undergrowth to where his horse would have to pick his way very slowly. She heard Erickson cursing, felt his anger thicken the very air around her. She paused, breathing hard, a stitch in her side. She was safe. At least until the next time.

She lowered her head in her hands. She didn't cry, there

was no purpose to it. Tears did nothing except make her eyes itch and her nose red. She waited, then waited some more. She finally walked due east, knowing that if Erickson MacPhail wanted to wait for her, he would be there, between the forest and Kildrummy Castle. There was a stretch of two hundred yards, ancient barren land cluttered with boulders and strewn with sharp-edged rocks, and farther on, the land had been gouged out by some clawing primeval fingers, leaving gashing crevices in the earth, some of them quite deep. On horseback, he would have to take care. He wouldn't be able to catch her easily.

She drew in her breath when she reached the end of the trees, looked toward Kildrummy Castle. She didn't see Erickson MacPhail. She drew a deep breath, picked up her skirts again, and ran as fast as she could.

When she heard hoofbeats just off to her right, she turned quickly to see how close he was. She tripped over a clump of black rocks and went flying into one of the narrow crevices that scored the earth.

5

TYSEN JUMPED OFF Big Fellow's back and ran to the girl who was lying half in and half out of a narrow, jagged cut in the hard earth. He saw that she wasn't unconscious from her wild fall, as he'd feared. She was lying on her stomach, breathing hard, not moving. Finally she pressed herself up on her hands and looked at him.

"You're the new baron," she said, her voice filled with relief. She took a deep, shuddering breath, then said more calmly, "I watched you ride away. Why did you come back? Not that it matters, but I am very grateful that you did, sir."

Tysen cocked his head to one side as he came down on his haunches beside her. "I came back because I realized that I wanted my daughter with me. I left her because I wished her to understand that I am still distressed with her, but I am her father and I love her dearly and can no longer hold out. I wanted her to see the village with me, meet the villagers who bought our extra eggs, smell the fish, meet the fishermen." He appeared surprised that he'd spoken at such length, but then he just shook his head and smiled. "Let me help you. Do you think you are hurt?"

"I don't know yet. Let me just lie here a few more minutes. What did she do to distress you?"

"She dressed as a boy and rode behind my carriage as my tiger all the way from southern England to Edinburgh."

"Oh, my, what a grand adventure! I would never have had enough courage to do that. How old is she?"

"Only ten."

"She's a very brave girl."

"What she is, is too young and foolish, and ignorant as a clod of dirt," Tysen said. It occurred to him that he was speaking about family matters to an unknown female lying half in a ditch. It both surprised him and appalled him. At the very least, it was very unlike him to spill his innards to a stranger. And here he was, chatting with her, smiling even. It wasn't like him at all. He said, "I believe I should get you out of that hole in the ground now. Do you know now if you're hurt anywhere?"

"Maybe, I still don't know for sure."

"I will go as easily as I can." Tysen reached out to clasp her under her arms. To his astonishment, she tried to scoot away from him. She moaned and grabbed her left ankle.

Tysen found himself again surprised. He cocked his head at her, making absolutely no move to touch her. "Are you trying to hurt yourself more? What is wrong with you? I don't believe this—you're afraid of me, aren't you?"

"I don't know," Mary Rose said slowly, looking up at him.

"You don't know what? If you're afraid of me?"

"Yes, that's it. I don't know you. I think you are probably too handsome for your own good. It must be difficult to be a good person looking the way you do. You're a baron now, too. Perhaps that gives you all the permission you need to be wicked."

Tysen said, all stiff and formal, "My brother is an earl. He isn't wicked. Well, he is, but not in the way you mean."

"You mean to say that your brother would rescue a lass in distress and would not attempt to take advantage of her?"

"Yes, that's exactly what I mean," Tysen said. "His name is Douglas and he is a fine man."

"One never knows about Englishmen," Mary Rose said, sounding all sorts of doubtful. "You brag about your brother, but what about you, my lord?"

She began rubbing her ankle now. "Oh, dear, I believe my ankle is swelling. This isn't good at all."

"I am not too handsome for my own good," Tysen said, and he began gently massaging her ankle for her. "I am just myself. It is my brothers who are handsome." Where had that errant nonsense come from?

"If your brothers are more handsome than you, then I fear for the sanity of ladies everywhere."

He blew out his breath, then stopped cold. He looked at his hand, now lightly curved around her ankle. He jerked it away as if she'd burned him. "I'm sorry. That was badly done of me. No wonder you would question my character."

"No," she said, "not at all."

"Whatever that means," he said.

"Perhaps you made my ankle feel a bit better."

He said nothing, just frowned at his hand that had been not only touching her ankle but massaging it. He had to get himself together. He was a man of God, and he must consider her as one of his flock and help her, not think of her in the way a man would perhaps think of a woman. Yes, he would help her. "Now, if you will contrive to trust me, I will get you out of that ditch."

"It's not a ditch, it's a crevice. There are a good dozen in this stretch. All the crofters call them sheep killers. Sheep are stupid, you see, and they just wander right up to them and step in and die."

"Just like you were so smart that you fell in."

She actually smiled up at him. "You do have a point there."

He blinked at her, then eased his hands beneath her arms and gently pulled her out. He leaned her against a rock and looked down at her. Her face was very white. She was obviously in pain. "If you will continue to trust me, I'll try to get that boot off your foot before your ankle is so swelled I'll have to cut it off."

He helped her sit atop a boulder, then stooped in front of her. It was difficult, but he finally managed to work the boot off her foot. He held that thick old boot, looking up at her to see if she was all right. She was crying, but she wasn't making a sound. The tears just gathered and ran down her cheeks. She scrubbed her fisted hand over her cheeks and gulped.

He said, "I'm sorry, but now it's off." He lightly touched his fingers to her ankle. It was appropriate that he do so. He said, more concerned now, "It feels hot and swollen. I fear you won't be doing much walking for a while."

He rose and reached into his pocket for a handkerchief. He didn't hand it to her, but rather dabbed it against her cheeks. Then he drew back, frowning. "It is odd of me," he said, "and I did realize that quite clearly even as I patted your face. I suppose you could say that I am a private man, in the usual course of things, not given to talking so much with people I don't know or people I do know, for that matter, or patting the tears from a girl's face, or assuring a stranger that neither I nor my brother is profligate. Does your ankle hurt still?"

She only nodded, then looked around. "I don't know what to do. I walked from Vallance Manor. It's nearly two miles from Kildrummy Castle, up the coast."

"Don't worry about anything. I'm going to take you back to the castle. Mrs. MacFardle surely has some ancient recipe to make you instantly better. Why were you running? Did something frighten you in the forest?"

"Just a man," she said. "Just a man who is profligate."

"You heard Big Fellow coming and you thought it was this man chasing you down?"

She nodded. Her ankle pulsed and throbbed, and she wanted to cry with the pain of it. But she'd already wet his handkerchief and knotted it, and what did tears matter anyway?

"Come along," Tysen said. He didn't think about it, he simply picked her up in his arms and carried her to Big Fellow, who was trying to worry a strange-looking plant from between two small rocks.

"No, boy," Mary Rose said, waving her hand at his horse. "Don't eat that. It'll make your belly swell up just like my ankle."

"What is it?"

"Damslip weed. It's not terribly common around here, but still you must be vigilant. One of the goats died just last year from eating damslip weed."

Tysen shoved Big Fellow back from the scraggy brown plant and said to him, "Now, you will be a gentleman. You will hold still, Big Fellow." And the horse stood there, polite as could be, blowing quietly as Tysen swung his leg over the saddle. He'd never before carried a female, not even Melinda Beatrice, had never before imagined climbing aboard his horse with a female in his arms, one with a painful ankle who was making a valiant effort not to cry again. "We made it," he said, settling her across his legs. "Are you all right?"

"Yes," Mary Rose said.

"Hold on to me."

She wrapped her arms around his back and buried her cheek against his shoulder.

"This is very strange," Tysen said as he clicked Big Fellow forward. "I don't know your name."

"Mary Rose Fordyce."

He felt a pooling of pleasure at the sound. "A musical name," he said. "This man you thought was chasing you, who is he?"

"Erickson MacPhail, a man who used to be my friend," she sighed. "My uncle wouldn't like it were he to know that I do not like Erickson now and I had told someone that he was profligate." Another sigh. She said, "Here I am sitting on a man's lap on top of his horse with my arms wrapped around him. I've never done this before."

"I have never before held a woman on my lap atop my horse either," Tysen said, looking right between Big Fellow's ears, ignoring the feel of her hair against his chin. "We shall both have to overlook it as a brief, necessary confusion. Who is this Erickson MacPhail? Why does your uncle like him?"

"He's a neighbor. Whenever I am out walking I must pay constant attention. This time he came along by chance, but in the past I know he's waited for me. Perhaps he was waiting for me this time as well. I do wish he would just leave me alone."

"Why hasn't your father or your uncle warned him off if you do not wish to be in his company?"

"I don't have a father. My mother and I live with my uncle and his family. I think my uncle wishes he was Erickson's father. Uncle Lyon admires him, thinks he's

brave and *braw*—that means 'handsome,' you know—
and ever so charming. He does not understand that I don't
want to be mauled by him, which is what he does, given
the least opportunity."

"I'm sorry about your father. I lost my father when I
was a lad of eighteen. I still miss him. The one and only
time I was ever here at Kildrummy Castle, he brought me,
just the two of us. It was a fine thing, having him all to
myself." Again—he'd done it again. Spoken freely, just
opened his mouth and let words fall out that hadn't been
approved by his brain.

She said nothing, just nestled closer and rested her
cheek against his shoulder.

"That's right, we're nearly there. Just lie quietly.
There's Oglivie opening the gates."

"Laird, what is the matter?" Oglivie called out.

The Scottish title gave him a bit of a start, but there
was no way around it—he was a laird and a baron now.
"The young lady took a fall."

Tysen thought Oglivie said something, but he
couldn't make out the words. He said against her hair,
"Just a few more minutes and you'll be more comfortable." Her hair was soft, smelled of the sea and the pine
forest and something else he couldn't identify. Roses,
perhaps?

As Big Fellow passed through the wide wooden gates
into the enclosed courtyard, he said, "You don't have any
brothers?"

She shook her head against his jacket. "Just my uncle."
He left it, but it wasn't right. He imagined a man bothering Meggie in five or so years, and a surge of intense
rage roared through him. It made his heart pound, made
him blink several times. Rage was something he'd never
really visited before. It was something dark and vibrant,

with a life of its own, all black and ugly. It pulsed violently inside him and made him cold.

He looked up to see the housekeeper standing on the top step to the castle. "Mrs. MacFardle," he said, "I am glad you're here. We have a young lady in need of some care. She hurt her ankle."

He tossed Big Fellow's reins to MacNee and very carefully eased out of the saddle, trying not to touch the painful ankle. "Perhaps," he said, "we should fetch a doctor to see to it."

"Mary Rose, och, is it you? What is this about, my girl?"

"I fell into one of the sheep killers."

"Ye must take a care with those blasted cuts in the ground. Well, bring yerself into the castle and I will see what ye need. My lord, just set her down and I will help her. No need for a doctor."

Tysen ignored her and carried Mary Rose into the main drawing room, a nice room that, despite its size, felt welcoming and cozy. But like the dining room, it was too dark. He would ask Sinjun for advice on wallpaper. Perhaps a pale cream and green stripe. No, that wouldn't work because the wooden walls were covered with countless paintings of long-dead Barthwicks and a series of beautifully worked tapestries showing Mary, Queen of Scots, from a child married to a French prince to the woman leaning down about to have her head severed from her body.

Perhaps he would ask Mary Rose. He laid her on one of the long, soft, gold brocade sofas and stood back. Mrs. MacFardle moved in. "Well, now," she said, "at least ye got yer boot off." She leaned over Mary Rose, clasped the ankle between her two big hands, and pulled.

Mary Rose yelled and lurched off the sofa.

Tysen was appalled at what the housekeeper had done. He said as he elbowed Mrs. MacFardle out of the way, "I have a way with sprains. If you will fetch some ice, ma'am, we will wrap it in towels around her foot. Ah, is there ice to be had in August?"

"Perhaps a bit," Mrs. MacFardle said and got to her feet, panting a bit. "Ye come to the kitchen with me, my girl, and I'll tie a wee bit of ice around yer ankle. Then ye can be off, back to Vallance Manor. Och, look here, it's the little miss, is it?"

"Yes, ma'am," Meggie said, walking into the drawing room. "Papa, what's wrong? Who is this lady with her foot without its shoe? Oh, I see, she's hurt. Goodness, your poor ankle. I know exactly what to do. Don't worry, I won't hurt you. Leo is always scraping himself and straining this and that. Bring the ice, Mrs. MacFardle, immediately."

Mrs. MacFardle harrumphed, gave Mary Rose a long look, and took herself off.

Tysen stood back and watched his daughter sit down beside Mary Rose. With the lightest touch imaginable, she lifted Mary Rose's foot onto her lap. "This is very impressive," Meggie said, leaning down to eye the swelling. "Leo would be envious. Oh, Leo is my brother. Your name is Mary Rose? That is quite lovely. I'm Meggie. Margaret, really, but that sounds like a saint, which Papa says I will never be even if I begin a strict regimen of good deeds at this very moment, which, I must tell you, isn't at all likely to happen."

"Meggie, we don't have saints in the Church of England, so it is irrelevant."

"Yes, Papa, I know. I was speaking metaphorically."

Mary Rose stared over at Meggie. "How ever do you know that word?"

"Papa uses many metaphors in his sermons. Some people in the congregation come up to me after services and ask me what they mean. Now, isn't that better? Your poor ankle, all swelled, and the colors are already coming. A very bright purple, I think."

Sermons? Mary Rose didn't understand any of this. Maybe she was hearing strange words because her ankle hurt so badly.

Tysen didn't know how Meggie had done it, but Mary Rose was sitting back against several pillows, her foot on Meggie's lap, her stocking magically off and folded neatly beside Meggie. Tysen stared at that small white foot, then cleared his throat. "I shouldn't be here. I will see both of you later."

"Papa, wait a moment. I believe Mary Rose should have a small glass of brandy. When I wrap her ankle, it will hurt."

Tysen walked to the large dark mahogany sideboard and poured a bit of brandy into a snifter that he wiped clean on his sleeve.

He held out the glass to Mary Rose. She hesitated, drawing back a bit. "The last time I drank brandy I was fourteen and wanted to be wicked with my cousin, Donnatella. She was only ten, and yet she was the one who decided we would drink the brandy. I was so sick I wanted to die."

"Just a few sips," Tysen said. "I once tried brandy when I was a boy. My brothers, Douglas and Ryder, dared me to drink it, as I recall. Then they laughed themselves silly when I vomited on my mother's rosebushes."

"Papa, truly, you did that? Uncle Douglas and Uncle Ryder were that wicked?"

"We were boys, Meggie. It wasn't edifying. You do not have to try it yourself. If Max and Leo try to taunt you into doing it, don't. Please believe me, it is awful stuff."

Meggie said thoughtfully, "Perhaps I shall taunt them into doing it."

And in that way, watching the father and the daughter, Mary Rose drank enough brandy to warm her belly and ease her mind so when at last Meggie wrapped towels filled with small chunks of ice around her ankle, she turned white, but she didn't cry out.

"You have magic hands," Mary Rose said to her. "I feel much better already."

Meggie looked up to see Mrs. MacFardle standing in the doorway, her arms crossed over her bosom. "I shall ask Oglivie to drive you back to Vallance Manor, Mary Rose."

"That would be fine, Mrs. MacFardle," Mary Rose said. "I don't believe I could walk there in a week."

"First you will stay for luncheon," Tysen said, walking around Mrs. MacFardle. "Then we will see."

"Papa?"

"Yes, Meggie?"

"You will have to carry Mary Rose to the dining room."

"Oh, yes, certainly. You're right."

"Oh, no, surely I can walk," Mary Rose said, seeing him hesitate. He didn't want to get near her. She tried to stand up.

Tysen shook his head, frowned, and leaned down to pick her up. Then he found that he was no longer frowning. Actually, he was smiling down at her.

He heard Mrs. MacFardle harrumph behind him. He wanted to tell her that he was being as careful as he could, but then he remembered how she had grabbed Mary Rose's foot and pulled on it. He didn't understand.

"Did I hurt you?"

"No, not at all."

Meggie followed behind her father to the dining room, where Mrs. MacFardle had laid out their luncheon. She was standing behind the laird's chair, her arms crossed over her bosom, a pose she seemed to favor. She looked disapproving. Nothing new there. Maybe this time she was concerned about Mary Rose. Meggie wanted to assure her that her papa was a saintly man, that he wouldn't dream of going beyond the line with any lady, particularly one who was hurt.

Tysen carefully eased Mary Rose down on a chair that Meggie held out, then slowly pushed it close to the table.

After he seated himself, he said grace. Meggie said matter-of-factly to Mary Rose, "Papa's a vicar, you know. He is more properly known as Reverend Sherbrooke. He is an orator of renown, recognized far and wide for his scholarship. My brother Max, though, he reads Latin better than Papa."

A vicar? Ah, a vicar gave sermons.

Mary Rose looked at the beautiful man who sat at the head of the long dining table. She'd only met two vicars in her entire life, both of them ancient relics, one of them smelling of nutmeg and the other of cedar. This man smelled of fresh air and warmth.

"My daughter exaggerates," Tysen said calmly. Then he smiled at her. "Ah, Meggie," he added, "you forgot to mention the richness of my metaphors, so rich, evidently, that many of my congregation don't understand what I said. I shall have to think about that."

Meggie giggled. "Papa is known widely for his metaphors as well. It's only a few people who will admit to not understanding your oratory, Papa."

Tysen said to Mary Rose as he handed her a bowl, "Would you care for some soup? I have no notion of what it could be, but it smells quite good."

"Cock-a-leekie soup," Mary Rose said, still staring at him, and she breathed in deeply. "You are truly a vicar?"

He nodded and watched as Mrs. MacFardle ladled some cock-a-leekie soup into her bowl. "It is made with chicken and leeks and a lot of pepper. You may sneeze, but then you will smile with pleasure."

She had practically accused him of being profligate, like Erickson MacPhail. "I am so very sorry," she said aloud as she watched Mrs. MacFardle ladle the soup into his bowl then Meggie's.

"Why ever for?" Meggie asked Mary Rose as she took a small taste of her soup.

"I was somewhat rude to your father," Mary Rose said. "I thought he might be another bad man."

"Papa?" Meggie looked down the table at her father and smiled. "How could you ever believe Papa to be a bad man? Goodness, the problem is that Papa is too good, much too straight and proper, and—"

"Meggie," Tysen said, pointing his spoon at her, "that is quite enough. Try the dish Mrs. MacFardle is holding out to you."

Mary Rose grinned. "Those are very English—potatoes boiled until they are mush, with butter running through them."

"Aye," said Mrs. MacFardle, "a lot of butter. My granny said that Englishmen thrived on plain, solid food. We want ye to thrive, my lord. Too many young Barthwick men dead. Don't want ye to be amongst them, because if ye do croak it, then what will become of us here in the castle?"

"Thank you, Mrs. MacFardle. I should just as soon not join them either. The luncheon is delicious."

Mrs. MacFardle turned to Mary Rose. Where there was only disapproval aimed toward Tysen, toward Mary Rose there was downright dislike. "Ye've eaten quite enough, my girl. Oglivie will drive ye back to Vallance Manor."

Tysen was appalled at his housekeeper's rudeness. He opened his mouth, only to be forestalled by Mary Rose, who said calmly, "I am ready to leave, Mrs. Mac-Fardle."

6

TYSEN WAS SITTING in a large cushioned chair behind
the battered oak desk in the musty, dark library that was
filled with so many books he was struck dumb with pleasure at the sight of all of them. Then he'd discovered that
most of them had yet to have their pages cut. The Barthwicks weren't, evidently, much for reading. Ah, but now
they were his books. He'd rubbed his hands together as
he took down Homer's *Iliad*, a dark-red book so old the
leather was cracked and peeling. He would have to have
someone go through the books very carefully and oil
them. He couldn't wait to see the look on Max's face
when he walked into this room. Max would want to be
the one to restore this magnificent, gloomy library. He
could also see his son carefully cutting each of the pages,
smoothing them down, pausing to read every few pages,
unable to stop himself. Tysen rose slowly when he saw
his daughter peering around the door.

"What is it, Meggie?" he asked, smiling at her, wondering why she was just lingering there and not dancing
through the room right up to his desk.

"You're smiling, Papa. It's very nice. I don't mean to
bother you, but I want to know why Mrs. MacFardle was
so mean to Mary Rose."

"That is an excellent question. I don't know. She just shook her head and pursed her lips when I upbraided her. At least we saw Mary Rose off in the dogcart with her foot resting on three pillows. Oglivie told me he took her right to the front steps of Vallance Manor."

"She has a lot of curly red hair, just like Aunt Alex."

"Yes, she does." Her hair had smelled of roses, he thought, and unconsciously drew another deep breath, but this time there was only the musty odor of a room left closed up for far too long. Tysen shook his head. "These wretched accounts. I will need help with them. I know Mr. MacCray told me about an estate manager, but I don't remember his name. Where is the man?"

"His name is Miles MacNeily. His mother died and he had to go to Inverness to see to things. He will be back in three or four days."

"Meggie, how do you know this?"

"I was out in the stables, making certain that Big Fellow was being taken care of properly, and I overheard MacNee and Ardle speaking of it. You know that servants know everything, Papa. When I offered them both some almond sweetmeats that Aunt Sinjun gave me, they told me how the old laird wanted to burn down Kildrummy Castle after Ian died, but none of the servants would let him do it. Pouder, they told me, flung himself on top of the old laird and pinned him down on the floor until the other servants dashed in to help him."

"Pouder? It is hard to imagine that. I can't see Pouder even able to flatten a fly. Of course, Old Tyronne was eighty-seven, but Pouder can't be more than a decade younger."

"I shall ask Pouder about it," Meggie said, grinning. "It must have been quite a sight."

Tysen said, "Old Tyronne's melancholy is understandable. Every one of his heirs was dead. Still, it is a pity that he died so embittered."

"Oh, no, he wasn't sad about that, Papa, at least according to MacNee and Ardle. They said he was angry at Miss Donnatella Vallance because she wouldn't marry him. Ranted that he could get another boy child off her and it was all her fault for being so selfish. Not his fault, never his. He'd done his best, but now he claimed he didn't care, and that was why he wanted to burn Kildrummy Castle. He wanted to burn it to the ground, make it hot enough so the devil would accept it in hell."

"Donnatella is Mary Rose's cousin, I believe."

"Evidently she is also a handful, at least according to MacNee, who is quite a handsome man, and I think perhaps he would like to flirt with her himself."

"Meggie, you will not delve into those particular matters, all right?"

"I was just listening, Papa."

Tysen let that go. He said, "I remember Old Tyronne as quite amiable. Of course, that was at a time when he had more heirs than any man I've ever known of." He wanted to know what else she'd learned, but he was her father, a vicar, and he didn't believe in gossip, really he didn't. And then his sweet daughter said, "Mary Rose and her mother live with Donnatella. Mary Rose's mother is mad, has been for nearly forever. Evidently Donnatella is very lively and terribly beautiful. She is spoiled, but she is so beautiful that no one minds too much when she throws a tantrum."

Tysen stared, mesmerized. Meggie's sources of information never ceased to amaze him. She'd learned all this just by distributing almond sweetmeats?

"Donnatella is younger than Mary Rose," he said slowly. "The old man was well into his eighties, and he actually expected a young girl to marry him?"

"That's right," Meggie said, and sidled farther into the room, sniffing the air. "Ardle said that Lord Barthwick believed Donnatella had the finest pair of hips in all of Scotland and was sure that birthing more heirs would be no problem for her. He also said that Lord Barthwick had more self-confidence than a man with two brains. Papa, I think we should open those windows. It is dreadfully close in here."

"You're right," Tysen said, knowing he should say something to Meggie about speaking of a woman's hips and childbirth, but he just wasn't up to it. Instead, he walked to the bank of heavy velvet draperies and jerked them open. Dust billowed into the air, setting him to sneezing. It took him a while to get the latch to open on the large glass doors. Finally, with a creak and a groan, the doors flew open, and father and daughter stood side by side looking out into a small garden, no more than the size of the library. It was completely overgrown—wild rose bushes, yew bushes, ivy, daffodils, and bright-red rhododendron bushes were all tangled together, choking each other to gain the bit of available sunlight.

"I had thought the entire manor formed a large square, what with the enclosed inner courtyard," Tysen said as he walked slowly out onto moss-covered stones outside the library. He turned and looked back. "Oh, I see. The library was simply cut in half to make this garden. Because it is facing the sea, it isn't obvious that it's here. A pity it has been let run wild. I wonder how many years since those glass doors have even been opened? Probably longer than you've been on this earth," he added, smiling down at her.

As for Meggie, his smile meant that he was no longer upset with her. It was a vast relief. He had, she thought, smiled more since they'd arrived here at Kildrummy than he had during than the entire past month in England. She said as she studied the tangled vines and branches, "There are many flowers buried under here, Papa. I'll be able to clean them up and then replant them around the castle. What do you think?"

"I think you are much like your aunt Alex. When she walks around the Northcliffe gardens, the bushes, plants, and flowers all come to attention. Douglas says the plants stand taller than his troops ever did when they were on parade."

Meggie was already rubbing her hands together. "I will begin this afternoon. I will write to Aunt Alex and ask her advice. Oh, yes, Papa, MacNee also told me about Lord Barthwick's cousin, Mrs. Griffin. She sounds rather frightening. She and her husband live in Edinburgh, but they were here much of the time, toward the end. MacNee said she was a real tartar and an old besom. What does that mean?"

"She isn't amiable," Tysen said and thought, Please, Lord, please keep the dear woman away.

"Well, MacNee said everyone prayed she wouldn't come back for at least ten years."

Tysen immediately joined in the prayers. "Donald MacCray didn't say anything about her," Tysen said. "I wonder why not?"

Meggie just shrugged, then said, "Oh, yes, Mrs. MacFardle wanted me to tell you that there is a message from Sir Lyon Vallance. He and his family will visit us here tomorrow afternoon at precisely three o'clock."

Tysen was pleased. He planned to speak to the man about protecting his niece from the likes of Erickson MacPhail.

Tysen nodded in greeting to Sir Lyon Vallance, a tall man with reddened cheeks, probably from too much drink. He'd once been a handsome man, but now he was running to fat. He was a bit beyond his middle years, but seemed bluff and good-natured. He pumped Tysen's hand up and down in a hearty grip. He was bald except for a very thin gray circle around his head. He beamed a long look around the drawing room and made a small sound of pleasure. Tysen nearly smiled at that. He didn't blame Sir Lyon. It was a cozy room, and he liked it despite its need to have new wallpaper and perhaps some new furniture and draperies as well. He would take care of that soon enough.

As for Sir Lyon's wife, Lady Margaret, she was a handsome woman, deep-bosomed, beautifully gowned, nearly as tall as her spouse, more than a glint of intelligence in her dark eyes. She was also quite a bit younger than her husband. Oddly, she was giving the room a rather proprietary look. As for their only child, Donnatella, Tysen realized that she was eyeing him more than was proper. Something of a cynic—a man of God couldn't escape a measure of cynicism, what with the indignity of human nature—he imagined that the lovely girl was expecting him to sigh over her hand, perhaps hold that delicate hand overlong, perhaps give her a dazed look to show her he was sufficiently bowled over by her charm. Just like Melissande, Alex's sister, who was, in truth, much more beautiful than Donnatella Vallance. After what Meggie had told him about her, he doubted he'd be bowled over even if he found her utterly charming. He merely nodded to her as he had to her father and mother. He girded his mental loins, and when everyone had a cup of tea in hand, he said pleasantly, "I am pleased to meet my neighbors. I trust Mary Rose's ankle isn't paining her too badly today?"

Lady Margaret arched a sleek black brow. "Her what, my lord?"

"Mary Rose's ankle, my lady," Tysen said, then took a sip of his tea.

"Oh, yes," Donnatella said, sitting forward in her chair, offering him an excellent display of her cleavage that was, indeed, quite lovely, almost as lovely as Mrs. Drakemore's, a widow in his congregation who displayed herself to him each and every chance she got. Truth be told, he'd been treated to many displays of feminine ingenuity since Melinda Beatrice had died six years before. Donnatella continued, giving Tysen another smile that surely invited intimacies, "Don't you recall, Mama? Mary Rose said something about falling into one of the sheep killers. She sprained it."

Lady Margaret obviously didn't recollect Mary Rose's accident. "She should take more care," she said, then looked long at Tysen. "You will be delighted to come to Vallance Manor for dinner, my lord. Perhaps Friday evening? Just you and the family. We can become better acquainted."

"I should be delighted," Tysen said.

"I shall give you a tour of the area tomorrow morning, my lord," Donnatella said. "I will come at nine o'clock."

"I have ridden both south and west," Tysen said. "I should be delighted to tour the north, perhaps to Stonehaven. I visited the town when I was here before as a boy."

He handed around a platter of Mrs. MacFardle's clootie dumplings, his first sight of them but an hour before. He saw Meggie cramming one into her mouth.

"Barthwick has been too long without a mistress," Lady Margaret said, her voice proprietary enough for a deaf man to hear. "Far too long."

"From what I have been told," Tysen said easily, "there has been no mistress here for more decades than I've been on this earth."

Sir Lyon guffawed in his tea. "A bit of wit, m'dear. Charming, don't you think?"

"Wit is only charming when it doesn't impede or otherwise obstruct the conversational direction I am taking," said Lady Margaret. "The furnishings—they are old and out-of-date. It is time a lady saw to things. A lady who has, perhaps, another, more experienced lady, to advise her—in short, her mother."

Tysen was afraid of that. Evidently Lady Margaret, after only ten minutes in his company, was ready to offer her daughter as his future spouse. But why him? Certainly Barthwick was a nice holding, but surely Donnatella could have her pick of gentlemen in these parts.

He had no intention of embroiling himself with any young lady. He did not want or need a wife, his children did not want or need a stepmama. His flock would perhaps appreciate a vicar's wife who would have their interests at heart. But if truth be told, even his congregation had appeared more content after Melinda Beatrice was gone. No, not content exactly. After all, Melinda Beatrice had always had their interests at heart; indeed, she was always telling him who needed to be fixed and how. It was just that when their interests hadn't coincided exactly with hers, then she had ground them under. He shook his head. Such thoughts were disloyal, unworthy of him, certainly more than unworthy of a man of God. He forced himself back to the platter of clootie dumplings and selected one. His nostrils quivered, they smelled so good.

Not ten minutes after the Vallance family had taken their leave, Meggie sidled out the front door to stand beside him.

"Mrs. MacFardle says that Donnatella Vallance is the most beautiful girl ever produced in these parts."

"You make her sound like a sausage," Tysen said, turning to face his daughter. "She is fine-looking, I suppose."

Then he shrugged. Perhaps he would have the opportunity to speak to Sir Lyon about Erickson MacPhail Friday evening when he went to Vallance Manor for dinner. He hoped Mary Rose's ankle would be sufficiently healed by then.

That evening, Tysen and Meggie stood together on the edge of Bleaker's Bluff, looking out over the sea, watching the porpoises dive and play, their honking noises filling the evening air. Oystercatchers spun and wheeled overhead, looking for schools of herring the porpoises churned up. The beach below was covered with large, rounded pebbles. Tysen couldn't begin to imagine how many centuries of tides sweeping over the beach had been required to smooth the pebbles to such perfect roundness. They covered the beach, making it dangerous to walk there. Seaweed wrapped around driftwood lay scattered over the pebbles, the wet green of the seaweed looking nearly black in the fading sunlight.

"Do you wish to sleep in my bedchamber again tonight, Meggie?"

She shook her head, her eyes on a baby porpoise that was diving madly around its mother. "I'll be all right, Papa. I am sorry to admit it, but that storm rattled me. But it's peaceful now, so I won't get scared."

Tysen nodded, breathed in the sweet, warm evening air. It was incredible here. He hadn't thought once about writing a sermon, which was odd of him.

It was then that Tysen looked up to see a man on horseback coming toward them. Another neighbor?

But when the man was close enough, Tysen felt himself drawing up. It was Erickson MacPhail, he knew it, not a single doubt. The confidence and arrogance in his very posture indicated a man who took what he wanted and damned the consequences and the wishes of anyone who chanced to cross him. Tysen took Meggie's hand and they waited, father and daughter standing side by side, until the man dismounted and left his horse to graze on the clusters of knicker weed sticking out of clumps of black rocks.

"I heard the castle had a fine new Englishman in residence," the man called out, striding toward them, tapping his riding crop against his Hessian boot. Then he noticed Meggie. "I had not heard," he added slowly, his voice thoughtful now, not so belligerent, "that the Englishman had a daughter."

"I am Lord Barthwick," Tysen said, surprised at himself for the show of formality, the touch of arrogance in his own voice. "This is my daughter, Meggie."

"I am Erickson MacPhail, Laird MacPhail, of Hyson's Manor. I am pleased to meet you, my lord, and you, little miss." He bowed to both of them, then straightened and looked out over the water. He breathed in deeply, his chest expanding. "This has long been one of my favorite lookouts. So many porpoises. As a boy I swam with them."

"Really?" Meggie stepped away from her father, stepped toward this unknown man. "You really swam with them? What happened? Did they hold you underwater? Flatten you?"

Erickson MacPhail smiled down at her, and it was a charming smile, open and friendly. "Oh, no. Porpoises are some of God's friendliest creatures. They welcome you, nudge you to play, stay with you."

"Oh, Papa," Meggie said, turning back to her father, her eyes shining, "I should love to do that. May we? Tomorrow, perhaps, if it is warm and sunny?"

"The water is always cold," Erickson said, grinning from her to Tysen. "You cannot stay in for very long or you will turn blue."

"Ten minutes, Papa? You taught me how to swim. It can't be colder than the Channel, can it?"

"Possibly," Tysen said, and felt something quite fresh and spontaneous blossom inside him. "Swimming with porpoises," he said. "I think I should like that as well."

"I saw you standing here and supposed you must be the new baron."

"Yes," Tysen said easily, eyeing the man who was constantly trying to catch Mary Rose alone and maul her. What sort of a man swam with porpoises, then tried to ravish a young lady? He was well made, fine-looking, he thought objectively. And dishonorable? He would know soon enough. "Meggie, why don't you go down to the beach and stick your fingers in the water? See how cold it is."

Meggie, excitement in every skipping step, was off.

"Pay attention to the path," Erickson MacPhail called after her. "It's an easy winding downward, but there are some sharp points."

Meggie waved but didn't slow. "If she takes a spill," he said, "she won't be hurt, just scratched a bit. You are an Englishman. Everyone has heard about it, but I wished to see for myself."

Tysen was watching Meggie's descent. He saw her skirt catch on a rock, pull her over, then he heard her laughter, sweet and clear in the evening air.

"I am just a man," Tysen said finally, looking back at the man who was probably several years younger than he was. Yes, Erickson MacPhail was handsome, also very well dressed. But there was dissatisfaction written around his well-shaped mouth, Tysen saw. Frustration, perhaps. Resentment? But why? "I hail from southern England, near Eastbourne in a small town called Glenclose-on-Rowan."

"I have been all over England. I found Brighton a lovely place, Eastbourne as well. You are part of the Sherbrooke family. Your eldest brother is the earl of North-cliffe?"

"That's right."

"I remember walking over the land where the Battle of Hastings was fought. It was moving, that spot, perhaps even atmospheric, but it is not Scotland. There is no land more beautiful, more filled with glorious memories than Scotland."

"It is quite magnificent here," Tysen agreed. "I met Mary Rose Fordyce yesterday."

"Oh? I saw her yesterday as well. She was coming out of the pine forest. She'd wondered about you and had been watching you leave the castle. That's what she told me. She likes to watch people going about their business. She is fanciful. She makes up stories about them, based on her observations of them."

"She hurt herself."

The man stiffened, his eyes darkened with concern. This was interesting, Tysen thought.

"Is she all right? What happened?"

"She sprained her ankle. Actually, she mistook me for you, chasing her down. She was running as fast as she could away from you. She tripped and fell into a sheep killer."

"There is no reason for Mary Rose to fear me," said Erickson MacPhail, and there was anger in his voice, and frustration as well. "I had already left her. There was no discord between us. I think it more likely that you misunderstood, my lord."

"Not likely," Tysen said. "She told me that you tried to maul her, that you even wait for her to come out and then you attack her. You have done this many times. I asked her why her father doesn't protect her, but evidently her father is dead. I have met her uncle, Sir Lyon Vallance."

"He is much admired in these parts. He used to be quite

the sportsman in his younger years. But when it comes right down to it, he stamps his big feet and bellows to the rafters, but there is no heat in him. If something needs to be done, he wants others to do it for him. I mean no harm to Mary Rose. I never have."

"She believes that you do."

There was contempt in the young man's voice as he said, "So she asked you, a stranger, an Englishman, to warn me away?"

"No, I have taken it upon myself to warn you off. She is a young lady. She should not have to worry about men waylaying her." Tysen wasn't used to this, but he said it, his voice clear and cold, "Is it rape you have in mind, sir?"

"Very strong words, my lord. Very strong, indeed. You are a stranger here. You are not a Scot. You know nothing. However, I choose not to take offense. I shouldn't want to bloody your face with your daughter nearby. You mistake the entire matter." He laughed. "Mary Rose, a lady?" Erickson MacPhail threw back his handsome head and laughed again, laughed louder than the squawking seagulls overhead. Then he waved to Meggie, turned to his horse and mounted in a single graceful movement. "Soon, my lord," he called, and wheeled his big gray gelding away. Tysen stood watching until he disappeared over a small hillock to the west.

The sun had set. It was chilly now, wind beginning to whip up from the sea. He called to Meggie, watched her wave back and begin her climb up the hill path to where he stood. It had rained the past two nights. Meggie didn't think it would storm tonight. Perhaps she'd given some almond sweetmeats to a local seer and been told it would be clear. He wouldn't be too surprised if that was the case.

Tysen sighed. He didn't understand this business between Mary Rose and Erickson MacPhail. He knew he shouldn't involve himself in local difficulties, but he'd been there, actually seen her fear. He didn't have a choice. Why had MacPhail really ridden this way?

7

∞

DONNATELLA VALLANCE ARRIVED at the exact same moment as an old carriage rolled into the inner courtyard through the gates of the castle.

Tysen heard Oglivie's voice, overwhelmed by a woman's imperious voice, then Donnatella said, "Oh, dear, it is Mr. and Mrs. Griffin, here from Edinburgh. I had hoped they would not descend on you quite so quickly. Mrs. Griffin was not pleased when it was announced that you were the heir. Oh, dear. She is a witch. Good luck."

"What about Mr. Griffin?" Tysen asked.

"Mr. Griffin has never expressed an opinion, as far as I know."

"What do you know about Mr. Griffin, I ask you, you impertinent chit? Sir, I am Mrs. Griffin. My lord, you will speak to me."

He stared at the lady who was striding toward him, like a major in the king's army, garbed in severe, unrelieved black, swinging a black cane with a golden griffin on its head, her voice as deep and sharp as a man's.

He said easily, "I am Tysen Sherbrooke, ma'am, Lord Barthwick. You were first cousin to the former Lord

Barthwick? Have I got it right? Is it possible that we are related?"

She had a thin black mustache atop her upper lip and masses of black hair, all twisted in coils on top of her head. Medusa had perhaps resembled Mrs. Griffin. The mustache quivered a bit as she shouted at him, "Related to you, sir? Good Gad, no! No paltry English blood in these veins. Well, no more than a dollop of English blood. I would allow no more. No, sir, I am a Scotswoman, through and through, very nearly.

"You are not a Scotsman. It is more than just a pity. It is more than a disaster, but God has cursed us for some heretofore unpunished sin and consigned all the worthwhile heirs underground. What are you doing here, Donnatella?"

"I am here to take his lordship on a tour, ma'am. I arrived just before you did." Donnatella then turned to Tysen and gave him a very warm smile. "Good day, my lord, it is ever so pleasant to see you again. Are you ready to leave?"

The black mustache quivered again, just a bit, over Mrs. Griffin's upper lip. Tysen wondered if Mrs. Griffin had a first name, but he didn't ask because then the lady laughed, a perfectly dreadful sound, all deep and hoarse, and said, "Ha! I'll wager one of my last groats that a tour isn't your objective at all, Donnatella. You are here to begin your flirtations with the poor man, who isn't poor at all since he now owns Kildrummy Castle, which the good Lord knows he doesn't deserve."

Well, that was the truth, he thought.

Mrs. Griffin turned back to Tysen, gave him a look that clearly told him he was grossly lacking, and said, "You probably do not have a chance, my lord. Donnatella is young, but she is wise in the ways of women, and thus, as a man, you haven't a chance. Hmmm. Donnatella is a

Scotswoman, however, and that is probably the only good thing to come out of this debacle. I would have married old Tyronne myself, but I was too old to give birth to another heir, and also, alas, there is Mr. Griffin to consider. A pity, but we will see."

Tysen looked beyond Mrs. Griffin to see a very tall, very thin gentleman, nattily dressed, his hair snow-white, thick and full, leaning against the door of the carriage.

"Sir," Tysen said, giving him a slight bow.

Mr. Griffin nodded, returned with a quick, jerking bow, and nodded once again. He walked up to stand just behind his wife. "My lord. We are here. We have returned, just as we promised ourselves we would. You have met my charming wife, I see."

"Yes, he has, Mr. Griffin. I am still standing outside, and I don't want to be here. Now, where is Mrs. Mac-Fardle?"

Tysen couldn't think of a single thing to say. He merely stood there gazing after the very tall lady who was old enough to be his mother and was probably even more vicious than his mother, who excelled at her craft. He prayed that neither Mr. nor Mrs. Griffin would remain for very long. He continued looking after her until she passed through the front door, Mrs. MacFardle now by her side. Mr. Griffin trailed gracefully behind his wife. She continued to swing her griffin-headed black cane back and forth.

"She is quite obsessed with Kildrummy," Donnatella said calmly, straightening the charming little riding hat she wore. A dark-blue ostrich plume curved around one cheek. "Do not have an apoplexy, my lord, for neither Mrs. Griffin nor Mr. Griffin lives here, thank the gracious Lord. Evidently she decided to see the new master of Kildrummy Castle for herself. She probably will not remain long. She detests the sea air. She says it makes her nose swell. I believe that her nose swells because she drinks so much smuggled French brandy. Mr. Griffin doesn't drink anything at all. He just stands there, all skinny and blank-looking, well dressed, his arms crossed, and stares at everyone. You have my profound sympathy, my lord."

Donnatella lightly laid her fingers on his arm. "Would you like to leave now?"

Tysen looked after the couple, Mr. Griffin still right on Mrs. Griffin's bootheels, nearly inside the castle now, and he wondered what his obligations were in that particular direction.

Donnatella laughed. "Don't concern yourself, my lord, truly, she will do just as she pleases without a by-your-leave. For the most part, she is harmless."

"And for all the other parts?"

"Whatever is involved, I doubt you will like it. She will boss everyone about. You will see that she and Mrs. MacFardle are quite the bosom bows—like to like, as my mother says. Also, Mrs. Griffin is quite rich, for Mr. Griffin owns a huge iron foundry outside of Edinburgh."

And so Tysen elected not to concern himself, at least not until he returned from his tour.

Donnatella took him all over the countryside. They visited Stonehaven, not at all changed from his boy's memory, all the houses still dark and dreary, hunkered down between a low, meandering cliff and the sea.

Tysen was beginning to believe that he had ridden by every single hillock, seen every tree, remarked upon every crofter's cottage by the time she stopped at a jagged outcropping of a cliff that hung dramatically over the sea about two miles northeast of Vallance Manor. She dismounted, walked to the edge, and stared down. She looked over her shoulder and called out, "Come, my lord. This is where Ian fell to his death. He broke his neck when he hit the rocks below. See there, since it is nearing high tide, you can barely see the tops of them sticking out of the water. There are no paths leading down to the water here. It was very difficult to bring Ian back up to bury him. Old Tyronne supervised the entire venture."

Tysen walked slowly toward her. He remembered Ian so clearly in that moment—so very young and strong, his white teeth gleaming when he smiled. He'd smiled so much as a boy, and he was filled with mischief. And then he had died before he reached his thirtieth year. The last heir. He'd been old Tyronne's last hope, his last grandson. Mr. and Mrs. Griffin's last hope as well, Tysen supposed.

As far as Tysen could tell, Donnatella Vallance hadn't flirted with him at all, thankfully. She'd just tried to ride him into the ground. Big Fellow was snorting, tossing his head. He was tired.

Tysen said, looking at those sharp black rocks with the frothy white waves whipping around them, "Donald MacCray, the solicitor in Edinburgh, wrote that Ian was drunk when he fell."

"That is what was said," Donnatella said, then shrugged. "Do you remember him from your only visit here? He was younger than you, wasn't he? Perhaps about two years younger?"

"Yes, I was ten at the time, and I believe Ian was around eight. I liked him. It is a pity that it happened."

Donnatella's chin went into the air, she drew in a deep breath of salty sea air and said, "He changed. At one time he was my hero—when he was twenty and I was only nine. I would have done anything for him. But then he changed, became sullen and withdrawn. I remember hearing of wickedness, of too much wildness in bad places in Edinburgh. Then, last year, when I decided to marry him, he was perhaps happy for a while, but evidently he drank too much one night and stumbled over this cliff. I doubt I will ever forgive him for that."

"I'm sorry, Miss Vallance. I did not know that you were his fiancée at the time of his death."

She turned and smiled at him, shrugged. "My father and mother wished me to be mistress of Kildrummy Castle. I did not love him, but I finally agreed to marry him." She paused then and gave him a sloe-eyed smile designed to make a man's knees go weak, a smile so beguiling it was superior even to those embarrassingly intimate smiles that Mrs. Delaney, the widow of a local draper, frequently sent his way. She was an extraordinarily confident lady who had made it her goal last year to get him into her bed. He would never forget what she'd whispered in his ear one evening after a town meeting regarding the bridge to be built over the river Rowen: "I want to bed you, Vicar, not wed you. Can you begin to imagine how I will make you feel?"

He'd had to admit to her that no, he couldn't begin to imagine. He had escaped without rudeness, surely a remarkable feat, given the lady's perseverance.

"Miss Vallance—"

"My lord, since we are neighbors perhaps you should call me Donnatella."

He said, "Very well, Donnatella. I am still very sorry about Ian. In the course of things he would be Lord Barthwick now, not I, and you would be his wife. It was a tragedy."

"But now you are here, my lord."

"Yes, now things have changed utterly, and I am here. To be honest, I had forgotten all about Kildrummy. I am a widower, ma'am. Perhaps you did not know that I am also a vicar. I am Reverend Sherbrooke of Glenclose-on-Rowan."

She gaped at him. It was particularly charming since it make her look silly, rather dull-witted, and thus quite human. "You are a vicar?" He'd never heard such incredulity in his life. He smiled at her and said, "Yes, Miss Vallance, I am a vicar."

She was looking at him, studying his face, still uncertain, still questioning. "But how is such a thing possible? Goodness, sir, I have seen paintings of John Knox, and let me tell you that he looked like what he was supposed to look like. But you do not. You, a vicar? No, it isn't possible. You are teasing me because you do not wish to engage at present in a harmless flirtation and thus you are trying to put me off."

He cocked his head at her. "Why isn't it possible, Miss Vallance?"

She looked at him as if he'd lost his remaining wits. She shook her head at him. "Because you are very handsome. You are also rich."

His Sherbrooke looks again. Well, there was nothing he could do about the way he looked or about the money that filled his coffers. Now that he thought about it, he himself had seen renderings of John Knox. The man's face made him shiver a bit. A fanatic in Presbyterian's clothing. He said, a smile in his voice, "You wish to see handsome gentlemen, you should meet my brothers."

"Well," she said slowly, looking even more closely at him now, trying perhaps to see if there was some sort of sign on his face that fit what a man of God should look like, at least in her view. "Thank heaven that you are not a priest, my lord," she then said, and touched her fingertips to his sleeve. "You are a widower. Do accept my condolences. We will have a late luncheon at Vallance Manor. My father requested that you come." She cocked her head to one side, the ostrich feather curling around her cheek, and said, "You may say grace to bless our food. It is rarely done. I cannot wait to see Papa's face."

Vallance Manor was an upstart, Donnatella told him as they reined in their mounts in front of a compact gray-granite house that looked more English than Scottish and wasn't old enough to have enjoyed a single soldier pouring boiling oil down on an enemy. It was a neat property, surrounded by pine trees, a graveled drive in front of it, beech trees lined up along the sides. It was inland from the sea, a good half-mile, but Tysen could still smell the sea air, and he liked that.

Donnatella tossed her mare's reins to a young boy who was missing his front tooth and was gazing at her with naked adoration.

She ignored him, waiting until Tysen dismounted and handed the boy Big Fellow's reins as well.

He realized he would soon see Mary Rose. Odd that he didn't think of her as Miss Fordyce. No, she had been Mary Rose from the moment he'd heard her name. He couldn't very well call her Miss Fordyce now. He would feel like a complete fool. He said, "I trust Mary Rose's ankle is healed today?"

Donnatella shrugged. "I don't know."

"I will soon see for myself," Tysen said.

"You are very kind to be concerned about her."

"She took a very bad fall. I was worried she had done herself a lasting injury."

"She didn't. She is fine."

He wanted to tell her that since she'd admitted that she didn't even know, how could she say with such certainty that Mary Rose was fine? Because no one had called for a physician?

He was met and briefly entertained by both Sir Lyon and Lady Margaret in the drawing room, a very modern room filled with furnishings to reflect the contemporary craze for all things Egyptian, from sofas with scrolled arms to chairs with clawed feet.

"How is Mary Rose?" he asked when there was finally a brief lull in the conversation. He was surprised that she wasn't here to greet him, a bit put out as well. He had saved her, after all, and yet she didn't care enough to thank him, or at least to acknowledge his presence.

Lady Margaret said, "Mary Rose, my lord, is fine. She naturally will not be dining with us."

"I don't understand," Tysen said slowly. "If she is fine, then why won't she be dining with us?" A look passed between Sir Lyon and his wife.

"Ah, of course the girl will eat with us," Sir Lyon said. "My lady was thinking that she had a prior appointment, but I do not believe it is so. Donnatella, my dear, why don't you fetch your cousin? Then we will have our luncheon."

Donnatella smiled at Tysen. "I think you will be quite relieved, my lord. You will see that she is fine now." And she left the drawing room, lifting off her charming riding hat as she went.

Sir Lyon, his voice all bluff and full of bonhomie, said, "Well, did my little beauty take you everywhere, my lord?"

"Yes, sir," Tysen said and thought of the dozen streams they had crossed, the ancient circle of stones they had seen, the ruins of a very old Scottish castle. "I believe I saw everything." He then asked about the history of Vallance Manor.

"It was said that Mary, Queen of Scots once stayed here," said Lady Margaret. "The manor was newly built then. I believe the year was 1570."

The door opened and in walked Mary Rose, no limp, thank the good Lord.

For a moment, Mary Rose and Donnatella were standing side by side. Mary Rose was tall, very slender, her dark red hair ruthlessly snagged back and rolled into a tight bun at the base of her neck. Her gown was an indeterminate gray from many washings, at least ten years old, he thought. But her eyes—they were the color of rich green moss, moss just rained upon, moss hidden from the sunlight, left in shadows to hold secrets and look mysterious. They'd been clouded with pain when he had seen her the first time, but not now. This was ridiculous—eyes the color of moss hidden from sunlight? He was suffering a flight of fancy that simply wasn't proper or appropriate. Had he ever even been visited by a flight of fancy before? Perhaps he felt a bit proprietary because he'd saved her. Yes, that was it. He turned purposely to Donnatella, who was smaller than her cousin, her figure lovely and rounded, her hair a rich, deep black, no red in it, her skin as white as a fresh snowfall. They looked absolutely nothing alike.

Mary Rose was—was what? Tysen frowned. She was a woman, not a girl like Donnatella. She also had a very strange look on her face. Those mysterious eyes of hers were narrowed, intent. She wasn't looking at him, she was looking at Lady Margaret.

He rose quickly and walked to her. "Hello, Mary Rose," he said and took her hand in his for a moment. He studied her face. "Your ankle is fit again?"

"Yes, my lord. I am perfectly fine now."

He dropped her hand, and she looked up at him now, full face, and wondered if he had already fallen in love with Donnatella. She knew well enough that she looked like a peasant next to her cousin—a maypole, a scarecrow stuck on a stick to frighten away birds in the fields. She was wearing an old woolen gown that had belonged to her mother when she'd been young. It was too short, far short of her ankles. Not that it mattered. She was nothing. Well, she didn't want to be anything, particularly to this Englishman—to any man, actually.

"Excellent," Tysen said, then took a step back. There was dead silence. Finally, Sir Lyon hefted himself to his feet. "Eh, my lord? Luncheon? I know it is late, but my beauty here wanted you to see everything before she brought you back."

"Yes," Tysen said. "Yes, luncheon would be very nice."

Without thinking, he offered his arm to Mary Rose. Donnatella laughed.

Over *forfar bridies*—sausage in pastry coats, tossed with onions—Donnatella said to the table at large, "I showed his lordship where poor Ian fell."

Mary Rose's fork fell from her fingers and clattered to the tabletop. But she didn't say anything.

Tysen said, "It is a tragedy. I remember Ian from the one time I was here so very long ago. I understand that he was to marry Miss Vallance. My profound sympathies to you all."

Everyone thanked him. Mary Rose picked up her fork, kept her head down, and continued eating something that Lady Margaret called *finnan haddies*, which, Donnatella told him, laughing, was simply haddock smoked over a peat fire. But the name was so quaint, didn't he agree? Yes, it was a very old Scottish dish that was much beloved.

"Would you care for some damson jam, my lord? It's delicious on Cook's scones."

"Thank you, Lady Margaret," Tysen said. He continued smoothly to Mary Rose, "I was standing with Meggie on Bleaker's Bluff last evening when we had a visitor. It was Erickson MacPhail."

Fear emptied all expression on her face. He'd scared her because he had decided it was time to bring Mac-Phail's dishonorable behavior into the open. But it wasn't well done of him. Before she looked down at her plate again, he saw something else in those very green eyes of hers. They held no secrets, no mysteries now. It was helplessness, he saw. She looked utterly helpless. If he hadn't been seated, he would have kicked himself.

Mary Rose calmly picked up her fork and cut up an overcooked carrot. She wouldn't be so surprised again that she dropped her fork. She had control of herself now. But why had Erickson sought him out? What had he said to Tysen? And why, she wondered as she looked over at him, her face perfectly blank now, had he brought Erickson's name up, here at luncheon?

Sir Lyon said, oblivious of the swirling undercurrents at his table, "Erickson MacPhail, a fine young man. His father was an excellent friend. Many of us were very distressed when he fell into one of those ridiculous sheep killers and broke his neck in a demned footrace with one of his crofters. Erickson is now the MacPhail laird." He gave a proud look toward his daughter. "He has been just one of many of our local boys to crowd upon my doorstep, all of them lapdogs for my dearest Donnatella. The day she turned seventeen, by gad, I thought I should have to keep my brace of pistols close about to scatter all those smitten young dogs."

"I have told Erickson no, Papa," Donnatella said calmly and took a bite of small boiled potatoes. "I told you that."

"But now Ian is dead, Donnatella," Lady Margaret said. "Perhaps you should reconsider Erickson's suit. Hyson's Manor is a fine holding. Except for Erickson's mother, who is a rather dreadful woman, it would be an excellent place to reside. The good Lord provides, however. If you married Erickson, she would doubtless have the good manners to die soon, don't you think?"

"It would benefit everyone," Donnatella said. Then she looked directly at Tysen. "We will see. Yes, we will just have to see, won't we?"

Tysen felt like a grouse on the run from hunters. He wondered where Sir Lyon kept his brace of pistols. He said, "MacPhail said he used to swim with the porpoises when he was a boy."

"Splendid young fellow," Sir Lyon said, and drank down his glass of wine in one long gulp. "Absolutely splendid." He wiped his mouth on the back of his hand, motioning immediately for the man standing just off to his left, probably the butler, Tysen thought, to pour him another glass, which he did. "Thank you, Gillis. I cannot understand, myself, how diving in and out of the water with bloody fish would be much fun, but to each his own."

Donnatella laughed behind her napkin.

"Mary Rose," Tysen said, turning to her, "you are acquainted with Erickson MacPhail." The moment the words were out of his mouth, Tysen wanted to shoot himself. Why in the dear Lord's name had he shoved her into the open like that? He held himself silent, waiting to see what she would say. Perhaps she would throw her jam pastry at him. Actually he knew very well why he'd done it. Tysen had never been content to sit about when something needed to be resolved. He wanted this situation faced and Sir Lyon properly informed so he would protect his niece. He was clumsy in his approach, but he would see her safe.

Mary Rose said after a long moment, "When I was a little girl, I swam with Erickson and the porpoises. They are mammals, Uncle Lyon, just like us. Not fish. Erickson taught me how to swim. He taught me that the porpoises wouldn't hurt me, that they loved to play and dive and plunge around."

"Surely you are wrong," Sir Lyon said. "They live in the water. Only fish live in the water."

"But you have seen Erickson recently, haven't you, Mary Rose?" Donnatella asked, her voice cool, a thread of something Tysen didn't understand running through it. "Not that I mind, of course," Donnatella added in a bright voice. "After all, I did turn him down, didn't I?"

"Yes, I see him often," Mary Rose said. "Too often."

Enough, Tysen thought. Very well, he would speak privately to Sir Lyon. He was Mary Rose's uncle. It was his responsibility to protect her. It didn't matter if he wanted Erickson MacPhail for a son-in-law, but even then, Tysen didn't want to see Donnatella taken in either. One thing was certain, he would never allow Erickson MacPhail to become Sir Lyon's nephew-in-law. Surely the news that MacPhail was trying to accost Mary Rose would make Sir Lyon reassess his opinion that the man was an excellent fellow.

Lady Margaret rose gracefully from her lovely Louis XVI chair. "Donnatella, you and Mary Rose come with me," she said, and swept out of the small dining room before the two remaining male persons had time to put down their forks.

When they were alone, Sir Lyon eyed the young man on his right and said, "Is there some sort of problem here, my lord? You need my assistance perhaps in some estate matter?"

8

TYSEN SAID SLOWLY, relieved that Sir Lyon hadn't drunk any more wine, "No, sir. There is no estate problem. It is much more serious. You see, the reason Mary Rose hurt her ankle was because she was running from MacPhail and tripped into a sheep killer. I believe he attempts to get her alone. He will probably rape her if he isn't stopped. You are her uncle; it is your responsibility to warn him off. It was imperative that you knew what was happening. I wish Mary Rose had told you, but since she did not, I have."

Sir Lyon looked at him for a very long time, no expression at all on his face. He rubbed his knuckles over his cheek. He drank more wine. He said finally, "And just what would your point be, my lord?"

Tysen could only stare at the man. "My point is that you are her uncle, sir."

"Listen, my boy," Sir Lyon said, sitting forward, his hands clasped beneath his chin. "You do not understand the way of things. I know you are a man of God. That particular calling perhaps sharpens your sensibilities, makes you question, perhaps, the means necessary to gain a needful end. Aye, Donnatella whispered to her mother that you were a vicar, and my Margaret whispered it to me right before we came in to luncheon. I am sorry that I forgot to have you invoke God's blessing upon our meal. The haddock was on the dry side. Perhaps a prayer from a vicar would have made it more tender. Now, my lord, you do not understand the situation here. You believe Erickson to be dishonorable. You wish, because you are a vicar, to question his motives, to deplore his actions, perhaps to flay him as a sinner."

"As a man of God, certainly I question his motives and condemn his actions. He is unnatural. His behavior is beyond the line. As a man, I also find that I would like to flatten him if he bothers her again. I am, however, no blood relation to her. You, on the other hand, are her uncle, her only male relative. It is your duty to stop him. She is very afraid of him."

Sir Lyon frowned into his remaining wine. "I know that he wants her, he has told me so. I don't know why, but he does. She is, after all, nothing compared to her cousin. What's more, she carries The Taint and it will always be there. Yes, Erickson will rape her if he must, but only if he must. He has assured me of that. He wants her. I have given him my permission. He can have her. She'll get no better offer."

Tysen felt as if he was listening to a language he had never heard before. He simply didn't understand. He rose slowly and placed his palms on the tablecloth. "I will not allow this man to rape an innocent young lady."

"I told you that he would rape her only if he were forced to. I have knowledge of this. I don't approve of it, but Mary Rose is very stubborn. She doesn't appear to accept what she is. Well, she does, I suppose, in a sense, but she has this stubborn pride that is completely misplaced. She gives herself airs. She believes herself to be above Erickson, which is utter nonsense. She won't listen to him. She won't accept him. She insists that she will not have him. She must be made to realize that Erickson MacPhail represents a tremendous triumph for her. Even her mother—when her wits are unclouded, which isn't often nowadays—hasn't said anything against Erickson.

"Perhaps you can assist us, my lord. Mary Rose must be made to see that if she weds him, mouths will be closed. All talk of what she is will stop. Erickson, as her husband, would ensure that all talk would end. If the lad has to force her, why, then, that is what will happen, and the consequences—namely, her marriage to him—will, by far, outweigh the rough-and-tumble methods."

"Of course I will not assist in this. She doesn't want to marry him. Trust her, she isn't being coy. I tell you, she is terrified of him. Do you really want your innocent niece to be raped? To be forced into a union she fears?"

"You grow melodramatic, my lord. Erickson wants to marry her. It is a wondrous thing for her to wed with him. To gain that end, I approve whatever it is he must do." Sir Lyon cocked his big head to one side, frowning until the light dawned. "My God," he said, blinking at Tysen, "you don't fully understand her situation, do you?"

Tysen was as baffled as he was angry. His voice was as cold as his brother's when he donned his magistrate's robes. "Understand what? This entire business should be distasteful to any civilized man."

Sir Lyon threw back his head and laughed and laughed. He took a sip of wine and spewed it out, and still he laughed. Finally he managed to say, "I apologize for not realizing that you are new here and thus do not understand. Ah, it is amusing. Of course Mary Rose is my niece, but here is where you labor under a severe misapprehension, my lord.

"Mary Rose isn't a lady. She is as far from a lady as

it is possible to be." Sir Lyon just shook his head at the young man's obtuseness.

"Mary Rose is a bastard, my lord. She is an embarrassment. She has no worth, no value. She is not a lady, she can never be a lady. For reasons unfathomed by either myself or her aunt, Erickson MacPhail is willing to marry her. Since she refuses to have him, I have told him he may do what he must to bring her to the altar. If she does not wed him, she will never have anything, never be anyone, never have respect or recognition or even a civil nod from the local gentry. Nothing. Don't you understand? She is and always will be a bastard."

"She will have her mother and her good name."

"She never had a good name."

"Of course she does. Just because her parents were not man and wife, she isn't to blame. Why can't you leave her be? Let her do what she wishes to do? Respect her for the good and honest person she is? Perhaps, if her situation is so very dreadful here, and will grow only worse as she grows older, then she and her mother could live elsewhere, where no one would ever know about her being a bastard."

Sir Lyon looked at Tysen with pity. "You are an optimistic man, my lord. You have high ideals. You believe the best of your fellow man. I, however, am not so sanguine. In my experience, some rare men are truly worthy, even selfless upon occasion, but usually men are weak and greedy and brimming with ill will toward those more vulnerable than they are.

"Ladies, too, aren't all that benevolent, my lord. They are malicious, they will shred the reputation of any female who strays outside the rules they themselves have set. It would not matter where Gweneth and Mary Rose chose to live. She would become known soon enough for what she is.

"Leave be, my lord. Let Erickson have her. All will be well. She will not be abused. He will treat her kindly— why should he not? He is a good man, I swear it to you. He will also be sympathetic to her mother, see that she has nurses, and surely you must agree that this is something to admire in him. Her mother, Gweneth Fordyce, you see, is quite mad, has been for years. She is my wife's younger sister, and she has lived with us since before Mary Rose was born. Leave off. Let the situation resolve itself in the way that it should. It is not your affair. Keep out of it, sir."

Tysen looked Sir Lyon right in his very sincere face and said, "Why did Donnatella say that MacPhail wished to marry her? That makes no sense."

"Ah, my little beauty," said Sir Lyon, now at ease again, twirling the lovely crystal wineglass between his fingers. "She told me that she turned Erickson down. It was then, she told me, that he went on to Mary Rose. So Mary Rose is his second choice. Perhaps that is why she is teasing him so. She is upset that she is second in his affections. But it has always been so. Donnatella is very beautiful, and even as a child her beauty drew the boys from all around. Now, about Erickson. I suppose it must gall Donnatella, just a bit, you understand, to have the young man so very quickly change the, er, recipient of his affection. My little beauty has hinted to me that perhaps Erickson wants to be close to her, and thus his willingness to wed Mary Rose. Well, let Donnatella believe what she will. Erickson is very fond of Mary Rose. Now, do not worry about her, there is no need. It is a play with a happy ending. Let it work itself out." And Sir Lyon smiled, replete with his lunch and with his wine, and more than pleased that he had so admirably performed his duty.

Tysen said, drawing himself straight and tall, "I will not allow this, Sir Lyon. If she doesn't wish to wed him, why, that is the end to it. If you will not speak to the man, then I will. I will not allow Erickson MacPhail to rape her."

Meggie was lying in her bed, the covers pulled up to her chin, for she had one of the long narrow windows open a bit and the evening air was cool. She said to her papa, "You are upset, Papa, and it is no longer about my sins."

Tysen forced his attention back to his very precocious daughter. "It is an adult sort of problem, Meggie. It is about Mary Rose and the man you met last night—Erickson MacPhail. I must deal with a problem that involves the two of them."

"Mrs. MacFardle said Mary Rose was a bastard. I overheard her talking about Mary Rose to Mr. and Mrs. Griffin when they were at luncheon. I asked Mrs. MacFardle later what that meant, and she said that Mary Rose's mama hadn't been married to her papa, that no one even knew who her papa was. Is that why there is a problem? Because Mary Rose doesn't have a father?"

"Yes, that is part of it. What do you think of Mr. and Mrs. Griffin? I was sorry that they weren't well enough to dine with us this evening."

"Mr. Griffin doesn't say much, just stands around looking at you, all disapproving, his mouth tight. Mrs. Griffin called me into the drawing room and told me to stand like a little soldier while she questioned me. She said I wasn't to speak too softly or too quickly. I answered a great many questions, Papa. She has a mustache, just like Mr. Clint's, in the village."

"What were some of these questions?" He was irritated, but he supposed that since he'd gone on Donnatella's tour, Meggie had been left to her own devices. Next time he would take Meggie with him. Her presence would keep

Donnatella behaving properly if she was inclined toward flirtation.

"She asked me all about our family. She was particularly interested in Uncle Douglas. She said it would have been less repulsive if he were the new Baron Barthwick because he already had a title, was a peer of the realm, and at least knew what was what. As for you, she said that a so-called man of God would find himself sauced up really fast here."

"She has a point there," Tysen said, wondering if he were sauced up, if it meant he would be laid low. He leaned down and kissed Meggie's nose.

"Did Mr. Griffin ask you any questions?"

Meggie shook her head. "No. Oh, yes, Mrs. Griffin wanted to know all about Mama."

Tysen stiffened. Beyond the line, he thought, that was well beyond the line.

"I told her that Mama died a very long time ago. I also told her that you didn't want a wife, so Donnatella wouldn't be able to seduce you."

He jerked back as if he'd been slapped. "Meggie, I am your father. I am a vicar. You are ten years old. Do not use that word again."

He eyed her. Meggie was smart, she was endlessly curious. "All right," he said, "where did you hear it this time?"

"I overheard Aunt Alex speaking to Aunt Sophie about a man named Spenser Heatherington and how Helen had probably seduced him without a by-your-leave. They laughed a whole lot then, Papa."

It was too much or not enough, Tysen was thinking, staring now beyond his ten-year-old daughter to the rumbling sea, which was loud this evening, waves crashing against the black, pitted rocks covered with the white bird droppings at the base of the Kildrummy cliff.

He drew a deep breath. Helen Mayberry and Spenser Heatherington, Lord Beecham. Actually, from what he'd heard about them, it was very likely to have happened just that way. Helen was a unique woman, Douglas had said, and laughed his wicked satyr's laugh. It was obvious to Tysen that Douglas admired the woman very much. Actually, Spenser and Helen had been married nearly four years now. They were, according to his brother, happy as loons, and they had two children.

Tysen cleared his throat. "Mrs. Griffin—did she say how long she and Mr. Griffin would remain here at Kildrummy?"

Meggie said matter-of-factly, "She said she was staying until Mr. Griffin was satisfied that you wouldn't run everything into the ground. But she said that Mr. Griffin didn't hold much hope that this debacle would end well, even when Miles MacNeily returns. Papa, what's a debacle?"

"That old bat," Tysen said, finally feeling a bit of irritation bubbling inside his belly. He rose to pace beside his daughter's bed, to calm himself. The room was chilly now, and he closed the window, latching it securely. He'd come to Scotland to become the Barthwick laird, a *my lord,* for heaven's sake, and now here he was, a debacle. It was time to beard the lioness, he thought, not the lion. The lion had no teeth. He was only a cipher. He said to his daughter, "I believe I will myself get to know our guests," gave her a nod, and left the room. "Strange how the both of them refused to come to dinner."

Meggie slipped on her wrapper, pulled on a pair of Max's socks that came to her knees, and slipped out after her father. Unfortunately, she came face-to-face with Mrs. MacFardle at the base of the grand central staircase.

"I wanted some milk," Meggie said without hesitation. She could always lie better than either of her brothers.

She'd tried to teach them the trick—always look the person straight in the eye when you lied. Otherwise you looked shifty and it was all over.

"Harrumph," said Mrs. MacFardle and led the way to the kitchen. Meggie looked back over her shoulder toward the closed drawing room door. Evidently her papa had found the Griffins.

The door was partially open, and she heard him say in his calm, deep voice, "I trust you are recovered from the malady that kept you from the dinner table?"

"If that is your roundabout way of asking if I am feeling fit now, the answer is yes. I am here in the drawing room, aren't I? I have allowed you to enter. I am even speaking to you, although it is difficult—"

Tysen cut her off. His irritation was building. "And has Mr. Griffin also regained his good health?"

"Mr. Griffin, I believe, is determining how long it will take you to destroy all the Kildrummy property. I, naturally, have asked him to do this."

He ignored that and forged ahead. "I would appreciate it, ma'am, if you would ask questions of me rather than of my daughter. If you wish to know about my family, ask me, and I will decide what you need to know."

"Why? She's a smart little gel," said Mrs. Griffin, dressed in the same stiff pervasive black, spread over nearly the entire sofa. She was holding that black cane, waving it just a bit. It looked like a weapon in her large hand. "She told me everything I wanted to know, whereas you would likely have perseverated. Besides, you went off with Donnatella and were not available to me. Now, to be blunt about all this—I quite despair of Kildrummy ever recovering."

"I don't," Tysen said. "However, ma'am, I think despair would be an excellent trait for you to cultivate."

"I have no idea what you mean by that, and thus it is

very likely irrelevant. Now, isn't Donnatella a lovely little chit? And you were with her for a very long time, weren't you? Alone." She gave him an arch, leering look that made him want to throw an old leather hassock at her.

"Aye," she continued, her leer even more pronounced as she looked him up and down, "if you weren't a vicar, I would believe that you had yourself a very fine time indeed. On the other hand," she added, the thin black mustache over her upper lip mesmerizing him, "it's possible that since you're an *English* vicar, you have no notion of what real sin is or isn't."

And even-tempered Tysen Sherbrooke, a man of cool detachment and sound judgment, leapt off the edge. He said, his voice utterly clipped and cold in his fury, "You are a malicious old woman. I do not wish you to remain here any longer, ma'am. You and Mr. Griffin will leave in the morning. Have I made myself clear?"

The black mustache quivered in outrage. Mrs. Griffin roared to her feet in a welter of black skirts and a great deal of energy. She swung up her black cane and aimed it at him, as if it were a blunderbuss. "You are a vicar, sir. You have insulted me, you have insulted my dear Mr. Griffin in absentia. You will beg our pardon."

And Tysen, still furious to his toes, said in a voice as rigid as his father's was whenever he'd been angry with his mother—not an unusual occurrence at all, "I apologize, ma'am. You and Mr. Griffin will still leave in the morning. I bid you good night and a pleasant journey back to Edinburgh."

"We'll just see what Donald MacCray has to say about this, my lord," she shouted after him. "He is the Barthwick solicitor, a man of singular and impressive standing, and he will pin back your wretched little English ears for your horrid behavior to me! Vicar—ha, I say! A plague on you, sir."

It was a fine parting shot, but he didn't turn back to the miserable old besom. He just walked out of the drawing room, nearly knocking over his daughter, who had obviously been plastered against the door. He saw a glass of milk on the floor beside her.

"If I could send you away as well, Meggie, I would," said Tysen and took the stairs two at a time, not looking back.

Two hours later, Reverend Sherbrooke was praying to God to forgive him for his illogical and highly odd anger, his unusual and passionately felt display of temper, his unquestioned rudeness in the face of rudeness that had, for whatever reason, driven him right over the brink. He'd landed facedown in an emotional quagmire. He'd wallowed in it, shamed his calling, riddled holes in his name. But, surely, what had come out of that dreadful woman's mouth still was of sufficient weight to justify what he had said to the old bat.

He realized in that moment that he was trying to justify himself to God. It appalled him that he had sunk so low, had let himself fall off a righteous path so easily. God was an integral part of his life, His presence and strength filled Tysen's very being. He was graced by God's love and it gave him endless joy. And yet he had left Him in a ditch somewhere in this wretched country and continued on alone. Look what had happened to him.

He finally said, his soul stripped of false pride, of pretense, "God, the fact is, I have sinned royally. I lost my temper, and there is no defense that is at all worthy. I was an ass. I brayed, loudly. I will try very hard not to do it again." There, he could think of nothing else to say. He was no longer angry at Mrs. Griffin, no longer wanted to swat Meggie's bottom. Well, maybe a bit.

No. He had to exercise better control of himself. He realized then that he was out of his element, far away from what he knew and understood, from everything familiar to him, all of it lying many miles to the south. He'd been tossed into an utterly different pocket of the world, where, to this moment, nothing was what it seemed. He felt like a blind man on a narrow path.

He finally opened his eyes, blinked, and saw that darkness had fallen in this land so very far north that it had to be nearly ten o'clock at night before the light finally faded away and the land was blanketed in blackness.

He felt at peace. He still had no intention of asking Mr. Griffin or Mrs. Griffin to remain. He wasn't a coward, though. He would show himself to them when they left. He would keep his mouth closed, no matter the provocation.

Mary Rose Fordyce was another matter entirely. She was a bastard. But that wasn't relevant. Saying that marrying Erickson would be a triumph for her made his belly twist and cramp with the unfairness of it. Evidently, though, it was of primary importance to everyone else hereabouts. No, he would not allow Erickson MacPhail to force himself on her.

He had come to a decision, and he meant it. He also realized, just before he fell asleep that night, that he would be pleased to have the old bat and her silent, disapproving husband gone from Kildrummy. Actually, he wondered what she would say to him when he stood there, perhaps giving a farewell nod and a little smile as their carriage passed out of the inner courtyard. He would, perhaps, even wave both of them happily on their way.

He smiled into the darkness. When the scream came, jerking him out of a deep sleep, he nearly fell out of his bed.

9

Tutene? Atque cuius exercitus?
You? And whose army?

TYSEN DIDN'T EVEN think of his dressing gown. He ran out of his huge bedchamber into the long corridor, his nightshirt flapping against his ankles. It was near dawn, the light dim and gray.

Another scream.

It wasn't coming from Meggie's bedchamber. It was coming from the guest chamber at the far end of the corridor. It was Mrs. Griffin, and she was yelling her head off.

Maybe Mr. Griffin, pushed beyond reason, was strangling the old witch.

Not a proper thought, he told himself as he ran down that corridor, wincing with each footfall since the floor was very cold. Not even a remotely acceptable thought for a vicar.

He threw open the door and dashed into a very dark room, with all the draperies closed, and he stubbed his toe. He drew up short, gritting his teeth at the shock of the pain, when he suddenly saw a candle flickering in the darkness, just a small circle of light, and in the center of that small circle of light was Mrs. Griffin's face. White as new snow; the mustache that topped her upper lip as black as a man's funeral armband. Her hair was tied in rags. It was a terrifying sight.

His toe still hurt. He called out, "What is wrong, Mrs. Griffin? I heard you scream. What is the matter? Where is Mr. Griffin?"

"Oh, it's you, Vicar," she said, gasping for breath. "I saw her. For the first time since I have been in this accursed castle, I finally saw her. Just last year I wanted to see her, I actually spoke into the empty room, asking her to show herself, but she did not come. She had to wait until I was furious and under great duress because I wanted to smack you in the head for ordering me to leave. I did not want to see her. I was not prepared to see her. Yes, she waited until I would be terrified into the grave with my fear. Mr. Griffin is right here, beside me, probably still asleep."

"Who came, Mrs. Griffin?"

"Why, the bloody Kildrummy ghost, of course," she yelled at him, her harsh, churning breath making her candle flicker. "She is right over there, in the corner, sitting there on top of the bloody commode." She shone the candle toward the corner. There was nothing there. "No, don't tell me that I am quite mad, sir. You know nothing at all. She was there, sitting right on the edge of the bowl, swinging her leg back and forth, just looking at me. I think she was whistling. I heard her whistling, surely a strange sound in the middle of the night, and so I lit the candle. And there she was. She kept whistling and now she's gone."

"I say, Mrs. Griffin, what is going on here? Why is the

vicar standing in our bedchamber in his nightshirt? By all the bloody saints, man, I will not let you seduce my wife! How dare you, sir! And you call yourself a vicar? You have gall, sir! I will kill you with my bare hands!"

Mrs. Griffin never turned to look at her husband, just raised her hand and hit him in the head. "Calm yourself, Mr. Griffin. In this case the man isn't trying to gain my corporal affections. He's too far away from me to succeed in any case."

Mr. Griffin said, "You told me he was a paltry fellow. Are you quite sure there is no attempted seduction on his part, Mrs. Griffin?"

"Yes, Mr. Griffin. You will see that he is keeping his distance. He has stepped only one foot inside our bedchamber. I believe he must have hurt himself—he was holding his foot for a while."

"My foot is fine now, Mrs. Griffin. Actually, it is my toe that hurts." Tysen shook his head at himself. He wasn't making any sense of this.

Seduce Mrs. Griffin?

He nearly fell to his knees with that blow. He cleared his throat, but didn't go any closer to Mrs. Griffin's bed. Mr. Griffin's face was now vaguely illuminated just beside his wife's. Tysen said slowly, "You believe you saw the Kildrummy ghost, ma'am? Who is this ghost?"

But Mrs. Griffin was now staring over at the commode with its large, flowered ceramic basin set on top, a water pitcher next to it. He followed her line of vision, but there was still nothing there, nothing at all.

"She is gone," Mrs. Griffin said, furious now that she was no longer afraid. She threw back the bedcovers and jumped out of the bed. She was wearing a dark wool nightgown that covered her from chin to heels. She seemed suddenly to remember that he was there, a man wearing naught but his own nightshirt, a man her husband feared was there to seduce her, and she yelled, "Begone, sir, begone! It is not proper for you to stare at a lady in dishabille. It is enough to raise the beast in any man, vicar or no."

And she flapped her hand at him. She needed but her griffin-headed cane.

"You heard her, sir," Mr. Griffin yelled, "begone before I rise out of my bed and thrash you within an inch of your life! Staring at my wife when she is wearing naught but her nightgown. You are not a gentleman, sir."

"But—"

Mrs. Griffin was looking again toward the commode. "She is no longer here. Ah, but her presence—I can still feel it. It is a moldy essence, and far too old. Can you not smell it? Mr. Griffin, do you not feel the mold crawling on your limbs? She doubtless came because the Englishman has taken over. She is upset, and she found her way into the wrong bedchamber. Do you hear that, ghost? If you want him to leave Kildrummy, you must secure proper directions to his bedchamber.

"Ah, but it is cold in here, like the grave she must spend some time in when she is not here, scaring me. Mr. Griffin and I are leaving this wretched place, right this minute. We will not remain in this room with this long-dead Lady Barthwick watching me from the commode."

It sounded like a fine idea to Tysen.

And so at dawn, not even an hour later, Tysen, now dressed and shaved, his toe no longer hurting inside his boot, stood on the steps of Kildrummy Castle to watch Mr. and Mrs. Griffin's carriage drive through the outer gate. He did manage a smile and a little wave. He could hear the driver muttering curses as he pulled the collar up to his ears. He saw Mr. Griffin's pale face glaring at him from the window. It was a chill morning with fog lying heavy just above the ground.

He walked back into the huge entry hall, shaking his

head. Life since his arrival at Kildrummy Castle had not been boring.

"Are they gone, Papa?"

"Assuredly they are, Meggie. I don't understand it. I don't believe in ghosts, never did, despite what everyone says about the Virgin Bride at Northcliffe Hall. I never saw her."

"Uncle Douglas did, several times. He just won't admit it. He thinks he will be called weak in the head if he does say that he saw her. He says only the ladies claim to see her, and that's because they thrive on the supernatural, that they gain attention from their claims, that they are, in short, weak in the head."

"Be that as it may," Tysen said, his voice testy, "I have never believed in the Virgin Bride or in any other ghost, not even when I was sleeping in that room once and— no, forget that. Whatever, Mrs. Griffin believed she saw a ghost in her bedchamber, and it quite terrified her. She informed Mr. Griffin that they were going back to Edinburgh."

Now that he thought about that strange sequence of events, he saw the humor in it and smiled, shaking his head. *Seduce Mrs. Griffin?*

Suddenly, with no assistance whatever from a spirit, Tysen realized quite clearly what had happened. He turned to carefully study his daughter's face. It did not require a great intelligence to understand what she had done. She was smirking, her eyes brimming with her triumph. He saw it before she could wipe it away.

"Meggie," he said slowly, "you have grown up with tales about the Virgin Bride at Northcliffe Hall and Pearlin' Jane at Vere Castle, who supposedly appears with great regularity to watch over your aunt Sinjun." He stroked his chin, never looking away from his daughter. "I will ask you only one time, Meggie. Were you the

ghost in the Griffins' bedchamber? Were you sitting atop
the commode? Whistling, perhaps? Swinging your leg?"

"Papa, it is time for breakfast. Would you like to have
some porridge?"

"Meggie?" His voice was very, very quiet. Meggie
gulped, then stared down at her feet.

She gulped again and said in a paper-thin voice, "Yes,
Papa. I'm sorry, but I had to do it. I was afraid they
wouldn't leave. She is so very dreadful, and he just stands
behind her and nods and looks like he's not even there,
and then last night I overheard Mrs. MacFardle tell Agnes
that Mrs. Griffin always did exactly as she pleased, that
Mr. Griffin never gainsaid her, and there was simply no
way she would allow an English vicar who just happens
now to be the laird of Kildrummy Castle to dictate to her.
Why, this was as much her home as her other home where
she lived whenever she wasn't visiting here. Mrs.
MacFardle went on and on, Papa, about Mrs. Griffin's
philosophy of life—she believes she deserves to govern.
I was worried she would go head-to-head with you. I
didn't want you to have to lose your temper. I didn't want
you to feel guilty over losing your temper. I was protecting you, Papa."

Meggie came to a halt, out of breath.

"Ah," Tysen said in an awful voice, one he reserved
for members of his flock who had grievously sinned and
weren't repentant, "so Mrs. Griffin is one of those bad
people I am too stupid to deal with, perhaps too dull-
witted to recognize even when I'm looking them right in
the eye?"

"You're not stupid, Papa, or really unaware, it's just
that you're too good."

"Meggie, I myself ordered them to leave. I recognized
Mrs. Griffin for what she was. She was leaving this morn-

ing, her spouse with her. Your performance only advanced their departure by an hour or two."

Meggie didn't say a single thing.

He became very still, then said slowly, "You believe I am weak? You believe that she could have succeeded in staying even though I ordered her to leave?"

"You are so very good, Papa," she said, barely above a whisper.

She had no faith in him at all. Tysen felt the blow hard and deep. Did she see him as good or as simply ineffectual? As a man who dealt in the spiritual realm and had little understanding of the real world?

Meggie said, her chin going up now, "Aunt Sinjun said a female always has to be prepared to act. She said that gentlemen many times don't have the fortitude to do what is necessary. She told me about the time she was willing to kill one of Uncle Colin's enemies. She didn't kill him, as it turned out, and that was good since the man hadn't been guilty after all, but she said to act, Papa. She said that a lady should never dither."

Tysen thought he would surely choke at the strange combination of irritation, bemusement, and despair mingling in his throat. He hiccuped, cleared his throat. "I am going back to bed." He began to walk back up the stairs, paused, then turned to see Meggie standing exactly where'd he left her, staring after him. "Did you really swing your leg at her?"

"Yes, Papa."

"Dear heavens," he said. "You must have whistled loudly to wake her up. What did you whistle?"

"A song Aunt Alex taught me about how women will one day rule the world and all men will become butlers."

Tysen could only shake his head. It was laughter rather than self-doubt that got the better of him just before he fell asleep again.

Vallance Manor

Mary Rose brushed her mother's thick dark-red hair that was still untouched by gray. It was long and smooth, perfectly straight, unlike her own hair, which curled and twisted, dancing about her head to some unknown but merry tune.

"It will be a beautiful day, Mama. No rain in the sky."

"Tell me about the new laird."

Mary Rose started at the sound of her mother's soft voice. As a rule, Gweneth Fordyce didn't speak all that much, but when she did, it sounded like lilting music. "He is very nice, Mama. He is an Englishman, a vicar, and he is also very handsome. Perhaps too handsome, but nevertheless, he is very kind. An honest man, to be admired."

Her mother said nothing more, just nodded, her eyes focused on the beech trees outside her bedchamber windows.

"His name is Tysen Sherbrooke, and his family is powerful in England. His brother is the earl of Northcliffe. Tysen is a widower. His little girl, Meggie, is here with him. She is precious, Mama. She helped me when I sprained my ankle."

"Donnatella will want him."

So soft her mother's voice, so gentle, like a whispering breeze through her hair. "Well, yes, she probably does. But I don't think he is at all interested—well, I don't know what he will do. She is very beautiful."

"Donnatella is just like her mother. She is a bitch wrapped in lovely packaging."

Mary Rose blinked at that. "Mama? You really don't like Donnatella? But you rarely even see her."

"I remember that the first word she ever spoke was 'mine.' What does that tell you? You know that everyone talks about everyone, Mary Rose. You know that. I hear everything. I even hear you speaking Latin to yourself when you're upset, or in a stubborn mood, or you're reading aloud one of those ancient books. I believe Ovid is your favorite."

Mary Rose gulped a bit. She did enjoy reading Ovid. It was terribly wicked, at least the parts she liked to read. She said, "Reverend Morley taught me Latin. I like it very much."

"I know. You can say anything you like about anyone and get away with it, since no one can understand you. Now, Mary Rose, you must take care, because Donnatella is still very angry at you about Ian."

It seemed to Mary Rose that her mother, quite suddenly and without warning, had fully recovered her wits. Perhaps her fragile mind, like a wheel that had gotten stuck in a ditch, was now back on its track. She'd prayed nearly every day of her life for that to happen. She said calmly, as if her mother really was with her completely, "There is no reason for her to be angry with me about Ian. The poor man is dead. I liked him very much, Mama. He was a good man."

"He was a gambler, Mary Rose. Perhaps it wasn't yet a vice, but I believe he would have become more ensnared as he got older."

"Well, it is a moot point. He is gone, all his virtues and vices with him."

"There is still Erickson. Like Ian, he turned from Donnatella to you. Keep your distance from him, Mary Rose, he is not to be trusted. Why does he no longer want Donnatella? Also, he is much too close to your uncle. I have seen them speaking quietly together, all alone. Whenever your uncle deals with another in that low, quiet voice of his, he is up to no good. Take care."

"I will take care, Mama."

Her mother jerked suddenly, and Mary Rose realized that she'd pulled the brush too hard through her hair. "I'm so sorry, Mama. Oh dear, are you all right?"

"Braid my hair for me, Mary Rose, on top of my head. I think I would like to go downstairs today, perhaps out in the garden."

"That would be wonderful," Mary Rose said, and crossed her fingers. Please, she prayed, let her come back to me. Don't let her mind cloud up again. "I want to work on my roses. You can give me advice."

Her mother was silent for a very long time. Then she said, "The English are untrustworthy. Not as untrustworthy as your uncle, but you still should never put your faith in one of them, even a vicar, Mary Rose, or you will be sorely disappointed."

"If you are thinking of the new Lord Barthwick, it's true he is an Englishman and a vicar, Mama, but he is utterly trustworthy. I would wager my last groat on that." Mary Rose paused a moment and smiled at the smooth braid she was plaiting. "I should have said that since I don't have a last groat—or a first groat for that matter— my belief in him will have to suffice."

"Does Donnatella still claim that Ian was going to wed with her, that he was her betrothed?"

"Yes, but it would have mattered only if Ian had lived. It doesn't matter now. Let her say what she will. She was very fond of him too."

"No, she wasn't. She just wanted him because he would be the new Lord Barthwick, and because he wanted you. She is dangerous, Mary Rose."

Mary Rose had nothing to say to that. She helped her mother dress in a lovely pale-yellow muslin gown that was many years out-of-date, but it didn't matter because her mother was beautiful and so was the gown. She found some yellow ribbons to weave into her mother's thick braids. "I wish Miles would soon return," her mother said.

"I do too. He is such a nice man, always so very polite to me. I very much like the way he's always come over here to visit with us."

"Oh, yes," said her mother.

Mary Rose dressed herself quickly and walked carefully beside her mother downstairs.

She saw Tysen standing in the entrance hall, looking up at them. Sir Lyon was at his side, looking up as well.

Her mother raised her hand in a small wave, looked at him for a very long time, and then she said to her daughter, "Do not trust an Englishman. He is far too handsome. When a man is that handsome there is inevitably sin in his nature."

"No, Mama, really, it's not true," Mary Rose said in a low voice, hoping Tysen hadn't heard her.

"I was told," Tysen said clearly, his vicar's deep voice carrying easily to every corner of the grand entrance hall, "never to trust a Scotsman."

Sir Lyon threw back his head and laughed.

Donnatella came out of the breakfast room. She said, looking for just a moment over her shoulder at Gweneth and Mary Rose, "Ignore her, my lord. She is only Mary Rose's mother, and she is quite mad."

Gweneth Fordyce said, her fingers tightly clutched to Mary Rose's arm, "I am mad when it suits me to be mad, Donnatella. You, however, are a bitch whether you wish to be or not."

Perhaps, Mary Rose thought suddenly—a revelation, really—that was the truth of things. Her mother purposely chose to live in a world of her own creation. Gweneth broke away from Mary Rose and walked gracefully down the stairs, her head back, looking like a queen. "I wish to have breakfast now, daughter. Bring the new Barthwick laird and I will question him."

"Yes, Mama."

Tysen gave her a brief bow. "I should be delighted, ma'am."

It had been a strange hour, Tysen thought later, riding beside Mary Rose. Because he had hours and years of experience dealing successfully with people of vastly diverse manners and behaviors and levels of impertinence, dealing with Gweneth Fordyce hadn't overtaxed him. She had, however, embarrassed her daughter very badly in front of him, and he was sorry for that. She shouldn't have kept harking to Mary Rose's blind faith, particularly in men, when everyone knew that men were created by the devil to ruin women.

Tysen had chuckled and said, "Sometimes I have held that opinion myself, Mrs. Fordyce."

"I am a spinster, Vicar."

"Yes, ma'am. Indeed you are."

"And perforce, my dearest daughter is a bastard."

"An appellation that perhaps fits the facts, ma'am, but not her character."

Mary Rose had stared at him, then abruptly choked on her tea.

When Mary Rose pulled her old mare, Primrose, to a halt beside a rushing stream, she said, "This is one of my very favorite places. Would you like to rest for a moment?"

He left their horses loose. Big Fellow had no interest at all in Primrose, probably because she was a gnarly old mare with a mean eye, so there were no problems there. Tysen sat beside Mary Rose on the bank of the stream, the sound of the roaring water like a low, continuous drumbeat. He raised his voice a bit to be heard over it. "Your mother did not seem at all mad to me, Mary Rose."

Mary Rose pulled up several water reeds and appeared

to study them closely. "I believe now that she has chosen her madness, that she prefers it to dealing with what is real." She shook her head, a spasm of regret, of hurt, in her eyes. "I realize, too, that her madness is a wonderful justification for saying exactly what she pleases."

"I am sorry, but you are probably right." A mother who wallowed in madness, leaving her child to fend for herself. Gweneth Fordyce was a beautiful woman, seemingly harmless, but he didn't think that was true. He didn't like the looks of her soul. She was selfish. She had locked herself away. No, she wasn't mad, he was very certain of that. He said, "Why does she dislike Donnatella so very much?"

"Because Donnatella is the daughter of the house and I am The Embarrassment. Mama also heartily dislikes her own sister, Lady Margaret. Now you're asking yourself why is it that we live at Vallance Manor if there is such discord."

"Yes, but I don't mean to pry if it distresses you."

Mary Rose merely shrugged. "The truth of the matter is that we have no place else to go. I am a bastard. There is no money. My mother has never told a soul my father's name. I look like her, so there are no physical clues."

"Your father was probably married—not an uncommon occurrence. It is a pity, though, that he provided no support for your mother. I imagine also that he was local. There have been no clues of any sort?"

"I have thought of that, but Mama is of no help at all. She has always just given me a blank stare whenever I have inquired into it in the past. You're right, of course. If he is still alive, his wife must be as well, else he would marry my mother, wouldn't he?"

"One would hope so."

"But who knows? It was twenty-five years ago, after all." She paused a moment, looking out over that rushing water. She turned to him and said with a half smile, "Ah, Tysen, it is a strange life, is it not? And no matter how strange life becomes, we still must deal with it."

"Yes," he said, "we must." He very much liked the sound of his name when she said it. That soft lilt lightly whispering against his flesh, warming him. That was ridiculous, like the ravings of a bad poet. Melodramatic enough for the likes of Lord Byron, the nincompoop.

"Your uncle has no idea who your father could be?"

She shook her head, sending a thick tress of red hair curling about her cheek. "No. If my uncle knew who my father was, then the whole of Scotland would know. My uncle isn't discreet. I am sorry that my mother insulted you."

"She did it with a good deal of heat and skill," Tysen said, and picked his own water reed. It was slippery between his fingers, but smelled strangely sweet. "It is hard not to admire that. It did not hurt me, Mary Rose. *Dinna fache yersel.*"

She grinned at him. "That sounded very Scottish, my lord."

"Aye, I am trying," he said.

"How are you dealing with Mrs. Griffin?"

"Mr. and Mrs. Griffin, my one-day guests, insulted me until I had no choice but to order them to leave. Meggie, who should be thrashed, doubted they would obey me and thus she took it upon herself to get them out of Kildrummy Castle at the crack of dawn."

"Goodness, how ever did she manage that?"

"She played a ghost and terrified the old besom."

"I should like to hear all about that. Meggie seems very resourceful. Mrs. Griffin has been about Kildrummy Castle forever. Mr. Griffin, I have heard, was quite the rake in his younger years. Irresistible, he was, I've heard it said. But you see, it is now Mrs. Griffin who holds the reins of power. She has for as long as I remember. No one knows how it came about. Is his deference to her merely an act? I don't know." She paused and smiled. "She's never paid me any attention at all, since I am a bastard. I wasn't even invited to have tea with her. Just Donnatella was."

"Mary Rose, do you want to marry Erickson Mac-Phail?"

She nearly slid into the stream, she jerked about so suddenly.

He grabbed her arm to steady her. "I'm sorry, but I had to ask you that. You see, your uncle believes you will come around once Erickson has the chance to really speak to you. Your uncle is certain Erickson can talk you into it."

"I would sooner be sent to Botany Bay than marry him," she said, that stubborn jaw locked, and he believed her.

She added, "He looks like such a charming young man, but he isn't. Actually, he isn't really a young man at all. He is nearly thirty."

Suddenly Tysen saw a pain in her eyes that came from something that had happened long ago, perhaps an awful memory. He said, "What, Mary Rose? What are you seeing, remembering?"

She slowly turned to face him. "Once, about ten years ago, I saw him accost my mother."

10

TYSEN SAT AT the laird's very old, scarred desk in the airless library, Miles MacNeily beside him. He had expected the estate manager to be a wizened old man with tufts of gray hair encircling his head, but he wasn't. He was older, certainly, but not over forty-five. He was tall and lean, very smart and quite fine-looking, his hair the burnished red so common to Scotsmen and his eyes very blue. He dressed well. Tysen wondered why he had never wed.

"Yes, my lord, you understand this all very well. It is because you come from great landholdings in England. All of this, well, it must seem paltry in comparison."

Tysen merely smiled at that intelligent face and shook his head. He would miss Miles MacNeily. He had learned a great deal from him in just the past day. It appeared that MacNeily's mother had left him all her holdings near Inverness. Mr. MacNeily would, unfortunately, be leaving within the month. He would be his own master. Tysen thought he would do very nicely as his own master.

"Actually, Miles," Tysen said, "it is my brother who is the earl, the lord of all he surveys. Don't forget, I am a vicar, I have always been a vicar. Anything I know I suppose I have simply absorbed over the years."

Miles gave him a charming smile. "Perhaps, but you have a fine brain, my lord. I have no doubt that I am leaving Kildrummy in good hands."

"Thank you. Even a vicar enjoys hearing such things said about him. Did you work well with the former Lord Barthwick?"

"Ah, Tyronne, the old laird, he could yell like no man I have heard in my life. I learned to move away from him quickly when I knew he was working himself up to a fury. I didn't wish to lose my hearing. It never took much to have him screeching his head off. Yes, my lord, we worked well together. It did not take him more than a dozen years to come to trust me. Kildrummy has been my home nearly all of my adult life. I have been happy here. I will miss it."

They worked for another hour, reviewing the situation of all the Kildrummy tenants, the problems they either faced now or would probably face in the near future. They spoke of all the Kildrummy holdings in the village, the number of flocks of sheep and herds of cows, improvements to be made. And on and on it went. It wasn't an immense task, but there were many details that Tysen knew he would have to commit to memory if he were to run Kildrummy well. He remembered then that he would be returning to England, to his home and his church, to his life that seemed so very far away at this point. What would happen to Kildrummy when he was no longer here to watch over things?

Meggie knocked and peered around the door an hour later. She grinned at her father and ducked a sweet curtsy to Miles. "I am here to fetch you to tea."

Miles, Tysen quickly realized, wasn't immune to his little hussy of a daughter, who was flirting shamelessly with him. Since she was ten years old, her twinkling eyes and smiles were given to a man she was ready to accept as a favored uncle. This appeared to delight Miles. Tysen just shook his head at her.

It was while Tysen was sipping his tea that he realized he had the solution to his estate problem; it was staring him in the nose. "Oliver," he said aloud.

Meggie turned to him, her head to one side. "What about Oliver, Papa?"

"Your uncle Douglas wants him to assist in the running of Northcliffe. I, however, believe it's Scotland where Oliver will make his way. I think Oliver might be just the man to run Kildrummy." Tysen rubbed his hands together, then told Miles exactly who Oliver was. ". . . so you see, my brother Ryder Sherbrooke has always taken in abused children—loved them, cared for them, and ensured that they were placed with excellent families or given the skills for the trade they wished. Oliver Dalrymple was one of his first children. He is now—is he twenty yet, Meggie?"

"Oliver is twenty-one, Papa. He just came down from Oxford in early June." She said to Miles, "Do you like his name? Dalrymple?"

"It sounds quite noble," Miles said. "There have been several Dalrymples who have figured prominently in the government."

"Yes, that is what Uncle Ryder told him. My uncle Ryder selected it for him, you see. Oliver didn't know who his papa was; then his mother died—it was due to something called blue ruin, Uncle Ryder said. I don't know what that is, but it killed her. All he knew when Uncle Ryder found him was that his name was Oliver. Now he sounds ever so elegant." She frowned a moment, then added, "And complete. Oliver is now complete."

"He is a very lucky young man," Miles said. "Just imagine, finding abused children and taking them in. It is an excellent thing your brother does, my lord."

"All of my uncle Ryder's Beloved Ones are lucky," Meggie said and poured him another cup of tea, beautifully executed because of the lessons her aunt Alex had given her.

Tysen was rubbing his hands together again. "I must write a letter. Miles, I will join you later. Meggie, keep out of trouble."

Tysen wrote a letter to Oliver and one to Douglas, and dispatched Ardle, one of his stable lads, with the packet to Edinburgh. Now, he thought, striding to the stables, it was time to beard the MacPhail laird in his den.

He found the MacPhail manor house without difficulty. It was about the same size of Sir Lyon's holdings, but Erickson's holding wasn't as nicely kept up. The lawn in front of the manor house needed a half a dozen men with sharp scythes, walls needed paint, stone needed to be replaced.

Erickson MacPhail wasn't at his manor house. The laird was riding, he was told by a pinch-mouthed housekeeper whose sleeves and hands were dirty.

Where would he be?

It was late in the afternoon. Mary Rose had ridden back to the rushing stream. When Erickson came some ten minutes later, she knew he'd seen her and followed her. "Marry me," he said.

"I don't want to marry you, Erickson." Mary Rose spoke calmly, her voice slow and patient, although her heart was beating so fiercely in her chest she thought it would surely burst out of her.

"You have told me that, Mary Rose," he said, his voice just as calm as hers, perhaps a bit patronizing because he believed her to be toying with him, and he thought it naught more than a silly woman's game, and he'd tired of it. He'd more than tired of it the day she'd raced back into the forest and he'd lost her.

She really was quite lovely, he thought now, knowing he would get his way because regardless of what she wanted, what she felt, he would have her. Aye, she wasn't at all plain. Her hair was rich, thick, a brilliant mix of colors, from the brightest red to a deep auburn. He raised his hand to touch it, then thought better of it.

And those eyes of hers, that soft green color. She had her mother's eyes. He remembered how Gweneth was so very beautiful and hot in her passion. Mary Rose's nose was narrow, her brows nicely arched. Her mouth—he did like that mouth of hers. He wanted to kiss her again, to feel whether her lips were as soft as he remembered. There was a line of light freckles over her nose.

She was looking at him, and the look wasn't promising. Why didn't she want him? No, it had to be a ridiculous woman's game. He was getting impatient with her. He had planned to go slowly, to woo her, but she wasn't cooperating. Damn her, she should be on her knees, kissing his hands, grateful to him for rescuing her, but no, she was shaking her head at him, that damned chin of hers up.

"Please believe me, Erickson. I'm not toying with you. This is no teasing game. I have never learned how to play those sorts of games. Listen to me now. I truly do not wish to marry you."

In that moment he finally believed her, and she saw that he did. Then, because he couldn't begin to comprehend why she wouldn't want him, he knew it had to be because she had given her affection to someone else. He asked, his voice rough in his growing anger, "Then who is the man you want?"

"There is no other man." Even as she spoke, he saw something in her eyes, something that betrayed her. But there was no other man about for her to—"By God, it's that damned vicar, isn't it? You've known the man for a week. Just because he is a vicar, a man pledged to God, you, you silly girl, believe he has to be kind, gentle, a soft creature who will always treat you like a bolt of silk. Given who and what he is, well then, that's probably true. He probably is soft and gentle. Damnation, he isn't the sort of man a woman needs."

She jumped to her feet. "Shut up, Erickson. How dare you insult him? I know him and you don't."

"I'll wager the pretty fellow wouldn't know what to do with a woman even if she were to stand naked before him."

"That is absurd. He has three children!"

"His wife must have guided him, told him how to accomplish his manly duty."

"Be quiet."

Erickson realized he wouldn't gain anything by continuing on this track. He still wanted to reason with her, gain her compliance. He said more calmly, with a bit of compassion in his voice, "You're being foolish, Mary Rose, shortsighted. He is the new Lord Barthwick. He comes from a noble English family. He won't marry you. But even beyond that, I honestly doubt he even comprehends what it is like to feel affection or lust for a woman. He's a vicar, for God's sake, he sleeps with his Bible, clasps his hands in prayer when he sees a man who would harm him."

He saw that her face had turned red, the freckles were standing out against her white skin. "Oh, leave go, Mary Rose. You're a bastard, for God's sake. Neither are you anymore a young girl. I'm the only one who wants to marry you."

"No."

"Very well," he said, his eyes on her breasts. She knew

there was no hope for it, not with that gleam of pleasure in his eyes, that gleam that bespoke a man's victory over a woman. Yes, Erickson was looking forward to this no matter her protestations. She shook her head, beyond words now. She knew he would try no more arguments to win her compliance.

"I have no money. A man with your responsibilities does not wed when there is no gain. It makes no sense. It would be very stupid of you. Your mother would not like it. She would forbid it."

"It doesn't matter. I will have all that I want. Trust me, Mary Rose. I can give you pleasure."

"No."

"Then it will be a bit rough for you. Perhaps you will not fight me overly much once I have given you a taste of lovemaking." He took a step toward her.

He was twice her size. Mary Rose had no choice. She took a deep breath and jumped into the stream.

She shrieked as she went under. She hadn't realized how numbingly cold the water would be. It knocked the breath out of her, froze her lungs, numbed her arms and legs instantly. She fought her way to the surface. The current had already swept her a good dozen feet away from him. She saw him standing on the edge of the stream, heard him yelling, and prayed he wouldn't jump in after her. He looked like he would, then he didn't. Only a fool would willingly leap into obviously frigid water.

At least the water wasn't over her head. The rocks were sharp and plentiful, however, the current so strong that she was hurled against every wretched rock in her path. She felt the shock and pain of it to her bones. She prayed that her only punishment for this outlandish action would be bruises, and not a broken neck.

The rocks were shredding her clothing and her flesh, the water freezing her, the ferocious current tossing her about like a rag doll. But at least she wouldn't drown, not unless she hurt herself so badly on the rocks that she was knocked unconscious.

She knew too that she had to get out of the water or she would die from the cold. Her poor mare, Primrose, was back where she had jumped in. She hoped that Erickson wouldn't take her with him when he left. Surely he had left by now. She realized then that he could simply ride beside the creek, dry and laughing, until finally, somehow, she managed to get herself out, and he would be right there, grinning down at her.

She saw that there were trees lining the stream along this stretch. He wouldn't get close enough to see her. She had to get out of the water now to have a chance of escaping him. If he caught her, she would be so weak she wouldn't even be able to kick at him.

She was swept directly beneath an oak tree branch that was bobbing up and down in the water. She managed to wrap her arms around the thin branch, praying it would hold her weight. Thankfully, it was still attached to the tree. She was sodden and cold, her fingers nearly numb, her body aching, but she wasn't about to let go of that branch. She took a deep breath and pulled herself slowly, every inch she gained sending waves of pain through her body, up out of the churning water. It frothed around her, pulling, pulling. She didn't know if she could do it. She saw Erickson in her mind, pulling her legs apart, looking at her, and she gripped the branch with all her strength. In the next instant, she was free of the water, her legs up and wrapped around the branch. Then she managed to pull herself onto the branch. It was bending dangerously low, nearly touching the water. *Please, don't break, don't break.* She pulled herself along the length of it for at least six feet. She nearly fell, flattened herself on the branch, then pulled herself along again. She made it. At last, she was hugging herself against the tree, taking huge breaths, thankful that she was alive and that Erickson likely wasn't close by. By now surely he had ridden farther down to where the trees fell away to reveal the myriad waterfalls, all of them at least a dozen feet high. She was grateful she hadn't had to go over them.

She was shivering violently as she climbed down the tree, going from branch to branch, her feet numb now inside her boots. Her gown kept tangling between her legs, making her slip, making her knees buckle with the weight. She was a mess. Her hair was hanging in her face, sodden and heavy. She pushed it back and kept moving slowly down the tree.

How far downstream had she been swept? A mile, perhaps more? She prayed it was much less. She was so tired and cold she was shaking now, her teeth chattering.

She panted for breath. When she felt the ground beneath her feet, she hugged the tree trunk for a moment. She was exhausted. She was also stupid. She couldn't believe she had jumped into that raging stream. Actually, truth be told, she would have jumped off the top of Ben Nevis to get away from Erickson MacPhail. Anything was better than being raped by him.

She began to walk back to where she'd left Primrose. Suddenly she heard Erickson yelling, heard his horse pounding through the underbrush. She froze in her tracks. No, he wasn't close. He was a goodly distance away, thank God. All she had to do now was find Primrose and get away from this place.

But where would she go?

She wondered if her uncle would allow Erickson in the house now when she told him what he had threatened to do to her.

Her head ached ferociously. Finally she found Primrose, lazily chewing on some slimy water reeds. She led her mare away into the thickness of the pine trees. She waited there, even though she knew she risked becoming ill. She couldn't risk running into Erickson.

Finally, when she felt like a pillar of ice, she mounted Primrose. When she neared Vallance Manor, the first thing she saw was Erickson MacPhail's horse being held by one of her uncle's stable lads in front of the manor.

She knew then, all the way to her bones, that she was no longer safe here in her own home. No, she thought, it wasn't her home, it was her uncle Lyon's home. He wouldn't protect her.

She didn't know what to do, but then it didn't matter. She turned Primrose south, toward Kildrummy Castle.

11

Nunc, vero inter saxum et locum durum sum.
Now, I really am between a rock and a hard place.

"GOODNESS, MARY ROSE, what are you doing out here? You are all wet and shivering. What happened? Did your mare throw you? Oh, my, look at all those cuts on your hands and face! Let me get Papa."

Mary Rose grabbed Meggie's arm as she slid off Primrose's back. "No, no, Meggie. No, please, I don't want to involve your papa in any of this . . . well, I guess it's a muddle. Nothing is good right now. I didn't know where to go. I can't see your papa, don't you see? He doesn't deserve any of this and—"

She knew she wasn't making sense. Meggie was only ten years old, she shouldn't be involved in this mess either, but now it was too late. She realized in a flash that this child was probably the only one who could help her. She got a hold on herself and said, "Listen, Meggie, I'm not hurt all that badly, just cut up and bruised a bit. But this isn't good. I've got to hide. Can you help me?"

Meggie didn't hesitate. She clasped Mary Rose's hand between hers and said, leaning close, "Yes, of course. First, let's take your horse to the stable. I will tell MacNee and Ardle to keep their tongues between their teeth. But why don't you want Papa to help you? At home he is involved in everything. All his parishioners call him whenever they have problems. He's really quite good at fixing things, even when a wife wants to hit her husband over the head with a board."

Mary Rose nearly laughed at that, but the hopelessness of her situation was sitting heavy as a board on her own head.

"Actually, Mrs. Crow did hit her husband on his head, and he lost his memory for a while. Papa thought he was just pretending, but it got Mr. Crow a lot of sympathy from his wife."

"I cannot, Meggie, trust me." She wasn't going to spit out that it would compromise him, place him between her uncle and Erickson MacPhail, or perhaps place him against the two of them. No, surely her uncle didn't know what Erickson had planned to do. Surely he hadn't given him permission to do what he had to do to gain her agreement to marry him. She just didn't know, and not knowing, she couldn't take the chance that her uncle would simply give Erickson the key to her bedchamber and tell him to do what he wanted. Her voice wobbled a bit as she said, "I just need to hide for a little while, until everything calms down. Your papa doesn't need to know I am even here."

"All right, Mary Rose. We'll figure all this out," Meggie said.

Mary Rose watched her hand over Primrose to Ardle, who just nodded, never stopped staring at her, which wasn't surprising, since he'd known her forever, and she knew she must look like a madwoman, all frowsy and wet. "Thank you," she said to him. "Really, Ardle, thank you."

"I'll take foin care of ol' Primrose, Mary Rose. Dinna ye fache yerself now, lass."

She was very grateful to him. She smiled, remembering Tysen saying the same thing to her in his starchy, clipped English accent. No soft lilt to his voice. "Thank you," she said again and lightly touched her fingers to Ardle's brown woolen coat.

Meggie whispered, clasping Mary Rose's hand, "Come, Mary Rose, you're terribly wet and cold. I know just where to hide you. You are beyond cold, aren't you? You're freezing. I don't want you to become ill. Hurry."

Meggie led her up the servants' back stairs, pausing at each landing to see if anyone was around. They heard Mrs. MacFardle humming a goodly distance away. "That sounds pretty," Meggie whispered. "I didn't know any sound she made could sound that nice. I'm glad we didn't see Pouder. He usually sits right by the front door but you can never be certain. I suppose you already know that."

"Oh, yes. Pouder has occupied that spot since before I was born."

"I have nearly tripped over him several times. He is Papa's valet-in-training, something he says he always wanted to be."

"I have always liked Pouder. He was always kind to me. He was very old even when I was a small child."

She wanted to giggle at the thought of Pouder seeing her, clutching his meager chest in shock, and expiring right there in his chair. She was becoming hysterical. It wasn't a good sign. She drew a very deep breath, trying to calm herself. She realized, of course, that what she really wanted to do was sink into oblivion, simply lie down in some corner and fade into the wainscoting. But she did neither. She docilely followed Meggie Sherbrooke to her bedchamber in the north tower. It was one of Mary Rose's favorite rooms. As a child she had spent many happy hours playing in this wonderful room. It had been Ian's bedchamber, but she didn't tell Meggie that.

"Take off your clothes, quickly, Mary Rose, and climb into my bed to get warm. I'll find more blankets. Goodness, I don't think I have anything you can wear. You're a bit larger than I am."

"Yes," Mary Rose said, managing a slight smile. "Yes, I am a bit bigger than you." She was stripping off her clammy clothes even as she spoke. Within two minutes her boots were on the floor beside all her wet clothes, and she was in the bed, shivering under all the blankets Meggie was piling on top of her. Meggie said, after she gently laid her palm against Mary Rose's cheek, "I'll find some clothes for you, don't worry. Yes, I will figure something out. You just stay there and I will fetch some hot tea. Hot tea is many times the best mediator. That's what Papa says. I don't know exactly what that means, but I think he's right. He usually is."

Meggie slipped out of the bedchamber, closed the door quietly behind her. Mary Rose lay curled up, trying to get warm, but the cold was very deep. Even her blood was cold, the very marrow in her bones was freezing her from the inside. She tried to take deep, slow breaths. She tried to calm herself. She was out of that stream, she was safe, Erickson was nowhere about. *Breathe slowly, yes, breathe very slowly. You can do it, Mary Rose. You're safe now. Breathe.*

It seemed like forever until, finally, she began to warm. She realized then that her old riding hat was still atop her head, the plume tangled in her hair. She must look ridiculous. She reached a hand out from under the mound of covers and pulled it off. Then she tried to spread out her hair over the pillow. It required both hands to draw most of the tangles out, and then she was cold again, so cold that she pulled the covers to her nose. Once she was warm, she quickly realized that every inch of her body hurt, fiercely. Well, it wasn't unexpected. The rushing water had slammed her against every boulder, every rock, every pebble in that wretched stream. She wondered if there'd been some fish she hadn't seen who'd taken a nip of her when the water had ripped her past them. She hoped none of the cuts or scrapes was bleeding. She didn't want blood on Meggie's bedclothes.

Her brain stopped when she heard footsteps outside the bedchamber.

Meggie, she thought. Please, it had to be Meggie. But of course it wasn't. It was boots, a man's boots, coming closer, coming to this bedchamber. There was a light tap on the door. Then Tysen's voice, and her heart nearly stopped along with her brain. "Meggie, are you there?"

Oh, God, what to do?

Then she heard Meggie say, her voice all delighted, so falsely full of pleasure that surely no one would be fooled by it, "Papa! Whatever are you doing here? Did you need me? Is there something you want me to do for you?"

Tysen hoisted an eyebrow and looked down at his daughter. "Actually I wanted to see if you would like to play a game of chess with me before dinner."

Absolutely nothing came out of his daughter's mouth, which was so unusual that, so far as he could recall, it had never happened before. Tysen said slowly, eyeing that tea tray, "Well, now, why do you have a tray with tea on it? Are you having a party in your bedchamber?"

"Yes, Papa, I would love to play chess with you."

"Meggie—"

"Oh, the tea tray. Well, you see, I was trying to write a song and decided that my throat was too dry to sing."

There was a moment of silence, and Mary Rose, whose

brain was still frozen, wondered if Tysen would believe that nonsense. Naturally he didn't.

"Meggie, what is going on here? No more of your storytelling. The truth, if you please."

Mary Rose knew she'd spill her innards if he asked her anything at all in that calm, utterly gentle tone of voice. She was getting cold again at the power of that voice. She held her breath, knowing that he would stride in at any moment and see her, and ask himself why the devil he had ever come to Scotland in the first place. If she'd had the strength, she would have slithered out of the bed and crawled under it. But she didn't have the strength. She just lay there, the covers now nearly to her eyelids, staring at that bedchamber door.

Silence, far too much silence, then a very small voice, Meggie's voice, saying, "Papa, don't make me tell you, all right? It's a promise I made to someone, a secret, and my soul will surely be damned to that bad place far below my feet if I tell anyone, even you."

More silence, then Tysen said, a hint of approval in his voice, "I suppose you will eventually let me know what you are up to?"

"As soon as I can, Papa. I swear."

He believes it is something inconsequential, Mary Rose thought, a little girl's whim, and she nearly yelled with the relief of it. She still didn't move, and evidently neither did Meggie, not until Tysen's footfalls had faded away down the long corridor.

Meggie was flushed to her eyebrows when she came back into the bedchamber. Mary Rose watched her turn the large key in the lock, then carry the tray over to set it on the small table beside the bed.

"Thank you, Meggie. I'm very sorry."

"I didn't have to lie to him," Meggie said, slowly pouring the very hot tea into a large, heavy mug, "and that's a relief. I hate to lie to Papa because he feels it so very much when I do, do you know what I mean?"

"Yes. His disappointment makes you want to sink into the ground, doesn't it?"

"Yes," Meggie said, handing her the mug, "it does. One would think that if you lied enough, you would not feel it so much, but it doesn't change. Oh, my goodness, Mary Rose, look at your poor hand, and your face. There are scratches all over you."

"Yes, I know, but they're not that bad." Actually Mary Rose didn't want to look. She just wanted to down every drop of that delicious, scalding tea in the chipped mug that Meggie had doubtless filched from a kitchen cupboard. She didn't say a word, just poured it down her throat. When she finished, she lay her head against the pillow again and sighed. "That was delicious, Meggie. I believe you have saved my life. You see, I jumped into a very fast-running stream and got swept over rocks. I got some cuts and scratches here and there, nothing to worry you."

Meggie poured her another cup of tea. She didn't say anything, just watched Mary Rose sip slowly. "It's Mrs. MacFardle's favorite mug. It's the biggest one." Meggie saw that Mary Rose's awful pallor was lessening and breathed a sigh of relief. "How long were you in the water?"

"Not more than ten minutes," Mary Rose said. "Too long, but I managed to catch onto a tree branch and pull myself out. Everything is all right now. Don't worry, it would have been difficult to drown, the stream isn't deep enough, even now when the banks are nearly overflowing." Surely Erickson realized that, surely he would never have left if he'd feared she could drown.

"But you couldn't go home?"

"I rode immediately to Vallance Manor. Then I realized I couldn't go inside."

She saw that Meggie was frowning. Obviously she wanted to know what was going on, she wanted to know why Mary Rose couldn't stay at Vallance Manor. How to explain to a little girl that this man would have raped her if she hadn't jumped into the stream? That he was there at Vallance Manor when she'd ridden there, and she didn't know why? She closed her eyes. "I don't feel very well, Meggie. Do you think I could just lie here for a little while, perhaps sleep a bit?"

"Yes, Mary Rose. I will go play chess with Papa. Perhaps it will distract him. Perhaps he will forget that I am keeping something from him."

"You know he won't," Mary Rose said, never opening her eyes. "I will leave just as soon as I am able," she added, and wondered if she would have to walk out of Kildrummy Castle stark naked. Her clothes were shredded and Meggie was ten years old. She sighed. She would worry about it once she'd rested. Yes, an hour, perhaps, to let her body warm and regain strength. An hour . . .

Meggie realized Mary Rose was asleep. She appeared to be breathing easily. But she was so very pale. Meggie stood over her, wondering what was going on, knowing it must be one of those adult sorts of things that they believed a young person, even a very smart one, wouldn't understand.

She gently touched her fingertips to Mary Rose's cheek and patted it. She had to leave now, find her papa and distract him. She looked one more time at Mary Rose before she let herself out of the bedchamber.

Meggie ate her dinner very slowly, gathering the peas one by one onto her fork, wondering all the while how she was going to get food to Mary Rose. Her father said, "You're learning quickly, Meggie. When you moved your queen, checking me, I must admit that I was worried for a moment." He hadn't been, but this was one of those untruths that made a child smile and try all the harder.

"Really, Papa?"

"Really. Now, after dinner I must leave you for just a little while. I must ride to see Erickson MacPhail. There are matters I need to discuss with him. He wasn't there earlier. I won't be long."

"Is it about Mary Rose, Papa?"

Tysen started to shake his head, but then he realized there was a thread of fear in his daughter's voice. What could she possibly know about this mess? He said, "Yes, Meggie, it is about Mary Rose. But don't worry, all right? I will make certain he understands the, er, situation."

Tysen sat back then, waiting for her to beg him to take her with him. To his surprise, she didn't say another word. She was studying the buttered potatoes in the center of her plate. Now this was strange, he thought, and he was soon frowning. Something was going on here. But what?

It was then that Mrs. MacFardle said from the doorway, "Excuse me, my lord, but Sir Lyon is here. He insists that he must speak to you. He won't be put off—not that I would, naturally, even if you were in your bed, sleeping."

"Thank you, Mrs. MacFardle. Tell Sir Lyon that I will be right along." Tysen tossed his napkin beside his plate and rose. He'd taken two steps when he realized that Meggie wasn't right on his heels. He was surprised to see her wrapping several slices of bread in a napkin.

He didn't say anything, but he planned to get to the bottom of whatever this was later. He strode out of the dining room. Sir Lyon was waiting for him in the entrance hall. Pouder was sitting in his chair beside the front door, his head down, nearly reaching his chest, apparently asleep.

"Sir," Tysen said. "Is there a problem?"

"Where is she, my lord?"

"I beg your pardon?"

"Mary Rose. She is gone. She never came home from her ride. She has disappeared."

He felt instant, corroding fear. He hoped it didn't show on his face. "And you believe she is here?"

"There is no place else she would go. Of course, her aunt claims that she would never come here, that she would be too embarrassed at her behavior, but I disagree.

"Come now, where is she, my lord? You must tell her that she is to come to me, at once."

"I'm sorry," Tysen said slowly, staring at Sir Lyon, whose face was becoming alarmingly red, "but I am afraid I don't know what you're talking about. Why would Mary Rose disappear? What has happened?"

"I do not know," Sir Lyon said.

Tysen said, "You do not lie well, sir. Come into the drawing room and tell me why Mary Rose felt she had to leave your home."

Sir Lyon bellowed at the top of his lungs, not moving an inch, "Damnation, there is nothing at all to tell, particularly to you, a bloody English vicar! She is my niece, in my care, curse her eyes, and I want her! Now."

Pouder jerked upright, blinking his rheumy old eyes, then shaking his head.

"She isn't here," Tysen said calmly.

"Aye," said Pouder. "Mary Rose isn't here. I haven't left my post for the past three hours and then it was just for a moment or two when I was needed to fold his lordship's cravats."

Tysen smiled at the old man, then said again, "Mary Rose isn't here."

Sir Lyon knew when most men were lying. And he knew to his bones that this damned young man, who was also a vicar, wasn't lying. His eyes were clear of deceit, and a man who deceived as well as Sir Lyon did certainly knew deceit when he saw it. No, the young man's voice was firm and unexcited. Sir Lyon also understood choler, knew what it felt like, what it sounded like. No, the damned young man, the cursed English vicar who was also the new Lord Barthwick, wasn't lying, damn his eyes. "Then where is she?"

Tysen said very slowly, his fear for Mary Rose rising with his level of anger at this man, "What in God's name have you done, man?"

"Nothing, I tell you. Nothing at all. The girl—no, she's not a girl at all anymore, curse her, she's a damned woman. She is flighty, too flighty for a spinster of her advanced years, and she is stubborn, more stubborn than her madwoman of a damned mother. She turned him down flat, and naturally he didn't like it."

Tysen felt his anger turn to rage. It was pouring through him, making his pulse pound, sending his blood roaring, ringing in his brain, making his eyes red. "MacPhail tried to rape her, didn't he?"

"No! Bloody hell, I don't know! She jumped in the bloody stream and was quickly swept away from him. He couldn't find her."

"Are you telling me that MacPhail just left and came running to you?"

"No, certainly not. He looked for her quite thoroughly, then rode back to where she had jumped in. Her mare was gone. Obviously she'd come back and taken her mare. Besides, even overflowing like that stream is now, it isn't deep enough to drown a goat, much less a person. But, curse her eyes, she didn't come home." Sir Lyon cursed long and low under his breath. Then, oddly, he looked as if he would burst into tears. "I just don't know where she has gone. Are you certain she isn't here? Perhaps hiding from you?"

"She isn't here," Tysen said, and then, of course, he knew that she was. He waited until Sir Lyon, his ire bursting loose, had ranted even more, until his face was so red that Tysen feared the man would collapse with apoplexy in his entrance hall. Pouder never moved in his chair, never said another word, just kept his eyes on Sir Lyon, no expression at all on his seamed face.

"You will keep me informed," Tysen said as he nearly shoved Sir Lyon out the front door.

"You will tell me if she comes here?"

"Very probably not," Tysen said. He didn't say anything more, just waited at the top of the steps until Sir Lyon had mounted his horse and was gone out the front gates. He turned slowly and walked back to the dining room, saying over his shoulder, "Don't worry, Pouder. Sir Lyon will calm down."

"He be a mangy one, m'lord," Pouder said, and still didn't move. "He may be old now, but ye have a care wi' him. Always a sneak he was, always."

Meggie wasn't in the dining room, not that he expected her to be.

What in the name of his beneficent God was he going to do? He took the stairs two at a time, then three at a time. She'd jumped into the bloody stream to escape MacPhail. He pictured that swirling, maddened water in his mind closing over Mary Rose's head, and his blood turned cold. At least, thank God, he knew she hadn't drowned. He was running by the time he reached Meggie's bedchamber. He didn't knock, just turned the handle. The door was locked.

He was a calm man, a man of judgment, of unclouded reason. He yelled at the top of his lungs, "Meggie, open this bloody door now!"

To his utter surprise, in but a moment the bedchamber

door opened. His daughter stood there, staring up at him, calm as a nun. "Yes, Papa?"

"Where is she, Meggie?"

But he didn't wait for her to say anything at all, he picked her up beneath her arms and set her aside. He strode into the bedchamber and came to a dead stop. The room was empty. Mary Rose obviously wasn't here. The bed was made, the counterpane not the least bit mussed. There was no sign of anyone at all.

He turned slowly. "Where is she?"

12

"WHO ARE YOU talking about, Papa?"

"I'm talking about Mary Rose, the person you were delivering tea to just a couple of hours ago. Listen to me. She's in trouble, Meggie, very deep trouble. Tell me where she is."

But Meggie didn't say a word. She swallowed convulsively, then she walked to her father and clasped her arms around his waist and buried her face against him. "Papa, I'm so scared. I was going to come to you. She's very sick, shaking all over, and Papa, she's all cut up, and bruised everywhere, and it looks bad. But she's got a fever and I'm so scared. I don't want her to die, please don't let her die."

Tysen put his arms around his daughter, kissed the top of her head. "It will be all right, sweetheart. I won't let anything happen to Mary Rose. You can trust me on this. Where did you take her?"

"I helped her into your bedchamber, Papa. I heard Sir Lyon carrying on and yelling and so I ran back up here and got her out. I knew Pouder wasn't in your bedchamber since he was seated next to the front door. I guess he finished rearranging all your cravats."

"Evidently so. He is still at the front door, snoozing again." He grasped her shoulders in his large hands. "You took her to my bedchamber? Why there, Meggie?"

"I knew Sir Lyon wouldn't demand to look in the laird's bedchamber, Papa."

Tysen felt her shudder and just pulled her more tightly against him until he felt her ease again.

"I wouldn't have allowed Sir Lyon to look anywhere, Meggie, but it's all right. Now, listen to me, here's what I want you to do."

Two minutes later, Tysen quietly opened the door to his bedchamber. The room was warm, a cozy fire built up. Meggie's doing, he supposed. The child had worked quickly. He walked quietly to the bed and looked down at Mary Rose. Her hair was fanned out about her head, still damp, tangled, looking red as blood against the white pillow. Her face was flushed. Meggie was right, she had the fever. He closed his eyes a moment, picturing her thrashing around in the rushing water of that nearly over-flowing stream. And the rocks, he thought, so many of them, jagged, sharp, no way to avoid them. There was no hope for it. He sat down beside her and lightly slapped her bruised cheeks. Her skin was hot to the touch. She didn't move. He slapped her again. "Mary Rose," he said, "come, now, wake up. Talk to me. You're safe now. I won't let anyone hurt you. Come on, Mary Rose, open your eyes."

She moaned then, a soft animal sound deep in her throat. He pulled the covers down to her waist, and smiled. She was wearing one of his nightshirts. He sup-posed that Meggie had put it on her. He laid his palm against her heart. It was beating slowly, but it was steady, thank the good Lord. He leaned close to her and listened. Yes, steady and slow.

He straightened, saw her hands then, bruised and

scraped, some of the cuts fairly deep, several of them
oozing just a bit of blood. Well, there was no hope for it,
there was no one else to help her. He pulled the nightshirt
down to her waist, and sucked in his breath. She was
covered with bruises, bright green, yellow, a bit of purple,
streaking her ribs, her belly, her shoulders. And the cuts,
myriad small slashes, none of them very deep, but ugly,
all of them. Tysen was a man of God, but as he looked
at her, pictured in his mind that stream and her struggling
in it, he knew deep, corroding fear, actually both fear and
anger at the damned man who'd driven her to jump in the
water.

What to do? Mrs. MacFardle had some medicinal
cream he could apply after Mary Rose was bathed. No,
he wouldn't say anything about her to Mrs. MacFardle.
He didn't want her to know that Mary Rose was here.
Further, she obviously didn't approve of a bastard being
treated like a person of value. He cupped his hand against
her breast again, pressing more firmly to feel the beat of
her heart. And he couldn't help himself. He looked at her
in those few moments as a man looks at a woman, and
he saw that she was nicely made, so very white, her flesh
smooth and her breasts wonderfully shaped. His fingers
flexed against her flesh, then he grunted at himself and
quickly jerked his hand away. He closed his eyes for a
moment. He couldn't think like this, couldn't allow himself to see her as a man who wanted her. She was very
ill. He heard a soft knock on the door. He pulled the
nightshirt back up and covered her again.

Meggie was there, holding a basin of hot water, several
cloths over her arm, and a bottle of ointment clutched in
her hand. "Excellent, Meggie. How did you ever get that
ointment from Mrs. MacFardle?"

"I had to lie to her, Papa. Since she doesn't know me

as well as you do, she believed me when I told her that you had cut your hand."

"You did well. Now, I want you to go back to your bedchamber."

"Papa, please let me help you. Mary Rose is—"

"Mary Rose is what?"

Meggie frowned toward the young woman lying in the middle of her father's bed. She struggled to find the words. "It's just that she's very alone, even though she lives in a houseful of people. I don't think there's anyone for her. Not even her mother. She needs me."

Just as I need you, Tysen thought, and smiled down at his precious daughter. He cradled her cheek in his hand. "I promise I'll take good care of her. No one is to know yet that she's here. If anyone asks about me, just tell them that I am not feeling well and am here in my bedchamber. Now, I don't want you to stay, sweetheart. Go now."

"You will call me if she worsens?"

"I most certainly will. I promise." Tysen waited until Meggie had slipped out of his bedchamber.

He locked the door, then walked back to the bed. Tysen hadn't ever taken intimate care of another person, except his children, of course, after their mother had died. He'd rocked them endlessly when monsters had invaded their dreams, wiped their foreheads when they'd been downed by fevers, held them when they vomited, rubbed their stomachs when they had belly cramps. But Mary Rose wasn't a child. She was a grown woman, and she wasn't his wife.

There was no choice. It was either that or ask Mrs. MacFardle to see to her, and that he couldn't, wouldn't, do. He remembered how she had purposely hurt Mary Rose's ankle just because she hadn't believed she belonged here at Kildrummy Castle, in the drawing room, in the same company with her betters.

"All right, Mary Rose," he said, staring down at her. "I'm all you've got."

He stripped her down, examined every inch of her, bathed her, rubbed the ointment that smelled like pine and lavender mixed together into every scratch, abrasion, and cut on her white body. No, he wouldn't think of her as having a white body, as having soft white flesh. He realized that she was shivering and quickly put her into his nightshirt again. He took his well-worn dark-green brocade dressing gown and wrapped that around her as well. He pulled the covers to her chin and smoothed her hair, only a bit damp now, from around her face. Her face was as badly bruised as her body. He lightly pressed his palms to her forehead, her cheeks. She was now cool to the touch.

He prayed she would stay that way.

He built up the fire, then pulled a very large leather wing chair at least two centuries old up beside the bed. He lit another branch of candles, picked up the book he'd been reading, and settled himself in to wait.

"I don't understand why you want to do this. You wanted Donnatella. Why me? Why now?"

He nearly dropped his book, Shakespeare's *King Henry IV, Part I,* one of his favorite plays.

"Mary Rose? Are you back with me?"

She wasn't. She twisted a bit, but the covers were heavy and she couldn't throw them off. *"I don't want to wed, don't you understand? I would never marry you, you were fondling my own mother. How could you do that? She is my mother!"*

"I know," he said, smoothing her hair, touching her face, to calm her. "Erickson MacPhail won't ever again be close enough to frighten you, Mary Rose. You must trust me on that."

"She's my mother!"

"Yes, she is. It's all right, I'm here now."

She started crying, deep, gulping sobs that seemed to be torn out of her chest, and tears, streaming down her face. He couldn't bear it. He sat beside her and pulled her up against his chest. He rocked her, speaking nonsense to her, holding her, stroking her back, his breath warm on her flesh, so that perhaps on some level, she would know she was safe. He remembered how he'd just stared at her when she'd told him about Erickson and her mother, crying quietly as she'd told him how even now she still wasn't entirely certain that her mother hadn't encouraged, hadn't, in fact, been his lover. Her mother had never said anything to her about it—understandable, Tysen supposed. He'd wanted to hold her then, comfort her, but he hadn't.

Nor had he been shocked. As a vicar, he believed that he had witnessed just about everything perverse, vicious, and brutal that anyone could possibly do. But he'd hated the fact that Mary Rose had seen the two of them, and had been so terribly hurt. Then, of course, she'd been embarrassed that she'd told him.

He leaned over and kissed her temple. He then nearly leapt off the bed at what he'd done, at what he'd felt at the touch of his mouth against her skin. He didn't let her go, he couldn't. He'd kissed her, a woman who wasn't his wife, a young woman who was defenseless, without protection. He closed his eyes. He'd had to take care of her, but that kiss, that wasn't well done of him. He touched his mouth to her cheek, tasted the salty tears, but this time he didn't kiss her, just held her close and closer still, and tasted her tears.

She calmed, her face against his shoulder, her breathing evening out. If she was still awake, he prayed that she wasn't still locked inside herself. "Mary Rose?" His voice was just a whisper against her cheek.

She was asleep. He gently eased her onto her back,

pulled the covers up. He rose slowly, looking down at her. He hadn't even known she existed until—was it even a week ago? Less? He couldn't seem to remember a day when she hadn't been there. No, that was ridiculous. He hadn't been interested in another female, not in this way, since three months after he and Melinda Beatrice had wed. He had to stop it, he was being disloyal, disremembering. Only he knew he wasn't, and he didn't like himself very much for admitting it. But it was true. There'd simply been no one else after Melinda Beatrice had died. He had long ago disciplined himself to master his own body and its demands upon him. And that control had been inviolable, until Mary Rose, a Scotswoman who was also a bastard.

Tysen wasn't a man given to curses, and so he didn't curse. Instead, he walked quietly to the large, blackened fireplace and stood there, deep in thought, staring down into the flames, not ferociously high now but sinking slowly and inexorably into the wood until all that remained was embers that glowed a soft, bright orange.

Mary Rose. He loved the sound of her name, the feel of it, both in his mind and on his tongue. Dear Lord, what was he going to do?

She awoke in the dark of the night. She was cold, so very cold that she knew if she breathed too deeply, she would shatter, just as the beautiful vase that had fallen off the mantel in her bedchamber had shattered and was no more. She, too, would be no more. She held herself stiff, but not for long. She began to shiver, her teeth chattered, and she simply couldn't stop it. The worse it became, the more fiercely the pain rippled through her. It dug deep, and she moaned with it.

"It's all right, Mary Rose, I'm here."

"Tysen," she whispered. "Is it really you? Oh, my, I'm so glad it's you. I don't feel very well. I'm sorry."

"You have a fever. I will deal with that, don't worry."

"I hurt—all the smacks and blows from those bloody boulders. I'm sorry."

"I'll deal with that, too. Now, I want you to lie as quietly as you can for just a moment, not more than three more minutes. Can you do that?"

"I'm sorry."

"Stop saying that. Just try to breathe deeply. I'll be right back."

It was a bit longer than three minutes, but then he was beside her again, his sleeves rolled up. He'd lit a six-branch candelabra and set it near the bed. He was surrounded by shadows, but the lines of his face were strong and calm and intent.

"I'm going to wipe you down with cold water. My nanny did it to me several times when I was a boy. It knocked the fever right out of me. I've done it to my own children. First, here's some laudanum to ease the pain."

He lifted her, and she drank the water laced with laudanum. "Good, you drank it all." He added as if to himself, "I must remember to keep you drinking." He paused a moment, his hand on the covers to pull them back. When he'd examined her before, she'd been unconscious. But now she wasn't. "Please just think of me as a physician, all right?"

"No, I can't," she said, and shuddered. "You're Tysen. You're something else entirely. This is very difficult."

"I know, but I won't hurt you, ever. Please trust me, Mary Rose."

"I trust you," she said, then closed her eyes. She didn't move.

He'd felt people's trust in him before, felt it as a burden or as a pleasure or as a simple obligation or duty.

It was not at all uncommon a thing, but those words coming from her mouth, words he knew she meant to her soul, made something shift deep inside of him, something that was warm and boundless, something that he hadn't felt in a very long time. It should have scared him to his toes, but it didn't. "All right, then," he said, and pulled the covers off her. He carefully eased her out of his night-shirt. Then he turned her onto her stomach and began wiping the wet cloths down her back and hips, over her legs, even to her arched feet. One of her toes was crooked. She'd obviously broken it many years before. His fingers closed over that toe for a moment.

Over and over he swept the wet cloth down her, then up again, feeling it grow warm from the heat her body was giving off. He dipped it into the basin of cold water once, twice, more times than he could count. He had to keep it cold. When he turned her onto her back, her eyes were open. She was looking up at him, saying nothing, just looking at him. He saw no signs of pain on her face, no fear, just that limitless trust. He smiled at her, covered his hand with the cloth, and began rubbing it up and down her body. Over her breasts, her belly. He closed his eyes. She was ill. He was a man of mature years, not a randy boy. He could deal with this. He knew well the demands of control. He would not dishonor her, would not shame himself by allowing his body to harden with lust. But of course his body did just that. He wondered briefly why God wasn't helping him here, but then he wanted to laugh at himself. Why would God concern Himself about a man's simple and inevitable reaction to a woman's body? Dear heavens, but she was beautiful. No, he wouldn't think like that. He kept rubbing her down. Wiping back up her body, he found, was harder. He tried closing his eyes, but it just didn't help.

The hair at the base of her belly was a deep red, just beautiful, a bit darker than the rich red hair on her head. He looked at her knees, very nice knees, then quickly brought the cold, wet cloth over them and rubbed them longer than necessary, staring at them, just at her knees, nothing either north or south of them.

He wasn't in good shape. But he was a man, not an immature boy. He would deal with this. He continued rubbing her down until he touched his palm to her cheek and she was once again cool. Thank the good Lord. Then she turned her cheek into his palm and for a moment, just a brief moment, he held her there. He quickly fetched another nightshirt from the ancient armoire and put her in it, smoothing it down over her legs, over her white feet.

He rolled up the sleeves so her hands would be free, covered her to her nose, then rose. She was still looking at him.

"Do you feel better?" He was actually surprised she was still awake, what with all the laudanum he'd put in that glass of water. He took a step away from the bed and prayed that a woman couldn't see the lust in a man's mind.

"Thank you," she said, her voice slightly slurred. "I'm sorry, Tysen."

"Be quiet."

He couldn't believe the harshness of his voice, but she simply smiled at him. "That's the first time you've ever shown impatience with me. Meggie told me that my uncle came here. She said you didn't have to lie to him because you didn't realize that I was indeed here, in Meggie's bed, until she helped me into the laird's bedchamber. She was afraid her bedchamber wasn't private enough, that anyone felt free to walk in on a child, but not on you, the laird. That's why I'm here. I'm s—"

Tysen just waved away her words. "Yes, Sir Lyon was extraordinarily upset that you weren't here. He knows you didn't drown, since Erickson searched until he saw that your mare was gone. He assured me that stream was too shallow to drown a goat. Did you ride home and see MacPhail there?"

"Yes. I saw his horse. I didn't know where to go. I hadn't intended to come here, truly, but then Primrose just galloped right to your gate. Meggie was out there and she brought me in. Up the back stairs so Pouder wouldn't see us." Suddenly she grinned. "I've always thought it remarkable that Pouder doesn't collect dust, since he's always there."

"He was collecting dust at a great rate until he realized that I, the new laird, did not have a valet. Since he only has two teeth left in his mouth, his smile at this discovery rocked me back a bit. You see, he's wanted to be a valet all his life, and now he had his opportunity." Tysen shook his head. "Only when he said that, he didn't say 'valet,' he said he'd always wanted to be a 'varlet.' It took me a while to figure all this out. Now I will find him at the oddest times in this bedchamber rearranging my cravats and straightening my razor and brushes."

She wanted to laugh, but she was afraid it would hurt too much. "He's a very nice old man."

"Yes, he appears to be. He also appears to be very proud of himself. I have told him that we would take his varlet training slowly so as not to disrupt his other, more important duties."

"You are very kind to him. Tysen, I know you don't like it, but I am sorry for causing you difficulties. I was thinking that tomorrow morning I can leave and—"

"Oh? You wish to leave? May I inquire as to what you would wear? I chanced to see the remains of your clothes in Meggie's bedchamber. Did you perchance intend to squeeze yourself into one of her gowns?"

"I will think of something," she said, his light dose of sarcasm floating through her mind. Her chin went up, a hard thing to do since she was so tired. "It's possible that

Mrs. MacFardle would have something I could borrow. Oh dear, I feel so very tired."

"No wonder. It's about time. I gave you a goodly dose of laudanum." He paused a moment, then the sarcasm was back. "All right, let us say that you are finely garbed in one of Mrs. MacFardle's castoffs. Where will you go?"

Along with the sarcasm, his voice was sharp, sharper than he'd intended. He saw her fold down, saw the helplessness of her situation wash over her, and felt like a clod. He took one white hand in his and held it close. He said very gently, "Mary Rose, we will think of something. You aren't yet well enough to think of wearing anything but my nightshirts. Go to sleep now and stop your mad squirreling about for a solution. I will think of something."

"But—"

He touched a finger to her lips. "No, be quiet. Let go of things and go to sleep. You'll feel better more quickly. Are you still in pain?"

"No, I don't hurt anymore." Two minutes later, her face was turned into the pillow. Her breathing was even. She was sound asleep.

Tysen tried to make himself comfortable in the wing chair. It wasn't too bad, but still, he didn't fall asleep for a very long time. When he awoke with a jerk, a moan coming out of his mouth, it was in the full darkness of the night. He realized he'd awakened from a dream of his own making, a dreadful dream that had him so scared he was struggling to find breath even as he lurched out of the chair and began pacing the bedchamber floor, his head still spinning from the terror of that damnable dream. When at last he managed to calm himself, he realized he was cold. He built up the fire, then lit one candle and walked to Mary Rose's bedside. He laid his palm on her forehead. She was blessedly cool to the touch, thank God for that, and sleeping deeply.

What had that wretched dream meant? All he could remember was the woman yelling, then a man's voice— slurred, weak, becoming indistinct, and then there was the feeling of death all around him, endless, irrevocable death, and he was there, a shadow, perhaps just a whisper of light, but he was part of it. Then, just as suddenly as it had begun, it was over.

He didn't understand. The fear was still stark inside him. He walked back to the chair and eased himself down. He cupped his chin in his hand and spent the remainder of the night staring into the flames.

The man's voice he'd heard—it was Ian, who had fallen off a cliff six months ago.

13

Dr. Halsey patted Mary Rose's cheek. "Aye, lass, that's it. Give me a smile. Then you can curse me for pouring this vile potion down your throat."

Mary Rose did smile up at him. He'd brought her into the world, so her mother had told her. "Where is Tysen?"

"Who? Oh, I see, you mean Lord Barthwick. Tysen— not much of a Scottish name, is it? Oh, well, I suppose that's to be expected since he's an Englishman. He's right here, standing not six feet behind me. I have this feeling his lordship will pound me into the floor if I cause you any more discomfort. How do you feel now, lass?"

Mary Rose consulted her body. "I feel battered."

"She should," Tysen said, stepping closer, taking her left hand between his two large ones. "As I told you, sir, she fell into that fast-moving stream and got knocked about until she managed to pull herself out with a tree branch."

"You always were a strong girl. You've a black eye, Mary Rose. It makes you look raffish, like a little red-headed pirate. Now, his lordship can go stand by the door. I must check you over, see that nothing is broken or needs my bonnie stitches."

Tysen said, "I have examined her, Dr. Halsey, and there are no nasty deep cuts that would need stitching. No broken bones, either. I have two boys of my own, and I know broken bones when I see and feel them. But she could be hurt internally."

Dr. Halsey gave Tysen a rheumy look, then straightened. "Aye, but there are other things that can be wrong. Now, Mary Rose, the fever is down and your lungs sound clear. You have no pain in your belly or your chest? Here, let me know if I cause you any pain."

He prodded her more gently than not, beginning with her head and moving slowly and methodically down to her toes. Then he smiled at her, and back at Tysen. "You will survive, lass. Now, you'll drink my tonic and I will see you again if you worsen."

Tysen saw the doctor out of the bedchamber. He heard Mrs. MacFardle's strident voice echoing down the corridor, "Ach, Dr. Halsey, it's a pitiful state of affairs we have here. Imagine, Mary Rose in the laird's bed, and him taking care of her, of all things, and here he is an English vicar. Had he but told me, why, I would have said that he could not, it wasn't proper. But he didn't mutter a single word to me, so what was I to do? Nothing good can come of it, ye'll see."

Her voice finally began to fade as she moved down the long hallway, but unfortunately it was still crystal clear to his ears. "Aye, come down and have a cup of tea wi' me and Mr. Pouder. I know he's awake, I heard him snort at Ardle, who is holding yer horse for ye."

Mary Rose, who was clutching the blankets to her chin, said, "You shouldn't have asked the doctor to come. He will tell everyone in the area that I am here in your bed, with you standing far too close to the bed where I'm lying. Mrs. MacFardle is right. I shouldn't be here."

Tysen just shrugged. "I would rather suffer gossip than

have you die on me because of my ignorance." Then he smiled. "Don't worry, Mary Rose. I am so relieved that you're going to be just fine, I believe I'll give you a cup of Mrs. MacFardle's cider."

When he returned with the cider not ten minutes later, having been snagged by Dr. Halsey for an inquisition on his opinion of the clearances, he saw that Mary Rose was asleep. He stood over her a moment. She did look a bit like a pirate, the black bruise circling her left eye like a pirate's patch.

He gently touched her forehead and found it cool. He imagined that he had no more than two hours at the outside before Sir Lyon would be back here, demanding to take her home.

But it wasn't Sir Lyon who arrived exactly one hour and forty minutes later. It was Erickson MacPhail.

> *You are a shallow cowardly hind, and you lie.*
> —Shakespeare, *King Henry IV, Part I*

Tysen walked slowly into the drawing room and closed the door quietly behind him. MacPhail stood by the fireplace, his arms crossed over his chest.

Tysen realized his own hands were fisted at his sides. Slowly, ever so slowly, he forced himself to ease. He was a vicar, and he believed firmly in God's strength, in God's compassion, but more than that, he was his father's son and he was like his brothers. Neither Douglas nor Ryder would lose his head and erupt in senseless violence whenever it pleased him to do so. And neither would he.

Erickson stepped toward him and said without preamble, "Dr. Halsey has told us that Mary Rose is here. He said he attended her. He said that she will be all right, that she is merely bruised a bit from getting knocked about in that damned stream. I was excessively worried about her. I am here to fetch her home, to Vallance Manor."

Tysen walked to one of the tatty old gold brocade settees and sat down, crossing one leg over the other. He wished his Hessians were polished more brightly. Old Angus had last polished them in Edinburgh. He eyed Mary Rose's nemesis for a moment, then said mildly, "Actually, you have saved me a good deal of trouble. I was on my way over to your home again to speak to you. About Mary Rose."

Erickson took a violent step forward. "Damn you, vicar, you will not put me off. Take me to her now, or vicar or no, I will beat you until you crawl to do my bidding."

Tysen arched an eyebrow, smiled pleasantly at Erickson, whose face was becoming alarmingly red. When he was older, Tysen imagined, his face would slowly become that unbecoming shade of red that results from too much choler. He said on a shrug, "I suppose you could try."

There was a marked sneer about Erickson's mouth that Tysen thought was singularly unattractive. "You dare to bait me? To set yourself up against me? You, a man who isn't really a man at all, but a gutless creature who exhorts real men from the pulpit? You threaten them with hellfire if they don't swallow their righteous anger and choke on it? You order them to become as weak-willed and spineless as you are? You tell them they are cursed unless they grovel before you?"

Tysen rose slowly to his feet. His heart had speeded up, but—strangely perhaps—he felt quite calm. All this litany of insults he had heard before, a number of times, beginning when he was at Oxford.

It made little impact, really, for it was naught but ignorant words, cruel words, sparked by unreasoning anger. There was, he had learned, too much unreasoning anger in this world. He said, "Do you love Mary Rose Fordyce?"

Erickson stopped dead in his tracks, a sleek dark brow up a good inch. "Good God, man, I want to marry her!"

"I see. So to convince her of your sincere regard, of your lasting affection, you were going to rape her? To escape you, she had to jump into the stream?"

"Damn you, there was never a question of rape. You're a vicar. You don't understand how females behave, what lengths they will go to in order to make a man grovel at their dainty feet. Mary Rose is very much a female. She is coy, she teases, she pretends to become hysterical, all to get her way. All her denials, her small dramatic gesture of jumping into that ridiculous stream, it was just a simple performance, a show of melodrama. She wants to marry me, to give her status, to give her a real name, for God's sake. She's through with her fun. She will marry me now. I will speak to her and you will see that she has quite changed her mind."

"All right, then," Tysen said, rising. "I will take you to see her. However, I will remain to ensure that you do not try to coerce her or bully her. I would say, though, that her jump into that stream—although you prefer to believe it merely a girl's teasing gesture—rather proves to me that she would do just about anything to escape you. No, you will not rant further. Be quiet and listen to me.

"She has been quite ill. You will not try to threaten her in any way, is that perfectly clear to you?"

Erickson stared at the far-too-handsome man, damn him, who was a bloody vicar, who was looking at him as if he was worth very little and full of naught save wind. He wanted to bash his face in, break that nose of his. Make him ugly. Yes, he wanted to beat him until he was so ugly Mary Rose wouldn't want to ever look at him again.

Was that why Mary Rose didn't want him? She wanted the bloody vicar who was also Lord Barthwick? He said slowly, "Why did she come here, to Kildrummy Castle?"

"To escape you yet again. Now, would you like to speak to her, to assure yourself that she indeed improves? I will give you five minutes, no more. She must rest. She is still very weak."

Mary Rose wasn't alone. Meggie was curled next to her on the bed, one of her small hands on Mary Rose's arm, both of them fast asleep. At the sound of her father's low voice, Meggie jerked up and blinked. She pushed her hair out of her face.

She shot a quick look at Mary Rose and whispered, "Papa, I wanted to guard Mary Rose, but I fell asleep. She is all right, isn't she? Oh, my, isn't that Mr. MacPhail with you? Why is he here?"

"He wants to speak to Mary Rose," Tysen said, his voice as emotionless as he could make it. He saw the change in his daughter's posture, in the expression on her small face, and wanted to smile. She drew herself up and said, "Very well—if she awakens. I believe she is now stirring. He may speak to her, but I will remain. He will not distress her."

"Well, MacPhail?" Tysen asked, turning to face the man, who looked both furious and bemused.

"For God's sake, man, she is a child. Make her leave."

"Oh, no, she considers herself Mary Rose's protector. Ah, yes, Mary Rose just opened her eyes. Remain where you are a moment and I will tell her that you are here." He paused, adding, "Naturally I will reassure her that you can attempt nothing that she would dislike."

He heard Erickson MacPhail cursing under his breath behind him. Rather vivid and varied animal parts, but not as colorful as his brother Ryder's Beloved Ones, who could spit out the most rank curses, even better than sailors raised in the king's navy. He walked to the bed, smiled down at Mary Rose, and took her hand between his. "Do not be alarmed. You have a visitor, but he will not upset you in any way. Both Meggie and I swear it to you. He simply wishes to assure himself that you are all right."

"I don't want to see him. Please, Tysen, he will—"

Tysen touched his fingertips to her lips. "Let him speak, Mary Rose, and then that will be the end to it."

"Yes," she said slowly, "you're perfectly right. I must speak to him and then it will be the end to it." She drew a deep, steadying breath and said, "May I have some water first?"

"You'll get through this in fine style." He lifted her head and put the water glass to her lips. He thought he heard MacPhail say something, but he ignored him. When she'd finished drinking, she sighed and sat up as Tysen fluffed a pillow behind her. Meggie moved even closer to her now, snuggling against her side.

Mary Rose watched Erickson walk toward her, every step announcing his anger, his frustration, his absolute bafflement that a vicar was standing at his elbow and a ten-year-old girl was squeezed next to her on that huge bed. She wondered if he still saw her as the woman he fully intended to have. She realized that yes, he did. She wondered if more men were like him, believing that any woman they wished to have was theirs. She also knew that Meggie was giving him a look that clearly said she would leap on him if he tried anything. She felt immense gratitude for the little girl plastered to her side.

Erickson stopped at her bedside and stared down at her, not saying a word for a very long time. Then, "You have a black eye."

"Yes," Mary Rose said, and she was tempted to smile, but she didn't.

"You are feeling all right, Mary Rose?"

He sounded like the man she'd known all her life, the man who had been her friend, so long ago, it seemed now. "Yes, just a bit sore. The fever is gone."

Then he became what she'd expected, even though he tried to keep his voice calm, cajoling, just slightly scolding, as if she were a child. "You should never have jumped into that stream. You were swept away from me before I could do anything. I was very worried about you. I searched and searched, but I couldn't find you. I was very frightened for you, Mary Rose. When I rode back, Primrose was gone, so I knew you were safe. You should never have jumped into that water."

She said, very clearly, "I would jump into that stream again, without hesitation, if you were threatening me."

He felt anger leap up, flame hot. He wanted to shake her, tell her that she shouldn't go against him, but he couldn't. He looked at the child, who was now even closer to Mary Rose than a minute before. He said formally, "Would you like me to escort you to Vallance Manor?"

Tysen thought she couldn't become any more pale, but she did, and now she was utterly without color. Meggie squeezed even closer.

Mary Rose shook her head.

Erickson said, "Your aunt and uncle and, of course, Donnatella, are quite worried about you. They're hurt that you felt you could not even come home, that you had to escape to this place."

"What about my mother?"

"No one has told her anything. Your uncle doesn't want to distress her."

"How could I go into Vallance Manor when I saw your horse in front? After what you tried to do to me, do you honestly believe I would take the chance of walking into a house where you seemed perfectly at home? Into a house where, perhaps, you would feel free to abuse me again?"

"Abuse? Again? Nonsense. There was no abuse, Mary Rose. You are disremembering everything. You know I would not harm a single curly hair on your head. I asked you to marry me. I was a perfect gentleman. You put me off, you played the clever, elusive female. What was I to think? I was merely going to try to convince you that I wanted you, prove my sincerity to you, that's all, but you decided to punish me, and you jumped into the water. I could not believe you did that. But now things are different. As soon as you are well again, we will wed. All you have to do now is accept me, and I will take you home."

Mary Rose closed her eyes a moment. Something wasn't right here. She opened her eyes and studied his face, but he looked just as he had a moment ago, all confident, a man clearly in charge, a very determined man. She said slowly, "Does my uncle wish me to marry you?"

"Yes."

"But that makes no sense. Donnatella wants you. Why does he not prefer you to wed Donnatella?"

"I have told him that I do not love Donnatella. I have told him clearly that I must have you."

"Will my uncle allow you to force me if I return home?"

The little girl was looking at him like he was a monster, even though she obviously didn't understand exactly what was happening here. The vicar, curse his eyes, looked faintly bored, but Erickson wasn't fooled.

"Forget your damned uncle. He has nothing to do with this. Forget this nonsense about forcing you. My mother is very fond of you, Mary Rose."

"Your mother, Erickson, refers to me as the Upstart Bastard in a very penetrating voice to anyone within hearing distance."

"She has changed, I promise you."

She spoke clearly, with no fear or hesitation. "Please, leave go, Erickson. We used to be friends. I wish we could be friends again. But nothing more. I do not wish to marry you. I am not being coy. I am playing no game with you. I have no wish to wed with anyone. I will not let you take me home. I do not trust my uncle, and that is a pity. Good-bye, Erickson."

He stiffened, saw that the little girl was very nearly ready to crawl on top of Mary Rose to protect her from him. It was too much. He threw back his head and heard his own laughter ring out in the room.

"Good," Tysen said. "A man who is laughing isn't thinking of mayhem."

Erickson said over his shoulder as he strode out of the bedchamber, "This isn't over, Mary Rose." He nearly knocked Pouder flat. "Good God, man, watch where the devil you are walking!"

"The cravats," Pouder said. "I must see to his lordship's cravats. I nearly have the hang of folding them properly now. I am his varlet-in-training."

Erickson stared at the old man he'd nearly knocked over. He'd known him ever since he was too small even to remember. "You're a varlet, Pouder? Oh, I see. Yes, see to the cravats," he said, and went slowly down the stairs to the grand entrance hall of Kildrummy Castle.

What the bloody hell was he to do now?

14

MARY ROSE HAD just eaten a bowl of too salty chicken broth under Tysen's watchful eye when Meggie burst into the room, out of breath because she had been running. "You'll not believe who is here, Papa! It's Aunt Sinjun and Uncle Colin!"

Sinjun stepped into the very large, very dark, melancholy bedchamber that had obviously had only a long line of men living there with no woman to perk the place up and quickly took in Mary Rose's vivid curly red hair, those incredible green eyes of hers, the bruises on her face, her pallor. And that leap of fear. She said to the room at large, which also included Tysen, who had just built up the fire and was now standing, wiping his hands, staring at her, clearly startled at her sudden presence, "I would have gotten here sooner, but Pearlin' Jane didn't tell me exactly where the trouble was or exactly who the trouble involved until last night just after Colin and I were all snuggled together in bed and—never mind that. Then I had to convince Colin that it wasn't some sort of absurd dream, brought on by a surfeit of—no, forget that as well. It isn't important either. Colin is, naturally, stubborn as a flea since he is a man, but he came around finally." Sinjun walked quickly to Tysen, who was now holding out his arms to her, still looking bemused, saying her name, and wrapped her own arms around him.

"Sinjun," he said again, kissing her, then holding her away from him, "you know I do not believe in ghosts. Even this Pearlin' Jane of yours. Now, will you tell me, with no embroidering of the facts, exactly why you felt compelled to drag yourself and Colin here to Kildrummy?"

"Of course I'll tell you, my dear, but first, who is this?"

"She's Mary Rose, Aunt Sinjun, and her hair is as beautiful as Aunt Alex's."

"Yes," Colin said, stepping forward and shaking Tysen's hand, then looking immediately over at Mary Rose, "I suppose that it is. I can see you've been hurt. I am Colin Kinross, the stubborn husband. What is going on here? I never believed Sinjun for a moment—well, perhaps for three or four very short moments, but no more than that—but she was so very worried that something bad was happening to Tysen that we came. I'm sorry, Tysen. If you are wishing us at Jericho, we will leave you be. But it looks as if my wife is correct. There is some trouble here."

Tysen said, "You have arrived at a splendid time. You can help Meggie protect Mary Rose from Erickson MacPhail."

"Oh, goodness," Sinjun said and was by Mary Rose's side in an instant, her cool hand on her forehead. "Of course there is trouble. Is Erickson MacPhail the man we saw striding out of the castle, looking like he wanted to blast everyone?"

"Oh, dear," Mary Rose said.

"It doesn't matter," Tysen said. "He finally realizes he has lost. Let him relieve his bile."

Sinjun said, "Now we are here, nothing else unpleasant

will happen to you." She smiled down at the young woman who had the most magnificent green eyes she'd ever seen. "Actually, with Tysen here, we're really not at all necessary, but—"

There was a swish at the doorway, then a loud, portentous clearing of the throat. Tysen turned to see Mrs. Griffin standing there, her hands on her abundant hips.

Tysen said pleasantly, "Sinjun, my dearest sister, I beg you not to leave. Now here is trouble that is possibly even beyond my ability to manage. Help me, Sinjun. I am clearly in need of reinforcements."

Mrs. Griffin said, striding into the bedchamber, swinging her black cane, "I do not wish to believe my eyes! But I cannot disregard what my eyes are seeing. There have been generations of Barthwicks who have slipped out of their mothers' wombs and then died on their own, usually of gnarly old age—at least some of them did—in that bed. Just look at her—all sunk deep in the lovely feather ticking, looking right at home, as if she belonged, as if she was the laird's wife. She is nothing but a bastard. No one has anything to do with her. She doesn't belong here, particularly in that bed. Ah, that raises a question."

Mrs. Griffin pumped herself up, her bosom attaining new prominence. "What is she doing in your bedchamber and in your bed, my lord?"

Tysen had always enjoyed his share of the Sherbrooke luck. But now it seemed that wondrous luck had deserted him. His bedchamber was very nearly overflowing with people, and poor Mary Rose looked as if she was going to expire on the spot. And now this ridiculous old besom was insulting her at a fine clip, and that made him very angry indeed. He said pleasantly, though it was very difficult, almost beyond him, "Mrs. Griffin, Mr. Griffin—I assume you are standing directly behind your wife, and that is why I don't see you?"

"Just so. We are here to see what is what."

"That is obscure enough," Tysen said. "Before you again take your leave, you can see that Mary Rose has been hurt. She is recovering from her injuries. This is all there is to it, this is your what is what. There is nothing that requires your assistance that I can think of. I hope your carriage is still awaiting you in front of the castle?"

"Rudeness isn't becoming, even though you are a vicar and an Englishman," said Mrs. Griffin. "Of course there is more to this than a mere what is what. I ask you, my lord, who are these people? Obviously they are more imported wretched English here to torment us."

Colin eyed the woman with the thin black mustache over her upper lip and her husband, who was still standing behind her, drew himself as tall as Robert the Bruce, wished he had a claymore to swing about, and said, "Ma'am, I am Lord Ashburnham. I am so Scottish that I wear my plaid to bed and even dream in Scottish, not English or Italian. Just who the devil are you?"

To Tysen's surprise, Mrs. Griffin gave Colin a very quick, very deep curtsy, ruined quickly enough when she opened her mouth. "I am Mrs. Griffin, naturally, my lord. I belong here. I have been coming here for so long that I once even considered marrying Old Tyronne so I could sleep in that bed. I did not marry him, of course, because of Mr. Griffin here, and he was still breathing then, as he is now. Poor Old Tyronne needed more heirs, but alas, I was a bit too advanced in years to provide one.

"Now, I can see that I am needed. There is a conundrum of magnificent proportions here. I—we—are here to resolve everything. First, get that girl out of that bed."

Tysen rolled his eyes. It kept him from marching up to Mrs. Griffin and either snarling something unvicarlike into her face or throwing her out the window, if only they were wide enough to accommodate her, which he doubted they were.

Sinjun said slowly, still absorbing the irrefutable fact that this woman actually existed and was standing here in Tysen's bedchamber, "Pearlin' Jane didn't tell me about you, Mrs. Griffin."

"Obviously this Pearlin' Jane person doesn't know everything," said Mr. Griffin, one shoulder showing around his wife.

"If Pearlin' Jane had told you anything at all about Mrs. Griffin," Tysen said to his sister, "I doubt you would have stirred from Vere Castle even if my head was under the guillotine blade. You would have written me a letter of condolence and kept your distance."

"I do not find you amusing, my lord."

"No, I imagine that you don't," Tysen said. "Now, why don't all of us leave Mary Rose to rest? Perhaps Mrs. MacFardle will provide us tea to pour down our respective gullets. Then perhaps you, Mrs. Griffin, will feel that the conundrum is well in hand and you are free once again to take your leave."

"I continue not to like your humor, my lord."

"Sometimes, Mrs. Griffin," Tysen said, swallowing his gorge since there was no choice at all, "I don't either."

"I insist that you satisfy me, my lord," said Mrs. Griffin.

Tysen said, "I doubt that I am capable of accomplishing that, ma'am. Come along now. Mary Rose isn't well."

"She doesn't deserve to be," Mr. Griffin said, extending his neck so that he could see around his wife's shoulder. "No one has anything to do with her."

I am not a violent man, Tysen said over and over to himself. Even if I were, I would not allow myself to strike an older man who has probably drunk more than his share of smuggled French brandy.

"You go ahead," Sinjun said, waving them all away. "I

wish to speak to Mary Rose. Colin, I wish you to remain and listen so that you may tell me things later that I am perhaps missing in all this."

Tysen didn't want to leave his sister with Mary Rose. He wasn't certain why, but he just knew, all the way to the scar over his left rib that occasionally ached when the weather turned unexpectedly, that it wasn't a good idea. Colin took his arm. "You have no choice," Colin said, sympathy and humor in his voice. "Sinjun must needs meddle, you know that."

"Yes, I know," Tysen said. "The first time she meddled, I believe, she was four years old and Douglas ended up under a rosebush, hiding from our father."

"Go, my dear," Sinjun said, giving him that special smile of hers that he had never trusted her entire life. "I will take care of things here. Trust me. Ah, I believe I was five that time."

Tysen sighed, smiled at Mary Rose. "I will see you soon. Try to rest. Try to ignore my sister." He then told Meggie not to flatten Mary Rose with too much protection and followed the Griffins out of the bedchamber.

"Now," Sinjun said, focusing all of her formidable intelligence on Mary Rose, "let me tell you all about Pearlin' Jane and what she said to me."

"Who is Pearlin' Jane?" Mary Rose asked.

Meggie said, "She is Aunt Sinjun's ghost. She lives at Vere Castle. She's been dead for a very long time, but she takes care of Aunt Sinjun."

"That's right," Sinjun said, and sat down in the big wing chair. "She came to me last night and told me that Tysen was in trouble, here at Kildrummy."

"He is," Mary Rose said. A tear rolled down her cheek. "I don't think I believe in ghosts either. I've never seen one, even here, and there are supposed to be at least six ghosts hanging about Kildrummy." She tried to smile through her tears, but it didn't help.

Meggie squeezed Mary Rose's hand as she came up on her knees beside her. "Oh, no, don't cry, please, Mary Rose. Papa will take care of everything. And Aunt Sinjun is very good at meddling, even Papa agrees that she is. Uncle Colin loves her so very much I even heard him say once that he would lock her in his bedchamber and visit her at his whim. That tells you something, doesn't it?"

There came a snort from Colin, who was seated in the wing chair, reading a newspaper.

"I would like to know what is going on here," Sinjun said.

"It's not his responsibility," Mary Rose said and sniffed. She hated herself. Tears were ridiculous. They did nothing but make her skin itch. "Pearlin' Jane could have been right, ma'am, but she's not any longer. I'm leaving. I will not allow Tysen to face any consequences that would harm him. Mrs. Griffin is right. I do not belong here. No one wants me here. I won't allow Tysen to be any more noble than he already has been. Would you please lend me a gown?"

Now this was interesting, Sinjun thought. This lovely ill young woman was in Tysen's bed, and she was worried about him and his blasted reputation but not at all about herself? Did she think so little of herself? If she did, it was understandable, given the horrid things that had spewed from that wretched Mrs. Griffin's mouth. Lovely hair, yes, Mary Rose had lovely hair, and a lovely face. But of course such things wouldn't weigh heavily with Tysen. She had never seen him like this. Melinda Beatrice had died six years ago. It was a very long time for a man to be alone. Of course, there were Max and Leo and Meggie, but children weren't the same thing as having someone to laugh with and talk to, to fight with, to make love to. Sinjun had worried about him for a very long time now. She looked at Mary Rose, at that pale face, the scratches, the horrible bruise around her left eye, and said calmly, "A gown? Certainly. I will do anything you need, Mary Rose." She smiled. "Do call me Sinjun."

"But—"

"You'd best give in to Aunt Sinjun," Meggie said comfortably. "She and Pearlin' Jane won't let anything bad happen."

Colin said, lowering his newspaper so he could see over it, "Yes, Mary Rose, you may trust my wife. I trust her with my life, and she has protected me very well indeed. Oh, yes, do call me Colin."

There was no way to rid himself of the Griffins aside from tossing them out into the courtyard on their respective ears. Not a bad thought. After two cups of strong tea, Tysen inquired yet again, "Why have you returned?"

"You see how he tries to be as imperious as Old Tyronne," Mrs. Griffin said to her husband. Then she turned her cannon on him with a goodly amount of enthusiasm. "It will not work, boy. No matter what you want, you will not marry Mary Rose Fordyce. I will not allow you to marry her. She is a bastard. If she is received anywhere, it is only because of her very respectable aunt and uncle. No, her sort will not be the mistress of Kildrummy."

Tysen lost every word in his brain at that moment. Wed with Mary Rose? Such a thought had never—no, he was merely protecting her, as a man of God, it was his duty to see that Erickson didn't rape her, that nothing or no one forced her to do anything against her will, that—he closed his eyes and managed to dredge up words for a simple prayer. They were very straightforward, those words that made up his prayer: *Lord, if I strangle this woman, will you find forgiveness for me?*

"My dearest wife is concerned about your reputation, my lord," said Mr. Griffin. "She is worried that you not besmirch the family name."

Mrs. Griffin saluted her husband over her teacup. It was her fourth cup, and Tysen found, despite being wordless and dazed, that one had to be impressed at her capacity. She then bent her look on Tysen, her black mustache quivering. "Even now, my lord, you may be certain that everyone north of Edinburgh is talking of how the new Lord Barthwick—namely, you—has an unmarried bastard female in his bed. According to Mrs. MacFardle, you *stayed* with her all night and took care of her *intimately*, and she is even wearing *your* nightshirt, and isn't that— one hesitates to say it, but I must—yes, it is utterly depraved, even for an Englishman."

Tysen, normally fluent in his speech, smoothly cultured, and quite self-possessed, lost not only his ability to reason and speak again, but also nearly every semblance of life. He stood rigid as a board, frozen in place, staring not at Mrs. Griffin but into himself, deep inside himself where one seldom has reason to look because there are many times shadows there, and doors that are better left closed. But he looked, regardless. What he saw, what he finally fully realized, what was staring him right in the face, was the realization that the miserable old hag was right.

Oh, dear God, he had taken intimate care of her, as if she were his child or his wife. He hadn't hesitated. By all that was holy, what had he done to Mary Rose? And all for the best motives, all to protect her, to save her, to be the buffer between her and MacPhail. She was wearing his nightshirt, he had taken care of her, looked at her, fully appreciated every white inch of her, which he shouldn't have done, but since he was a man, there'd been no hope for it.

"Well, my lord? Have you nothing to say for yourself? Did you bed Mary Rose? One doubts she was a virgin because a bastard is seldom a virgin, no matter her age. Will she, a bastard, deliver another bastard into this world? Her dear aunt and uncle, so well respected in these parts, in all their goodness, allowed her to be raised with their own sweet Donnatella. Mary Rose should never have remained in a respectable home. Just look what has happened. She is upstairs lying in your bed. And you, my lord, you allowed it. You freely partook in it. And still you let her stay."

Tysen slowly shook his head, back and forth. He had looked deep into himself, seen the truth, recognized what he must do, and now he must act. He turned and walked out of the drawing room, the sound of his boots striking the tile in the front entrance hall sharp in his ears. Those boots of his might be a bit dirty, but they made loud, sharp sounds as they hit the tiles. And yet, deep inside himself, he heard nothing. He felt waves of guilt and shame, but now, thank the good Lord, they were receding in the face of his resolve to make things right. He heard Mrs. Griffin's voice calling after him, but he didn't understand her words. Indeed, they weren't even words to his mind.

When he opened the door to his bedchamber, he saw Colin still seated in the big wing chair, still comfortably reading a newspaper, obviously still at his ease. Colin, excellent man that he was, had learned years ago that it was best just to give Sinjun her head.

Sinjun was now seated on the bed, close to Mary Rose, speaking to her, and his dearest Meggie was on her knees next to Mary Rose, holding her hand, nodding at whatever Sinjun was saying. Then Mary Rose looked up and saw him.

"Hello, Tysen," she said, and he would have had to be a blind man not to see the leap of pleasure in her eyes at the sight of him, the smile that hadn't been there but a moment before, there now, sweet and honest, and it was for him, and he thought, She should not so openly give me her joy. Is there no hope for it?

15

THEN ALL HER joy died on the spot and she said, looking down, "I am going to Vere Castle with Sinjun. I plan to be a nanny to Fletcher and Jocelyn. She doesn't want me to be, but I have to do something to earn my keep, don't I?"

She was leaving?

"I'm not ignorant. I speak Latin. I can instruct Phillip, perhaps I can also teach Dahling to play the bagpipes. I don't play them well, but I do know several tunes. I do know how to do things. I won't be useless."

"You speak Latin?"

He was gaping at her, distracted for the moment.

"Yes, and also a bit of French, although my accent is not terribly pleasant. Since there are no longer Latin speakers about, why, then, no one can criticize my accent."

She spoke Latin? How ever had that come about? He got himself back on track, just shaking his head at her. "You're not leaving Kildrummy Castle," he said, and he even managed to smile at her. Sinjun opened her mouth, but then he saw that she was staring at him as if she'd never seen him before. Slowly, very slowly, Sinjun got off the bed and stood beside it for a long moment. Then she held out her hand to her niece. "Come along, Meggie. You, Uncle Colin, and I are going to explore the castle. Will you give us a tour?"

Meggie had no idea what was happening here, but she knew it was something very important, something between her papa and Mary Rose. Mary Rose knew Latin? Goodness, what would Max have to say to that? She nearly leapt off the bed and took her aunt's hand.

Colin calmly folded his paper and rose. He gave Tysen one long last look, then lightly touched his hand to his wife's shoulder. Tysen heard Sinjun say, "We don't have to see that dreadful woman, do we?"

"No, we won't go near the drawing room," Meggie said. "I want to show you the hidden garden behind Papa's library. I believe Mr. MacNeily is working in there. He's Papa's estate manager, you know. He is very nice. I wish he would stay, but he is leaving Kildrummy soon now. Oliver is coming to take his place, at least Papa hopes he will."

Colin said, "That will make Douglas gnash his teeth."

He heard Sinjun laugh. "Oliver would do marvelously well here at Kildrummy."

Tysen closed the bedchamber door, locked it. He said as he walked back to the bed, "Just forget this nanny business, Mary Rose. Forget teaching Latin to Phillip and bagpipes to Dahling. You aren't going anywhere."

Mary Rose had scooted up, feeling more strong and fit than she had even five minutes before. She hadn't taken her eyes off him. As he spoke, she noticed, for the first time, that stubborn jaw of his. "I must," she said, and it hurt to say it, but there was no choice. "Surely you see that."

"No, I don't see anything of the kind. Listen to me. We all do what we must. The must to be done in this situation is this: you must marry me. You will be the mistress of Kildrummy Castle in Scotland and you will be a vicar's wife in my home in England. I live in a village called Glenclose-on-Rowan. My house is officially called the Old Parsonage, but it's been known for years and years as Eden Hill House."

"That is a very romantic name for a parsonage."

"I suppose so."

He thought inconsequentially that even with that awful pallor, she looked quite lovely sitting there in his nightshirt, her red hair in soft curls around her head and over her shoulders. Her mouth opened again, but nothing came out. He waited. He was good at waiting. Many times it took a parishioner a goodly number of minutes to screw up his courage to confess a sin.

"I cannot. Surely you know that, Tysen."

"You cannot what? Marry me? I don't see that there is anything else for you to do."

"I will not do that to you," she said, and her voice had firmed up now, and color was coming into her cheeks. "I came here because I wasn't thinking straight, because I was afraid to go into Vallance Manor with Erickson's horse wandering around outside the house, just like he was used to being there, as if he belonged there.

"But no matter. I was wrong, very wrong, to come here and involve you and Meggie." She drew a very deep breath. "I will not allow you to sacrifice yourself because I was a fool."

He smiled, a calm, clean smile that showed his lovely white teeth and lit up his blue eyes even more. "Forget this sacrifice business. It is nonsense. I should have told you this sooner. I have three children. Max, my scholar and wit, is nine; Leo, who sings like an angel, gets into more mischief than a devil's spawn, and stands on his head, is seven. You already know my precocious Meggie.

They are all good children, but perhaps you wouldn't wish to be saddled with three stepchildren."

"Meggie has told me all about Max and Leo." Then she seemed to fold down. She just sat there, shaking her head back and forth. "No, you are purposely misunderstanding me. Please, Tysen, you know I would love your children dearly. I had accustomed myself to not having children. No, I won't speak of that. You are being stubborn."

"I would be interested in knowing if you spoke Latin better than Max."

"Yes, I probably do. I probably read Latin better also."

"Who instructed you? I cannot see Donnatella enjoying Latin lessons."

"The very old Presbyterian minister who died some three years ago. He was pensioned off when I was very young. He was lonely." She shrugged. "He taught me many things. He, like everyone else, deplored my antecedents, but he taught me nonetheless. He also preached to me, but I think it was more to keep in practice than to save my soul." Then she actually smiled at the memories.

"We have to get back on track here, Mary Rose. Do you find me that distasteful? You believe me no better than Erickson MacPhail?"

Mary Rose threw back the covers and swung her legs over the side of the bed. His nightshirt had come up to her knees, and now he looked at those knees he'd thought were the prettiest knees he'd ever imagined when he was wiping her down with the wet, cold cloth. She was standing now, his nightshirt dragging on the floor, the sleeves a good six inches beyond the ends of her fingers. She walked right up to him and stood there, not a foot from him, and poked her finger in his chest. "I have to face you. I cannot remain lying there, a pathetic victim with a black eye, a woman you must see as nauseatingly pitiable. You will not tell me what to do. You feel guilty and responsible. That is nonsense. I will not marry you. I will not serve you such a turn, Tysen. I will go to Vere Castle with Sinjun. I will learn. I will become a proper nanny. I will speak Latin to everyone."

"No," he said, crossing his arms over his chest. He looked thoughtful for a moment. She decided he was finally coming to his senses. She'd been noble. She would deal later with the vast wasteland deep inside her.

He said, "We will have to post bans. I suppose things are the same here as they are in England?"

The wasteland disappeared, but she knew it made no difference. She grabbed his arms and tried to shake him, but she couldn't even begin to budge him. "You will make yourself sick again," he said, not allowing himself to touch her. That wouldn't do at all. He held firm. "Get back into bed, Mary Rose."

Then she smiled, a sudden, quite lovely smile. "Tysen, you are a very good man. You have the most beautiful eyes I have ever seen. And your mouth—no, I shouldn't have said that. Listen, I have no intention of making you regret your inheritance. I will not drag you down and bring you disgrace. I am a bastard. There is nothing to be done about it. When will you accept that as an unchangeable fact?"

"Yes, I know that you are a bastard." He shrugged. "Who cares?"

"Everyone I have ever known cares a great deal," she said honestly. "When I was a little girl, Donnatella would call me a bastard and laugh and laugh. I didn't think it could be all that bad because Donnatella was, after all, much younger than I. But I finally asked my uncle Lyon. He told me that I didn't have a father. From that day onward, everything changed. I knew then that I didn't belong, I realized then that everyone—the servants, my aunt, my uncle—treated me differently. I realized I was at Vallance Manor only because my mother was the sister of the mistress of the house."

"That could not have been pleasant, but it is past now, Mary Rose. I am sorry that it happened, but it is over and done with. I will say it again. Who cares?"

"Don't you understand? You belong to a noble English family. I could never belong."

"Are you quite through yet?"

"You are sounding like a long-suffering man faced with a hysterical female."

"You, hysterical? You assured Erickson that you weren't. But it doesn't matter, as it happens. As a vicar, I deal quite well with hysterical females. In truth, however I do not wish to be married to one. My first wife perhaps tended toward hysteria—no, forget that. You have struck me as very commonsensical, Mary Rose. Also you have a beautiful name. I think your eyes are far more beautiful than mine, although the Sherbrooke blue eyes are touted throughout southern England." He laughed, just shaking his head. "I don't care that you never had a father. It's simply not important. If it truly bothers you, then we won't tell anyone in England. It matters not, either way. Marry me."

"You don't know me."

He was smiling now, those white teeth of his just lovely, and his hands came up to close around her shoulders. "We will learn all about each other over the next forty years. I do not believe I snore. If I did, Meggie would surely tell me, since she and her brothers sometimes curl up around me in the wintertime when it is very cold. There are also two cats, Ellis and Monroe. They aren't racing cats, but—"

She was instantly diverted, as he'd hoped she would be. "Racing cats? I have never heard of such a thing. What are racing cats? I can't imagine getting a cat to race. Cats always do whatever pleases them. Come, you're teasing me."

"Oh, no. Cat racing is quite the sport in southern England. The season is from April to October, and the races are held on Saturdays, at the McCaulty Race Track near Eastbourne. If you like, I could try to get you a racing kitten to train. I once met the Harker brothers, the premier trainers in all the sport. They are at Mountvale Hall, the home of Rohan Carrington."

Her eyes were shining as she said, quite without thinking, "Oh, goodness, to teach a kitten to race. What fun that would be, what—" She drew up short. "No," she said. "I must not think about things like that. I cannot. It simply isn't right. I will not change my mind, Tysen, I cannot."

"It might prove difficult. The Harker brothers are very particular about whom they trust to properly train racing kittens."

"You really must stop this. I will not think about racing kittens, I won't."

Without conscious thought, at the end of his tether, Tysen tightened his hold on her shoulders and pulled her slowly against him. He leaned his head down and kissed her, his mouth against hers, both closed. It didn't matter. It was a revelation. It was as if his body had suddenly come alive, sending every last bit of him reeling, exploding in awareness and bone-deep pleasure, more pleasure than he could even begin to imagine. "Open your mouth," he said, appalled that he'd said such a thing to her, and praying with every fiber in his body that she would. Where had that come from? To his utter surprise she did, immediately, all soft and warm, and his tongue gently touched her lower lip before entering her mouth. Oh, God, he knew he was going to die then, die from this immense, overwhelming joy. He would shudder himself to death if nothing else.

He pulled back, his heart pounding hard, heaving, unable to get hold of himself, feeling so urgent, so very good, he didn't quite understand what was happening to him. Whatever it was, he didn't want it to stop. He wouldn't mind if he exploded with these feelings.

"I didn't know," he said slowly, looking down at her, absolutely amazed at what he had felt, his entire body aching now because he wasn't touching her, didn't have his tongue in her mouth. He shook his head at himself, utterly dismayed. He dropped his hands to his sides and took two quick steps away from her. His body ached, simply ached. "I just didn't know," he said again, and it was true. He didn't understand what had happened. But he knew it was wonderful, and he was still trembling from the onslaught.

Her mouth was shiny from his kissing her. He watched her touch her fingertips to her mouth, as if she couldn't quite comprehend what had happened, either. Then she blinked and stared up at him, at his mouth, and that ache was taking him over, making him shake and want to cry with the urgent wanting he felt. She said, with great inadequacy, "That was quite nice, Tysen."

Nice? She thought it only *nice*? He was quaking like a tree ready to be toppled over. That cataclysm that had nearly sent him to his knees was only nice? As in a summer day was nice? He simply couldn't help himself. He was pulling her against him again, hard against him, and his arms were around her this time and he was kissing her wildly, his fingers kneading and caressing her back. He at least had the sense not to let his hands go below her waist. She wasn't yet his wife. But he couldn't stop kissing her, that wonderful mouth of hers, her jaw, the tip of her nose, her eyelids. There was so much, so very much to see, to feel, to taste.

"Marry me," he said into her mouth. "I cannot bear this, Mary Rose. You must give me my way in this. Everything will be all right. You will speak Latin better than Max, and he will glow with pride. Ellis and Monroe will curl around your ankles and sleep against the backs of your knees. We will all deal well together. Marry me."

Actually, he was beginning to believe that he would simply fall down and die if she didn't marry him, if she didn't allow herself to become his wife and belong to him. He couldn't stop. He kept kissing her until she made a small noise into his mouth. That nearly whispered little sound shot mindless lust throughout his body. He realized in one last flicker of reason that it was simply all over for him.

He nearly leapt away from her, breathing so hard, so fast, that for a moment he couldn't get hold of his body. When he did, he smiled at her shocked white face. Dear God, he had frightened her. He heard himself say with absolute honesty, "I want to do that to you until we are both very old and doddering."

"I—" She gulped. "Yes," she said then. "I would like that very much. I have never done that before. I am twenty-four years old, on the shelf, everyone says. I have never done that, Tysen, never known that one person could make another feel all these strange things. They're frantic sorts of things. I want them desperately. I don't want them to stop. I don't understand."

"Feel what things exactly?" He couldn't believe he'd asked her that, but he didn't take it back. He wanted to know.

He watched her hand fall to her belly and lightly press inward. He watched her fingers press downward a bit more. She didn't realize what she was doing, but he did, and he nearly collapsed on the spot. It was all he could do to prevent himself from leaping on her again and throwing her on her back on that soft, giving bed.

"It is like I am somehow hungry, my stomach is hot, and I feel like I want to touch you everywhere."

He nearly swallowed his tongue. Control, he thought. It had been so many years since he'd felt these ungovernable, roiling feelings that made him want to fly and howl and shout for joy. Go slowly, he thought, go gently. "Mary Rose, if you were my wife, then you could touch me everywhere, just as I could you. There is incredible pleasure when a husband and wife come together, so I have heard. I believe you and I would know that pleasure."

"I was afraid when Erickson tried to hold me like you did. No, I was beyond afraid, I was terrified. Isn't it peculiar that it is so very different with you? That it is all I can think about? Er, Tysen, could you please kiss me again? Perhaps let me press myself against you, all of you? You are very different from me."

As God is my witness, I will not go beyond the point where I cannot stop myself. "I will kiss you and hold you if you promise to be my wife, Mary Rose. I am a vicar. I am not allowed to enjoy myself in such a way without God blessing our union. Surely you understand how I am constrained. I have done things in my life that now, knowing how life is, I would do differently, but despoiling you, giving in to a man's lust—that I will not do."

"Yes," she said, so disappointed she wanted to cry, and yet at the same time she admired him tremendously, "I understand. I'm not at all good, Tysen. For many years I was jealous of Donnatella. I am impatient with my mother. I would have shot Erickson if I'd had a gun and knew how to load it and fire it."

"Are you making some sort of point here?"

"I don't know if I would make a very good vicar's wife."

"Nonsense. You are human, Mary Rose, delightfully so. Jealousy, anger, frustration—those are not bad things, they're just things that all of us feel because they're there to be felt. They cannot be ignored, at least not all of the time.

"You wish to know what I see when I look at you? I see a beautiful young woman. I am not blind. Looking at you delights me—your hair, your mysterious eyes, that wicked little smile of yours, and your nose, Mary Rose. It's straight and narrow and really quite a nice nose."

She was trying very hard not to laugh, not to fall to his knees, and weep her eyes out. "Tysen, stop it, just stop it."

"Oh, no. I also see great kindness in you, Mary Rose. I see no petty meanness in you, just caring. You have been alone too much. You have not been cherished. I also think that you feel things very deeply. Perhaps, someday, you will feel deeply about me." Oddly enough, at that very moment, he knew it was right to make this girl, a girl he hadn't even known existed a simple week ago, his wife. It was the thing to do. It was what he wanted to do. Then he nearly laughed at himself, at all his mental machinations, all his man's justifications. He also wanted to make love to her until both of them collapsed. He remembered vaguely the awesome desire he had felt for Melinda Beatrice when he'd been all of twenty years old and she was his goddess. He'd prayed for valiant deeds to perform to prove his devotion to her, but there hadn't been any.

The fact of the matter was, however, that his union with Melinda Beatrice was a very long time ago and they had both been so very young. He was a man now. He had tried his best then, but he'd been so ill-prepared. There'd simply been so much he had never experienced, had not known how to deal with—from his wife to all the people in his congregation. And then he'd been a father and Melinda Beatrice had died.

But things were different now. He was different in many very important ways. His children had changed him, made his life richer, given him more compassion, more patience. The many men and women in his congregation had changed him as well. He had tried to be a good man, a man to minister to them as he should.

But never before in his life had he comprehended the simple joy another human being could bring him, the endless warmth, the caring, the immense joy of the world. And the excitement of just looking at her, a smile on his mouth without his even realizing it. Now she had come into his life—so completely unexpected. She fascinated him even as she brought out every protective instinct he had buried deep inside. This quite pretty girl, who wasn't a girl anymore but a woman of twenty-four years, was now standing in his nightshirt not two feet away from him, and this was the only woman he wished to have by his side. Forever.

Dear Lord, give me the words to convince her that this is a very good idea.

16

Vallance Manor

"SHE WON'T MARRY me."

Sir Lyon was disgusted with the young man who was sitting in front of him, his hands clasped between his knees, looking bewildered and defeated. He'd had such faith in him, not only in his good looks but in his ruthlessness. He'd believed him utterly dedicated to this task, but he'd failed.

Sir Lyon said, "Stand up and pull your shoulders back, damn you. You have hardly tried. Good God, man, get her away from that cursed vicar, and it will be done."

Erickson raised his head. "He won't even allow me to be alone with her. Neither will his daughter. She was practically crouched over Mary Rose to protect her from me. What am I supposed to do? Pound a man of God into the bloody ground? Lock the little girl into a closet?"

"No, of course not. If you did that, you'd be hung up by your heels." Sir Lyon drank down a snifter of his fine French brandy. He rubbed his chin. He felt a clump of hair that his valet, Mortimer, blast the fellow, had missed when shaving him that morning. Sir Lyon said slowly, rubbing his palms over the brandy snifter, "There has to be a way to get to her, to spirit her away from Kildrummy Castle. Then the vicar would be out of it. What could he do? Nothing at all. Damnation, boy, I can't believe she actually jumped into the stream. I always believed Mary Rose an obedient, diffident little thing."

"She's changed, sir," Erickson said, and for a moment, he was puzzled by it. But it was true. Rather than freezing like a doe in a hunter's sights, just days before, she'd run away from him into the pine forest near Kildrummy. He said slowly, "I can remember her as a little girl. She was quiet, obedient, just as you said. I remember that she was always standing on the outside of things, watching, listening. Maybe she's changed slowly, small things that I just haven't noticed. But she's managed to keep herself away from me for a very long time now. I have tried every tactic, but nothing has worked.

"As I told you, she escaped me last week. She actually managed to run away from me. And she escaped me again yesterday. She moved very fast. I was reaching for her, and then she was in the water, being swept downstream. She's a strong girl. She pulled herself out, since there was no one else about to do it."

Sir Lyon wasn't much impressed. "She's a female. Find a way to get her. Hold her down so she can't run away."

Erickson looked toward the fireplace, its grate empty now, and the painting of Sir Lyon's great-grandfather, William Thatcher Vallance, hanging above it. He'd been a terrifying old man who had left more bastards in the area than anyone before or since. He said, "When Ian and I were boys, we were always searching every nook and cranny of Kildrummy, trying to find secret passages. We didn't find any, didn't see a single ghost. We just got tangled up in a lot of spiderwebs and our boots run over by a battalion of rats. But we did find a very private way into the castle, through a very narrow ivy-covered door that gives onto a private garden just outside the library. The Kildrummy steward, Miles MacNeily, spends a good of time in there, but he is soon to leave, I hear."

"Yes, he came into an inheritance," Sir Lyon said. "A good-sized one, I hear. Miles wouldn't care what you did with Mary Rose, in any case."

"The odd thing is that I believe he would. I remember he was always asking about her, always seemed to enjoy seeing her. I also remember that he was always very nice to her when she was younger, gave her treats, that sort of thing." Erickson rose and began pacing back and forth in front of Sir Lyon. He looks heroic, Sir Lyon thought, a very fine-looking young man with clear eyes and a noble brow, possibly even more handsome than poor Ian, who shouldn't have died stumbling drunk over a cliff. He still didn't understand how it could have happened. But Ian was long gone now, and how it had happened simply didn't matter anymore.

What mattered was right here, staring him in the face. Erickson MacPhail, the man who was willing to buy his niece and overlook her unfortunate parentage. And his dearest Donnatella would benefit once she got over her snit. He would take her to Edinburgh, introduce her to every suitable gentleman between the ages of twenty and eighty. She would be fawned over, poetry written to her lovely eyebrows; she would be feted, spoiled rotten. That would make her happy, perhaps even content, once away from her cousin, who had somehow managed to steal Ian away from her. No one could credit it, but it had happened. Sir Lyon had marveled at it. He doubted now that anyone remembered Ian had wanted Mary Rose. No, most folk would think of Mary Rose, see her next to her cousin, and it would be Donnatella who'd lost her betrothed in that dreadful accident. And Donnatella, bless her lovely self, never corrected anyone who showered condolences upon her beautiful head for her Ian's death. And Donnatella, who surely couldn't have been involved in Ian's death.

Sir Lyon said now, "Whatever, Miles MacNeily isn't important. I suppose you could try your plan. As you know, however, the Griffins have returned and also Lord and Lady Ashburnham, Lord Barthwick's sister and brother-in-law, have come to visit. What with the servants also hanging about, there are a lot of folk for you to avoid. Do you know how you're going to get her out of there?"

"Not as yet, but I shall think of something. Time grows short."

"Aye, it does," said Sir Lyon. "However, I myself have a few other strategies to try before you attempt it."

He didn't see Donnatella standing quietly behind the drawing room door.

Kildrummy Castle

Mary Rose's voice was as thin as the stem of the yellow rose that sat in a vase atop the mantel when she said, "Do you really think I am kind?"

He raised an eyebrow. "Kind, did you say?"

"Yes, you are the one who said I am kind. I want to know if you really believe it."

A touch of acrimony, just excellent, and yes, he'd also heard just a tiny thread of hope there as well.

He laughed, he couldn't help himself. He grabbed her and hugged her tightly. Then he closed his hands around her waist and lifted her above his head. Her hair swirled about her head, falling in a rich red curtain of curls about his face. He breathed in the sweet scent of her, a woman's unique scent. It had been so very long. He hadn't forgotten, but since he couldn't act on such thoughts, he'd shoved them way back to the recesses of his brain and avoided ever going there in his thinking.

Tysen looked up at her, this girl with her wonderful scent, hair so rich and deeply red he wanted to bury his face in it, but now he wasn't smiling. He looked more serious than a vicar—namely, a man like himself—in a roomful of pickpockets. "Enough is enough, Mary Rose. I will hold you off the ground until you say yes to me."

Her hands were on his shoulders, her fingers kneading him. "You will truly ask the Harker brothers to give me a racing kitten?"

"I promise. However, they must deem you worthy and responsible. A racing cat requires great commitment, I've heard Rohan Carrington say. That means that you must begin to have a better opinion of yourself. If you do not believe yourself worthy, then why should they? Now, why would you ever doubt that you are kind?"

"You are the first person in my life who has ever said that. Why should I attribute something to myself when no one else has?"

"Because I'm telling you to, and since I will be your husband, since I haven't told an outright lie since I turned eighteen years old, you must trust what I say."

"What do you mean, you've told no outright lie?"

"One must shade the truth a bit on occasion, to avoid wounded feelings. I learned to do that very quickly. That, or one simply keeps quiet. Now, to prove my worthiness to you, if the Harker brothers decide you would make a good mistress, I swear that if the racing kitten upsets Ellis and Monroe, I will not complain. I will not force it to live in the stables."

He would swear that at that precise moment, he saw a gleam of wickedness in her eyes, a wickedness to match Sinjun in her finest moments. She said, all demure as a nun, "If I say yes, Tysen, will you kiss me again?"

Dear Lord, he thought, and found that all he could do was nod, mute as the village idiot.

"Wait. What if after we are married you discover that you do not like me overmuch?"

"I even like your toes, and that includes the crooked one you must have broken when you were younger."

Any wickedness was long gone. She looked utterly appalled. Her fingernails dug into his shirt. "You looked at my toes? I mean, why would you look at my toes? No one I know looks at toes. Oh, my goodness, when?"

He kept his voice very matter-of-fact. "I had to wipe you down when you had the fever. No, don't start twitching. No maidenly yells. There was no one else to do it, Mary Rose. You have not even heard me complain about that, have you? I have not upbraided you for keeping me awake nearly all that night. So you see, I am a good-natured fellow."

"You saw my broken toe," she said again, and he would swear that in that instant he'd never seen a more mortified face in his life. "You saw even more than my broken toe."

"Well, yes."

"It's very embarrassing, Tysen. Only I have ever seen myself without my clothes on. Oh, goodness, you're a man."

"Well, yes, I am. Mary Rose, if you do not tell me yes very soon now, I just might drop you. Though you are not large, you are beginning to push my limits here."

Still, her face was full of questions. To his utter relief, she slowly nodded, to herself more than to him. "Very well, then, Tysen. Because I do not want you to be bent over like an old man, moaning and clutching your back, I will say yes."

"Say it."

"Yes. I am hopeful. I am also still so embarrassed I want to swallow my tongue. All right, then, I will say all of it. I will marry you, sir, and I pray to God that you will not regret your gallantry."

He lowered her very slowly, his muscles nearly locking tight at the feel of her against him. To prove to her that he was a man of his word, he kissed her, just as he'd promised.

It was a lovely afternoon, sunlight flowing in through the westerly windows. As soon as Meggie and the countess of Ashburnham had left the room, Donnatella looked down at her cousin and said, "You look perfectly dreadful, Mary Rose. Would you like me to brush your hair?"

Mary Rose only smiled. Not too long ago, had Donnatella said something like that to her, she would have felt like a prune pit ground underfoot. But now she didn't think anything Donnatella said would faze her. She didn't doubt at all that her hair had more rats in it than the Kildrummy stables, but it didn't matter, hadn't mattered to Tysen. She was so very happy, all she could do was smile stupidly up at her cousin. "That would be very nice, Donnatella. You look very beautiful with the sunlight shining in your hair."

"Yes. Thank you."

"How is my mother?"

"Mad, as usual," Donnatella said as she walked over to Lord Barthwick's dresser and picked up his brush. She said over her shoulder, "She hasn't said much, really. Mother simply told her that you were visiting the daughter of the house here at Kildrummy. Nothing else was necessary. She left the room humming." Donnatella saw light hairs in the brush. Tysen Sherbrooke was a lovely man, she thought, and obviously in need of a wife. Given he was a vicar, likely without much spine at all, all his thoughts spiritual and not at all to the point, he would be easily managed. It was something to think about, just in case.

She pulled a dark blond hair from the brush, a small smile on her lips as she walked back to the bed. "Mrs. MacFardle tells me that you must leave the vicar's bed. Indeed, she's yelping that you should have never been in this bed in the first place, that soon everyone will be talking about it, and poor Lord Barthwick will be quite ruined."

"Yes, I can well imagine her saying that. I am feeling much better. Perhaps this evening I will move back into Meggie's bedchamber. Her bed, just like this one, would hold six people without touching."

Donnatella sat down beside her and lifted a handful of hair. Such a common color, she thought, as she smoothed out the tangles. "Meggie is the vicar's daughter?"

"Yes, she is precious. And very smart. She loves her father very much."

Donnatella hit a snag. Mary Rose flinched. Donnatella worked on the knot until it was free. "I saw Erickson just a while ago at Vallance Manor. He is very upset, Mary Rose."

Donnatella felt the sudden bolt of fear in her cousin, making her all stiff, and she studied more tangles in Mary Rose's hair. She said, "Really, Mary Rose, being afraid of a man is quite ridiculous. He would never hurt you. I do believe he loves you. Now, what is the matter with you? Marry him, for God's sake, and then you will control him well enough."

"I don't think so," Mary Rose said slowly, staring straight ahead. "I know you could manage a husband quite well, but I? I'm not sure about that. I have never thought that Erickson loved me. You are wrong about that."

"Then why does he want to marry you so badly?"

"I don't know. Even if I did marry him, I cannot imagine controlling him. You could. You are very strong, Donnatella."

"A woman has to be strong or she will become nothing more than a rug to be trod upon." She hit another snag, and this time Mary Rose jerked.

"Ah, nearly done. Hold still."

"When I was your age, I wasn't so firm about things. I have always admired that in you." Mary Rose thought about Tysen treading on her, and knew, all the way to the soles of her feet, that he wouldn't. "I cannot marry Erickson," she said, lightly closing her fingers about her cousin's wrist. Her scalp was burning, surely it was enough. Donnatella lowered the hairbrush and said, "Now your hair is mixed with his."

Mary Rose just shook her head. "I don't love Erickson, I never have. You're quite wrong about his feelings for me, else why would he try to rape me?"

"Rape?" Donnatella actually laughed—such a sweet sound, Mary Rose thought. How jarring it was with that awful word that had come trippingly off her tongue.

"Yes, rape. He has tried twice. Thank heaven I managed to get away from him both times."

"I've heard," Donnatella said, lowering her voice to a near whisper, pulling close to Mary Rose's ear, "that he is a splendid lover. He has bedded several women in the village, and believe me, they smile like loons when he leaves them." She gave a delicate shiver. "Perhaps you should simply trust him, Mary Rose. Let him have you. Enjoy him, use him. Men are ever so easy when it comes to that. I will teach you how to do it."

"I have never felt the slightest desire to let him make love to me. Really, Donnatella, I cannot imagine such a thing." She frowned, looking toward the now lowering sun through the windows. "I don't understand why he wants to marry me. It makes no sense. I am a bastard. He truly did try to rape me. He isn't a good man to so easily want to do that."

"A man in love may be excused many things," Donnatella said. "A man in love, I have always believed, is singularly stupid. Perhaps I should offer him my assistance in bringing you around. It would be far more efficient."

"I would that you not, Donnatella."

Donnatella laughed. "Yes, men in love—or in lust—it is one and the same to all of them. I have seen it several times now. It is really quite amusing to watch. However, Erickson spoke to you earlier. He saw you looking like this, and he still wants to marry you. Doesn't that convince you that he is blinded by his feelings for you?"

"No."

Donnatella walked to the long row of windows. She flung one of them open and leaned out. "I have always loved Kildrummy Castle. I knew when I was a little girl that I belonged here, that it had to be mine someday. Isn't it strange how everything worked out? I thought to marry Ian and be mistress here, but then Ian died. So senseless the way he died. Now there is another master here, and he isn't married. It's as if he came here, knowing I was close, knowing this was always what I wanted. I thank God that the vicar is so very handsome. Have you noticed his eyes? They are an incredible blue. He also appears not to have a patch of fat on him, and that is a wonderful thing." Donnatella turned to look at Mary Rose, who was sitting on the bed, her arms clasped around her knees.

Donnatella went on, "I will think about all this. I will spend time with Lord Barthwick. I will watch him become stupid because he lusts after me. Isn't that a thought? A vicar, lusting after a woman. Is that even possible? However, I cannot imagine being the mother of a little girl who is only half my age."

"He also has two little boys, Max and Leo. They are nine and seven."

Donnatella arched a perfect brow. "Three children? I had no idea that a vicar indulged himself so generously in the marriage bed. I wonder what his wife was like. Has he said anything about her?"

"No."

"Oh, well, she's dead, no longer important at all. I think you should come home with me right now, Mary Rose. If you are afraid that Erickson is lurking about Vallance Manor, ready to grab you and haul you away, why, then, I will protect you. You can even sleep in my bed. I won't let him come near you. Does that make you feel safe?"

Mary Rose felt her heart begin to pound, fast, hard strokes. Donnatella wanted her back at Vallance Manor? Why, for heaven's sake? Slowly, she just shook her head. "I cannot."

"So you will remain and ruin the poor vicar's reputation?"

There was a knock on the door. Mary Rose wanted to run to the door and let whoever it was in, quickly, so she would not have to answer that sticky question, but she just wasn't up to it, and that had been why Tysen had finally left her. He'd wanted her to sleep, and she had, until Meggie and Sinjun had brought Donnatella to see her.

She didn't expect it to be Erickson, but nevertheless, she was as rigid as the post at the foot of the huge bed, waiting, waiting. It was Tysen, and he wasn't smiling.

He nodded to Donnatella. "Mary Rose, I am sorry to disturb your visit with your cousin, but it appears that your mother is in a carriage outside in the courtyard. She wishes to see you. She also refuses to come inside. What do you wish to do?"

"Mother is here, truly? I must see her, Tysen."

He smiled then. "It is no problem. My back has sufficiently recovered." He fetched his dressing gown, quite aware that Donnatella was watching his every move, and brought it to Mary Rose. "Can you stand up? Good, I'll put it on you."

Donnatella said, laughter lurking, "It is pleasant to see a man occasionally play servant to a lady, sir, but do allow me. I will bring Mary Rose downstairs."

"That isn't necessary," Tysen said, not even turning to look at her. "Keep upright, Mary Rose, don't collapse on me now. Yes, just hold on to me." He wrapped her in his dressing gown and tied the belt around her waist. "Your feet are bare, but it is very warm, so it will be all right. Are you ready?"

She nodded.

Tysen picked her up in his arms and simply walked out of the bedchamber, leaving Donnatella to stand by the window watching him and frowning slightly, wondering what was going on here.

Tysen said as he walked down the long corridor with her, "I don't mind at all being your servant. Do you know something? You aren't quite as heavy when I'm walking."

She laughed. For just a brief moment, she rested her head against his shoulder, her warm breath against his neck. Mary Rose wished at that moment that she could stay in Tysen's arms for as long as his back held up. She breathed in the scent of him, dark and rich, with a touch of wildness, like the barest hint of white heather in the air.

"Your mother looks quite beautiful," he said as he carefully walked with her down the main staircase. The front door was open, spilling in bright afternoon sunlight.

"She usually does," Mary Rose said. "When we wed, what will we do about her?"

"I will give that some thought. Don't worry, Mary Rose. Everything will work out all right." But how could it? Her mother was a very odd woman. At worst, she was indeed mad. More than likely, she used madness to gain her what she wanted. Her mother never left Vallance Manor. Her mother also knew who her father was and refused to tell anyone. And now her mother was here, in a carriage. It was hard to believe. What had happened?

17

GWENETH FORDYCE HADN'T ridden in a carriage for six months. Her last time had been that dreadful ride to Aberdeen to her mother's funeral. She'd hated the old lady, but both she and her sister, Margaret, knew they had to don black and veils and pretend to a bit of grief. Her jaw dropped open when she saw the new Lord Barthwick walk out of the castle with Mary Rose—wearing his dressing gown—in his arms. Her feet were bare. Gweneth knew, knew all the way to her soul, that there was something between this man and her daughter. Nothing illicit, for after all, he was an English vicar. But something, something that was more than a man trying his best to protect a woman. No man that she'd ever heard of carried a woman around with her feet bare.

When the Vallance coachman opened her door, she gave him her hand to assist her down. She stood there, looking at the vicar, at her daughter, and she said, "You will come home with me now, Mary Rose. I am sorry, my dear, but as your mother, I cannot allow you to remain here with an unmarried man. I know he is a vicar, but that doesn't matter. Spiritual trappings do not matter in a case such as this."

"Hello, Mother. Forgive me for coming to you like this, but I'm still not feeling quite the thing again."

"You look just fine, Mary Rose. There is color in your cheeks, you are the very bloom of health. Even your toes look healthy. You needn't worry about clothes. We will go directly back to Vallance Manor and you can stay in your bed there. Vicar, please put my daughter in the carriage."

"I don't think so, ma'am," Tysen said. "Mary Rose doesn't feel safe at Vallance Manor."

"That is absurd. It is also unimportant. I am her mother and she will obey me. There is no chaperone here. Come along, Mary Rose."

"Hello, ma'am. I am Lady Ashburnham. I am his lordship's sister and he invited me here to chaperone Mary Rose."

Excellent, Gweneth Fordyce thought, smiling at the lovely young woman striding toward her, long-legged, full of energy, looking quite a bit like the vicar. Yes, she had the same dazzling blue eyes as her brother.

What an absolute relief. She'd kept her promise to her sister and to Lyon. She'd argued and ordered, and now this. It was hard not to laugh her pleasure aloud. Now she didn't have to say anything more. She'd been trumped by the appearance of Lady Ashburnham, and even Lyon at his most critical would have to agree that she'd done all she could.

"A pleasure, my lady," she said to the young woman, who also had a sparkling smile. A handsome pair they were. The vicar was very smart indeed. "Now I must go. Mary Rose, attend me. You will endeavor not to be a burden to his lordship."

"No, Mama, I'll try not to be. Won't you stay for a cup of tea?"

"Oh, no," Gweneth said and nodded to the coachman,

who quickly assisted her back into the carriage. She straightened her shawl, smoothed the ribbons on her bonnet. She looked toward the people standing not six feet away from the carriage. The last sight she had of Mary Rose was her smiling shyly up into the vicar's face.

Be happy, my darling, she thought, and waved to her daughter.

The carriage rolled out of the inner courtyard.

"That is your mother, Mary Rose?" Sinjun asked.

"Yes," Mary Rose said, and she was frowning at the carriage dust billowing into the clear air. Her mother had said all the right things at first, all with the objective of getting her to go back to Vallance Manor. But the fact was, her mother hadn't wanted her to return to Vallance Manor with her, not at all. But why?

Tysen said thoughtfully, "At the beginning, I didn't care much for your mother, but this time, after she spouted the nonsense, she was genuinely pleased with things just as they are. Yes, I like your mother, Mary Rose. She isn't like all that many mothers I've met to date, but she loves you. I wonder what she would have done if Sinjun hadn't chosen to show herself?"

"Meggie came into the drawing room and grabbed me. She told me I had to be a chaperone, quickly, because she was just a trifle too young to have anyone take her seriously, and so she pushed me out the front door." Sinjun looked thoughtfully after the coach that had disappeared through the front gates. "She didn't want you to go with her, Mary Rose, despite everything else she said. Now, isn't that strange?"

"No," Tysen said. "She knows that Erickson MacPhail would probably be invited into Vallance Manor and allowed to carry Mary Rose out over his shoulder. She's protecting her. It was well done."

Meggie wandered out now, but she wasn't looking at

them, she was looking at the gaggle of geese that were now honking loudly at the sight of her. They'd been hovering close by her for the past three days. Just yesterday, they'd come right up to her, honking just as loudly, and she had given them all the bread she could steal from Mrs. MacFardle's kitchen. Now she knew them. In minutes, they would be surrounding her, their chicks hovering close. "Oh, dear," Meggie said, picking up her skirts and running back into the castle. She called over her shoulder, "I'll be right back with some bread for them!"

Tysen laughed. "Maybe they can nibble on that crooked toe of yours, Mary Rose."

"What crooked toe?" Sinjun asked and picked up Mary Rose's foot.

"Oh, my, don't, please, Sinjun. Tysen has already seen my toes."

"He has, has he? Now isn't that interesting?"

"Be quiet, Sinjun. Oh, here is Donnatella. I'm glad she came down. I believe you have enjoyed quite enough of her delightful company?" He cocked a brow at her.

"Yes. She wanted me to come back with her to Vallance Manor. It seems that everyone wants me back there. How is your back?"

"I believe I will put you down in the drawing room and pour tea down your gullet. I am too blown to make it back up those stairs carrying you."

Sinjun could but stare after her brother as he walked back up the steps into the castle. He wasn't acting the way he usually did. He wasn't being depressingly serious with nary a smile anywhere near his mouth. He was actually smiling, a beautiful smile, and it seemed to suit him very well.

Now he was amusing, he seemed to understand wit very well. But the most remarkable thing—he seemed happy. He was overflowing with it. So many years since she'd seen him like this, nearly more years than she could remember. She'd been so very young when he'd decided he wanted to be a man of God and had become as serious as an abbot and so pious she'd wanted to shoot him. Sinjun decided on the spot that she would kill for Mary Rose if ever the need arose.

When they walked into the drawing room, there was Colin standing next to Donnatella, who was leaning toward him, her hand on his sleeve.

Sinjun recognized the signs immediately. Donnatella was extraordinarily lovely, however, and it appeared to Sinjun that Colin wasn't looking at all hunted, like he usually did when the ladies tracked him down and cornered him.

Sinjun said, "Would you mind if I stuck my fist in your cousin's face, Mary Rose?"

"Perhaps you'd better not. You know, Sinjun, his lordship is very handsome," Mary Rose said. "Donnatella very much likes handsome gentlemen."

"Not this handsome gentleman," Sinjun said and marched right up to her husband and the little hussy who was clutching at his sleeve, laughing overly much at something Colin had said, something that probably wasn't all that amusing at all. Still, he was looking down at her like he indeed was the most charming, the wittiest male in the known world.

She said sweetly, "Colin, my dearest love, the love of my life, the man who praises my beauty endlessly. Do you remember how you promised me that we would visit that cave Meggie told us about? The one that is quite hidden, ever so private? The one where we can—well, never mind that. I do not wish to be indelicate. I am quite ready to please you now." She moved closer until she actually pushed Donnatella away from him. She stood on

her tiptoes and whispered in his mouth, "I have plans for
you that will curl your toes."

"You are transparent, Sinjun," Colin said, caressing her
cheek. "The truth is that you are jealous. No matter the
amusement I am currently enjoying, your jealousy still
pleases me. A cave, you say? You will curl my toes?"

"Harrumph," Sinjun said, grabbed his hand and turned
to face Donnatella, a sunny smile on her mouth that
would, hopefully, offset the murder in her eyes. "Do forgive us, but we are still newlyweds and must hie ourselves
off to dark, cozy places. My husband is a demanding gentleman. Good day to you, Miss Vallance."

"I thought they had several children," Donnatella said,
staring at the now empty doorway. "I shouldn't mind
making love with him. He is a beautiful man. Ah, well.
Mary Rose, you are looking ever so well again. Are you
ready to come back with me to Vallance Manor?"

"Miss Vallance," Tysen said easily as he lowered Mary
Rose onto a dark-blue brocade settee, "not just yet. You
will have to amuse yourself without your cousin's company."

"For how much longer, sir?"

"I haven't yet decided," Tysen said. "We will see. I
will send a message when Mary Rose is ready to return
home. You may return home now."

Donnatella looked undecided, an expression that Mary
Rose had hardly ever seen before on her cousin's face.
Donnatella always knew what she was doing—but not
now. She merely nodded to Mary Rose and walked out
of the drawing room.

Nothing much was said until Pouder, leaving his post
by the front door, walked sedately into the drawing room
and cleared his throat. "My lord, Mrs. MacFardle is in a
snit. I don't know what to say to her. Your lordship is
required to deal with the situation."

"Thank you, Pouder, I shall." Without thinking, Tysen took the old man's arm and gently steered him back to his chair. It was well padded, a good thing, since Pouder looked to be all bones.

Tysen called out over his shoulder, "Mary Rose, you converse with my daughter when she returns from feeding the geese."

"I will speak with her as well," Miles MacNeily said, walking toward them. He gave Tysen a small salute and smiled at the sight of Pouder, whose head had already fallen forward to his chest.

Tysen tracked down Mrs. MacFardle in the vast Kildrummy kitchen. With no preamble, he said in a calm, very cool voice, "Mary Rose is lying on a settee in the drawing room. She is doubtless hungry. If you are not carrying a silver tray loaded with delicious cakes and nicely hot tea to her in the next ten minutes, you will leave Kildrummy Castle. If you are not smiling and respectful to Mary Rose when you deliver that tray to the drawing room, you will also leave in the next ten minutes. Do you quite understand me, Mrs. MacFardle?"

"But she is a bastard, my lord! She doesn't belong here. She doesn't belong anywhere where there are respectable people. Folk hereabout will believe you too democratic, too lax in your morals—er, no, that isn't quite right, is it? Perhaps, because you are a vicar, you have to continually watch yourself not to care too deeply about people who don't deserve it. Yes, it is a matter of having too much kindness, my lord. It isn't what Lord Barthwick should do. Mary Rose mustn't sleep in your bed. If she is still too ill to return home, then she may sleep in the servants' quarters, up just one short flight of stairs to the third floor. There is this quite charming room that—"

Tysen felt waves of anger washing through him, and it appalled him, this emotional reaction that came from deep within him, destroying his control. "You have said quite enough, Mrs. MacFardle. Mary Rose Fordyce has agreed to marry me."

Her mouth gaped open. She looked utterly horrified.

"Either you will accept her as your mistress, as Lady Barthwick of Kildrummy Castle, and treat her with respect, or you will leave, in the next minute, actually. The decision is yours. Now, we await tea in the drawing room. Ten minutes, Mrs. MacFardle, no longer." He said not another word, not even when he heard her suck in her breath behind him.

He turned at the doorway and said over his shoulder, "You are the first person to hear our news. It might be a very polite thing if you were to congratulate me on my good fortune."

"Oh, dear," said Mrs. MacFardle. "Change of this nature is unwelcome. I knew that an Englishman would bring disaster. However, congratulations, my lord."

He had forgotten about Mrs. Griffin. When he walked into the drawing room, she was sitting in a deep, faded chair that she'd had Mr. Griffin pull over to within a foot from where Mary Rose sat on the settee. She was tapping her foot, lightly tapping her cane on the carpet at her feet as she said in a loud voice, "I have had quite enough of this, Mary Rose. I have decided that I will take you to Edinburgh with Mr. Griffin and me."

"Mary Rose has agreed to marry me, Mrs. Griffin."

Meggie jumped to her feet. "Papa, really? Oh, this is wonderful! Mary Rose, you will really marry Papa? You will live with us?" She dashed across the drawing room, rubbing the bread crumbs on her skirts, and dropped to the floor at Mary Rose's feet and hugged her knees. "I hadn't really expected this to happen, but it is ever so nice. We will all have such fun, you will see. Oh, I am so very happy."

"Child, you will hold your tongue now. You should be in the nursery or sitting quietly reading sermons, or whatever it is that children—"

Tysen was grinning from ear to ear, he just couldn't help it. "Mrs. Griffin, my daughter needs to get acquainted with her future mother. Now, tea is to arrive shortly. Pouder, what is it?"

The ancient old man was leaning against the doorframe, grinning widely, showing each of his remaining teeth. He was nearly wheezing as he said, "Congratulations, my lord. Oh, this is a miraculous thing! I am needed now more than ever. I am learning to be a varlet. Perhaps Mary Rose will also teach me to be her maid."

Mrs. Griffin continued, as if she hadn't been interrupted, "Mary Rose, we will leave in thirty minutes, right after we have had some of Mrs. MacFardle's tea. It is a great imposition, but I suppose that it must be done. You may be my companion, my maid, perhaps you can even set the fires in the mornings. I will contrive to pay you a bit, just enough for the occasional gewgaw. Now, get up, Mary Rose, and put on your clothes. This is—"

Tysen said then, "Meggie, I wish you to go outside and see that your geese have eaten enough. No, don't argue with me, just go." No one said another word until Meggie, her step slow, finally was gone from the drawing room. As for Miles MacNeily, he had left to help Pouder back to his chair. Only the three of them were left. He wished that Mary Rose was safely hidden away, but she wasn't.

It had to be dealt with, now.

"That will be quite enough, Mrs. Griffin," Tysen said. Then he looked over at Mary Rose as he spoke and nearly lost what little control that remained. She was crying, tears streaking down her pale cheeks, not making a sound, just tears and more tears. The cruelty, so much cruelty she'd endured, mean words that cut deep, and they'd finally cut so deep she couldn't hide her pain. He'd thought that the careless cruelty simply didn't touch her, but it did. He wanted to kill Mrs. Griffin, and after her, Mrs. MacFardle.

Rage made him feel hot, strong, and vicious. He was ready to go into battle. He was ready to kill. He strode to stand right in front of Mrs. Griffin. "I want you gone from Kildrummy Castle in five minutes. No longer. You are a malicious, nasty old woman. You and that nonentity of a husband of yours are despicable. I wish never to see either of you again. You are no longer welcome at Kildrummy. Do I make myself perfectly clear?"

Mrs. Griffin, her face scarlet with fury, leapt to her feet, but Tysen very calmly continued, "Get out of my house, both of you. Now. This time, if you dare to return, I will have you thrown out. No—I will do it myself."

He heard Mrs. MacFardle give a shriek. She was late with the tea tray, he realized, at least five minutes late. A clean sweep, then. He turned to see her trying to hold the tray and commiserate at the same time with Mrs. Griffin. He said, "Mrs. MacFardle, you will leave Kildrummy Castle. Perhaps Mrs. Griffin would like you to accompany her back to Edinburgh. I believe she needs a companion, a scullion, a maid, and a valet. You could, I doubt not, fill each and every one of those roles for her. Perhaps she will even pay you a pittance to buy some gewgaws."

He heard a sound from Pouder, but when he looked over at the old man, his chin was still on his chest.

Once the drawing room was empty of Mrs. Griffin and Mrs. MacFardle, he closed and locked the door. He went to Mary Rose, who was looking up at him, sniffing, rubbing her hands over her eyes. He was still shuddering from the ferocious rage that had come from the deepest part of him. "I'm so very sorry, Mary Rose. I should never have allowed that miserable old witch to continue her vicious tirade for as long as I did. I should never have allowed her to remain when she dared to come back here again.

"Oh, my dear, please forgive me. I was blind, quite blind. But it won't happen again. Also, Mrs. MacFardle will be leaving. She and Mrs. Griffin belong together."

He sat down beside her, simply because he couldn't stand that awful pain he saw in her eyes. "Mary Rose," he said, and pulled her onto his lap. He rocked her, then just held her, his cheek against the top of her head. "It will be all right now. I'll take care of you. There will be no more cruelty, no more spite. Trust me, all right?"

She said nothing, just lay limply against him. They sat quietly for a very long time. Tysen didn't know how long they'd remained together until he heard Meggie's voice and her light knock on the drawing room door.

He leaned back, looking down into Mary Rose's face. She looked beaten down, defeated, and he hated it. But no more pity. He'd never found that to be good for anyone. He kissed the tip of her nose. "Do you know where we can find someone to cook dinner for us?"

18

Id imperfectum manet dum confectum erit.
It ain't over 'til it's over.

MARY ROSE HEARD the whisper of sound so very close, nearly in her ear. It was a man's voice, soft and low, telling her something, but what? Then she jerked awake, realized it wasn't a dream, and opened her mouth to yell. A fist slammed into her jaw, and she fell back against the pillow.

Erickson smoothed the hair off her face and just looked down at her for a moment in the dim light of the one candle. He had to do this, there was simply no choice. He cursed under his breath as he pulled the covers off her. She was wearing that damned vicar's nightshirt. It didn't take him even a moment to realize that she would also shortly be wearing the damned vicar's dressing gown as well.

Once he'd wrapped her in the dressing gown he hauled her over his shoulder, then walked quickly to the bedchamber door, cracked it open, and looked out. Nothing. No one. It wasn't all that dark, since several of the bed-chamber doors were open and bright moonlight poured through the windows and out through the open doors. He didn't need a candle.

All he had to do was get her back down to the library, out the door that was covered with draperies, and into the garden. Then it was easy, just through that narrow ivy-covered gate and to his horse, tied a good hundred feet from the castle. Everything was going splendidly. He had known immediately that it was an excellent plan. It was a pity that he'd had to tap her on the jaw to keep her from yelling, but it wasn't much, after all, and surely she would forgive him. A new bride, perforce, had to forgive her husband. He wondered for a moment if his mother had ever forgiven his father anything. No, that was impossible. He firmly believed that his father had died to escape his mother.

It was just past midnight, and everything was quiet. Erickson paused a moment, listening. He thought about his mother telling him at dinner the previous evening how simply everyone in the area now knew that the new Lord Barthwick—a vicar!—had kicked out not only the Griffins but also poor Mrs. MacFardle, who had surely worked there longer than anyone could remember. Erickson remembered that he'd always hated Mrs. MacFardle, the old witch, for the way she'd treated Mary Rose. He frowned as he thought about that. Actually, she'd been a witch to most everyone, particularly the children. He felt Mary Rose's limp weight over his shoulder, felt her bouncy hair touch his face. No, he refused to feel guilt about what he was doing. He had no choice.

One step at a time. He was very quiet. Mary Rose didn't weigh much, so that didn't bother him. Then, with no warning at all, he heard giggling. Good Lord, giggling? From the room just down the hall.

There was obviously a woman in that room, and she was awake and giggling. Only one thing that could be about. Then he heard a man shout, not loud, then laugh, and another damned giggle. He heard bare feet running across a wooden floor. He stood, frozen, in the middle of the corridor, waiting, wondering what to do, when a door flew back and a woman, dressed in a flowing white nightgown, ran out of the room, still giggling, looking over her shoulder at the man who was running after her. The man who came out of the bedchamber was naked. For an instant, Erickson thought it was the vicar, and he was chasing a woman. But it wasn't. It must be the vicar's sister and her husband. They were the only ones left in the castle that the vicar hadn't kicked out. But what were they doing, running around out here in the corridor? For God's sake, wasn't there a bed in that bedchamber?

Suddenly the woman eased back into the shadows and stood still as a statue. She wasn't more than ten feet away from him.

The naked husband ran beyond where she was standing silent and still, then pulled up sharp, held a candle high, and looked right into Erickson's eyes.

It wasn't fair, dammit, just not fair. Erickson cursed, ripe, full-bodied curses. Damnation, his was an excellent plan, and it had gone perfectly until he'd had the rotten luck to have an amorous couple want to play in the corridor.

"She's mine, damn you!" He was so furious, so frustrated, that he yelled right in Colin's face, "I'm taking her!"

For a moment, Colin couldn't believe his eyes. "My God, you puking little bastard, you've got Mary Rose. Sinjun, come quickly!"

Erickson saw the flash of a white nightgown, saw the man hand her the candle. Erickson didn't wait. He turned on his heel and ran down the long corridor as fast as he could with Mary Rose bouncing up and down on his shoulder, the naked man nearly on his heels.

Then Mary Rose groaned, reared up, and shouted, "No, Erickson! This is madness! Let me down, you fool!" She stiffened right up, knocking him off balance. She grabbed his hair and kept pulling even as she leaned as far back as she could.

"Damn you, Mary Rose, stop it! Trust me. We're leaving this place, together."

They went down, Erickson falling on his back, half on top of her. Mary Rose yelled, Colin came to a stop to stand over them, and Sinjun, her white gown fluttering about, was holding a candle over them.

"He's smashing me," Mary Rose gasped, trying to breathe, then, "Thank you both for coming out for whatever reason I don't yet know."

"It is no problem," Colin said, coming down to his knees beside Erickson, who was just lying there, staring up at him. "You're bare-assed, man," Erickson said. "Have you no sense? There is a lady present."

Colin looked briefly over at Mary Rose. "Close your eyes." She did. Colin jerked Erickson off her, and Erickson came up fighting. He was strong, a dirty fighter, and he would have had a chance if it hadn't been for Sinjun. She gave a low growl when Erickson sent his fist into Colin's belly. She threw the candle at him. The iron base hit him in the jaw, then bounced onto the wooden floor, sparking flashes of flame as it hit.

"You asinine idiot," she yelled, "trying to steal Mary Rose," and she joyfully jumped at him.

Erickson knew he was in very deep trouble. He was doing his best to hold the woman off, even as he realized that she smelled wonderful, a sort of violet smell, before the naked man was ripping his arm out of the socket. He smacked his fist against the woman's shoulder, sending her reeling back into the naked man, who let him go to catch his wife. Then Erickson was on his feet again, running as fast as he could. The only thing was, he didn't know of a way out of the castle that lay in this particular direction. But it didn't slow him.

And then directly in front of him, a door flew open and a man came running out, fastening his breeches as he moved. This time it was the damned vicar. At least he wasn't altogether naked.

"I don't have her," Erickson yelled. He briefly considered trying to knock the vicar senseless, but thought better of it. It was ridiculous for a man of God to look strong and mean, but this one did. Erickson turned quickly, only to run into both Colin and Sinjun. All three of them went down. Tysen looked up to see Mary Rose running toward them, his dressing gown held in one hand above her knees so she could run faster, the other hand carrying the candle that thankfully hadn't set the castle on fire or even gone all the way out. It was flickering wildly, but hanging on.

"He tried to steal her, Tysen!" Colin shouted, coming to his feet, giving Sinjun his hand to pull her up as well. "Ah, it's you, Mary Rose. Close your eyes again."

Instead, Mary Rose quickly shrugged out of Tysen's dressing gown and thrust it toward Colin, her eyes shut tightly. Colin laughed as he put it on and belted it around his waist. Then the three of them stood over Erickson MacPhail, who, in truth, was too smart to stand up and get pounded. He didn't like this, couldn't believe he'd failed, cursed himself, cursed Mary Rose for her damned stubbornness, and cursed Mary Rose's damned uncle for getting him into this in the first place.

Tysen, legs spread, stared down at the man, well aware

that he was getting less calm, less reasoned, by the moment. In a very low voice that didn't sound like him at all, Tysen said, "Did he hurt you, Mary Rose?"

"He hit my jaw to keep me quiet, but it's not bad."

Tysen looked back at Erickson. "You were going to steal her and rape her?"

"No, damn you," Erickson said, flat on his back, not moving. "I was going to ask her to marry me. Again. Don't you understand? I am wild for her. I must have her. I will not rape her if only she will see reason and agree to become my wife. Damnation, I want her. No one will dare call her a bastard when she is my wife. She will be safe. She will be protected."

The blood was pounding through Tysen's head. He did something he'd never done as an adult—he lost all control. He leaned down and grabbed Erickson by his shirt collar, jerked him upright. He pulled him close. "That is all nonsense and you know it. I don't know why you want her so badly, but I will find out before I let you leave Kildrummy. Now, you miserable excuse for a man, I'm going to kill you."

He didn't hear Mary Rose's yell or Sinjun's voice telling him to calm down, to remember who and what he was. But he did hear Colin saying, quite clearly, "Let me kill him when you're through with him, Tysen."

Tysen hadn't struck another man since he'd left home. There, naturally, he'd fought every day of his life with his brothers. He'd learned to fight as dirty as they did in order to survive. He hit Erickson in the face, then in the belly, in the kidneys. He threw him against the wall, smiling when he heard his head hit hard against the oak. Erickson shook his head and came out fighting, fists pounding into Tysen.

"Oh, yes, come on," Tysen said, and grabbed his right

arm, bending it back until Erickson managed to kick him in the leg and pull free.

"I didn't do anything, damn you," Erickson yelled and sent his fist toward Tysen's face, but he didn't make it because Tysen blocked him at the last instant.

"You bastard," Tysen said, and he was on him again, this time beyond himself, hitting and hitting him until he felt hands dragging at his arm. He tried to shake off the hands, and then he realized it was Mary Rose, and she was crying.

Mary Rose crying? Why was she crying? They'd saved her, and he was in the process of killing MacPhail, who should have been strangled at birth. He shook her off and grabbed Erickson again, who, having caught his breath, came back swinging. He got Tysen in the belly, and the two men went down, rolling over and over, slamming their fists, hurling yells and groans of pain. Finally, Tysen managed to twist Erickson onto his back and hold him down. The moment he straddled him, Tysen felt thunderous joy roar through him. He smiled down at Erickson, then slammed his fist into his jaw, once, twice.

"That's enough," Mary Rose yelled in his ear. "Stop it, Tysen."

"Yes, it's nearly my turn," Colin said, striding up. "She's right, Tysen. You've pounded him enough. You've probably even pounded him more than your share. Now give me a go at the bastard."

Tysen didn't even look up. He hit Erickson again. The man was nearly unconscious, not fighting back now.

"No," Sinjun said. She was standing over her brother, her eyes wide, still trying to understand what had happened. Tysen had bashed the man, bashed him good, but he hadn't stopped. He was holding him around his neck now, not trying to strangle him, thank God. She could tell that at last he was calming down, that finally he was gaining control. No, she was wrong. He was strangling him again. She laid her hand on his bare shoulder and said very gently, "Tysen, my dear, you must stop now. It's over. You've punished him quite well enough. Stop or you won't like yourself very much. I know you very well, so believe me. I don't want you wallowing in guilt, consigning your own soul to hell. Stop. Now."

It was her last words that finally cleared away all the rage from his brain, made him aware of the nagging and various pains in his own body. His blood was no longer furiously pumping through him. Everything was slowing now. He felt his heart steadying, slowing back to normal. He rose to his feet and stood over Erickson MacPhail. He said very calmly, as he stared down at the man, "If I ever see you again within fifty feet of Mary Rose, I will kill you. Do you understand me?"

"All of us will kill you. We will take turns, each with a gun or fists or a knife," Sinjun said. "God will forgive my brother his violence toward you because you are such an evil fraud that you deserve to be sent to hell."

Colin said, "Now, like my brother-in-law, I want to know why you want Mary Rose so desperately. A man who truly loves a woman doesn't try to coerce her, doesn't try to rape her, certainly doesn't steal her away in the middle of the night. Why do you want to wed her? Come, tell us the truth and perhaps we will let you live."

Erickson, his nose bleeding, his lip split and oozing blood, his belly caved in, his neck and jaw so sore he could barely talk, said, "You're wrong about all of it. I have no base motive. I love her. I must have her for my wife. I am not lying, there is no other reason, just my sincerest affection for her." Then he looked over at Mary Rose, standing there, pale, the vicar's nightshirt nearly covering her toes and her fingers. "You must marry me,

Mary Rose, you must. My life cannot continue if you do not."

Colin frowned. "You are lying. I want to know why you must have Mary Rose as your wife."

Erickson shut his mouth so fast he bit his tongue.

Colin said very quietly, "Mary Rose, bring the candle over here so I can see this idiot very clearly. Yes, that's good. His nose is bloody. It adds interest, don't you think?"

"No," Mary Rose said.

Colin stood right over him. "She's right. Now, we will have all the truth out of you, or I will hold you down while Tysen finishes stomping you into the floor. Do you understand me, you treacherous sod?"

Erickson sighed very deeply, he looked defeated and desperate. Then shook his head. "No, I won't say any more. There is nothing more to say. I am innocent of anything except my passion for Mary Rose."

Colin came down on his haunches, grabbed Erickson's shirt collar, lifted him up a bit, then, with no warning, no hesitation, he pounded his head against the floor. Erickson moaned.

"There is not a dollop of love in you for Mary Rose, probably not a bit for any woman. The truth, all of it. Now, or I will kick your brains into the wainscotting."

Tysen was leaning against the wall, his arms crossed over his chest, saying absolutely nothing.

Erickson yelled at him, "You're a bloody vicar! How can you allow this man to smash my head? I'm already half-dead since the lot of you attacked me. Stop him, for God's sake."

"Not unless you tell us the truth," Tysen said, examining his sore knuckles.

"There is no bloody truth to tell you, damn it."

"Would you like me to take over, Colin?" Tysen said, taking one step toward them.

Both Mary Rose and Sinjun crowded in, keeping Tysen back, both of them staring down at Erickson as if he were a slug that was peering up at them from under a rock.

Colin leaned forward again, grabbed his collar.

Erickson groaned. "No, not again. Damn, I can feel one of my teeth loose in my mouth. I have nothing to say. If you kill me, then you will hang for it."

"Tysen, where are you going?"

"It's all right, Sinjun. I'm going to get my gun. I can't take the chance that he will try tomorrow or the next day to rape Mary Rose and force her into marriage. I have to kill him. He won't tell us why with all this dramatic charade we're playing. There's just nothing else to do."

"We'll draw straws," Colin said.

"I want to draw a straw as well," Mary Rose said. "I don't want to be afraid of him anymore. They can't hang all of us, can they?"

"No, they cannot," Sinjun said. "Get the gun, Tysen."

Erickson looked from one grim face to the next. He believed them. He felt defeat fill his craw. There was no way out of this. He drew a deep breath, swallowing his pain, and said, "All right, damn all of you to bloody hell. I must marry Mary Rose because she isn't poor. She's rich, very rich. She's got a trust from her father—no, I don't know who he is, only her mother knows, since she would surely remember pulling up her skirts for a man. There is evidently a lot of money in the Bank of England in a sort of trust for her. Mary Rose receives it when she is either married or turns twenty-five. Damn you all, I must have that money!"

Erickson looked up at Mary Rose, whose face was in the shadows since she was holding the candle. "You will be twenty-five next month, Mary Rose. You must marry me before your birthday so I may have the money. I need it. Donnatella only has five thousand pounds—it simply isn't enough."

"How much money?" Sinjun asked.

"I don't know. Sir Lyon said it was thousands upon thousands. He said this old man who is the trustee wouldn't tell him the amount, just that it was more than even a greedy man could imagine."

Tysen was sucking in air hard again because he nearly couldn't breathe. He shoved Sinjun and Mary Rose out of his way, leaned down, jerked MacPhail up and began hitting him as hard as he could, which was very hard indeed since this new wave of rage had turned his vision red, made his heart pound so hard it should burst through his chest. It was Colin who grabbed Tysen and pulled him off. Tysen turned to hit him, but Sinjun yelled, "Stop it, Tysen! Calm down, it's all over. At least now we know the truth. Stop it! The little worm has lost, well and truly lost."

Mary Rose walked slowly between the two men. She pressed herself against Tysen and locked her arms around his back. He felt her mouth against his bare chest, her warm breath. Slowly, so very slowly, he lowered his arms, and squeezed her to him. He rested his face on the top of her head. He breathed in her scent, tasted her hair, curls bouncing into his mouth.

"Did you have some sort of agreement with Mary Rose's uncle?" Colin said now, standing over Erickson, his hands fisted, but he knew the man wasn't going to try to get away. He knew Tysen might just snap again and this time he might just kill him. He knew deep in his soul that he couldn't allow that to happen. Such an act, he knew, would destroy Tysen, crush his soul, damn him forever.

"Yes," Erickson said finally, knowing he'd failed,

knowing it was no use. "I was to give him ten thousand pounds when I wedded Mary Rose and he would see that she was available to me at Vallance Manor so I could properly woo her there, if she didn't accept me elsewhere."

Mary Rose turned slowly, not releasing Tysen, holding him, perhaps, even more tightly. "What about Donnatella? She's the one you have always wanted, isn't she?"

Erickson rubbed his aching jaw, felt blood from his nose and split lip, as he said, his voice filled with dislike now, "Yes, you're nothing compared to Donnatella. You're not stupid, Mary Rose, you have eyes. Since you live at Vallance Manor, you see every day how beautiful she is."

Mary Rose didn't pull away from Tysen at all, just continued to look at Erickson. "If you married me then you couldn't have Donnatella. She would never be your mistress. You know that, Erickson. None of this makes any sense. You would have my money, but surely you would be miserable married to me and not her."

Erickson said, "My mother is very strong-willed, you know that. She said that all would be well, in the not-too-distant future. She said she would have the money and I would have all that I wanted. That would have to be Donnatella, wouldn't it?"

"You mean your mother planned to kill Mary Rose?" Sinjun was staring down at the man, revolted, but yet not wanting to believe such evil existed.

Erickson only shrugged, which was a difficult movement since every bit of him hurt, even his knee he'd hit when he went to the floor with the damned vicar. He said, furious, "That is bloody lunacy. My mother wouldn't kill anyone. I don't know what she planned to do, but she wouldn't kill anyone."

Sinjun lifted her nightgown, baring her leg to the knee, and sent her foot into Erickson's ribs. He moaned, clutching himself. "You're lying, you paltry—I can't think of anything strong enough to call you that would fit. Believe me, in the stables at Vere Castle I have heard many singularly wonderful terms for paltry men. It's obvious that your mother would kill Mary Rose, or you would, and after Mary Rose was dead, then you would have her money *and* Donnatella. Bloody hell, you are an evil man. As for your mother, she should be taken out and shot. Immediately."

Mary Rose said against Tysen's chest, "I can't believe it. I'm rich then? Why didn't my mother ever tell me? Why did she make me believe that we were the poor relations, completely dependent upon her sister and Uncle Lyon?"

"Perhaps your mother didn't think you would believe her," Tysen said. "Would you have?"

"No, probably not. But she should have tried." Mary Rose felt pain flow through her. She simply didn't understand her mother, never had. She said, "But how does Uncle Lyon even know about the money?"

Erickson said, holding his head, not looking at any of them, knowing the rest of it didn't matter, so why not tell them, "Your uncle told me that he threatened to have both you and your mother kicked out of Vallance Manor. I think he wanted to bed your mother and she refused him. I don't blame her for refusing him. He's an old man and his breath is nasty. I guess your mother had to tell him about the money. She assured him there were buckets of it because your father was very rich. She promised she would give him some if he didn't kick you out and if he left her alone. He came up with this plan after, of course, he went to Edinburgh to make sure she was telling him the truth." Erickson turned over on his side and very slowly began to pull himself upright, using the wall for support.

"Wait," Mary Rose said. "If all this talk about an inheritance comes from my mother, then perhaps it doesn't really exist. My mother has been mad, on and off, for a very long time. Maybe she asked this man in Edinburgh to lie for her."

Erickson shook his head. "No, she didn't. Your uncle found and confronted the man who holds the trust for you. He wouldn't tell your uncle who your father is, but he confirmed that there is a trust in your name, confirmed that it was a lot of money."

Mary Rose just stared at him, still trying to take it in. She was no longer a poor relation. She had worth.

Colin said, "But you had to marry her before she turned twenty-five or you wouldn't get a dime?"

Erickson nodded, on his hands and knees now, breathing hard, trying to get hold of himself.

"That's right," Sinjun said slowly. "If Mary Rose were twenty-five, then she would get her dowry and she and her mother could go anywhere they pleased, do anything they wished to do."

"It's still so hard to believe," Mary Rose said. "I never knew, never guessed. Perhaps my father loved me, since he left me so much money. I never considered that even possible."

Tysen wanted to tell her not to consider it now, but he didn't. He raised his head and looked at Erickson's neck, his fingers clenching at the remembered feel of choking him. No, he shouldn't remember that with fondness. He was shaking his head at himself when he looked Erickson right in the eye. "I'm going to wed with Mary Rose, didn't you hear? She will be my wife. You have lost. It is all over."

Erickson nodded. "Yes, Mrs. MacFardle has told everyone that you're marrying the Bastard, and she doesn't understand it except that she's saying that Mary Rose planned it all. She wet herself down in the stream, rolled about in some briars, and came here with the purpose of gaining your pity and then seducing you. And because you're a bloody vicar—you have all this honor and nobility—you'd feel yourself forced to marry her."

To his own surprise, Tysen threw back his head and laughed. He hugged Mary Rose very close and laughed harder. He said finally to Erickson, "Can you even begin to imagine Mary Rose seducing anyone?"

Erickson was forced to shake his head. His belly was starting to roil and ache. His ribs pulled and poked against the inside of his skin. He held himself perfectly silent. He wasn't going to bear the humiliation of vomiting on the corridor floor of Kildrummy Castle. He moaned and rolled back, hitting the wall, his eyes tightly shut. "That's why I had to act quickly. If Mary Rose were to marry you very soon, then all would be lost."

"I see," Tysen said. "Or you could have tried to kill me too."

"No, I'm not a murderer."

"I'm rich," Mary Rose said, wonder in her voice. "Now," she said, not loosening her hold around Tysen's back, perhaps squeezing him even more tightly, "now you don't have to marry me." Slowly, she leaned back against his arms and looked up at him. "I release you, sir. You are free of me now."

"Actually," Tysen said, "no, I'm not."

Erickson was holding his belly, lying on his side. He felt a small surge of hope. "That's right, Mary Rose, you don't have to marry him now. Now you can think more clearly about this. You've only known the vicar for a week. You've known me all your life. I've always been kind to you, never baited you about being a bastard. You swam with the porpoises, and I taught you, remember? Listen to me—a vicar doesn't need money. A vicar needs only to have a roomful of captive people for him to exhort about their endless string of sins. That's why there are churches. Once they file in, they close those huge doors. No one can get out. Then the vicar yells at them, makes them feel guiltier than dirt. Once they fill the collection plate, he pats them on the head and they feel all right again, and he feels superior."

"I cannot believe that you and your mother have survived this long without someone trying to murder the both of you," Colin said.

"My mother means no one harm. She just wants me to be happy. However, she wants herself to be happy as well. She wants to attend balls and routs in Edinburgh, rub elbows with Society. Mary Rose, listen to me, the vicar doesn't need you, not like I do. He's a man of God, and even though he nearly killed me—something he'll roast in hell for doing—he isn't really a man, as in a man a woman would find pleasure with and—" He stopped cold, shook his head at the possible further pain his words just might bring down upon his body, and said, desperation bubbling very close to the surface, "Please, marry me, not him. Be free of him, don't let him talk you out of it. I'll only force you if I have to, only if you refuse me and—"

Sinjun kicked him again.

19

THE FOLLOWING MORNING at the breakfast table, Miles MacNeily told everyone about his adventure escorting Erickson MacPhail back home, there to be dealt with by his fond mother. "He didn't even have a chance to explain," Miles said. "She started yelling at him from an upper window. If I hadn't wanted to pound him into the ground some more, I would have felt sorry for him." Miles shook his head and looked at his eggs, which had been cooked so long they looked like clumps of yellow rocks. "The woman's a terror. I heard her call him an idiot, loose-mouthed, a rotten seed of her womb. I left as quickly as I could. It's strange. Erickson has the reputation of being very strong, very determined. But, evidently not with his mother." He eyed the eggs again and forked down a bite, choked, and grabbed for a glass of water.

Mary Rose winced as she watched him. No one else had as yet touched the eggs. She said, "I'm sorry, Miles. I've never made eggs before. I suppose that I did fry them a bit too long."

"Perhaps just the slightest bit, Mary Rose. Don't worry about it. You tried," Miles said, but he smiled at her, and it was a very sweet smile, Tysen saw. He felt something vaguely like jealousy rolling around in his gut, and it shocked him. Shocked him so much he just stared down at his dirty boots. Miles MacNeily was old enough to be her father.

Tysen said finally, "Miles is right. Don't worry about the eggs. We are all grateful."

Sinjun said suddenly, "I didn't know you were in the kitchen, Mary Rose. Are you certain you feel well enough to be up and working like this?"

"I feel fine, Sinjun."

"Nonetheless, until we can find a cook, I will see to the meals. Colin, please assure everyone that I am a splendid cook."

Colin choked on his coffee. It really wasn't his wife's claim that bowed him over, but rather the rancid odor and taste of the coffee. He couldn't seem to stop coughing until Meggie smacked him hard on the back.

Once Colin was upright again, a glass of water in his hand, his eye on that coffee in his cup, Meggie said, "I heard Pouder talking to MacNee about a new cook. Pouder said Mrs. Golden from the village needs money to take care of her grandchildren. He was of the opinion that she would be ready to come to Kildrummy today, so you don't have to cook us any meals, Aunt Sinjun. He also said that she would make a splendid housekeeper as well."

There was a moment of stunned, very grateful silence before Tysen said, "Meggie, despite all the arguments you put up to me, despite all your endless complaining, I was right to force you to come with me to Kildrummy Castle. You have been of invaluable assistance to me, and I thank you."

Meggie didn't even blink. "Thank you, Papa. I live to serve you."

The table shook with all the laughter. As for Meggie,

she sat back, her arms folded across her chest, the little queen who had brought down the house.

Three hours later Mrs. Golden was happily humming and baking bread in the Kildrummy kitchen. The smells floated through the castle.

But there was no more laughter.

Tysen, standing on the top steps of the castle, was yelling at the top of his lungs. "You will not leave, Mary Rose! Where did that carriage come from? You will remain here and you will marry me. I don't want you to free me. I have kissed you—perhaps even more than kissed you, at least in my imagination. You have been compromised. You have seen my bare chest, hugged me. You have breathed against my bare shoulder. That's beyond being compromised. Now, come back into the castle this minute or it will be the worse for you."

But Mary Rose kept walking to the waiting hired carriage, carrying a valise that Miles MacNeily had reluctantly loaned to her.

"Oh, Papa, no, she can't do this," Meggie said, coming to a skittering halt beside her father. "I had no idea what she was planning. It's her honor, Papa, she said that it was choking her. I didn't know what she meant then. Oh, goodness, I think Mr. MacNeily helped her, and that's because Mary Rose talked him into it. I think he's hiding because he doesn't want you to thrash him like you did Erickson MacPhail. You can't let her go, Papa. You have to stop her."

Tysen wondered in that instant if the world hadn't tipped onto its side and put him in danger of falling off. Here he was, standing on the top steps of the castle, his hands on his hips, his face red, and he was yelling like a madman. He could actually feel the hot blood roaring through his veins. This was utterly ridiculous.

Meggie was tugging at his hand. "Please, Papa, you have to stop her. Mary Rose means to do the right thing— it's just that she sometimes doesn't realize that what she believes is the right thing is stupid."

"Yes, I will stop her, and yes, this is an incredibly stupid thing she's doing." He ran down the long, curving stairs into the inner courtyard. "You will stay put, Mary Rose!"

She was about to let the coachman assist her into the carriage when Tysen grabbed the man by his collar and simply flung him away, sending him skittering on his backside into the dirt. "Now, as for you—"

"Tysen, you shouldn't be here. You were supposed to be in the village."

"I was and now I'm back, thank the good Lord. Meggie is right, this is one of the stupidest things you've done to date, Mary Rose. Now come along."

She kept pulling and tugging. "You must see reason here. It is good reason, solid reason. I can see it. It's not stupid. Why can't you see that it is the right thing to do? You don't want me as your wife. I'm a bastard, you can't change that. Your brother—the earl—would rip off his wig and stomp it into the ground in rage, if it were the last century and he wore one. No, you can't have a bastard in your family, it would be a travesty, you—"

Tysen heard the geese, Willie leading the way, honking so loud he could no longer hear his own furious heartbeat. He heard Meggie yell, "Papa, I've got her valise. No, no, Willie, don't nip at my arm. I'll get bread for you, but you must be patient."

He briefly saw Meggie from the corner of his eye tugging at Mary Rose's valise, slowly pulling it back toward the castle, the geese stampeding madly after her.

"No more," he said, looking down at Mary Rose. "No more." He grabbed her and hauled her over his shoulder.

"Tysen, oh, goodness, this isn't what a vicar should do. Put me down. This is ridiculous. I'm doing what is best. Listen to me. Mr. MacNeily went to a lot of trouble to get this carriage here for me—"

To Tysen's utter surprise, he smacked her bottom. "You are going nowhere." To his further utter surprise, his palm lay on her bottom for a good second longer than necessary to deliver the hit. He raised his hand as if scalded, then stared straight ahead, determination freezing his face, and walked back to the castle.

Still, she reared up, but it did her no good. She could kick, she could pound him with her fists, but because she didn't want to take the chance of hurting him, she was, effectively, not going anywhere.

Mary Rose saw Meggie tugging with all her might at the valise, the geese honking louder and louder, Willie pecking at Meggie's feet. Dust flew up and Mary Rose thought, I must plant trees and shrubs here. There is too much bare earth and black dirt. Then she shook her head, tried to relax as her stomach bounced up and down on Tysen's shoulder.

The coachman picked himself up, brushed off his trousers, and stared after the man—a vicar!—who was carrying the lady over his shoulder, followed by a little girl dragging the dratted valise with geese nearly on her heels, making more racket than his own dear wife in her finest moments.

Miles MacNeily stood just inside the castle door, in the entrance hall. Pouder, standing next to him, looked mildly interested. When Tysen came through the door, Miles said, "I'm sorry, my lord, but Mary Rose, she is very special and she didn't want you to feel responsible for—"

"Miles," Tysen said, not looking toward his steward as he strode through the entrance hall, "you're fired."

"But, my lord, I'm already leaving, in but two weeks now."

Meggie managed to pull the valise into the hallway. Willie was honking loudly outside on the steps. Pouder was waving his gnarly old hands at the goose, yelling, "Begone, ye miserable white-feathered sot! Ye'll nae bite the lass's heel!"

Willie's beak came around the side of the wide front door. He honked, then retreated. Tysen couldn't help it, he started laughing. The woman over his shoulder had tried to leave him, and yet he was laughing. He felt her belly on his shoulder, knew that if he pulled her just a bit closer, his face would be touching her hip. He was hugging her thighs. The feel of her, it made him shake.

What was happening to him?

He saw Meggie, his precious girl, pulling that ridiculous valise past Pouder, who was just staring down at her. Miles MacNeily leaned down and scooped it up.

He heard Meggie said, "Thank you, Mr. Miles. You shouldn't have let Mary Rose talk you into that carriage. She is promised to my father, and I have already written to my brothers telling them that we will have a new mother."

"Er, would you like me to post your letter, Meggie?"

"Yes, sir, that would be very kind of you. Oh, goodness, Mary Rose, what is in that valise? It weighs more than I do."

"I gave her my two prized candlesticks," Miles said, "for her to pawn in Edinburgh. Since I haven't yet come into my inheritance, I don't have any money. Perhaps I should give them to your father as restitution."

Meggie, a practical girl, who was racing after her father and Mary Rose, turned briefly and said, "I suppose it is the least you could do for your treachery."

Where had Meggie learned that excellent word?

And then Tysen thought, two blasted candlesticks! It was too much. He felt laughter bubbling up again, and seamed his mouth together. He said, "I imagine that you needed the candlesticks to live on until your twenty-fifth birthday?"

Mary Rose nodded.

"I suppose you would have written to your mother for the name of the solicitor."

She nodded again, not a word out of her mouth.

"And then you would have been up bright and early, ready to camp on the solicitor's doorstep? Then once you had all your wealth, you would have brought your mother to Edinburgh?"

Another nod.

He walked toward the staircase, paused a moment, and called out over his shoulder—actually, over Mary Rose's bottom—"You're not fired, Miles, at least not for another two weeks."

"Thank you, my lord. I'll see to the coachman. I'll take Mary Rose's valise back to Meggie's bedchamber."

"I don't want your candlesticks," Tysen said, "just swear to me you'll keep them hidden from Mary Rose."

"Yes, I swear, my lord," Miles said. "I can see now that this is for the best. I won't listen to her again."

Mary Rose called out, raising her head from Tysen's back, "At least you listened to me once, sir."

Tysen was again picturing Meggie yanking and jerking on that ridiculous valise. Actually, he thought as he walked into the drawing room, he knew what he wanted to do was to simply ease his arms up and splay his hands over Mary Rose's bottom.

It didn't occur to him that he was committing sins of lust in his brain, that he was actually compounding sins by the moment. All he was aware of was the closeness of Mary Rose's bottom. It wasn't until some time later, after he'd given her over to Sinjun with instructions to sit on her if she tried anything else stupid, that his sins started coming home to roost.

Even while he was contemplating those sins, the list compounding itself by the hour, Pouder informed him of their newly-arrived guests.

When he saw Sir Lyon, he decided he would rather spend eternity cataloguing his sins than be in this man's company again. However, this time Mary Rose's mother was with him. It was mid-afternoon, and there were more delicious smells sweeping through the castle. The freshly baked bread had everyone sniffing the air.

Tysen just stood there watching Sir Lyon sniff the baked bread, then escort Gweneth Fordyce into the drawing room. Why had she refused to come into the castle before? Why was she coming in now?

Mary Rose, thankfully, was upstairs, now in Meggie's bedchamber, being entertained by his daughter, who, at his instruction, was keeping a very close eye on her. Sinjun, he'd been told, was visiting ever so often, just to make sure that Mary Rose hadn't climbed out a window. As for Colin, he was in the stables determining what stock was needed to purchase.

"Sir Lyon, Mary Rose's mother," Tysen said, not knowing what to call her. "Thank you, Pouder."

"I will adjourn to your bedchamber, my lord, and see to the freshening of your clothes."

"An excellent notion, Pouder. I wanted to thank you for the fine ironing of my cravats." He turned to his guests.

"Would you like to be seated? I can have Mrs. Golden prepare some tea."

"Mrs. Golden shouldn't be here," Sir Lyon said, then seemed to realize that this approach wasn't at all conciliating, and added, chin out, "Mrs. MacFardle, for all her abilities, is a bitch. You're better off without her. That bread smells delicious."

"I shall have her bring some bread with the tea," Tysen said and gave orders to Pouder, who hadn't yet left his chair by the front door to freshen Tysen's clothes upstairs.

When he returned to the drawing room, Gweneth Fordyce spoke. "I have many times wanted to poke a knife through her middle. Over the years, she was very unpleasant to my daughter. She wasn't to me, because she was afraid of me, the madwoman."

"I don't doubt that she will find a suitable position," Tysen said. Once everyone was seated, he stood by the fireplace, his arms crossed over his chest, and simply nodded.

Sir Lyon cleared his throat and cleared it yet again. He shot a sideways look at Mary Rose's mother, then said, "My lord, I understand that a very few minor difficulties arose here last night."

"No, nothing that we couldn't handle," Tysen said, nothing more, and just waited.

Sir Lyon girded his loins and said, "As Mary Rose's uncle and her guardian, I am willing to give Mary Rose my permission to wed you, if she is willing to provide me with payment from the dowry provided by her father, for all the money I have spent on her and her dear mother over the years, over a very lot of years. Nearly twenty-five to be exact."

"I see," Tysen said. "Knowing that you were charitable and kind to your sister-in-law and her child aren't sufficient?"

"No, they are not. Tell him, Gweneth."

Mary Rose's mother rose very slowly. She looked down at Sir Lyon, and there was no liking at all on her still-lovely face. "Ah, so that's it. Tell him what, Lyon? That I have always thought you a pompous bully? That now I think you are merely pathetic? You are, you know, trying to extort money from Lord Barthwick."

Sir Lyon's face turned so red, Tysen feared that he might fall over with apoplexy. Sir Lyon jumped to his feet and shouted, "You are ungrateful, Gweneth! Damnation, woman, I opened my home to you and your bastard. I have never begrudged you anything. You have been part of my family." He paused a moment, and if anything, his heavy face grew even redder. Tysen tensed his muscles, preparing to catch him when he collapsed. "Damn you, Gwennie, I am beginning to believe that you are not mad at all, that you were never even remotely mad, that you have merely pretended to madness so you wouldn't have to do anything yourself for your poor daughter."

"No, I am not mad," Gweneth said. "Actually, the madness kept you away from me—at least for the most part—until recently. I was a fool to tell you about Mary Rose's trust from her father. I never considered that you would go to Erickson and bribe him to marry my daughter so you could get even more money. You are a pathetic human being, Lyon."

Sir Lyon shouted, "That is a lie! You will be quiet! Dammit, I need the money!" He pinned Tysen again, and he was panting from his anger. "Attend me, my lord, if I do not receive the money to which I am entitled, I will wed Mary Rose to Erickson MacPhail."

Tysen regarded the man with his red face, his fists bunched atop his knees. He waited until Sir Lyon's face began to recover its natural color. He then motioned for the man to be seated. Once he was, Tysen said, "Ten thousand pounds, wasn't it? I believe this is the amount you and Erickson MacPhail agreed upon?"

Gweneth Fordyce, who had sat down again, now leapt to her feet. She stared down at Sir Lyon, so much anger getting ready to erupt that Tysen said quickly, "No, ma'am, please be seated again. I have something to say to both of you that perhaps you do not know. I have already been in contact with Donald MacCray, Tyronne Barthwick's solicitor in Edinburgh. He tells me that Mary Rose Fordyce has no legal guardian, that you never applied for such a position. Therefore, Sir Lyon, you are here to extort money from me or from Mary Rose, and you have no leverage at all. I would suggest that you consider praying to God for forgiveness for this elaborate deception." He didn't add that he would be doing quite a lot of praying himself, for that quick and clean lie about the guardianship. He realized he was right, of course, just looking at Sir Lyon's face. He'd been caught out. It was there for all to see.

Sir Lyon didn't jump up this time, just shouted at the top of his lungs, "So I am not her legal guardian. It wasn't necessary. I am the bloody girl's uncle! Gweneth, you will set this aright, you will see to it that I get the ten thousand pounds, or you will never again be welcome at Vallance Manor. Damnation, it's probably a very small part of what her father left her."

Gweneth looked down at her brother-in-law for a very long time. Then she smiled at Tysen. "My lord, he forced me to come with him today, hoping I would help him. I did not know what he intended, but I knew it was likely something dishonorable. As to the amount of money her father left her in trust, I do not know the exact amount. Her father simply assured me that it was very substantial. Now, would you mind if I had all my belongings and Mary Rose's sent here to Kildrummy?"

Tysen bowed to her. "I would be delighted, ma'am."

Gweneth Fordyce looked down at her brother-in-law and said, "I assume that you will allow me to have our things taken from your precious manor? You will provide me a carriage to come back to Kildrummy?"

He had no choice at all, Sir Lyon realized, or before nightfall he would be known as not only a bloody fool, but also a bounder. "Of course," he said, and wanted to strangle her. He knew he had to think. Nothing was going the way it should. He hadn't managed this well. He never should have trusted Gwennie to come with him today and plead his case. He should have known she'd turn on him. Damnation, he still wanted Gwennie in his bed, but faced with the economies he would be forced to make, even that desire was fast fading into the woodwork. With outward calm, he bade Lord Barthwick—the damned vicar who should have been easy to outwit and intimidate—good-bye and escorted Mary Rose's mother back to the carriage.

He drew in another whiff of that delicious freshly baked bread as he walked out the front door of Kildrummy and realized he hadn't even gotten to taste a bite of it.

That evening Gweneth Fordyce, along with three Vallance Manor footmen, arrived at Kildrummy Castle with a mountain of luggage.

20

THE NEXT MORNING Tysen was seated in the library, writing a letter to Donald MacCray to find out the truth of things. He looked up when Mary Rose said from the doorway, "My lord?"

He raised an eyebrow at her. "So formal?"

"Well, I still feel that you are angry at me for trying to leave yesterday, even though I know it is still the best thing to do, the proper thing. You did not wish to speak to me last night. Indeed, you avoided me, so I came to you."

"You don't know anything," he said, and eased his quill back into its onyx stand. He sat back in his chair and leaned his head back against his arms. "What is happening now that I must needs know? More outpouring of guilt on your part? You will shoot yourself now to spare me from sacrificing myself? Or is it that you disapprove of something else I have done for your benefit?"

"No," she said, then sighed and fiddled with the lace at her wrist. She was wearing one of her own gowns that her mother had brought with her. "Thank you for inviting my mother here. She is very happy. Meggie likes her very well, and naturally, my mother believes Meggie to be the brightest child in all of Scotland. Meggie has a new grand-mother, and thank the Lord she isn't mad. I believe my mother is going to teach Meggie how to draw. She is excellent with watercolors." She paused a moment, then added, "It's true, isn't it? My mother really has been pretending to madness all these years? It was all a ruse?"

He nodded.

"I suppose I understand it. She was pregnant, unwed, and what was she to do? But why madness, particularly when she was at Vallance Manor with her own sister and brother-in-law?"

Tysen sighed. "Evidently your uncle wanted her in his bed and he wasn't above using blackmail. Your mother was quick-witted. She chose madness as her defense against him. I suppose it became a habit with her."

Mary Rose thought about that a moment. "It would seem to me," she said finally, "that there are very few honorable gentlemen on this earth."

"Bosh," Tysen said. "When we are home, I will surround you with honorable gentlemen. They abound. My brothers are honorable. You will like them and their wives and children. I will admit, however, that your uncle and Erickson MacPhail could strongly influence one's opinions."

"I do not understand why my father did not help my mother."

"Your father was undoubtedly married."

"Yes, of course, but still. I was thinking, Tysen."

"The good Lord spare me. Another plan to escape me?"

"I was thinking that when I am twenty-five, just next month, I can repay you for taking care of me and my mother. You've even allowed her to move in with you. It is very generous. Oh, goodness." Mary Rose actually felt her jaw quiver, she just couldn't stop it, and it was hard to swallow.

Tysen said with no sympathy at all, "If you cry, Mary Rose, I will haul you over my shoulder again, ride to that stream, and toss you in. We can see just how long it takes you to climb out this time. Now, you have caused me no end of trouble simply because I am doing the right thing. If only you would finally recognize me as the end to all your misery, and your mother's as well. You still have tears in your eyes. Stop it now."

She sniffed.

"That's something. Now, I'm writing a letter to see if, just perchance, the lie I so smoothly told your uncle yesterday happens to be the truth. I believe it is. Your uncle didn't gainsay me, but it's best to have it in writing."

She stared at him. "You lied? You actually knew you were going to do it, and knowing, you still lied? Oh, Tysen, it is all my fault, that is a sin and you committed it and you are a man of God and—"

"Be quiet and listen." And he told her the very believable tale he had concocted for her uncle's benefit.

She said slowly when he had finished, "I have never before been told that Sir Lyon was my guardian. Indeed, I can't imagine that my uncle would ever have willingly wanted to be my guardian. He was embarrassed that a bastard was living under his roof. It was difficult for him to feel magnanimous, his shame was so great. You know, I wonder if Ian discovered this?"

"I have no idea. I will ask Mr. MacCray, if you wish. Regardless, you and I are going to be married on Sunday, by special license. I spoke this morning to Reverend Mac-Millan, a very nice old gentleman who says he has known you all your life and thinks you will make a fine wife for a vicar, even though the vicar is foreign. He is, however, concerned that in my nobleness, I am rushing you into this. He is concerned that you might wish to change your mind. I told him that your fondest wish was to wed a vicar, namely me, and move to southern England where you wouldn't know a soul, present yourself to a gaggle of new relatives entirely unknown to you, and become a mother to three children not your own. I believe he wanted to laugh at that, but he choked so badly trying to hold it back that I had to thump him soundly on the back."

She was standing there, pale, her face still bruised, her light blue gown a bit loose on her, for she'd lost flesh during the past week—no wonder. She didn't laugh, didn't crack even a little smile.

He said very gently as he rose from his chair, "Give over, Mary Rose, give over. Marry me. It is the right thing to do. We will do well together."

He didn't look away from her.

Finally, she said, her voice barely above a whisper, "All right, Tysen. I will marry you this Sunday."

And so it was that the following Sunday morning, in the drawing room of Kildrummy Castle, the Honorable Tysen Edward Townsend Sherbrooke, Reverend Sherbrooke of Glenclose-on-Rowan, brother to the earl of Northcliffe, took his second wife, Mary Rose Fordyce, spinster, of Vallance Manor. Gweneth cried delicately into a lovely lace handkerchief, and Colin Kinross stood beside Tysen as he calmly spoke his vows. As for Sinjun Kinross, she stood beside Mary Rose and lightly squeezed her shoulder upon occasion, perhaps to encourage her to speak up, but no matter.

Neither Mary Rose's uncle, aunt, nor cousin was present, having sent their regrets, and that was no surprise at all, rather a relief. Also there had been no word at all from the MacPhails, neither mother nor son.

Mrs. Golden prepared a delicious wedding luncheon,

and Miles had managed to secure half a dozen bottles of rather decent champagne. She had hired an additional six girls from the village. Two would remain to help her at Kildrummy—a good thing, Tysen thought, for he had very few clean shirts left.

As for the new Reverend and Mrs. Tysen Sherbrooke, they would remain at Kildrummy Castle until the middle of September, exactly two weeks away.

There was one additional guest at the wedding besides Miles MacNeily, and that was Donald MacCray, the Barthwick solicitor, from Edinburgh. Given, however, that this was Reverend Tysen's wedding day and Mr. MacCray had no wish to intrude, he merely said to Tysen, "There is no reason for you to worry. As it turns out, Sir Lyon was never your wife's guardian. He lied to you. As for your, er, deception, it proved to be a sound deduction." Whenever Tysen happened to look at Mr. MacCray, he was drinking champagne and staring at Gweneth Fordyce. Meggie whispered to her father that she'd wager their solicitor had drunk at least one whole bottle by himself.

Late that evening, Meggie happily followed her father and Mary Rose into his huge bedchamber, chattering, never taking a breath, laughing very gaily.

"Your aunt Sinjun gave you a bit of champagne, didn't she, Meggie?"

"Well, yes, Papa, just a bit, yes. It's nasty stuff and I can't seem to stop talking." She beamed at him, then hugged Mary Rose tightly. "We will all do very well together. You are not to worry, Mary Rose. Max and Leo will believe I did well to bring you home. Now, shall we talk about your new duties as Papa's wife?"

And Meggie sat down in the middle of the great bed, her legs crossed, beaming at her father and her new mother.

He didn't know what to say. Neither did Mary Rose.

Tysen finally was preparing to open his mouth when there came a knock on the bedchamber door.

"Yes?"

Gweneth Fordyce peered around the door. "Ah, Meggie, dearest, there you are. I am very much in need of your assistance. I have this wretched headache, brought on, I daresay, from excessive attention from Mr. Mac-Cray. Would you bathe my forehead for me?"

Meggie was torn. She looked from her father to Mary Rose's mother, then sighed. "Papa? Mary Rose? Do you mind if I see to your mother? She's now my grandmother, you know. I shouldn't wish her to suffer if there is something I can do."

"No, Meggie, we don't want her to suffer, either. That would be very nice of you." Tysen kissed his daughter. "Mary Rose and I will see you in the morning."

Meggie frowned a bit over that and cocked her head to one side in question, identical to the way her father did it. "Mary Rose, aren't you coming with me to your bedchamber? Why did we come to Papa's bedchamber at all?"

Tysen said, very carefully, "Meggie, Mary Rose is now my wife. That means that she will stay close to me, both during the day and during the night. She will be staying with me now in this bedchamber."

"But Papa, I—"

There was laughter, muted, from the doorway. Then Gweneth Fordyce came in and held out her hand to Meggie.

"Meggie, dearest, this headache of mine grows severe. Now, your new mama has to get used to your papa. That's what marriage is all about. This means that they will spend a lot of time together, get to know each other much better, talk about so many things. You are not to worry about anything, all right?"

"I suppose so," Meggie said. "Do you want to stay here with Papa, Mary Rose? Do you want to talk to him all night?"

"Yes, Meggie, I do."

Meggie raised on her tiptoes, and Tysen held her against him, kissed her forehead. "Good night, sweetheart. Mary Rose and I will see you in the morning."

And they were gone.

Tysen said, six feet away from his bride, "That wasn't terribly romantic, was it?"

Mary Rose didn't say anything at all. He saw that she was scared witless.

He was too, he thought, and quickly walked to the fireplace and built up the fire. It was chilly tonight, yet it was only the first of September and shouldn't have been.

When he turned back to her, she still hadn't moved a bit.

He walked to her, took her shoulders in his hands and said, "There is no reason for you to be afraid of all this. If you don't wish to have me with you tonight, you have but to say so."

The instant those words were out of his mouth, Tysen wanted to slit his own wrists. He waited, in agony, while she stood there, still scared to her toes, and he knew she was thinking that offer over. Then, finally, she said, "When you kissed me and held me, it was very nice, Tysen. We are married now. I suppose that we should get it done. It's expected."

"Well, yes, but that doesn't matter. No one will know one way or the other. No, it's up to you, Mary Rose. We don't know each other all that well. If you would prefer to wait—" He finally managed to get his mouth to shut up. What was wrong with him? Had he lost all control of his brain?

Very slowly, Mary Rose nodded. But she still just stood

there, her hands clasped in front of her, still wearing that very lovely gown her mother had made over for her. It was pale pink with a lot of lace at the neckline and just a straight fall of skirt to her ankles. He was surprised that the pale pink was so very nice with her bright hair.

Tysen cleared his throat, hoped he didn't sound like a man about to be felled by lust, and said, "I am very fond of you, Mary Rose. And I know you are of me as well. I know that lovemaking must seem very strange to you and—"

His precious bride waved away his words. "Yes, perhaps," she said, and took a step toward him. "Could you please kiss me?"

And so he did. Very soon, he realized that he wanted her more than he could even begin to imagine, and yet she was a virgin and he remembered Melinda Beatrice, her awful pain, her sobs that first night when he came into her, her sobs after he had come out of her, her sobs when he had wanted her again so very badly he'd nearly cried.

He shook his head. He'd been a boy, hadn't known a single thing about how to give pleasure, how to take pleasure when it was offered. Not that he knew much more now. But he had, he admitted to himself, during those first months of his marriage, listened to his brothers whenever they spoke of matters of the flesh, which wasn't a rare occurrence at all. So, he supposed, he had a good deal of theory down very well.

"Let me unfasten your gown for you. Then, if you like, I can go out into the corridor while you put on your nightgown."

She pulled her thick hair out of the way, and Tysen found that his fingers were extraordinarily nimble on all the buttons of that wretched, beautiful gown. He forced himself to step back when her white back was bare.

"There, it's done. I'm sorry I didn't think to place a

screen in here." He left her then, quickly, and paced outside the bedchamber door, up and down the corridor. He found himself drawn to the sound of a woman's quiet voice. It was Sinjun. She and Colin were speaking in their bedchamber, and the door wasn't closed.

He, a vicar, a man who would give a good lecture to any of his children were they to eavesdrop, walked closer to that cracked open doorway. He heard Sinjun say, "But Colin, Tysen was only a boy when he married Melinda Beatrice. He knew nothing. He was always so pious and proper that naturally he wouldn't know anything. He isn't at all like Douglas or Ryder or you, and never was, for that matter. I'm just concerned that—" She stalled, but Tysen already knew everything she would have said; it was crystal clear in the quiet air.

Then Colin said, "Listen to me, Sinjun. Tysen isn't a clod, nor is he a fool. He's still a Sherbrooke, and I swear to you that the Sherbrooke men are born knowing how to make love properly to a woman. Leave be. Come to bed and I will let you seduce me, if you promise to go very slowly so I will have enough time to respond to you."

Sinjun giggled. Then, "You're sure it will be all right? You don't believe you should perhaps speak to Tysen, ask him if he has any questions or perhaps wishes to discuss things? Colin, wait! What are you doing? Oh, goodness, you are an evil man."

Tysen heard his sister, his baby sister, giggle. Then he heard only silence. No, that was a very deep breath someone in that bedchamber just drew in.

Tysen quickly walked away. So he'd been born knowing how to please a woman, had he? Well, he'd never succeeded with Melinda Beatrice. But that had been so very long ago, and Sinjun was right. He'd been a boy, untried, bowled over with those rampaging feelings he couldn't control, so eager he'd nearly spilled his seed on himself.

He would simply have to trust himself. As his brother Ryder always said, "If a man can make a woman laugh, she is his."

Laughter. How the devil did a man make a woman laugh when the man couldn't think beyond those raw, very urgent surges in his groin?

He came back into the bedchamber. Mary Rose was lying in the middle of the bed, propped up on pillows, the covers to her chin. He smiled at her. He went methodically about the room, pinching out the myriad candles. When there was only a single candle lit near the huge bed, he moved away into the shadows and undressed. He pulled his nightshirt over his head. He came to a halt beside the bed.

"I'm not wearing one of your nightshirts," she said. "I think you look better in it than I do."

He pulled back the blankets and came in beside her. He said, looking down at her beloved face, "Do you know we had never even seen each other before a very short time ago?"

Mary Rose pulled her hand out from beneath the mound of blankets and lightly touched her fingers to his face. "Yes, and it both frightens me and makes me believe devoutly that God had very good plans for me. You're quite wonderful, Tysen."

Her words stirred inside him, moved him, and he said, "I don't want you to think that I married you simply because of my honor, because I want to protect you, save you from the machinations of your wretched uncle and Erickson MacPhail. I am very fond of you, Mary Rose. I am very glad that you are now my wife." He looked away from her a moment, then said, "And we are man and wife now. Or vicar and wife, if you would prefer." That was an attempt at humor, but it didn't yield anything except perhaps a tiny smile.

"I can barely see you, Tysen."

"Well, one doesn't have intimate relations in full daylight," he said, although he imagined that his brothers even had intimate relations in the gardens, beneath the oak trees. But he never had. He'd always believed that a wife was precious and should be protected from a man's lust, her modesty never to be violated. "I don't wish to shock you or embarrass you," he said, his voice austere.

"Thank you," she said, but there was something odd in her voice that he didn't understand, and he said quickly, "Please don't be frightened of me. I might not be much good at any of this, but I wish to try. I'm going to kiss you now, Mary Rose, kiss you until I've gotten all the way to that crooked toe of yours, and I will kiss it as well."

She grinned. Aha, nearly a laugh. "All right," she said, and closed her arms around his neck.

"You taste like strawberries," he said, "and your hair is as soft as my mare's mane."

She giggled when he at last touched her breast. Then she jumped. He closed his eyes a moment, wondering what to do. He knew he was in a bad way, and that surprised him, but it didn't matter. He said, "I want you to hold still, and I will try not to hurt you."

He eased her nightgown up, felt her soft flesh, and prayed fervently that she was ready for him, that he wouldn't hurt her too much. She didn't pull away, did nothing to escape him. And her kisses had been so very enthusiastic. He had to control himself. So very long, he thought, so very long since he had been with a woman, and that woman had been his first wife. He regretted that in his inexperience he might hurt Mary Rose, that he might deny her pleasure. Then he realized he could only do his best. He could, as a matter of fact, do exactly what he wanted to do, and surely that wouldn't be bad. He was a Sherbrooke male, after all.

He gritted his teeth, knowing the moment was upon him, and came inside her, pushing slowly, his blood pounding through his body, nearly splitting him apart with lust, but his determination not to hurt her was profound. He was a man, not the boy who had mauled Melinda Beatrice. He moved very slowly indeed. He stopped. "Mary Rose?"

She was looking at him, but she wasn't smiling now, ready to kiss every bit of his face, ready to let him even put his tongue in her mouth. She was scared stiff, rigid as a log beneath him.

"Yes?"

"I'm inside you. Just a bit more. You're doing very well. I can feel your maidenhead. Can you feel me feeling it?"

"Yes."

Then it was simply too much. The man and the vicar broke; he lost himself and all his good intentions. He couldn't stop himself, he pushed hard until he broke through her maidenhead and went deep. Dear God, he was touching her womb. His heart pounded, his body was more alive than he'd ever felt in his entire life. He was on the edge of a cliff, and he wanted to leap off that cliff right this very instant, but he heard her crying. "Mary Rose? Are you all right?"

"Yes, Tysen, I swear it to you. That maidenhead part was a bit difficult, but you're not moving now and it isn't too bad." She added, wonder in her voice, "I knew that a man came into a woman's body, but I just never imagined it like this."

Oh, dear God, he thought, he was so crazed with lust, so over the edge with a need that was eating him alive, that he thought he would die. It was soon over, and he'd never imagined anything like it in his life. He had died, he thought, a wonderful death. He was hanging over her, balanced on his elbows, breathing so hard, feeling his heart pounding against his chest, still beyond words, beyond any rational thought. It was wonderful, what had just happened. He'd forgotten—that, or he'd never experienced it. It was beyond wonderful.

Mary Rose wasn't moving.

He said, once he could speak coherently, his voice all stiff with guilt, "I am sorry that I hurt you. That won't happen again. Can you forgive me?"

"Yes, of course. You're my husband, and I suppose things have to happen that aren't always pleasant. I don't know, Tysen."

"I didn't make you laugh," he said, and he slowly came out of her. He lay beside her and pulled her into his arms. He realized that he'd jerked off his nightshirt and that he was naked and she could feel that he was naked. He could imagine that it would send her running from the bedchamber. "Let me put on my nightshirt," he said, but Mary Rose just shook her head against his shoulder. "No, please don't. You are so very warm, Tysen, and hard. I love the feel of you."

He nearly swallowed his tongue. A woman—his wife—had said that to him. He didn't say a thing because he simply couldn't think of anything to say. Did a man thank a woman—his wife—when she said something like that to him? He didn't know. He was, however, immensely grateful that she was still in her nightgown. That was for the best, given how her words had made him feel. It was sinful, what he was thinking, it was excessive, what he wanted to do again, and boorish and probably so pleasurable that he nearly groaned. No, it was time to sleep, time for her to ease with him, perhaps forgive him for hurting her, though she hadn't seemed upset with him.

He snuffed out the single candle, then he was lying on his back, in the dark, and he could feel her pressing against him. She was soft and warm and her breasts were against his side. Yes, God be blessed that she was wearing a nightgown. He knew he should say something. It was difficult to tell her to trust him when it came to matters of the flesh, since he was such an ignoramus and a clod, but he tried. "Trust me," he said, kissing her cheek when he missed her mouth. "Trust me."

"I would trust you with my life, Tysen," she said, her breath warm against his flesh, and he shuddered. He didn't trust himself to say anything more. He just might start begging her to let him have her again.

He held her against the length of him. He wanted to come inside her again, right now.

He remembered overhearing Douglas and Ryder talking about how a man should never be a pig, it wasn't worthy. He held himself very still, and eventually, he slept.

Mary Rose didn't sleep for a very long time. How very odd, she thought, looking off into the darkness and feeling him so very warm and alive pressed next to her. He was a man, and he had actually been inside her, and he'd touched her, he'd kissed her. It hadn't been awful. Well, not too awful. She knew he had enjoyed the business. No, for her it hadn't been too bad. She sighed. She realized then how very wet and sticky she was. She heard Tysen's breathing even out into sleep. Slowly, carefully, she eased away from him. She stripped off her nightgown and bathed herself. She was sore, muscles pulled. It was all quite strange. She grabbed up her nightgown and pulled it back over her head. It was chilly in the large bedchamber. The embers had burned themselves out.

She slipped back into bed beside him, nestling close. This part was nice, she thought, and laid her palm over his chest. Her palm wanted to go down his body, but she knew that wasn't done, that wasn't what she should want to do.

When at last she fell asleep, she felt optimistic. Tysen cared about her. He'd been sorry to hurt her, but she wondered if he truly had been all that sorry. She'd seen something in those beautiful eyes of his, something hot and pleased even as he'd been apologizing so sincerely. But how could she begin to understand him? He was, after all, a man, and she simply couldn't grasp what they were all about. She wondered if any woman grasped anything about the thoughts of a man.

21

Dawn was turning the bedchamber a soft, vague gray. Tysen awoke, instantly alert, instantly aware of the wonderful soft and giving body beside him. He then realized it was freezing. He didn't want Mary Rose to be cold when she awoke. He eased away from that wonderfully warm body and rose to light the fire. He was shivering when he returned to bed. He warmed himself, then came onto his side over her. "Mary Rose," he said, and just saying her name made him as hard as the black basalt rocks below the castle. He was more than warm now, he was burning up, and it was from the inside out. He was roaring with heat, like a furnace that was being stoked so fast it was in danger of exploding.

He didn't wait for her to stir. He began kissing her. Her flesh was flushed and warm, and he could see her lovely face now, pale and calm in sleep, her glorious red hair wild about her head. He realized that she was wearing his nightshirt and wondered how that had happened, but it didn't matter, of course. He had that nightshirt off her in under two seconds. She wasn't fighting him. She wasn't stuttering with fear, wasn't trying to stop him at all. She even lifted her hips for him to get the nightshirt off her.

When she was naked and he'd hauled her up tightly against him, he felt all of her, every small bit of her. He moaned into her mouth when he realized that she was kissing him back. He felt so very urgent, nearly frantic in his need, that he simply didn't think about it being daylight in the room, that he would shock her, that she knew he could see her body and she would be mortified.

Mary Rose was kissing him back, wildly now, and when he said against her mouth, "Open, I want to taste you," she did, and he was shuddering with the power of it. When he kissed her breasts, his hands all over her, she made little mewling sounds, and they nearly drove him over the edge, those sounds and her mouth and her hands, now stroking his belly. He tried to arch up so she could touch him. When she did, he nearly became a pig. It was a very close thing. He pulled away from her, heaving from the effort, and then everything suddenly was very clear to him. He wanted to kiss her everywhere, something he'd never done before, something that hadn't really occurred to him before, but now he wanted it more than anything in the entire world. It seemed utterly natural, something he had to do if he wished to keep breathing. He came down her body, kissing and kneading her belly, then his hot breath was lower, and his mouth was on her and his tongue as well, hot and wild.

Mary Rose froze for a moment at what he was doing to her, but not longer than a moment. "Oh, my," she said and pressed herself against his mouth and felt his fingers, stroking over her, easing inside her. "Tysen," she said, nearly on a yell, then realized something incredible was happening to her. She lurched up, grabbed fistfuls of his hair, and screamed.

Then she fell back against the pillow, saying his name over and over, begging him not to stop, never stop, please, please. On and on it went, with her wild beneath him, and

Tysen felt her frantic pleasure washing over him, coming deep inside him, and it shook him to his core. Never had he felt anything like this in his entire life. Slowly, he lessened his pressure, it just seemed the natural thing to do, and when he felt her ease, he raised his head and looked up her body. He could see her clearly in the morning light pouring through the windows. Her face was flushed, her lips parted, and she was staring at him, but her eyes were vague and soft, and she said, "Oh, goodness." And then she held out her arms to him.

He'd never moved so fast in his life. He said as he came over her, "I hope you like this as well," and he was inside her, deep and moving hard and fast. This time there was no doubt at all in Tysen's mind that he was going to die. And it didn't matter. He was ready to leave this earth. When he raised his head, arched his back, and yelled to the ceiling, she held him very close, and he felt her breath on his chest, and she was kissing his chest as well, her hands stroking everywhere, even between their bodies on his belly.

He fell flat on top of her, his head beside hers on the pillow. He felt her hands slow now, lightly stroking down his back, and every once in a while she kissed his ear, his neck, any part of him she could reach.

She said against his ear, "That was a very incredible thing, Tysen. I had no idea that being married could mean having feelings like that."

He hadn't either. He was floored. He thought of his brothers, who were worldly men and enjoyed making love to women immensely. They'd never been at all shy about speaking about such things. He'd always believed it was a sin, perhaps a sin of overindulgence, what his brothers did with great regularity, perhaps even a sin that they enjoyed their wives so very much. He'd felt superior to them, felt that they hadn't achieved his ability to rely on his intellect, to let his spirit and his mind control his body. It had to be a sin, for didn't it make a man forget himself, forget who and what he was, forget what was important in life and what wasn't?

Had he truly been such a pompous idiot? Such an obnoxious prig? He grew hard inside her again, and he couldn't help it, he started laughing. He laughed because for the first time in his thirty-one years, he finally knew the incredible joy of being a man and having a woman enjoy him as much as he did her.

He managed, finally, to bring himself up just a bit, and he kissed her mouth. "Mary Rose," he said between light, nipping kisses, "can you feel me inside you?" He started moving slowly, easily, and the pleasure made him want to shout and sing, perhaps even dance.

"Yes," she said, leaned up and kissed his shoulder and moved beneath him. "Yes, I can. It is a wondrous feeling, Tysen. Thank you for showing me what was what."

He saw their two bodies together, and he realized that it was the first time in his life that he had ever had a woman's body pressed against his. "Are you sore?"

"Yes, but it doesn't matter. I rather like this, Tysen."

And he laughed again and kissed her, still laughing, and then he wanted very much to touch her again, to feel her tense and go wild when she gained her climax, and it just happened. He slid his hand between them and found her and watched her eyes go vacant. He was, he thought, a man who was very happy. Surely that wasn't bad, a husband who enjoyed his wife. Surely.

There was a knock on the door.

Tysen opened an eye but didn't move. He said, "I don't care what is going on, even if Erickson MacPhail is back intending to steal you away again, I don't want to move. Don't you move, either. You've got to be safe from him since you're lying beneath me."

She laughed, squeezed him hard, and called out, "Who is it?"

"It's Meggie."

Tysen opened an eye. "I have a daughter. I also have two sons. At the moment I can't remember their names." He smiled a bit at that. "At least Meggie knocked."

They'd just managed to pull apart when the door opened and Meggie stuck her head in. "Good morning. It is nearly eight o'clock, you know. Shall I bring you breakfast, Papa? Mary Rose, are you all right? Are you still talking to Papa? Telling him things? Do you still like Papa?"

Tysen sighed deeply and said, "She adores me, Meggie, and yes, we would love some breakfast."

"Yes, Meggie, I still like your papa."

The door closed and Tysen turned to face her. He pulled her hard against him, felt her breasts, her belly, the length of her smooth legs. "So what do you think of being married to me so far?"

"I lied to Meggie," she said, and pushed back the covers. "I more than like her papa. Being married to you so far is splendid. I had never in my life imagined feeling such things." She started to get out of bed, remembered that she was naked, and stopped cold. She turned quickly to see her new husband, the covers at his ankles, also quite naked, and he was staring at her as if he didn't know what to do either.

She didn't move, just kept staring. He didn't move either, and he also just kept staring. She swallowed, and her hand fluttered, then fell back to the sheet. "Tysen, we are unclothed."

She was staring at him, not at his face but at his sex, and he felt pinned. It was the first time a woman had ever seen him naked, and this woman seemed to be very interested in him. Melinda Beatrice had always averted her eyes whenever he'd chanced, by accident, to be naked with her anywhere near. "Mary Rose?"

"You are a beautiful man, Tysen," she said, and stood. She started to cross her arms over her breasts, then, almost defiantly, she dropped her arms back to her sides. "I suppose it is ridiculous for me to be embarrassed, since you saw me while I was so ill."

"That's right," he heard himself say, as if from a great distance, and then he took his own turn looking at her. "It's different now, though," he said. "You see, now you're smiling at me, and you're moving about and you are very alive and warm and your face is a bit flushed and your hair is incredible, Mary Rose."

She squeaked and dashed to pick up her nightgown from the floor near the washbasin. She pulled it over her head, then chanced to look at the basin. "Tysen, oh, my God."

Her voice was a thin, wispy sound that had him out of bed in a flash. "What's wrong?"

He was at her side in a minute.

She could only point to the bloody water in the basin.

"It's from your maidenhead," he said, vastly relieved. "It's nothing to worry about, I promise you."

She turned then, looked him up and down, mainly down, her look very interested, and he flushed, couldn't seem to help himself. He reached for her and pulled her close, both, he supposed, to preserve his modesty and because in truth he wanted her against him again. He breathed in the scent of her, the light rose smell of her hair, the smell of himself, and the smell of sex.

"Do you forgive me now, Mary Rose?"

She pulled back slightly, looking up at him, feeling him against her, and she couldn't quite comprehend what had happened. "Oh, yes. I think you are the finest husband in the world." She pulled back more and looked down at him. "And the most beautiful. A man—you are so very different from me. I think you are incredible, Tysen." And she reached down and touched him. He moaned and jerked, but he didn't pull away, just kept holding her against him, wishing she would touch him again, and knowing it was best if she didn't.

He didn't say a thing. He couldn't think of a thing to say, in any case. She thought he was beautiful? That male part of him? He held her even more tightly. He was hard, and he didn't know what to do about it.

Luckily for him, there was a knock on the door. He slowly separated from her, sighed, and fetched his own dressing gown.

"You have a letter from Douglas," Sinjun called out when Tysen and Mary Rose, holding hands now, both smiling like loons and trying not to look self-conscious, came down the front staircase.

Colin came through the front door, windblown, wearing only black knit breeches and a flowing white shirt, and grinned at the two of them. "Good morning. I trust both of you are quite well?"

Mary Rose said, "Oh, yes, Colin. Everything is quite excellent." She blushed, turned nearly as red as her hair. Tysen, without thought, leaned over and kissed her cheek. He thought she looked luminous, the morning light stark on her face, her green eyes bright, her mouth laughing. He was a married man, he realized at that instant, and she was his wife, and he decided he was quite pleased about it.

He had become Lord Barthwick, come to Scotland, and gotten himself a bride. God's plan was as yet unclear to him, but given that Mary Rose was now his, it had to be a good plan.

"Hmmm," said Colin, and after eyeing the two of them

a bit longer, he turned and gave his wife a wicked look. "I am not at all surprised," he remarked to the entrance hall at large, which included Pouder, napping in his chair by the front door. "After all, Tysen is a Sherbrooke."

"Be quiet, Colin," Tysen said pleasantly as he took the letter from Sinjun and began to read it. "You're embarrassing my wife." How strange it was to say that word aloud. He continued reading, then raised his head and said, "Douglas is rather irritated with me, but he says it won't last because Oliver is so excited about learning the management of Kildrummy Castle, and thus what can Douglas do? Oliver is on his way to Scotland. He should be here quite soon. Douglas said he was so eager that he was throwing his clothes into his valise so he could be gone. He says also that I am now in his debt."

That very afternoon, Oliver arrived, all his luggage with him, a big smile on his face, and an enthusiastic yell at the sight of Kildrummy Castle.

"Oh, Reverend Tysen," Oliver said, pumping his hand up and down. "It is more than I deserve. Oh, my, now you're Lord Barthwick. You're my lord now. And you are Mr. MacNeily, sir? You will assist me, sir? You will not leave until I know enough not to bankrupt this beautiful place?"

"I will not leave," Miles MacNeily said, laughing as he looked closely at this very young man, "until I am convinced that you will raise Kildrummy Castle and its lands and tenants to new heights."

When Oliver met Mary Rose, Reverend Sherbrooke's bride, he simply stopped cold and stared at her.

"Oliver," Tysen asked, "are you all right?"

"It's that you're married, sir—my lord—and I simply hadn't ever thought of you with a woman, that is, she is your wife and—"

"It is a pleasure to meet you, Oliver," Mary Rose said, and shook the young man's hand.

"It is time," Tysen said to Mary Rose. She knew it was, and yet she was afraid, afraid of what she would learn.

Mr. MacCray had left earlier, Colin and Sinjun were riding, Meggie was helping Pouder arrange Tysen's cravats in his bedchamber, Mrs. Golden was preparing their dinner, the new maid was washing their clothes, and Oliver and Miles MacNeily were ensconced in the library, surrounded with ledgers.

"I asked your mother to meet with us," he said. He paused, then added, squeezing her hand, "She knows it is time that you're told, Mary Rose."

To their surprise, Miles MacNeily was not with Oliver in the library. He was with Gweneth Fordyce in the drawing room. He rose slowly when Tysen and Mary Rose came into the room.

Tysen didn't say a word, just stood quietly, waiting.

Mary Rose looked from her mother to Miles MacNeily and said, "Sir, are you my father?"

He smiled at her and said, "I wish that I were, my dear, but I didn't come to Kildrummy Castle until you were nearly ten years old. For the rest of it, however, your dear mother has agreed to marry me."

Mary Rose weaved a bit where she stood. She felt Tysen cup her elbow, holding her steady. "I don't understand. You have always been very kind to me, sir. Is this why? You have always loved my mother?"

"Yes, I have loved your mother for a very long time. However, I could not afford to make her my wife until recently, when I inherited property and money from my mother. You see, if she had married me, we would have been forced to live here at Kildrummy since there were no cottages available." He paused a moment and smiled down at Mary Rose's mother. He said now, "As for you, Mary Rose, I saw you, your beautiful red hair flying around your little face, all skinny, your slipper hanging off your left foot, and you gave me this big smile, and I fell in love. You also had the most beautiful teeth. No, my dear, I love you for yourself. Do you mind? Can I now be your stepfather?"

Mary Rose turned to her mother, who'd said nothing, just sat on the settee, gowned in lovely light-blue muslin, looking both pale and worried and quite happy. "Mama?"

"Yes, my darling, I would very much like to marry Miles." She drew a deep breath, rose slowly. "You see, he could love me because he was the only one to whom I was never a madwoman. It has been a long time, for both of us. But now you are settled and it is time."

Tysen said, "I congratulate both of you. Mary Rose, what do you think about this?"

"I just don't know. So many things have happened. I thought Mama would come with us back to England, that I wouldn't be alone in a foreign country, that—"

"Oh, dearest," Gweneth said, her hands outstretched, walking quickly to her daughter. "We can wait if you wish. I will accompany you and your husband back to England."

Mary Rose was shaking her head. "No, Mama, that was very selfish of me. I am so very happy being married to Tysen that I cannot imagine you not having that happiness as well." But as she said those words, Mary Rose thought of her mother and Miles MacNeily in bed together, their clothes on the floor, pressed together like she and Tysen had been last night, Tysen's mouth all over her, and she simply couldn't imagine such a thing. She stared at the toes of her slippers. "Oh, goodness," she whispered.

Tysen said, "Excellent. We have need of some champagne." He paused then and said, "May we end it here, ma'am? It really is time, you know. Time for Mary Rose to learn about her father, to learn about the trust he left for her."

"Yes," Gweneth said, "it is past time. It's just that there is tragedy as well, Mary Rose, and it will hurt you to know."

"How can learning who my father was be a tragedy?"

"Because your father was Ian's grandfather."

Tysen could only stare at Gweneth Fordyce. "You're saying that Old Tyronne was Mary Rose's father? That he left her money?"

"Yes," Gweneth said. "He was past sixty when I met him. His wife had died, and he was desperate to have more heirs waiting in the wings. It had become an obsession with him.

"I had come to visit my sister and her new husband. I met Tyronne. I was fascinated by him." Her hands fluttered a bit, and she turned away from all of them to walk to the large row of windows. "I'll never forget that he told me he wanted sons, he had to have more sons, that life was too uncertain, too fragile, even with the male heirs he had at that time. Five males, I believe."

She turned then, splaying her fingers, as if beseeching her daughter to understand. "I was intimate with him, Mary Rose, and you were the result. He refused to marry me until he knew if you would be a boy. You weren't, and so he said that he had to find another woman to birth him another boy child.

"He told me about the trust he would set up for you in Edinburgh. The only requirement was that his identity as your father had to remain a secret. I hated him. I wanted to kill him. But I kept silent because he'd promised to provide very well for you. He said that I could never tell you that he was your father or he wouldn't keep the money there for you. I suppose he didn't want you hanging about all his heirs.

"I had nothing at all. I moved in with my sister and Sir Lyon and very shortly thereafter began my madness. It was Sir Lyon, you see. He wanted me. It was the only way I could discover to keep him at bay."

"Mama," Mary Rose said, barely above a whisper, "I am so very sorry."

"No, wait, that isn't all of it, dearest. There is Ian, Tyronne's last heir. As you know, Tyronne never married again. There were so many boys—sons, grandsons, nephews, cousins—but slowly, each of them died. Until there was only Ian, and he wanted to marry you, Mary Rose. But, naturally, he couldn't. You were his grandfather's daughter."

"Ian died," Mary Rose said. "He got drunk and fell over that cliff."

"Perhaps," Gweneth said. "But I know that Tyronne told him that very same day who you were, that he was your father. And then Ian was dead. It was all over."

Mary Rose couldn't, wouldn't, believe it. "No, I will never believe that Ian killed himself."

"I don't know. I pray that he didn't."

Without another word, Mary Rose turned and walked to her husband. Tysen opened his arms and drew her close. He said nothing, merely held her, resting his cheek against her hair. Finally he said, "Is that all of it, ma'am?"

"Yes. I do not know the amount Tyronne left in trust for her. It is probably a vast amount. He more than hinted that it was. I do have the name of the old gentleman, the only person in the whole world, who knew what had happened. I will give it to you now. It is your right."

22

September 15, 1815

TYSEN AND MARY Rose left the bedside of Mr. Mortimer Palmer, solicitor, a very old man who was propped up in bed, all wrapped up in woolen scarves. He'd given Mary Rose a thick envelope, then blessed her in the manner of a Catholic cardinal and proceeded to cough until Tysen feared he would fall out of his bed with the effort. He was frankly relieved that Mr. Palmer had survived their visit. He wondered what would have happened to Mary Rose's envelope if Mr. Palmer had died before she'd come.

They were walking back to Abbotsford Crescent to Sinjun and Colin's town house, enjoying the warm, sunny weather, breathing in the smells of Edinburgh. Tysen was listening to all the lilting English that he scarcely understood, looking over his shoulder every once in a while at the castle, high and stark on the hill in the middle of Edinburgh. Mary Rose was walking beside him, her brow furrowed, silent and thoughtful, clutching that envelope to her bosom.

"You may as well open it now, Mary Rose," he said after a while, smiling down at her. "Don't worry so. It will be all right." He led her into a small park and motioned her to a small bench.

"I'm afraid," she said, looking at him, then at that fat envelope clutched in her hand as if it were a snake poised to bite her. Finally, after more hesitation, she thrust it into his hands. "Please, Tysen," she said, "you read it."

Tysen opened it. There was a single sheet of paper wrapped around another smaller, very thick envelope. He opened the single sheet of foolscap first and read aloud:

My dear daughter:

I am dead and you are either twenty-five or married, and thus are reading this, my letter to you. Your mother was a beautiful woman and I was hopeful she would breed me a son and another heir, but she did not. She birthed you, a female. I prayed and prayed for a son, but God didn't heed me. No, you are not a son and that is a pity. This is why I couldn't marry her. She hadn't proved true. But you are here now and what am I to do? Because I am an honorable man, I am providing you with a dowry.

Your father,
Tyronne, Lord Barthwick

Tysen wadded the single sheet of foolscap in his fist and shook it northward, toward Kildrummy Castle. Then he got hold of himself. He read the letter again, to himself this time, and he laughed, an honest laugh. He said, "What a pathetic old curmudgeon. He believed it was a pity that you weren't a son? Thank God you're weren't, else we wouldn't be here together, you still looking all battered down. Listen to me. Old Tyronne had a full measure of cruelty, not to mention he was more obsessed with begetting heirs than the devil is with stealing souls. The old buzzard also enjoyed a full measure of arrogance. Actually, he was a dreadful man, Mary Rose." He waved the envelope again. "You will not let this hurt you. The old man's mind was long gone when he wrote this drivel."

She cocked her head at him in a way that he found very appealing. She laid her hand lightly on his forearm. "It's all right, Tysen, truly. I remember him when I was growing up, and he was always strange. Because I was a girl, I suppose, he didn't pay me any attention. At that time I just accepted it, didn't really think anything about it. I remember clearly Ian telling me that every evening at dinner, whatever male children were present, he questioned each one of them to determine his state of health. Ian was always laughing about it, said he and his cousins would make up strange symptoms just to watch Old Tyronne turn pale and wring his hands and talk about the dread diseases that the symptoms could be." She stopped talking then and grew very still. "He was rather pathetic, wasn't he?"

"Yes, he was. I'm glad he was never in your life, at least as a parent. He wouldn't have given you much of anything, Mary Rose."

"I know. It was better just seeing him from a distance, hearing the bizarre stories about him. At least he was interesting—as an eccentric."

Tysen handed her the smaller sealed envelope. It was thick, very thick indeed. Slowly, Mary Rose opened it. It was so old, it shredded in her hands and out spilled pound notes, scattering like snowflakes. They gathered up the notes and counted them.

Then they both burst into laughter.

Tyronne, Lord Barthwick, had left exactly one hundred pounds for his daughter's dowry, all in one-pound notes.

"It was amazing," Mary Rose said later to Sinjun, Colin, and Meggie, who was standing beside her father. "Once we stopped laughing, we realized what a very fine jest it was. What if I had married Erickson MacPhail? He believed I was rich, and here he went to all that trouble to try to snare me, and as it turns out, Old Tyronne left me only one hundred pounds."

"Will you tell your mother about this?" Colin asked.

"No," Tysen said. "Mary Rose doesn't want anyone to know what the old curmudgeon did." He gave her a big grin. "She decided to let Erickson always wonder how wealthy he would have been had he coerced her into marrying him. Now he will marry Donnatella and be miserable with her five thousand pounds. I wonder what his dear mother will have to say about it?"

"I doubt she will say very much," Mary Rose said. "Donnatella is a force to be reckoned with. Erickson's mother wouldn't have a chance against Donnatella. As for Uncle Lyon, I suppose he will simply have to economize. None of them will like that very much."

"Sir Lyon will probably immediately marry Donnatella off to Erickson," Tysen said. "Ah, Mary Rose, you have made your mark," he continued to his bride. "You leave a mother who is quite content now with Miles MacNeily, a good man who will take good care of her, and a suitor who is gnawing on his knuckles and will always think of you as the pigeon who escaped him." He touched his palm to her cheek. "And now it's time for you to make your mark in that foreign land where you will come to live."

Mary Rose sighed and lightly rubbed her cheek against his palm. "Meggie told me that a wife must cleave to her husband, that she must follow her husband, even into a snake pit."

Meggie said, "I assured her, Papa, that there were only a few snakes near where we live."

Eden Hill House
Glenclose-on-Rowan
Southern England

"Who are you?"

Mary Rose had just wandered around the side of the vicarage. She looked about and saw a lanky young boy standing on his head just behind a hedge close to the front door of the vicarage.

"Isn't that awfully hard to do?" she asked, coming down to her knees beside him. This, she realized, must be Leo, the athletic boy who loved horses, couldn't spit out a single word of Latin, had the sunny disposition of his uncle Ryder, and drove his sister quite mad with his pranks. Tysen and Meggie had told her that both boys were staying with their aunt and uncle at Northcliffe Hall.

"No," he said, "it simply requires a very sturdy head. Papa says I have a head made for being stood upon."

"I'm Mary Rose."

"I'm Leo. Are you here to see Papa? He's the vicar, you know. He's in Scotland being a new lord, and I don't know when he will return."

"Well, to be perfectly blunt about this—"

"Leo, come up to your feet, if you please."

"Papa!" Leo gracefully flipped over frontward, ended up on his feet, whipped about, and flung himself into his father's arms. "We didn't know—Max tried to wager that you would be here by next Sunday, but I only have three shillings left and I can't afford to lose them too. I know he cheats, Papa, I just can't prove it."

"I'm home, and I'm glad you didn't lose your three shillings," Tysen said, and Mary Rose saw him hug the boy tightly to him, briefly closing his eyes as he held him. He held him at arm's length then, studying his face, and said slowly, turning a bit toward her, "It's very good to see you, Leo. What are you doing here? You're tanned and look repellently healthy. Ah, I see you have met Mary Rose?"

Leo turned to look at her. "She told me her name, but that's all. I hope she isn't a governess, Papa. Max would make her want to clout him, since he brags he already knows everything. But she doesn't sound all proper and educated like a governess should. She talks funny. Perhaps she is a new maid? Oh, yes, Uncle Douglas lets us visit home while Max is having his lessons with Mr. Harbottle."

Tysen said mildly, still holding his boy, loath to let him go, "I'll write immediately to your uncle and tell him I'm home and have decided to let you stay here with me. Now, Mary Rose knows more Latin than Max does. What do you think of that?"

Leo really looked at her now, up and down, several times. She was wearing one of her old gowns, a pale gray muslin with no particular style, and now she wished she'd worn one of her two new gowns that Sinjun had had made for her in Edinburgh. "I didn't know that girls could speak anything but English. Mr. Harbottle says that's why he doesn't tutor girls, they just can't learn. Max told him about Meggie, how she can out-argue even him, but Mr. Harbottle wouldn't believe him." He frowned at her now. "You really do talk funny."

Mary Rose said, thickening her accent a bit for his benefit, "It's Scottish, and Mr. Harbottle sounds quite anti-quated."

"Meggie says he's an old dimwit and doesn't know a bean from a strawberry. You're really from Scotland? Papa brought you back from Kildrummy Castle?"

"Yes."

"Leo," Tysen said, squeezing the boy's arms, "Mary Rose is my wife and your new mother."

Leo became very still. Slowly, he turned and stared at her with new eyes, eyes that didn't appreciate what they were seeing. A mother? He scratched his head. "Papa, I haven't had a mother for years. I don't think we really have use for one. No, Papa, I don't need a mother. None of us does. Besides, how can she be my mother when I don't even know her?"

"Shut your trap, Leo!" It was Meggie, and she was scurrying around the side of the vicarage. She came to a stop not six inches from her brother's nose. "I didn't know you were here or I never would have let Mary Rose leave me and wander about by herself. Listen to me, codbrain, I know her, and I will tell you right now that she is exactly what we want." She added, her voice quite vicious, "Don't even think about torturing her, Leo, or I will hurt you very badly."

"Well, that's a good start," Mary Rose said, laughing. She sounded more dazed than amused, and Tysen couldn't blame her. He said to Leo, "I'll hurt you too, Leo. Just get to know her. I think you'll find she's very nice. Now, is Max back yet from his lessons with Mr. Harbottle?"

Leo, sticking very close to his father, looked up at him, frowning, and said slowly, "That was funny, Papa. Are you all right?"

"Why, yes, of course."

"Well, Max is with Mr. Pritchart. I believe they are arguing a theological point, in Latin, naturally." Leo said to Mary Rose, "Mr. Pritchart is Papa's curate. He's the one who takes us back to Northcliffe Hall after Max's lessons. Mr. Pritchart is even older than Papa but he doesn't yet have a wife. Maybe you could marry him instead of Papa."

"Once married," Tysen said, "it's forever. Mr. Pritchart will have to find his own wife."

"Can you argue in Latin?" Leo said to Mary Rose. He was now plastered against Tysen's side.

"I don't believe I have ever enjoyed an occasion where this was possible," Mary Rose said. "Perhaps Max will show me how it's done."

"Your hair's red," Leo said.

"Leo," Meggie said, her eyes narrowed, "you will carefully guard what comes out of your mouth. It's a pity you didn't receive my letter telling you all about Mary Rose. You could have practiced holding your tongue."

"I didn't say anything vicious," Leo said.

"Yes," Mary Rose said, "very red. Do you like red hair, Leo?"

"My aunt Alex has red hair. Yours is even redder. Your hair is all thick and curly just like hers. My uncle Douglas—he's Papa's brother and the earl—evidently he really likes red hair. He's always playing with Aunt Alex's hair. I saw him rub her hair against his face once and then he licked it. I thought that was revolting."

Mary Rose very nearly burst into laughter, but held herself together in time. What had she expected? Little boys who would take one look at her and vow to love her to distraction?

She blinked at her husband, a child on either side of him now, facing her, and she was standing there, alone, beside the vicarage that was now where she would live forever.

"Papa's different," Leo said slowly, eyeing him again.

"He's funny and he hasn't stopped smiling. He didn't even say anything when I talked about the three shilling wager with Max."

"Papa's just the same," Meggie said. "Just shut up, Leo." She frowned at her brother until she was sure he would remain quiet. Then she did a little skip over to Mary Rose, hugged her, and said, "What do you think of your new home? Isn't it lovely? All this peach brick and the ivy, so much ivy. Papa's said he fears the ivy will creep into his bed and wrap him up and then Monroe and Ellis won't be able to knead him. But it's pretty inside, and large enough for all of us, you'll see, Mary Rose. Well, to be honest, the drawing room is very dark, but I expect that you can order all the draperies burned."

"There is a lot of ivy," Mary Rose said. "It is lovely. Should I really burn the draperies?"

"Actually, yes," Tysen said. "I've just never thought to do it."

"That's because you're a gentleman, Papa, and gentlemen aren't capable of seeing things in their homes that need to be done."

Tysen grinned down at his daughter. "I swear to you, Meggie, I will look at things differently now that Mary Rose is here. Let's go inside," he added to Mary Rose, taking her hand. "You need to meet Mrs. Priddie, she's our cook and housekeeper. We have two maids who come in daily, Belinda and Tootsie, and Marigold, the tweeny. There is Malcolm who sees to the stables, you already met him." He paused a moment, then said on a smile, "I trust you will find Mrs. Priddie more acceptable than Mrs. MacFardle."

"Oh, there's also Monroe and Ellis," Meggie said. "They love Papa. And since you sleep with Papa so you can talk all night, Monroe and Ellis will probably be right there too, climbing all over you and purring."

"Ellis just spit up a big fur ball," Leo said. "Mrs. Priddie yelled at him and tried to whack him with the broom, but he was too fast for her."

"Ellis," Tysen said, and he smiled at her, thinking that smiling was something very natural now, "undoubtedly has racing blood. He's long and lean and so fast he's sometimes a blur."

"But he's lazy most of the time," Leo said. "I try to get him to play with a ball and he puts up his tail and walks away. Papa, you're still smiling."

"Leave Papa alone, Leo," Meggie said. "Now, the reason Ellis leaves is because you're boring. Accustom yourself to it."

"Well, at least I wasn't walking around with my drawers showing and—"

"Do you want me to kill you again, you little crabhead?"

"You'll never catch me!"

And they were off, Meggie chasing Leo, out of sight into the vicarage garden. Tysen just shook his head. "She won't hurt him badly," he said, and realized he was still grinning widely. It felt very good.

After meeting Tootsie, Belinda, and Marigold who giggled and gaped at her, and Mrs. Priddie, who was full of stiff civility, Mary Rose briefly toured all the downstairs vicarage rooms. Thirty minutes later, Tysen was trapped by a Mrs. Flavobonne, who insisted only the vicar would do, and Mary Rose went upstairs with Mrs. Priddie. When Mary Rose was finally standing in the middle of her new bedchamber with its adjoining door to Tysen's room, she heard Meggie outside her window, in the vicarage gardens below. Mrs. Priddie excused herself, said she had to rescue Reverend Sherbrooke from that oily Mrs. Flavobonne, and left her alone. Mary Rose walked closer to the window and looked down.

"You just batten down your hatch, Leo," Meggie said, and then she poked her finger against his chest, hard, and pushed him back into a mess of the infamous ivy.

"But he just found her in Scotland, Meggie. We don't need another mother. Everything is just fine the way it is. I don't want her here. She doesn't belong here. She's a foreigner and a girl. Why do you?"

"I'm a girl, goat face, and I belong here. Half the people around are girls. Get used to it." Meggie poked him hard again, and he landed on his bottom in a rosebush. He hollered and jumped up. "A thorn got me in my left cheek. Just because I don't like her, you don't have to kill me, Meggie. You just got home. You should be happy to see me."

"Not if you're still a moron," Meggie said, then frowned. "You've grown. It's been only a month and you've gotten bigger than I've gotten. But I can still break your legs, so don't you forget it."

Leo said, "I'm going to be as big as Papa. Maybe by next month. By Christmas, for sure. You won't be able to beat me up for much longer."

"I will always be able to beat you up," Meggie said, hands on her hips, "because I'm going to be bigger than even Papa. Now, don't you dare say anything bad about Mary Rose to Max when he gets back from Mr. Pritchert's house, do you hear me?"

"Mary Rose—that's a silly name. It sounds all spongy and soft, like she doesn't have a backbone. Why did Papa marry her? He didn't do it to get us a mother, because we don't need or want one. It's not like we've asked him to get us one. Why?"

"Papa married Mary Rose because there was this awful man who tried to steal her away to make her marry him, and she didn't want to."

"Oh," Leo said, rubbing his bottom where the thorn had stuck into him. "Well, all right then, I can understand that.

He married her because he's so bloody honorable and he felt sorry for her. It's a good thing a man can only have one wife, otherwise Papa would have married a good dozen ladies by now, all because he felt sorry for them and rescued them from something or other. But you know, Meggie, he's laughing. He's saying funny things. It sounds very strange. What happened?"

"He's happy. Perhaps he has changed a bit. Hmmm. Well, he does laugh a lot now. I like it."

"Yes, I suppose I do too," Leo said.

"Oh, dear." Mary Rose backed away from the window. "Oh, dear," she said again to the empty bedchamber that was horrible. Well, she'd eavesdropped. What did Leo mean that Tysen had changed? Of course he laughed and grinned and said funny things. It was the way he was.

She walked to the middle of the room and just stood there for a moment. She'd deserved what she'd heard. Leo was a little boy. It would take a while for him to get used to her. She looked around her then. She didn't want to spend another minute in this dismal place. It had been Melinda Beatrice's bedchamber Mrs. Priddie had told her. It hadn't been touched since the mistress had passed on some six years before. Didn't Mrs. Sherbrooke think it simply lovely?

Mary Rose wanted to puke, a word she'd never really even thought before, but it fit this particular circumstance. She would end up on her knees over the chamber pot if she had to stay in here. It was perfectly dreadful, not that it was ugly or anything like that, it was the feel of it, the way the air smelled, the way it was creeping in on her, closing her in. She was an idiot. This was ridiculous. It was just, simply, that the room wasn't hers.

She was standing in the center of the room, not moving, wondering what to do when the door opened and Tysen came in. He didn't even ask her what the matter was, just said without hesitation, "I don't wish you to be in here. I have never cared for this room. My bedchamber is quite large enough for both of us. Why don't we have this room redone into a sitting room? If that doesn't work, we can lock the boys in here for punishment?"

She ran to him and threw her arms around his back. Mrs. Priddie harrumphed behind Tysen. She said quite clearly, "You dealt with Mrs. Flavobonne very quickly, Reverend Sherbrooke, perhaps too quickly. This is the home of a man of God. It is a vicarage. If you were yourself, Reverend Sherbrooke, there would be no matters of the flesh. You would be above that. This isn't what I'm used to, sir."

"But I'm no longer just myself, Mrs. Priddie. I'm now married." And, he thought, a smile blazing, he wasn't above much of anything, particularly when it came to Mary Rose and where he touched her. Tysen very slowly dropped his arms. He turned to Mrs. Priddie. "Let's show Mary Rose her new bedchamber."

Mrs. Priddie harrumphed again. Both cats—Ellis, so long and skinny that he seemed to be wrapped around fat Monroe, with his yellow eyes and fur blacker than a sinner's dreams—were on top of Tysen's bed. Ellis cracked an eye open, saw Tysen, and yowled once, then twice, unwound himself from Monroe and leapt. Tysen, used to this, caught the cat in mid-flight and simply brought him to his shoulder. "Have you been a saintly cat, Ellis?"

The cat was purring so loudly that Mary Rose, who had never before heard the like, just stood there staring at him.

"He stole a pork chop right off the kitchen table, Reverend Sherbrooke."

"Well yes, Mrs. Priddie, he is fast, isn't he?" He rubbed the cat's stomach, hugged him, then finally set him back down beside Monroe, who was just looking at everyone, not even twitching a whisker.

"Monroe doesn't do much," Tysen said, and petted the cat in long strokes down its back. The cat stretched out, and Tysen continued to pat him until Ellis, jealous, swatted at Tysen's hand.

"Just wait until we're in bed with them," he said to Mary Rose, and Mrs. Priddie harrumphed yet again.

"I can't wait," Mary Rose said, and Ellis looked at her, then stretched his neck toward her. She gave him a light pat. Ellis jumped back onto Tysen's shoulder.

23

Antiquis temporibus, nati tibi similes in rupibus
ventosissimis exponebantur ad necem.
In the good old days, children like you were
left to perish on windswept crags.

MAX SHERBROOKE, STANDING straight and tall, his
shoulders back, said firmly, "Girls do not speak Latin."

"This girl does," Mary Rose said easily.

"Even if a girl were able to repeat the words, she would
have no comprehension of what she was saying."

Mary Rose raised an eyebrow at that pompous pro-
nouncement from a boy who had blue eyes—Sherbrooke
blue eyes—just like his father's and Sinjun's and Leo's
and Meggie's, and a very stubborn chin. The boy would
break hearts when he grew into manhood. She stroked her
fingers over her chin. "Hmmm. Do I perhaps hear the
antiquated Mr. Harbottle speaking?"

"Certainly not," Max said, frowning just a bit, "although he does not hesitate, even on good days, to point
out the weakness of the female sex."

"Why do you have such a low opinion of the female brain, Max?"

"Yes," Tysen said pleasantly, coming into the very dark drawing room with its soon-to-be burned draperies, "tell us where you got this asinine notion."

"You said—" Max, pinned by his father's stare, managed to squirm just a bit. "Well, perhaps it isn't precisely what you said, sir, but I've never believed that you thought any girl, with the exception of Meggie, of course—"

"Of course."

"Well, that any girl could do much of anything except have babies and—"

"Yes, you're quite right, Max. I've never said anything so absurd, or believed such a thing either. Now, you'd best just stop right where you are. If you were to continue, I fear that your new mother would shoot you."

Max was staring hard at his father. "Leo said something about how you were different, but I thought he'd just been standing on his head too long. I don't know, Papa, but—" Max stopped talking, stared at that smile on his father's face.

Max continued to stare at his father. Mary Rose knew she wasn't their mother, and she wished Tysen wouldn't call her that, particularly now, particularly when they looked at her and wished her back in Scotland. But she managed to laugh, fanning her hands in front of her. "Max, please, none of this is important. Here we are arguing about Latin and which sex can or cannot speak it— a very dead language that is excessively common, after all, and a language that is very likely not nearly as interesting as the Egyptian hieroglyphics, don't you think?"

"Don't tell me you can speak hieroglyphics," Max said, raising an eyebrow identical to his father's.

"Er, no. Not really. Actually, you don't speak them,

you read them, but no one can just yet. I've been reading about the studies done on the Rosetta stone. That perhaps it holds the key to translating the hieroglyphs. A Mr. Young is currently working on deciphering them."

Max moved a step closer to her, a heartening sign. "I have heard that the symbols are simply pictures, that there is no alphabet. Mr. Harbottle believes it is all heathen in any case, and therefore who cares?"

Tysen decided at that moment that Mr. Ellias Harbottle would not ever again open his mouth around Max. To think he was paying the man for lessons. Why hadn't he ever realized before that Harbottle was indoctrinating his son with such rubbish? Actually, maybe he should turn Meggie loose on Mr. Harbottle.

"No one is certain yet," Mary Rose said mildly. "Not about them being heathen, but about the hieroglyphs being an alphabet and an actual language or just pictures. Since your father knows most of the scholars at Oxford, however, when something definitive is discovered, he will find out about it very quickly. Then he will tell us."

"Yes," Max said slowly, staring at his father. "You will know, won't you, sir? It's a serious sort of thing, very scholarly. Perhaps there are even some religious aspects to it, so it should be of interest to you."

"Do you possibly believe it could be more interesting than you are, Max?" Tysen said, and his son blinked at him.

"I'm not at all sure, Papa," Max said, giving his father a confused look. Then he did a little skip, his Sherbrooke blue eyes alight with excitement. "Just imagine looking at all those symbols and drawings and actually reading them! I believe I will go to see Mr. Harbottle and tell him it's important that we know about everything, heathen or not."

And Max left the room, humming softly, a sign, Tysen

knew, that he was deep in thought. He had to find another tutor for his son, but able scholars were scarce.

Tysen said to Mary Rose, "You at least deflected him, Mary Rose. Well done. I don't think Mr. Harbottle is a particularly positive influence on my sons. I hadn't realized." He frowned a moment, then replaced it with a smile, cocking his head to the side.

"Oh, goodness, Meggie does it just the same way," Mary Rose said, charmed.

"What?"

"The way you just tilted your head."

"Yes, but now I have something important to say. I had never realized that your name sounds all soft and spongy. Isn't that what Leo said? Not that you were eavesdropping, of course."

She sighed. "I shouldn't have listened, I know, but I just couldn't help myself. And no, I hadn't thought either that I sounded soft and spongy."

"I know this is only your first day here," he said, coming to catch her hands up in his, "actually, only your fourth hour here, but it appears that everyone in Glenclose-on-Rowan knows that the vicar has taken a new wife. Mrs. Flavobonne probably told Mrs. Padworthy, and even though she's probably older than those stones on the Salisbury Plain, she can get around. The good Lord knows what else is being said. Mrs. Priddie just informed me that many of the ladies are on their way here, bringing cakes and biscuits and scones, since you're Scottish. I can't imagine that their husbands are pleased with their sudden defection at what is almost dinnertime."

"Oh, dear," Mary Rose said. "How much time do I have?"

"About five minutes."

The vicar met the dozen ladies who streamed through the vicarage front door and congregated in the entrance hall, clutching their plates and dishes to their respective bosoms.

When they were all assembled, finally, in the drawing room, and Mrs. Priddie had relieved them of their offerings, Tysen said, "Ladies, please let me present to you my wife, Mary Rose Sherbrooke."

Mary Rose stepped into the drawing room. Meggie slithered in behind her, staying behind the ladies' backs. She sent Mary Rose a little wave, then leaned against the window.

"I am delighted to meet you," Mary Rose said, and gave what she hoped was an enthusiastic smile. "It is so kind of you to come so quickly to welcome me. All the food you have brought smells delightful. Please sit down. I should like to meet each of you."

Tysen left some ten minutes later, having downed a bite of scone that left the taste of flour heavy in his mouth, and certain that everything would be all right. Some of the ladies he didn't trust an inch, but they seemed to be behaving themselves. It was Miss Glenda Strapthorpe, though, who worried him. Perhaps he should have mentioned her to Mary Rose. He was aware that the ladies were eyeing him a bit strangely by the time he quit the drawing room. Well, he supposed he had laughed, perhaps even grinned a bit. Several of the ladies had looked at him as if he'd grown another ear. He hadn't changed that much, had he?

He hadn't allowed himself to worry about how Mary Rose would deal with the members of the town and his congregation. Actually, truth be told, he hadn't thought about much of anything since he'd made love to his bride on their wedding night. That was about all he could think of. His own pleasure at seeing that wonderful look of astonishment in her beautiful eyes when she yelled that first time, still had him feeling like the most accomplished lover in all of England, perhaps even as excellent as his brothers. He hadn't been able to have her since they'd left Sinjun and Colin's house in Edinburgh, for Meggie had slept in their bedchamber every night on the way back home. It had been difficult, lying there, Mary Rose not three inches from him, and not being able to do a thing because Meggie was on a cot two feet away from their bed. He'd wanted to weep by the third night. He had the feeling that his new wife wanted to weep too. That was a wonderful thing.

Now they were home, and he could have her this very night. Maybe he could have her twice this very night. Surely God wouldn't think that too self-indulgent. He looked around his study, stuffed to the ceiling with more books than he could read in two lifetimes, most of them so hideously boring that it would be better to have a dead brain in order to get through them. But this was his home, this was where he wrote the words he spoke to his congregation each Sunday, words of God's expectations of his noble creation, God's punishments meted out fairly but harshly, and God's continual demands of His disciples.

He sat at his desk. There was not a speck of dust. It was as if he'd never been gone. Except for the large pile of correspondence, neatly stacked. He began reading.

Thirty minutes later, Meggie, panting, her face pale, stuck her head into Tysen's study. "Papa, it's Mrs. Bittley. She's being so mushy nice, you know how she can be. I'm afraid she's just preparing herself to take Mary Rose apart."

Tysen was at the drawing room door in under thirty seconds. He paused a moment next to the partially open door, listening.

Mrs. Bittley, Squire Bittley's shrew of a wife who'd been a fixture for as many years as Tysen had been on this earth, was standing in the middle of the drawing room, her bosom overpowering in deep purple, a purple feather sticking out of the sausage curls behind her ears, and she was facing Mary Rose, a muffin in one hand. "How delightful for you, a foreigner just to our north, to be married to our own dear vicar, an Englishman to his bones."

"Yes, very delightful for me, Mrs. Bittley. Thank you for remarking on it. Mrs. Markham, would you like another cup of tea?"

"No, Mrs. Sherbrooke—how difficult it is to say that name when you—a perfect stranger—and not even a perfect *English* stranger—are very suddenly and so very unexpectedly wearing it."

Mary Rose just smiled at the very thin woman who was so fair her hair looked nearly white in the dim afternoon light. Tomorrow, she thought. Tomorrow there would be light in this room. She would have it painted a pale yellow, perhaps. She stopped herself. She had to remember that this was just barely her home. She turned her attention to Mrs. Markham and said easily, "I suspect you were a bit surprised for a while to hear yourself called Mrs. Markham when you first married your husband, were you not?"

"That is neither here nor there," said Mrs. Bittley. "You have admitted that you are Scottish, have admitted that you are a foreigner."

"It is not something one can readily hide, don't you think?"

Mrs. Padworthy, an ancient old woman, tiny and stooped, waved a veined hand. "Now, Mrs. Bittley, haven't I told you that I have always liked the Scottish people? They bring such exotic music to the world with that wheezing bagpipe, a strange-looking thing that sounds like a gutted cow, don't you think? And all those quaint combinations of colors in their endlessly clever plaids, so popular amongst them—at least they did until they went against God's rightful king and we had to plant our boots on their necks. Wasn't the last time in 1745?"

"Ah, ladies, I trust you are enjoying your visit with my wife. Mrs. Bittley, won't you be seated? Mrs. Padworthy, how is your dear husband? Well, I trust?"

The thin mouth thinned even more. "He is nearly dead, Vicar. I expect him to be breathing his last by the time I arrive home. You did not ask about him before."

"We will pray that he lasts a while longer," Tysen said. "Ah, yes, Mrs. Bittley, I see a chair just over there. Meggie was just telling me that I should disclose to you, since you are all my very good friends and have only my best interests at heart, exactly how I went to Scotland and came home with a bride."

"You went to Scotland, Vicar," said Mrs. Padworthy, "because you inherited a Scottish title and a castle that likely is so old it is in ruins and smells of damp. You are now Lord Barthwick. That is why you went. You didn't go there for any other reason at all."

He smiled at all of them, each one in turn. "True. However, I found, quite simply, that when I met Mary Rose I knew—yes, ladies, I knew all the way to my very soul— that she was special. It took me a very long time to convince her to marry me and live here with me in England. Her arguments were sound: she didn't know anything about the English, for to her, you see, we are all foreigners, with different beliefs and manners, perhaps we even commit different sins, although she and I did not discuss any specifics.

"I assured her that everyone here would be delighted to meet her, to welcome her, to befriend her, for the English were a sunny-tempered race, very important since it rains here so very much, a gracious people, a kindly people. Ah, here I am going on and on and it isn't Sunday, and thus this is not a sermon, just a devout plea from my heart for your understanding. Forgive me for disturbing you, ladies. I will remove myself and let you continue getting to know each other."

He gave each of them an austere smile, the sort of Sunday smile, Mary Rose thought, that was aimed at people who were seriously considering committing major sins.

"This is very unlike you, Vicar," Mrs. Padworthy said. "I shall tell my husband about your very lax conduct if he is still breathing when I return home. We will see what he has to say about all this."

"But only if he is still breathing," Tysen said, smiled at all the ladies again, and left the drawing room. Mary Rose could swear that she heard Meggie's voice just outside the door. Actually, she wanted to run after him and leap on him and kiss him until he was silly with it.

She drew a deep breath and said, "Ladies, I very much admire my husband. He is a wonderful man."

Mrs. Bittley said after a moment, very much aware that the other ladies were no longer quite so ready to hurl themselves into the attack, "It did not take the vicar all that long a time to convince you to marry him. He wasn't gone for any time at all. It was very quickly done, too quickly done. Evidently you did something quite severe to him. He isn't what he was. We will have to study this. There is a mystery here. We will all hope that your English will improve when you have lived here a while."

"Or perhaps," said Mary Rose, "some of you will begin to speak with the soft lilt of Scotland, perhaps a bit less bite and clip in your speech. What do you think?"

Mrs. Bittley harrumphed. Mary Rose wondered if she and Mrs. Priddie were related.

Mrs. Tate, the very young, quite pretty wife of the local blacksmith, Teddie Tate, cocked her head to one side, her lovely black hair sliding across her cheek, and said, "I believe I would like lessons in a lilt. What do you think, Glenda? You haven't said anything at all. Come, tell us, what do you think about learning to lilt?"

Glenda Strapthorpe, just turned nineteen and well aware that she was the prettiest young lady in these parts, actually, in many other parts as well, turned her lovely pale face toward Mary Rose. "I believe a lilt would sound terribly common, Bethie. Mayhap vulgar. Rather like red hair, I think."

Bethie Tate wasn't certain what to do with that, and so she said quickly, "Mrs. Sherbrooke, do tell us about Kildrummy Castle. Just imagine, Reverend Sherbrooke is now Lord Barthwick. I wonder what his brother, the earl of Northcliffe, thinks about that."

24

Northcliffe Hall
Near New Romney

THE EARL OF Northcliffe, Douglas Sherbrooke, was reading Tysen's short note at that moment. He finished reading and looked blankly toward the fireplace, which was quite empty since it was warm out today. He read it again, then one more time.

"I don't believe this," he said, and looked up to see his son Jason peering around his estate room door.

"What don't you believe, Papa?"

"Come on in, Jason. It's time for your chess lesson, isn't it? It's a letter from your uncle Tysen. He's gotten married. She is Scottish and her name is Mary Rose. He, er, sounds quite happy, very lighthearted, indeed. Quite unlike himself, actually. He writes about how Meggie dressed like a boy and played his tiger all the way to Edinburgh. He said he nearly expired on the spot when she was unmasked, so to speak. I wonder why he didn't write of this when he wrote before to take Oliver away from me."

Jason sniggered behind his hand, then cleared his throat and stared down at his boots. His father grew very quiet. "Did you know what she would do?"

"No, really, not quite, Papa. Just the idea of it is worthy of note, don't you think?"

"No, I don't think." Douglas knew his beautiful son, knew he was more stubborn that a stoat, knew that he'd never get any more out of him, particularly if it would get his cousin in trouble. He said, "Thank God she came to no harm. An idiot thing for Meggie to do. They have just arrived back at the vicarage."

"You said that Uncle Tysen found a vicaress in Scotland?"

"Hmmm," said Douglas and tapped the letter with a fingertip. "Tysen was smiling when he wrote this, I'm sure of it. I can see him smiling, laughing, his mouth all wide. Maybe even dancing a bit, at least his feet are moving. What is going on here? I think perhaps we should all pay a visit to the vicarage. What do you think, Jason? We could return the boys' clothes."

"Do you think she's ugly on the outside?"

"Why would you say that?"

"I overheard you saying to Mama once that Leo's mother was close to an abomirat—"

"An abomination?" Oh, Lord, Douglas thought, he was continually forgetting that children's ears were so sharp they could hear a mouse eating cheese in the corner of the pantry.

"Yes, that's it. And I've heard Uncle Tysen say that the flesh isn't important, that it's what is in the soul, and in the heart, that makes a person ugly or beautiful."

Douglas stared at the small human being who had come from his loins, and had excellent hearing, and very likely had looked up "abomination" in the dictionary. "Yes," he said slowly, "your uncle is perfectly right. We shall just have to see, won't we? Listen to me, Jason—you will not ever say the word 'abomination' in your new aunt's hearing, do you understand me?"

"Yes, Papa, but do you think she will be as, er, unpretty as Leo's mama was? Although, of course, I don't remember her."

"I have no thoughts whatsoever on the subject. Forget it, Jason."

"Yes, Papa, but it will be difficult."

"You're strong. You can do it." However, Douglas found himself clearly remembering Melinda Beatrice, Tysen's first wife. He remembered that Tysen had believed her a goddess, the perfect wife for a vicar, his soul mate, his helpmeet—and he had been quite wrong. He winced. Well, Tysen had been very young, much too young to have his brains working properly. And any joy, any fullheartedness, that he'd had, that twit Melinda Beatrice had crushed right out of him. But now Tysen wasn't very young, and he seemed changed, and it was for the better. God be praised.

"You're always telling Mama how beautiful she is," Jason said.

"Your mother is very special, Jason. Her insides are just as beautiful as her outsides."

"I'll go tell James, Papa. Maybe our new aunt won't be able to tell me and James apart and we can pretend to be each other and gather information."

"I request that you don't."

But he knew that Jason was already coming up with scenarios that would make Douglas's head ache. They would drive the poor woman distracted, pretending to be each other.

"Can we play chess a bit later? A new aunt—maybe she'll have presents for us."

"Greedy little beggar." After his son left the estate

room, likely to wander with his twin in the Northcliffe gardens and ogle all the naked statues, Douglas rose and went to look for his wife, to give her the news.

He found her in the music room, practicing her new harpsichord. She was endeavoring to get through a Scarlatti sonata that had a goodly number of high, tinkly notes. It was to be played very fast, and she was trying, but the result was regrettable. She played with verve, however, just as she did everything. He rubbed her shoulders lightly, then leaned down to kiss her ear, then her nose, and then her mouth. She turned on the bench, her hands closed around his back, and she rubbed her cheek against his shirt. "Ah, bless you, Douglas. I was ruining my ears." Alex sighed. "It isn't very easy."

It wouldn't have occurred to him not to lie cleanly and quickly, and so he did. "It was wonderful, Alex," he said, kissed her again, and added, "I will just give you a little respite. Read this letter from Tysen."

"Oh, dear," Alex said, blinking several times, when she finished the letter. "Goodness, she has two names, just like Melinda Beatrice. Do you think she has no bosom either?"

Douglas laughed and laughed. He remembered how Ryder had said that no girl should have two names and no bosom. Well, Tysen had married another girl with two names. He wondered if Ryder had received a letter yet and if he was thinking about his new sister-in-law and the rather astounding change in Tysen.

Chadwyck House
Between Lower Slaughter and Mortimer Coombe
The Cotswolds

Ryder Sherbrooke had one little boy tugging on his left arm, another little boy clinging to his right leg, and a little girl with her legs locked around his middle, laughing in his ear, her skinny arms clasped around his neck. He was laughing himself, even as he tried to free just one hand. "Don't strangle me, Linnie. I must read this letter. It was just delivered, and it's from your uncle Tysen. I don't like letters delivered like that, it usually means something is wrong. All of you need to let me go for just a minute. That's right, I'll be a prisoner again, just let me sit down first."

Ryder sat down in a very large chair, made exactly to his specifications. It fit one adult and at least three small children or two larger children. "And," he'd said to his wife, Sophie, rubbing his hands together, "I'll even be able to hold one of the very little ones as well."

Ryder smoothed out the piece of foolscap and let the children gather in close. As he read, he was stroking little Theo's arm, nearly healed now.

Dear Ryder:

I am writing to tell you that I have brought a wife home with me from Scotland. Her name is Mary Rose and she is lovely. When I left Kildrummy Castle, Oliver was dancing about, exclaiming over everything he saw, so excited that he could barely speak. He sends his love and tells you that he will do just fine as my manager there. Many things happened—I dealt with the strangest people—but all worked out, and I did gain a wife, who, to be perfectly honest about it, is adorable. She fills me with pleasure. My love to all your children. You will meet my Mary Rose soon.

Your brother Tysen

"By all that's amazing," Ryder said slowly, staring over Linnie's head at nothing at all, unable for the moment to believe what he'd just read. "This is something indeed. No, don't any of you worry, it's not bad news. It's incredible news, actually. It appears that perhaps my dour, righteous brother has changed a bit. Maybe more than a bit. Hmmm, we'll have to see.

"Now, Theo, I saw you frowning just a moment ago. Does your arm pain you? No? Good. Linnie, my shoulder's a bit numb. As for you, Ned, you may just stay right where you are and hug me as tightly as you want."

"What is it, Uncle Ryder?" Linnie crawled closer and plastered herself to his side. As for Theo and Ned, they were each sitting next to him, each pressing against part of him, each touching him, from his neck to his knee. Now that he'd finished the letter, they moved even closer, something that was always possible even when you'd wager it wasn't. He'd learned there was always more room for a child, he'd learned that wondrous fact many years before. He hugged them all, leaned his head back, and closed his eyes. They were still so afraid, he thought, afraid that they would suddenly find themselves back in the hells where he'd found them, afraid they'd feel pain again, the humiliation and helplessness, the god-awful hunger that had shrunk all their small bellies. He felt the pain deep inside him, and rage, knew he would feel it until he died. He realized how very lucky he was to have them, and he smiled at them, patted them, and stroked their small faces. They would get better. They would learn to trust. He had had few failures over the years, thank God. And they would learn that they would be loved forever. He felt Linnie snuggle up under his armpit. He dropped the letter to the floor and gathered them all even closer to him in that big chair.

"Do tell us, Uncle Ryder, who writted to you?" Theo

was very young and had learned to talk from a gin-soaked thief in the back alleys near the docks in London. But he'd improved tremendously in the four months he had been here, and his arm, finally, was mending well. Ryder said easily, "It was a letter from one of my brothers. He's your uncle Tysen. You met him, Theo, do you remember, just after I brought you here? Just at the beginning of summer? He is the vicar and he brought his three children."

"Meggie taught me how to climb a tree," Linnie said. "I fell on her, but she just laughed. She showed me how to hit a boy, too, so he'd really hurt."

"Maybe I don't want to hear any more about that," Ryder said.

Linnie said, "Meggie told us not to bother her papa, that he had very serious thoughts in his head, and that those serious thoughts occupied all of his time. She said he needed her close to protect him because he was so very unworldly."

She knew her father very well indeed. Ryder smiled, imagining Meggie's precious little face as she'd said that. He said now, "He had very serious thoughts for many, many years. But now? A new wife? I wonder what has happened to Tysen? I wonder what Meggie thinks of her?"

"Leo taught us how to race," Ned said, "around the big oak tree, jumping over the yew hedges, and around the pond back to the house. Leo taught the winner how to flip over backwards."

"Max was teaching us Latin," Theo said.

"*Vos amo*," Ryder said, and kissed each of them.

"What does that mean, Uncle Ryder?" Linnie asked.

He gave each of them another quick kiss and a hug. "It means 'I love you.' "

"*Vos amo*," each of them said, then repeated it again

and again, until it became a chant. Ryder rolled his eyes, knowing that Sophie would hear nothing else from any of the sixteen children for the next month. As for Jane, the directress of Brandon House, which stood only one hundred yards from Ryder and Sophie's own home, Chadwyck House, he didn't doubt that all the children would be chanting it to her in unison until she was ready to throw up her hands and run from the room. Of course, she would be smiling because it would also wring her withers.

Theo said, "Max taught us *'Diabolus fecit, ut id facerem!'* "

Linnie said complacently from Ryder's armpit, "That means 'the devil made me do it.' "

"He said that never failed to make adults laugh," Theo said. "He said any mischief followed by that would likely save you a hiding." Theo frowned. "But how could that be true if the adult didn't speak Latin?"

"It couldn't," Ryder said and laughed. He didn't stop laughing for a very long time.

He looked up to see his own daughter, Jenny, standing in the doorway, her head cocked to one side, listening carefully, a smile on her lovely face. She was seventeen now, looked like him, nearly mirrored his expressions, only she had her mother's soft green eyes. She was slow in her thinking and in her speech, but she had a beautiful soul and a very sweet disposition. She also loved all the children.

"Vos amo," Ryder called out to her. "That means 'I love you.' "

Jenny gave him her sweet smile, and said softly, to all of them, *"Vos amo,* too."

Ryder moved Ned and brought Jenny down on his legs. Ned, without hesitation, climbed up on Jenny's lap. Ryder closed his eyes. He was blessed. He also had a feeling that he would probably be losing his daughter to Oliver, now in Scotland, managing Tysen's Kildrummy Castle. He also believed that Oliver loved Jenny more than anything, even more than himself, and that was an excellent basis for a marriage. They'd grown up together. As far back as Ryder could remember, Oliver had always protected her. As for his Jenny, he fancied she quite worshipped Oliver.

Everything would be fine.

He hugged her closely to him and felt her soft laughter against his neck. "I miss Jeremy," she said. "When he comes home from Italy, do you think he'll stay here or go immediately to Scotland to visit Oliver?"

Ryder thought of Sophie's younger brother, born with a club foot, and it didn't matter a bit. He was a bruising rider and fighter, a fine young man.

"I don't know," he said slowly. "We'll just have to see."

Jenny missed Jeremy? Not Oliver? What was this?

Ryder sighed and closed his eyes. Life, he supposed, would always be life and that meant twists in the road and surprises to hit you in the eye.

Jeremy? Not Oliver?

Eden Hill House
Glenclose-on-Rowan

> *Credo fatum nos coegisse.*
> I think fate brought us together.

He loved to kiss her belly. He loved to rub his cheek against the soft, warm flesh. He would sigh with pleasure even as she giggled at the feel of his scratchy morning beard against her. And then, in such a short time, she would be free to yell his name as she climaxed because his palm covered her mouth. No chance that the servants or any of his children would come running.

He was smiling at her as he watched her sip her tea, knowing she was worried about their visit around the town, to bid all his parishioners hello and for them to meet her. Meggie was coming, insisting that everyone had to see that Mary Rose was very welcome at the vicarage. He was also thinking about nibbling her crooked toe.

An hour later, Tysen was still smiling, for most folk wished him well, because they liked him, he supposed, and believed that Mary Rose would be a helpful addition to the town.

"Mrs. Bittley is a fishwife, Papa," Meggie said and squeezed his hand.

"Yes, but she has always been one. There is no change there. That is gratifying, I suppose. At least it's expected, so one is never surprised."

"I like change," Meggie said, giving her father a sideways glance.

"Yes," Tysen said absently. "Now, it's time to have our last—hopefully small and of short duration—bride-welcome, at the Strapthorpes'. They live just over toward the forest, Mary Rose, a ten-minute walk. Grattling Grange—a strange name for a house. Mrs. Strapthorpe tells everyone that it comes from a German count who built it in the fourteenth century. I have no idea if this is true."

Meggie said, her voice far too grim for a ten-year-old, "I'm sorry, Mary Rose, but you'll have to face Miss Strapthorpe. But I won't leave you. At least now she will have to stop flirting with Papa. And the way she's always treated me and the boys—" Meggie shuddered.

"She was rather quiet when all the ladies visited the vicarage our first day back," Mary Rose said, tilting her head up so the sunlight could fall full on her face. It felt wonderful. She felt Tysen's warm breath on her cheek as he lightly kissed her. She stopped, looked up at him, her heart in her eyes, and said, "Did she really flirt with you, Tysen?"

"No. Meggie is exaggerating." He kissed her again, on her ear.

Meggie rolled her eyes.

They heard a noise that sounded like a giggle. It was Mrs. Snead, the local seamstress, who had been examining a swatch of muslin. A soft pink muslin that, Tysen thought, would make up a beautiful gown for Mary Rose. He smiled at her and introduced his wife, who complimented her on the beautiful muslin. Tysen then asked Mrs. Snead to make his beautiful Mary Rose a gown.

Mrs. Snead sighed, a palm over her heart.

"Well done, Papa," Meggie said when they were on their way again.

"Mary Rose looks beautiful in pink," Tysen said, and kissed her ear.

Meggie began humming at that. As for Mary Rose, she was happy to her toes. She was also feeling very confident. It didn't matter if Glenda Strapthorpe had flirted with Tysen and was very pretty. Mary Rose was wearing the pale yellow muslin walking dress that was a gift from Sinjun, and she knew she looked very fine in it. Meggie had told her so at least three times. As for Max, he had frowned at her, looked her up and down, and said, "Just look at you, Mary Rose. You look all soft and fluffy, like a yellow dessert with red hair, and that's why you shouldn't be able to speak Latin."

"*Quis est qui inquit*, Max?" Mary Rose said, and grinned at his father, who was closing a large hand around his son's throat.

Meggie asked, her brows lowered at her brother, "Just what does that mean?"

"It means 'Who said that,' " Max said. "Why, Mr. Harbottle says that, that's who."

Tysen shook his head, perplexed. He'd been thinking that Mary Rose looked edible, at the very least, until his ears had finally picked up Max's words. He said, "I don't wish you to listen to Mr. Harbottle again, Max. Do you understand me? I can't believe that I never before realized what a fool the man is. I have made inquiries, Max, but there just aren't many tutors about who know more than you do. Is it possible for you to simply learn from him and not adopt any of his absurd philosophies?"

"You mean like girls are worth very little?"

"That's it exactly."

"I will try, Papa," Max said.

"You're such a shortsighted little dolt I doubt you'll be able to manage it," Meggie had said, and smacked him in the shoulder.

Now Meggie said to Mary Rose, "I don't trust Glenda Strapthorpe. She's a cat. She's wanted Papa for more than a year now, and he's had to be very wily to escape her. Remember that time she trapped you in the vestry, Papa? I heard two of the ladies saying behind their hands that she tried to assist you out of your robe."

"Er, yes," Tysen said, and Mary Rose saw him blush. Then he shook himself. "No matter. I'm married now, and she will quickly accustom herself. She has probably long forgotten me and is searching out fresh quarry."

Mr. Strapthorpe was monstrously fat, with gout and at least three chins. He admired Tysen not because he was a devoted town leader and an excellent vicar but because he was the brother of an earl, a very wealthy earl with a great deal of power. Mr. Strapthorpe was still in trade, although he'd removed himself physically far away from his factories in Manchester, and his new status as a wealthy man and the most important man in Glenclose-on-Rowan had made him look to Tysen as a possible son-in-law.

But he was philosophical, if nothing else, and greeted Mary Rose with gallantry while his pinched and meager wife poured tea and complained about the servants that one had to deal with in a small town.

Glenda Strapthorpe made a lovely entrance not three minutes later, her eyes on Tysen as she came into the overly warm drawing room, wearing so lovely a gown that Mary Rose felt suddenly like a dowd. Evidently Meggie agreed, because she moved closer.

As for Tysen, he rose to greet Glenda and said charmingly, "You are in fine looks, Miss Strapthorpe, as is my own lovely wife. When she has settled in, we shall begin entertaining."

Glenda paid no heed to this or to the vicar's new wife. She said, without preamble, "I need to show you something, Reverend Sherbrooke. In the conservatory. Mama, we will be back shortly."

Her mother shot her a nervous look, nearly spilling the tea she'd just poured. Her father looked as if his gout suddenly pained him. Tysen knew Mr. Strapthorpe didn't like this forwardness in his daughter, but Glenda ruled the house. Her parents were there to serve her, and everyone knew it.

Tysen smiled at Mary Rose and his daughter, and took Glenda's arm. He said over his shoulder, "No sugar in my tea, Mrs. Strapthorpe. We will be back very quickly."

Glenda Strapthorpe had no sooner closed the door to the conservatory—it was just a room so far as Tysen could ever tell—than she said in a wonderful, throbbing voice, right in his face, "How could you, sir?"

"How could I what, Miss Strapthorpe?"

"I wanted to marry you, sir, and instead you brought back that creature from Scotland! All you had to do was ask me. I would not have kept you dangling overly. I would have refurbished the vicarage, perhaps added to it, removed some of those worm-eaten old graves and built another wing that would cozy right up to the church so you could be closer to your flock. You would also have greatly appreciated my beauty. You should have already appreciated my beauty. It is remarkable. Just look at me, sir, then at her. There is no comparison."

Tysen looked mildly interested. "No," he said, "there is no comparison."

"Yes, I waited and waited, but you didn't ask me. What do you possibly see in her? Surely she has no dowry to bring to you. I am nineteen years old. She is old, nearly the age of my mother!"

Tysen decided in that instant that he hated conservatories. It was time to bring this monologue of hers to a close. "Forgive me for disappointing you, Miss Strapthorpe. Mary Rose hasn't quite gained your mother's years. Now, what did you wish my advice on?"

"Are you blind, sir? Are you an idiot? Without a brain or any sense at all? I just said that I wanted you, and you were beginning to appreciate me when you had to leave for Scotland. Now you are Lord Barthwick, and my father is more than pleased, and he wanted you for a son-in-law. And you had the gall to bring her back, that foreign creature with no style, no claim to beauty—"

Tysen said slowly, cleanly interrupting her, "Yes, Miss Strapthorpe, perhaps I have been a bit blind. The fact is, however, that I am now married. I was raised with the notion that a person of breeding was always civil, even in the face of disappointment, distress, or regret. If you have no need for advice, then let us return to the drawing room."

He heard her angry breathing behind him as he opened the door and stepped back to let her pass in front of him.

"Be nice to Mary Rose," he said, looking at her straight in her lovely eyes. "I would appreciate it very much. It would be the polite thing to do."

She looked like she would rather gut trout.

"Well, we survived," Meggie said, when, finally, a half hour later they were walking back toward the vicarage. "Well, Papa, did she try to seduce you in the conservatory?"

"No," Tysen said. "Meggie, curse you, I don't want you to know about that word and its meanings. 'Seduce' isn't a good word for you. You're only ten years old. Contrive to forget it."

"Yes, Papa. What did she want with you?"

"She wanted to upbraid me," he said. "She was angry that I brought back a wife when she saw herself as waiting to marry me." He sighed.

"Oh, dear," Mary Rose said. "There might be problems."

"Nothing we can't deal with," Tysen said. "We have done our duty. You have met nearly everyone except for Mr. Thatcher, who spends a great deal of his time beneath his table, dead drunk. But he is always sober on Sundays, and you will meet him then, Mary Rose."

It was strange how they responded to Tysen, she thought—both with wonder and, perhaps, with a bit of confusion. It didn't make much sense to her. Then she realized that she'd been blind—what had concerned everyone was that most people simply didn't know what to make of her, a foreigner dropped suddenly in their midst. They very likely wondered why he would marry her, of all the possible women available to him.

Mary Rose brooded about it, at least until dinner that evening.

25

Vivere, amare, discere
Living, loving, and learning

OVER A VERY fresh turtle soup at the dinner table, Tysen announced, "The weather is very warm. We're going to visit Brighton. I asked Mr. Arden—"

"That's Papa's solicitor," Meggie said to Mary Rose.

"Yes, and he immediately found us a house. I didn't want to tell you until I was certain we could go. We will spend a week there. What do you think?"

His two boys stared at him. Leo said slowly, "Papa, you have never before taken us to Brighton. You have never taken us anywhere except to visit our uncles. You have always believed that doing nothing much of anything at all is a waste of time."

Had he really believed that?

"We would love to go," Max said, frowning a bit toward Mary Rose. "Perhaps having her here isn't such a bad thing."

"I agree with you, Max. She is nice to have here," said

his father, and thought briefly about kissing her behind her left ear, breathing in her scent, and maybe then sliding his mouth to her—well, no, that would be rushing things a bit. He realized his children were looking at him. He coughed behind his hand and tried to look blank.

"Oh, I see," said Leo.

"Dolt," said Meggie.

The regent wasn't in residence at the Pavilion, and so Brighton was thin of the London society who dutifully followed the prince here during the summer months. It was late in September now, but the weather remained glorious—sunny and mild. They quickly settled into the small rented house on the Steyne.

Mary Rose saw the young man again on their fourth day. She had seen him before, quite a lot, really. She was sitting beneath an umbrella on the beach, watching Leo, Max, and Meggie playing in the sand.

Tysen had gone off to buy some tea cakes for them all when the young man cast a long shadow beside her. "Excuse me, ma'am, for intruding on your solitude, but I heard from some friends of mine that you are from Scotland. My name is Bernard Sanderford."

She remembered that Tysen had spoken to him, that she had seen him about a good half-dozen times now, and so she smiled and said easily, "Why, yes, I am Mary Rose Sherbrooke, sir."

"Ah, yes, the lovely Mrs. Sherbrooke. Your husband is a vastly fortunate gentleman. One has but to look at you to know that."

Mary Rose thought immediately of Erickson MacPhail. She'd rather hoped that Erickson was one of a kind. Evidently not. She didn't say anything, just watched Mr. Sanderford. He was as handsome as Erickson. Perhaps that was the key to a rotten character. She wasn't the least bit afraid of him, not since she'd had a goodly bit of experience with Erickson.

Even when he came down on his haunches beside her, Mary Rose only looked at him, her face still. He was a bit too close, but she knew she could blight him easily if the need arose. It was odd that there was no one else on the beach, just the children, playing near the breaking waves.

He said, his eyes so intimate that she wanted to throw sand in his face, "Actually, your husband is very well occupied at this moment, ma'am. Does he perhaps bore you and thus you sent him away on an errand? I know you saw me, and so you sent him away. Ah, I have been watching you, and I saw how you looked at me. Perhaps you and I could get to know each other. Perhaps we could meet later?"

"Are you related by any chance to Erickson MacPhail, sir?"

"No, that is a foreign name, ma'am. Surely I would not be related to a foreigner. Now, perhaps—"

"Mama!"

It was Meggie, covered with wet sand, her hair in tangles around her face, and on her heels were Max and Leo, looking windblown, sunburned, and quite alarmed. Meggie planted herself in front of Mr. Sanderford, hands on her hips, and demanded, "Sir, who are you?"

"Meggie, love, this is Mr. Sanderford. He was just paying a bit of a visit."

Max said, "Our mother doesn't entertain gentlemen when our father isn't available."

"Surely," Mr. Sanderford said, appalled, "you are not the mother to these children? You are far too young."

"Mama is nearly thirty-five years old, sir," Leo said. "She just looks young. She says that we keep her looking young. She's very happy with Papa and with us. She tells us that all the time, don't you, Mama?"

"At least twelve times a day," Mary Rose said.

"I see," Mr. Sanderford said slowly and rose. Even though he was young, his knees creaked a bit. He dusted off his knit britches, looked at each of the children, and said, "I never loved my mother as you do yours. You are fortunate to have her."

"Yes, sir, we know," Leo said, and waited there until Mr. Sanderford had left them. When he was sure the poacher was gone, he sped away to turn a series of cartwheels right down to the water's edge.

Mary Rose laughed.

"He reminds me of Erickson MacPhail," Meggie said thoughtfully as she watched him walk back up the beach to the path.

"Odd you should say that," Mary Rose said. "You three were right here. How ever did you know that he wasn't being a gentleman?"

"Pompous Max might be a blind looby," Meggie said, eyeing her brother, "but he knows when a flash cove has the light of wickedness in his eyes."

Mary Rose could have handled Mr. Sanderford, but she was pleased to her bones that the children had been so possessive of her. "Thank you all," she said.

Then Tysen was back, his hands filled with cakes and tarts, apples and oranges. "Who was that man speaking to you?"

"Father," Max said, "that was no gentleman. He was trying to flirt with Mary Rose."

Tysen blinked at that. Slowly, he lowered himself to the blanket. "What happened?" he said to Mary Rose.

"He is very much like Erickson MacPhail," she said matter-of-factly, "and I could have dealt with him, but

Max, Leo, and Meggie came running to protect my virtue."

Tysen wanted to bash the man's face in. He was on his feet in an instant, his face red with outrage, but Mr. Sanderford was nowhere to be seen. Then he cursed under his breath. Meggie heard him and stared, her mouth dropping open.

"I'm sorry," Tysen said. "I should not have said that."

"Papa, we didn't let him do anything at all," Max said. "Here comes Leo. Just ask him. There is nothing to worry about."

"Yes," Mary Rose agreed as she picked up an apple. "Just a small drama. Now, Max, I do believe you have a nasty scratch on your foot. When we return home, you must let me put some ointment on it."

"*Num mihi dolebit hoc?*" Max wanted to know.

"What does that mean?" Meggie asked.

"That means 'It won't hurt a bit,' " Mary Rose said. "Unless, of course, I want it to."

"*Abeo,*" Max said, and ran toward the frothing waves.

"*Abeo?* What does that mean?" Meggie said, shading her eyes from the sunlight to watch Leo, who was now walking on his hands down the beach.

"He said he was leaving," Mary Rose said, and laughed.

"Have I told you recently that I love to kiss your belly?"

Her heart was pounding, slow, powerful strokes, waiting, waiting, and she felt his warm breath on her skin, felt her muscles tighten, felt the need for him building, always building, and flowering, opening her, and she managed to say, "No, but I rather believed that you liked it. You seem to spend a goodly amount of time on my belly."

"And elsewhere," he said, lifting his head to smile at

her. He nearly crossed his eyes when there was a sharp knock on their bedchamber door.

"Oh, dear," said Mary Rose, her eyes nearly crossed in disappointment.

It was Leo, and he had a confession to make: he and Max had made a new friend, who, it turned out, was a wily gambler, and wicked, and both of them had lost their shoes in a wager.

Tysen didn't want to know what the wager had been.

Their stay extended for another five days, until finally rain came crashing down upon Brighton, dark clouds and wind whipped up the water, and the temperature plummeted.

Then, because Samuel Pritchert had already prepared the congregation for at least another month of sermons to be written and delivered by himself, Tysen slapped him on the back and told him he was taking his family to visit their cousins.

Samuel Pritchert inquired in his emotionless voice, "How long do you plan to stay away this time, Reverend Sherbrooke?"

"Ah, that remains to be seen, Samuel. I can trust you to keep the spiritual ship on course." And he laughed and rubbed his hands together. Samuel Pritchert looked over at Mary Rose and the boys, all of them looking tanned and bright-eyed from their extended visit to Brighton, and wondered what sort of a place this once very serious and upright vicarage would become.

They remained two weeks at Northcliffe Hall, and late one afternoon Mary Rose found herself walking in the Northcliffe gardens with the countess. "These are very private gardens," Alex Sherbrooke said, then sighed. "I suppose, however, that the boys discovered them a very long time ago. The boys can always sniff out anything that perhaps even smacks of a bit of wickedness." And so it was that Mary Rose saw the endless number of Greek statues, each copulating in one way or another, some so delightfully shocking that she blinked and nearly swallowed her tongue. "Goodness," she said for the fifth time when she paused in front of a large stone man whose face was buried between the legs of a woman who looked to be in ecstasy. "That is Sophie's favorite, I believe," Alex said. "You know, I don't believe Tysen ever spent any time at all in these gardens. Indeed, I know that he found them dreadful and altogether godless. Do you think he might enjoy them now?"

And Mary Rose, who was still staring, her eyes glazed as she thought of Tysen and her doing the very same things, said on a croak, "I plan to show him as soon as he returns with his lordship."

"His name is Douglas. He will feel offended if you continue to be so formal."

"But he looks like he should be treated with great formality," Mary Rose said.

"Perhaps, sometimes," Alex said.

"Your sons are the most beautiful boys I believe I have ever seen. Tysen had told me they were identical twins. But to me they aren't at all alike."

Alex Sherbrooke sighed. "Most people can't tell them apart, and that leads to a lot of mischief. As to their confounded beauty, it's unfortunately true. It quite drives poor Douglas mad. You see, the boys are the image of their aunt Melissande, and she is the most beautiful woman in all of England. Douglas despairs for womankind when the boys reach manhood. On the other hand, Melissande's son is the very image of Douglas. Perhaps you will meet my sister and her husband soon. Now, come along, Mary Rose, there are more very interesting, er, presentations for you to investigate."

And Mary Rose was nothing loath.

That evening, just before dusk, Mary Rose led Tysen to her favorite statues, deep in the private gardens, and they didn't emerge until a light rain began to fall at nearly eight o'clock.

Douglas Sherbrooke just shook his head, amazed, heartened, and very, very pleased.

The Sherbrookes then traveled to the Cotswolds and spent three weeks there. They took both James and Jason with them, who had pleaded on their knees to their earl father and their countess mother to let them see Uncle Ryder and all his children. All in all, it was an excellent performance, and it gained them what they wanted.

All the children stayed in Brandon House, not for the purpose of giving Tysen and Mary Rose privacy but because a house filled with nearly twenty children was bedlam, with an endless parade of fights, laughter, mischief, jests, some tears, and abundant amounts of food.

It was November now, and it should have been cold and dank and dreary, but it wasn't. There were a few more warm, sunny days remaining before the fall weather made itself known. On those days Tysen enjoyed lying on his back, his head in Mary Rose's lap, in the apple orchard. The afternoon sun was streaming down through the leaves, and it was warm, the light breeze carrying the smell of honeysuckle.

In the distance they could hear the voices of a good dozen children. But here, they were alone.

Tysen leaned over and kissed her belly. "Too much material between thee and me," he said, and closed his eyes when he felt her fingers stroking slowly through his hair. He sighed. "I don't suppose I can drape all your clothes over the apple tree branches?"

"Not just yet," she said and bent to kiss his mouth. She was silent for a moment, her eyes closed. "It's like we're out of time here," she said slowly, leaning back against the apple tree trunk. "Like it's not only a different place and time, but we're also apart from the world and all its realities and demands. Do you miss being the vicar of Glenclose-on-Rowan? It's been nearly three months now."

Tysen thought about that. He thought about all the people who had wished him and his new wife well. He thought of his children, their smiles, their laughter, the ferocious fights among the three of them, all of them won by Meggie. And he thought of his own laughter and joy just watching them, and just being with Mary Rose. Waking with her in the mornings, at the Vicarage, Ellis and Monroe stretched across the both of them, purring madly, listening to her speak to his children, seeing their smiles, just knowing that she was there and that she was his and his alone, just as he was hers. And the vicarage—it seemed lighter, and not just because the drawing room was now painted a pale yellow and those dreadful dark draperies had been taken down. No, it just felt as if the house itself had shaken off years of gloom and emerged into the light. It was a very happy place, with Samuel Pritchert the only gloomy face to be seen. Even Mrs. Priddie was smiling now. He'd actually heard her singing once while she baked some haddock in the kitchen.

He frowned. "Have I changed, Mary Rose?"

"Not that I know of," she said, rubbing her fingers over his brow. "You have always been the same to me, always saying just the right thing, taking care of things. And your laughter, Tysen—I have always loved your laughter, the way you tease me, tease the boys and Meggie. Why would you ask such a strange thing? Haven't you always been as you are now?"

He didn't want to examine that. Perhaps he was even afraid for her to know that he had been at one time, perhaps, a bit stricter, a bit less humorous, perhaps even a bit on the stodgy side, even pompous and too austere in his notions, with everyone. "How do you like your new family?" he asked, grabbing one of her hands and holding it against his heart.

"Well, Douglas—the earl. When I first saw him I thought he must be dreadful, you know—stern and autocratic and very lord of the manor."

"He is a natural autocrat."

"Perhaps, at least until Alex happened to tickle him under his left arm and he laughed and grabbed her and then he pulled her down behind that settee and her petticoats went flying.

"Your laugh is a lot like his, Tysen. As for Alex, she is amazing, truly. Max has said that he now approves red hair. He said that an aunt and a stepmother have overcome his reservations." She laughed. "They're coming around, Tysen. They are grand children."

"What do you think of Ryder and Sophie?"

"I think Ryder could seduce any woman between the ages of eighteen and eighty."

"Even you?"

"Oh, no, I'm the only woman who wouldn't succumb to him with a lovely sigh. You have some of him in you as well. You're both so filled with kindness and laughter, and everyone seems to shine brighter when you're near. You walk into a room, and everyone just seems to turn toward you, ready to smile. It's the same with Ryder."

He was like Ryder? His fun, carefree brother who'd enjoyed seven mistresses at one time?

"But there's some of Sinjun in you as well, or perhaps you in her. Sophie manages to hold her own with

Ryder—very difficult, I imagine. She's quiet, just gets things done with no muss or fuss, and I believe that Ryder would crawl on his belly if she wanted him to. Such love and patience both of them have for all the children."

"Oliver was one of Ryder's first children," Tysen said. "He knew only his first name, and hunger and endless cruelty. When Ryder found him in an alley in London, he was dragging his broken leg, trying desperately to find a pocket to pick so he could get some food."

"But look at Oliver now. He is a man and he is smart and knows he belongs. Ryder did very well by him. And just look at you, a man of God, who cares for everyone in Glenclose-on-Rowan, prays with them, helps them overcome tragedy and unhappiness, and shares happiness with them. You are an excellent man, Tysen. Have I told you that I am the luckiest woman in all of southern England?"

"No, you hadn't yet told me that."

"I would be certain of it if only I could manage to get a racing kitten."

"Hmmm," Tysen said. "I will write to Rohan Carrington and see what the Harker brothers have to say."

"I will be philosophical about it if I am rejected by them. Perhaps Leo is right. Perhaps Ellis would make a good racing cat. I saw him running from Mrs. Priddie once, and he flew across that kitchen, skidded on a polished patch, turned an entire flip in the air, and was gone again.

"Now, Tysen, I saw a good dozen of the children climbing all over you this morning."

"It's because I had the wit to stop in Lower Slaughter and buy all of them presents. They hope to get more out of me if they swamp me with attention."

"If I swamp you with attention, what will I get?"

"Ah," Tysen said, raising an eyebrow and looking up at her, "I just had a very great desire for the private gardens at Northcliffe Hall."

"I have an excellent imagination."

"And I have an excellent memory."

26

Eden Hill House
Glenclose-on-Rowan

SAMUEL PRITCHERT, TYSEN'S curate for three years now, a stickler with a rigid soul, a man with a face so morose it was rumored that his own mother cried when he was born, said in his flat, deep voice, "Reverend Sherbrooke, I regret to report that the local ladies—so many of them—feel cut adrift from you, their pastor. They do not feel that you are truly back to minister to their needs. As the lovely and very young Mrs. Tate said, 'Our dear reverend seems inattentive since he finally came back after his months and months of absence. He no longer cares about us.' "

Tysen just stared at him. He'd always thought it amazing how everyone spilled their innards to Samuel Pritchert within minutes of his appearing, despite the fact that Samuel always looked nearly ready to burst into tears—that, or simply sink into a pit of gloom. But everyone did speak to him, frankly, many times too frankly.

Tysen himself trusted Samuel implicitly to keep his finger on the emotional pulse of his flock. Samuel had just given his prologue. He was ready to move forward with but a nod from his vicar. Tysen didn't want to hear this. Truth be told, he was afraid to hear more, but he knew he had no choice.

And so Tysen lowered his quill to his desktop, leaned back in his chair, and rested his head against his crossed arms. He said mildly, "I have only been home for eight days, Samuel. It is true that this will be my first sermon in three months, but you did an excellent job. I felt particularly moved by your sermon this past Sunday, for you presented it quite well. It would seem to me that any flock would like an occasional change of the guard in the pulpit.

"Now, tomorrow is Sunday, and I will once again be before them, my time away from them over. Why, Mary Rose and I visited with everyone before we went to Brighton and then on to visit my brothers. I have been home to stay for a week now, and everything is back to normal. I have seen everyone in these past days, spoken to everyone, commiserated with everyone, prayed with everyone. Surely both Mary Rose and I have taken tea with nearly everyone yet again, and I will say that everyone has been quite civil. So please tell me, Samuel, how could they possibly come to this conclusion, a conclusion that is nonsense, of course?"

"Be that as it may, sir," Samuel said, not answering the question because he deemed it irrelevant, "I must tell you that I always strive to communicate God's word to his flock, and to communicate the flock's words and feelings and thoughts back to you."

"Very well. Tell me what I haven't seen." At Tysen's nod, Samuel gently cleared his throat. Tysen could see that he was striving to find a tactful way of delivering the blow. He said finally, reluctantly, "I feel it my duty, sir, to remind you that you are no longer in Scotland, surely a place of sufficiently strict Protestant ethics, a place that surely holds no more sinners than we have here. But nonetheless, the Scottish people are still not our sort. Perhaps they changed you, sir, presented you with problems that made you think differently from the way you've always thought, made you yell and howl when normally you would speak quite calmly, perhaps even whisper, made you perhaps question—perhaps even deny—all the spiritual and pious philosophies you have hitherto always firmly believed and espoused."

"Although your words flowed quite nicely, Samuel, I am not entirely certain I understand what you just said."

"You would have understood before you left for Scotland, sir. You would have answered me in the same vein—before Scotland. Ah, it is difficult, Reverend Sherbrooke. I will endeavor to clarify my sentiments. The Scottish people, sir—they are, quite simply, not like us. They do not share the exact breadth, complexity, and depth of our beliefs. They do not comprehend or appreciate the ways we look at ourselves and at the world. They are different from us, sir."

"Ah. What sort are we, Samuel?"

"We are Englishmen, Reverend Sherbrooke."

"I begin to see. And my wife isn't."

"That is correct, sir. From what I've learned, our people are striving out of respect for you to tolerate her if you will but return your former self to them. That means, sir, that they want you the way you were before you left for Scotland. They want the *real* you to come back to them." As Tysen's eyebrow was still elevated, Samuel added, near desperation in his voice, "They very much want you to try very hard to be yourself again. No one else, just your old self, the very introspective and devout self that was in full bloom here before that old and revered self left for Scotland."

"The way I was before I went to Scotland," Tysen repeated slowly. "What do you think they mean by that, Samuel?"

"I have even spoken at length with many of the men and the ladies in our flock, Reverend Sherbrooke. They have sought me out, actually, many of them. They wanted to speak to me. Mr. Gaither, who now owns the Dead Spaniard Inn—he just purchased it this past week from his older brother, Tom the Wastrel—something you didn't know and it would have been nice if you had but known and commented upon it.

"Ah, yes, my point is that Mr. Gaither was the men's spokesman. He told me that they have all discussed the situation amongst themselves. I have to say it, sir—though it smites me to have to—they have even gone so far as to smirk and leer. They are jesting at how a pretty woman has brought you—a devout man of God—as low as a young man rutting his first female, as low as a young man who has no thought, no caring for anything save his own fleshly desires. Mr. Elias even reported that he saw—actually saw—you kissing your wife, sir. He said it nearly knocked him on his, er, arse."

Tysen nearly roared out of his chair then, ready to separate Samuel Pritchert's head from his shoulders. He caught himself with effort, and simply nodded.

"It has quite bothered me, sir, because they now see you as one of them—no longer a man of God who has always been set apart from them, set apart from the base desires that seem to plague men and bring them low time and time again.

"They see you, quite frankly, as now being as weak and as much of the flesh as they are, as consumed by matters of the flesh as they and their neighbors are, as all their friends and enemies are. They fear for you, sir. You have fallen low. You are, in their eyes, no longer their spiritual leader. You have fallen from grace."

Matters of the flesh. Tysen froze. He thought of the last three months, all the glorious nights and glorious mornings, each and every one of them filled with endless delights, endless tenderness and discovery, and dear God, endless lust that bowed him to his knees, made him heave and pant and yell with the utter joy and wonder of it, and emptied his brain of what he was, what he used to be.

Samuel was right. He wasn't the same man now as the one who had traveled to Scotland. He realized that he'd been smiling for at least three months now, smiling at nothing in particular, something he hadn't done since he'd been a very young man, since before he'd decided to become one with God, a spiritual man of the Church, before he'd met Melinda Beatrice.

He saw himself clearly then, the before and the after. After that decision so long ago, he'd become dour, so very serious, that he was humorless, unable to see anything that brought simple joy to life. From that point, he'd had only one goal, only one focus. Over the years, that focus had been on the people for whom he alone was responsible. They were to look up to him, to depend on him to tell them how to solve their problems and to succor them in their time of need and pain. And these people expected certain behavior from him, he'd known that very well, and he'd never let them down, before he'd gone to Scotland, before he'd wed Mary Rose.

Certainly he'd always loved his children, but he'd never given them his unstinting attention or the unfettered joy he now lavished on them and on himself and on his new wife.

Mary Rose. His wife. He'd made love to her that very morning, kissing her awake, his hands all over that smooth, warm body, feeling such pleasure, such overwhelming need that seemed to grow greater each time he became one with her. He'd awakened, he remembered, with a wondrous smile on his face, and hard as the oak planks of the bedchamber floor.

Tysen rose and walked to the windows. It was gray and cold outside, a nasty, dreary drizzle streaking down the glass. It had moved from fall to winter in such a short time. He realized he was cold, cold all the way to his bones. He said nothing to Samuel, just walked to the fireplace and built up the fire. Then he drew in a deep breath and turned back to his curate, who hadn't moved, just stood there, silent and still.

Samuel said at Tysen's nod, "I will be blunt, sir. Our people do not want a foreigner here. They want you, but they want you the way you were before you went to Scotland and brought her back."

"Go away now, Samuel."

"There is just a bit more, sir."

"Very well."

"It seems it is your laughter, sir."

"My what?"

"Your laughter, sir, your unconcealed lightness of spirit, your unexpected flow of charm, your wit. It makes them uncomfortable, it makes them feel as if their spiritual leader has become a stranger. It is your lack of seriousness, sir, that alarms them, your lack of proper gravity and conduct, of proper perspective on what is important in life. You have changed into a different man. All have remarked upon it. You are no longer their spiritual leader. You have diminished in their eyes. Their faith suffers because of it. There, I have said it. I hope you will forgive my bluntness."

"I thank you for your bluntness, Samuel. Go away now."

Tysen didn't move until Samuel was out of his study. He turned to stretch his hands to the fire. He rubbed his neck, feeling knots he knew hadn't been there ten minutes before. Then he realized that it was only eleven o'clock in the morning and he was again hard with lust for Mary Rose. He'd made love to her three-and-a-half hours before, and now he wanted her again. She filled his mind, she filled his heart—perhaps even his very soul, which, until she'd popped into his life, had been filled only with God and with God's mission for him on this earth.

No, she didn't own his soul. No, that wasn't possible. He hadn't sunk that low yet. But she'd changed him by giving him her body, by giving him her trust, by giving him all the love that filled her, and it was abundant.

He knew she loved him, although she hadn't yet said the words. She was open, guileless, her love for him shone in her eyes. And what did he feel for her, his wife? The woman who had changed him utterly?

He didn't want to think about it, he simply couldn't. He'd become single-minded, a man lost in his own appetites, in the gratification of his own selfish needs.

It repelled him even as he accepted that it was true.

Even at twenty years old and newly wedded to Melinda Beatrice, he'd never felt this overwhelming intensity of need for another person, this frantic desire. Yes, call it by what it is—lust. But it was more than that. Melinda Beatrice had tried to yield to him because she'd loved him, had told him she loved him countless times, and she'd wanted to be his wife and his clerical helpmeet, but it hadn't lasted. Very quickly he'd visited her bed only when he realized he had to so that children could be conceived. And life had become, he'd supposed, what it had needed to become, what it was meant to become, and he had gained what he'd sought.

He was surely respected, surely admired, surely needed, since he'd tried with all his being to fill his role as the spiritual adviser to nearly an entire town of people.

Ah, but now here was Mary Rose. She was his. Just to be near her, to touch her, to feel her pleasure when he touched her with his fingers, with his mouth, was something he'd never even considered before, but with her it had seemed so very natural, so important somehow to share her own pleasure with her, to know that he was giving her pleasure. And when he came into her, when he heard her crying out his name over and over when she reached her climax, he'd felt blessed. He'd felt beyond himself. He'd felt more than he was.

She made him feel like a man who was cherished, and surely that was something blessed.

Not only was she loving and giving to him, she was dealing well with his stubborn boys, even telling Max the previous evening at the dinner table to eat his broccoli— in Latin. Max laughed so hard he had to hold his stomach. In fact, Tysen had heard Max mumbling several times at the breakfast table just this morning so he wouldn't forget: *"Aut id devorabis amabisque, aut cras prandebis."* Mary Rose, when asked by Meggie what that meant, gave them all a sunny smile and said, "It means 'You'll eat it and like it, or you'll have it for breakfast tomorrow.' "

Yes, he'd laughed so hard he'd nearly fallen out of his chair, just like his son. So he wasn't sufficiently serious anymore, was he? He laughed too often? He was too lighthearted? And this diminished him?

Dear God, what was he to do? He knew Samuel was right. He knew his flock was right. Everyone had seen the incredible changes—everyone except him.

But now he did.

He had changed.

It wasn't a respectful, devout change.

He had become a man seduced by all that was unimportant to the salvation of his soul.

It was a licentious change.

He moved to his desk, read the pages he'd written for his sermon. He felt a shaft of pain as he read, and surprise at what he'd written so naturally, so easily—so joyfully. He closed his eyes for a moment. Then he tore the pages in half.

Tysen didn't remain at the vicarage for lunch. He went to the Dead Spaniard Inn to have Mr. Gaither's barmaid, Petunia, serve him a cup of spiced tea and a cold plate of chicken and warm bread. He felt the damp from the thickening rain and cold to his bones.

He ate and waited for Mr. Gaither to show himself, which he did after Tysen had taken only two absentminded bites of the chicken and wondered yet again what had become of his life.

"Ah, Reverend Sherbrooke, it's delighted I am to see you home again. You were away far too long, sir. Many good people lapsed a bit, didn't attend Mr. Pritchert's sermons. A good fellow, but long-winded he is, poor man. But Samuel Pritchert is always there, always ready to shoulder another man's burdens, to counsel him, to help him wipe clean his plate when it's dirty. But tomorrow you're finally back in the pulpit. Everyone will be in church."

Mr. Gaither was wider than his apron, and his heart was as big as his belly. He was a good man, a man Tysen had respected for the entire eight years he had been the vicar in Glenclose-on-Rowan. Mr. Gaither had dealt more than fairly with his wastrel older brother, who had, evidently, just taken a ship to the Colonies, to find new victims to fleece.

"Have you ever traveled to Scotland, Mr. Gaither?"

"Not I, sir. Born and raised here, been here all my life. I believe it's best for a man to know his roots and stick close to them."

Not very subtle, Tysen thought, and took a bite of the warm bread.

"I saw your wife, sir, just yesterday afternoon, with little Meggie, over at the draper's shop on High Street. They were laughing, sir, over nothing at all as far as I could tell, as far as anyone else could tell. She's a looker."

"Yes, Meggie looks a great deal like her aunt Sinjun," Tysen said.

"No, I meant your wife. All the, er, men think so."

Tysen wadded the piece of bread into a ball in his fist. His heart began to pound, death-hard strokes. Now Mr. Gaither wanted Tysen to believe that Mary Rose was a strumpet to be ogled? He remembered Mr. Sanderford in Brighton. Mary Rose hadn't wanted him to flirt with her, she hadn't, and Tysen felt a leap of rage at this insult, and nearly choked on the bread he'd been chewing. He managed to calm himself. He said, after he'd motioned Mr. Gaither to seat himself, "My wife and daughter are very fond of each other. Naturally they laugh together. Now, I don't know precisely what you mean, Mr. Gaither, by this 'looker' business. You have met my wife. Did you not come to the vicarage just three days ago with your dear wife to share tea with us?"

"Naturally, my lord. Mrs. Sherbrooke was very gracious to everyone. It is just—oh, dear, I surely meant no insult to you or to her, Reverend Sherbrooke."

"Perhaps you should try for an explanation, Mr. Gaither, one that is readily understandable."

"Dear heaven—the pain, the embarrassment—to speak of it, sir. No help for it. Your wife flirted with Teddie Tate! Shameless, it was."

"Ah," Tysen said, utterly confused now. The only man Mary Rose had ever flirted with in her life was him. Again, he remembered Sanderford, and he nearly smiled, remembering how Mary Rose had compared him to Erickson MacPhail.

"Poor Bethie Tate, well, dear Bethie was in tears, sobbing her heart out to Miss Strapthorpe."

"I see. It is Miss Strapthorpe who mentioned this to you?"

"Oh, Miss Glenda mentioned it to everyone, Reverend Sherbrooke."

"Other than flirting with Teddie Tate, is there any other sin my bride has committed?"

"Oh, sir, now you're upset and I never meant for you to be. I know, I know, Miss Strapthorpe fancied you for herself, and thus you think this is all a lie to discredit your wife, that it is nothing more than the spite of a rejected female."

"That's it exactly, Mr. Gaither. Miss Strapthorpe is a single-minded young lady. I fear I offended her by not giving her what she wanted—namely, myself and the vicarage, which she wanted to expand into the graveyard."

"You don't say! What a thought that provides. Just imagine drinking your tea atop old Mrs. Beardsley's coffin, and she's been down under for over fifty years now."

"I believe Miss Strapthorpe had visions of removing the coffins."

"Oh, dear," said Mr. Gaither and shook his head. "Aye, and I'll wager you were plain-speaking with her too, sir, and not unkind."

"I suppose so."

Mr. Gaither stroked his fingers over his clean-shaven jaw. "It's true that her disappointment is great, according to Mrs. Bittley and Mrs. Padworthy. I heard them talking just outside the tavern, while they were waiting for their husbands to down their final mugs of ale. Proper sods, their husbands were that day. Aye, it is a strong possibility that Miss Strapthorpe perhaps exaggerated the thing a bit."

"More than a bit. Now, all that is distraction, Mr. Gaither. Tell me what this is all about."

"I will try, sir. You see, everyone remarks on the fact that you have quite lost your head over your new wife, that you have fallen snare to a man's weakness. An ordinary man's weakness. And that is it, sir."

"I see," Tysen said slowly, and thought, well, I have certainly heard enough of this before, and he rose from his chair. It was all very clear to him now. "I am very sorry that everyone believes that I have somehow changed when all I've done is gotten married."

Mr. Gaither looked at him sadly. "A very melancholy thing to happen to a man of God, Vicar. A disastrous thing."

Tysen felt his heart pounding again, only this time each deep stroke sent a deep, searing ache through him. His head rarely ached, but it did now, a biting pain just over his left temple. He said, "Is laughter such a bad thing, Mr. Gaither?"

"If it exposes naught but more laughter, Reverend Sherbrooke," Mr. Gaither said, pity in his eyes now, "then I fear it likely is, at least for you, sir."

Tysen left, turning right on High Street, nodding, speaking, looking all his parishioners in the face as he met them. Few met his eye. He wasn't kissing Mary Rose, he wasn't laughing. He probably looked as serious as if he was conducting a funeral. He ignored the rain, falling more heavily even now, and walked to the beautifully tended old graveyard beside his church. Glenda Strapthorpe had wanted to take away all the graves and build a wing onto the vicarage? It boggled his mind.

He was still shaking his head in disbelief as he walked among the graves, eventually wending his way through the stones to his favorite. The man buried here had been a violent warrior, yet when Tysen came to the grave, he felt peace, a measure of serenity. He laid his hand on the ancient headstone, feeling the centuries-old texture that was still changing, year by passing year. It was just possible to make out the nearly obliterated lettering: Sir Vincent D'Egle, born in 1231, died in 1283. There were fresh flowers on the grave, leaning against the marker. Meggie had brought them, he knew, because she'd long known that he somehow identified with this one particular grave. They were bedraggled now, the rain tearing them apart. He felt as bedraggled as those wretched flowers. He moved just a bit away from it and sat on the long stone bench. He looked up at his church, at its magnificent spire, rising so tall above every other building in Glenclose-on-Rowan. The thick gray stone looked solid and timeless beneath the gray-clouded, weeping sky. He'd sat here many times listening to the bells rung by his sexton, Mr. Peters, feeling the incredible sounds seep into his very soul.

He closed his eyes and prayed for a very long time.

27

THE VICARAGE WAS crammed to the attic rafters. Douglas and Ryder and their families had all descended, unannounced and unexpected, late that Saturday afternoon, piled into three carriages that overflowed the vicarage stable.

The vicarage was filled with shouting children, laughing adults, a housekeeper who was nearly in hysteria from the pressure of it all, and him and his wife.

Mary Rose was gowned in the new dress Sinjun had given her, a dark-green wool with lace at the neckline, long fitted sleeves, banded with a dark-green satin ribbon beneath her breasts. It looked, he thought, very well indeed on her.

Mary Rose was overwhelmed, he knew, but looking at her now, not as her husband and a man who was coming to know her, but as a stranger would, he thought her nervousness wasn't obvious. She smiled, she was gracious, she dispensed tea and small cakes and tarts, she listened intently to any child who happened to engage her, and she smiled happily at him whenever she had the chance.

As for Tysen, he wanted to close himself in his study and remain there, in the darkness, steeped in the pain and doubt and uncertainty that had penetrated to his very soul. But he couldn't. His brothers and their families had come to visit, only the good Lord knew for how long, because neither Douglas nor Ryder would say. All they did was poke him in the shoulder and laugh. He sat there quietly, a teacup in his hand, saying nothing, just listening to everyone talking, arguing, all of it so very normal and, yes, lighthearted. Just a bit over a week ago, he'd held Max up by his ankles as punishment for saying *merda* to his cousins. He closed his eyes against the pain of it, against the inevitability of it.

Mary Rose didn't know what was wrong. Tysen was acting strangely, and it wasn't brought on by the visit by his siblings—no, he'd been abstracted for the full hour before they'd arrived. When he'd come in, his hair plastered to his head from the hard-blowing rain, she'd skipped up to him, laughing, scolding, smiling, so filled with pleasure at the simple sight of him, sodden but here with her again, and she'd come up on her tiptoes to kiss him. He'd not moved.

Slowly, slowly, her arms had fallen away and she'd stared up at him. "What is wrong, Tysen? What happened?"

"Nothing," he said and left her.

She'd wanted to yell after him to get out of his wet clothes, for he was probably soaked to the bone, but she didn't. She just stared after him.

Now he was acting as though the world was going to end at any moment, and he didn't know whether he was going to heaven or to hell.

What had happened?

Because Mary Rose was worried about her new husband, she wasn't particularly nervous about the unexpected visit of her new family in her own home. Besides, she knew them now, had seen naked statues with Alex and had made an apple pie with Sophie. Still, Meggie stood by her, her hand on her shoulder, her small protector, and she felt a rush of love.

Meggie said, "In this darker light, your hair and Aunt Alex's look exactly the same color."

"I know," Alex said. "In the bright sunlight, Mary Rose's hair is shinier and richer, altogether more charming."

"I wasn't intending that exactly," Meggie said, and grinned at her aunt.

"You have no guile, Meggie," Alex Sherbrooke said, and popped a small apricot tart into her mouth, closing her eyes as she chewed. She said then to Mary Rose, "As I told you at Northcliffe Hall, we are both cursed and blessed, you and I, what with all these curls and twisters and waves. At least there is so much hair, we should never go bald in our later years."

Mary Rose offered Alex another apricot tart and took one herself.

"You'll also never become flat-chested," Sophie Sherbrooke said, eyeing her sister-in-law's bosom. "What do you think, Mary Rose? Don't you think that God was overly generous to Alex when he handed out bosoms?"

Mary Rose laughed. "Very unfair, indeed."

"What is this about breasts?" Douglas Sherbrooke said, walking lazily to where his wife sat, sighed as he looked at her bosom, and lightly kissed her mouth.

"Douglas, that is not at all appropriate," his wife said.

"I have told you, dearest, that 'bosom' is a very faint vague sort of word used only by females. What you have are breasts. Thank God."

Sophie cleared her throat. "Actually, whatever we were speaking about, Douglas, it wouldn't hold your interest. Do go torment poor Tysen. To be perfectly blunt, our conversation isn't for your tender ears, my lad."

Mary Rose said a few minutes later to Sophie Sherbrooke, after Douglas had strolled off, an eyebrow arched upward, a smile on his lips, "I so enjoyed meeting all the Beloved Ones. I have never seen Tysen shouting and laughing quite so much as when a dozen of the children had taken him to the ground and were holding him down and sitting on him."

"He did enjoy himself," Sophie said, and frowned slightly as she looked over at him now. Mary Rose knew what she was seeing. A man who was distracted, a man who wasn't really with them, but off somewhere, deep in his thoughts, and she'd bet those thoughts weren't wonderful.

Sophie turned to smile at her husband as she said, "It is bedlam." She saw that Ryder was standing in the middle of the drawing room, holding Leo's head under one arm and Max's head under the other, rubbing them together. "Ryder loves them all so. Give him a crying child and that child will be smiling within moments. You know he is also a member of the House of Commons. That job and the children keep him very busy."

"You make it sound like you do nothing at all save sit about eating sweetmeats," Mary Rose said. "Remember, I was there at Chadwyck House. I saw how you never slowed from dawn until dusk."

"Well, I quite enjoy being responsible for all our tenant farmers. I can tell you the very best sheep-breeding methods, the most efficacious manures to be plowed into our fields, the best milking cows to be had—goodness, I am quite the expert on crops. Just let me tell you all about barley and rye sometime." She laughed gaily, adding, "In addition, naturally, I have to keep my dear husband under control, always a fascinating and demanding job."

"I saw that it was," Mary Rose said.

"Ha," Alex said, poking her elbow into Sophie's side.

"Ryder dotes on you. He gets within three feet of you and he's licking his lips. It's embarrassing, Sophie."

"And just what about you, Alex? You're one to talk. I can see Douglas staring at your bosom from across the room, and he is supposed to be attending to what poor Tysen is trying to say."

Mary Rose listened to the good-natured bickering between her sisters-in-law. She liked them both, impossible not to. They were open, friendly, and didn't seem to mind at all that she was from Scotland and spoke with a lilt.

Alex said then, "Max was telling us all what he said to you at dinner one evening when you first came. Something about he wouldn't eat his broccoli—and he said it in Latin. Then you answered—also in Latin. Well done, Mary Rose. Max seems so much less, well, how do I say it? He seems more lighthearted, more ready for fun, than he ever has before. It's amazing, don't you think, Sophie?"

"Oh, yes," Sophie said thoughtfully. "And Leo. He simply couldn't sit still at Chadwyck House. He was just telling me that he likes to ride, primarily with you, Mary Rose. He said that you could sing to a horse and the horse would start running faster than the wind."

Mary Rose thought about that small jest with Leo, still so surprised that her borrowed mare, Dahlia, had actually nearly run her legs off when she'd sung that Robert Burns ditty. "They are both dear boys," Mary Rose said, "unlike Meggie here, who gives me nothing but trouble. She is always criticizing me, always telling me what I should do and what I shouldn't do."

Meggie only laughed and pulled Mary Rose's earlobe.

Sophie and Alex looked at each other. They'd been pleased before when a laughing Tysen had brought his bride to visit them. They were even more pleased now. Tysen had chosen well this time.

Meggie said, "Mary Rose has nearly as sweet a smile as you do, Aunt Sophie."

"Very well," Sophie said on a sigh. "You may wear my garnet bracelet, Meggie."

"Thank you," Meggie said.

"That was well done," Mary Rose said, tilting her head at Meggie. "Am I as easy as your aunt?"

"I haven't yet tested you, Mary Rose. We will see."

Mary Rose later went to the stables with Leo to see his uncle Douglas's stallion, Garth, a brute with a vile temper, Leo told her, that made Uncle Douglas laugh with pleasure when he tried to fling him off his back. She was to sing a Robert Burns ditty to Garth, and then they would see. She opened her mouth and managed to sing nearly one complete verse to the huge horse before he did his best to trample them. She moved nearly as quickly as Leo.

Yes, Mary Rose thought as she dressed for dinner, her new family were very nice people, delightful really, and they seemed to like her very much—the Scottish bastard who was now, magically, an English vicar's wife. She'd even brought her husband a hundred-pound dowry.

She managed to find beds for all their guests. The three boy cousins would sleep with Max and Leo, and she imagined that they would be awake most of the night. Grayson, Sophie and Ryder's son, was a mesmerizing storyteller, despite his meager eight years, or maybe because of them. In the dark of the night, Ryder had told her at Chadwyck House, his boy could make his listeners' hair stand on end. He'd told his first ghost story at three years old, and his old nurse had run screaming from the nursery.

She gave Meggie's bedchamber to Douglas and Alex, and once again Meggie would sleep in their bedchamber. It was a pity. She wanted to know what was bothering Tysen.

At dinner that evening, just the adults present, he was quiet, his expression austere, his speech, when he was required to say something, really quite cool, detached. He simply sat there at the head of the table, eating little, just listening to his family toss jests and insults to and fro across the table. He was, Mary Rose thought, uninvolved, and she hated it. Had it been just the night before, he would have been laughing as much as they were now. Dear God, she missed his humor, his lightness of touch, his kindness.

What had happened?

What was wrong?

When at last the house was quiet and Meggie was asleep on her cot against the wall on the far side of the bedchamber, Mary Rose came up on her elbow, bent over her husband and kissed him.

What he did was the last thing she expected.

He didn't move. His mouth stilled beneath hers, and he said, "Don't."

She whispered, "But I love to kiss you, Tysen. It's been far too long. I won't wake Meggie. Just another kiss." He was wearing a nightshirt because Meggie was in the room, and Mary Rose hated it. Her hand strayed to his belly. She loved to touch him, feel his entire body tense, feel the power of him.

He grabbed her hand and lifted it off him. "Go to sleep, Mary Rose."

Slowly, she pulled back. She couldn't see his expression, just the shadow of his face in the dark of night. "Do you feel all right, Tysen?"

"Yes."

"Have I done something to upset you?"

"No."

"Something has happened. Won't you talk to me?"

"There is nothing to say. Go to sleep."

She lay on her back, gazing up at the darkened ceiling, wondering what was wrong, wondering why he wouldn't talk to her.

The following day was Sunday. All the Sherbrookes went to church. Gathering the children together was a task for Ryder, the most patient of all the adults in the house. As they walked from the vicarage to the church, the bells were ringing, the air was clear and sweet with the smells of late fall, and the gray clouds and rain wafted away early that morning. They filed into the pews, an adult assigned to every two children.

Tysen hadn't come into the church with them. He'd told her that he and Samuel Pritchert would go in through the vestry.

The organ, Mary Rose thought, was just a bit out of tune, but it was played very well by old Mrs. Caddy, whose fingers were gnarled and bent with arthritis.

It was the first time Mary Rose had seen her husband as a vicar. He came in quietly, wearing his black robe, his linen very white, standing back while Samuel Pritchert gave out all the announcements, led the congregation in the singing, and offered a single prayer for God's grace, a rather long prayer that had the children twitching.

Then Tysen walked forward to stand tall behind his beautifully carved walnut pulpit. When he spoke, his voice was deep and resonant, reaching every ear in the large church. His Sherbrooke blue eyes were clear, radiant in the gentle morning light that streamed through the stained-glass windows into the church. She found herself mesmerized, looking at him, thinking no angel could be more beautiful than he.

But when he spoke, his eyes were intense, his expression bleak. He became an avenging angel, here to warn the people of the consequences of their sins. He spoke at length of one's duties to God, of not allowing worldly considerations to pull one away from one's focus on God and his commandments. He spoke of God's expectations of those who believed in him and devoted their lives to him and his teachings.

He spoke eloquently, intelligently, his words severe, stark, and, in truth, Mary Rose thought, many of his thoughts so intricate and complex that they seemed to her to be fitted more to a roomful of clergymen than to a church filled with laypeople here to worship.

She became very still as she listened to her husband speak to the nearly two hundred people packed into the church. There was not a hint of levity or laughter in his voice, no message of redemption or joy in any of his words, no assurances of God's boundless love and compassion, no encouragement to marvel at the daily endless beauty of God's bounty.

He was intelligent, she thought, so very austere and clever in his harshness. And he was very cold. Mary Rose realized that his brothers and their wives saw nothing amiss with what he was saying or how he spoke. That was what they were used to? No, that didn't seem right. Her husband, the man who had enveloped her in his caring, his kindness, his immense ability to make her feel very good about herself, he wasn't to be found in this vicar. This was a very different man, a man she didn't know. How could it be? She realized suddenly, in a flash of insight, that his siblings looked disappointed. Was that possible?

She didn't like that distant, harsh sermon or this stranger who spoke with such cold passion about God's endless demands, His countless tasks for man to perform to earn His approval. This stranger was pious and hard and demanding on God's behalf; he was ready to smite both the sins and the sinners into eternity.

Thankfully, the service finally ended. Mary Rose sat

there, stunned. Mrs. Caddy began playing a loud, energetic recessional, and Mary Rose stood with everyone else.

Tysen, Samuel behind him, walked down the center aisle, past his family, not looking at them, or at her, not pausing to speak to them, or to her. He stationed himself just outside the great church doors, in the light of the early-afternoon sun, not smiling, seriously greeting each of his parishioners, shaking hands, bowing over others, speaking quietly, not even one stingy smile ever showing on his mouth.

When Mary Rose paused in front of him, he gave her only a curt nod, as he did his brothers and their wives. As he did his own children and nephews.

No one said a word to Mary Rose. Max, Leo, and Meggie stayed close to her, but they didn't speak to her. They were talking low among themselves. She knew they could see that she was completely smashed down. She also knew they realized if they did try to comfort her, she would burst into tears. She couldn't begin to imagine how Max and Leo would react to that.

28

$\mathcal{T}$YSEN CAME THROUGH the narrow garden gate. He stood at the back of the garden, his palms pressed against the pale peach stone wall, the ivy touching his fingers. He pressed his forehead against the wall. The sun had disappeared behind wintry gray clouds. It was chilly, but still not all that cold. Nevertheless, he felt numb to his bones. He closed his eyes and wondered what he was going to do. He could, quite honestly, think of no more prayers no more pleas to God to show him his duty, to give him guidance, to help him see what His plan was for this one simple man. Perhaps it was because he already had God's plan, that he'd performed exactly as God wished him to as his chosen emissary. But it was cheerless, that plan. He felt deadened all the way to his soul, and surely that was blasphemy.

He had prayed himself out. Now he felt utterly alone, and he knew in that moment that he'd always been alone, until Mary Rose. Dear God, he couldn't bear himself. He hated the pain that was crouched inside him now, burrowed in so deep he doubted he would ever be free of it.

Douglas said, "Just what the hell do you think you're doing, Tysen?"

Wearily, he turned to face his brothers. Both Douglas and Ryder were standing not six feet away, their posture aggressive, their faces hard.

"Yes, that was some performance," Ryder said after the silence had continued for too long. He looked at Tysen, his confusion and frustration plain. "You gave a ringing sermon about sin and the dreadful consequences of sinning and wickedness and man's duties and obligations to God. Endless and unforgiving, all those duties. Then you offered up a thundering prayer in that god-awful cold voice of yours, exhorting everyone to forget everything but their obligations to God. All else, you said, was sacrilege.

"Then, you damnable ass, you leave your wife, ignore both her and your children and the rest of your family, to go off by yourself to greet your parishioners. What the devil does God say about your duty to your wife? What the hell is wrong with you? What were you thinking, you damned prig?"

More unblinking silence.

Douglas said as he took a step toward his brother, "Alex said that Mary Rose was stunned, that she was very hurt by your actions. For God's sake, I myself saw what you did, saw her shock, her utter surprise. I saw how all your parishioners looked pleased when you did that, nodding their bloody heads because their vicar of old was back, the man who had no humor, but nonetheless, they knew him, didn't want him to change.

"And your children—no, that can wait. Tysen, I've a good mind to knock you down and smash your bloody face into the dirt."

Ryder said, stepping forward to stand again by his brother, "You marry her and now you treat her like she's some sort of unwanted stray who happened to wander into your house. An unwanted, *foreign* stray. You ignore her.

You simply cut her in front of all your parishioners. You're acting like a bloody ass."

"I know," Tysen said, and he said nothing more because, simply, there was nothing more to say.

"What the hell do you mean by those idiotic words?" Douglas said, and now his hands were fists.

"I mean only that I know how I'm acting. I am at last acting the way I am supposed to act. The past three months have been an aberration, a mistake. I am back to being myself now. All is as it should be."

"An aberration? A bloody mistake?" Douglas said, a thick black eyebrow slanted upward. "Aberration? Damn you, what sort of bloodless word is that? Tysen, Mary Rose is your wife. We have observed how much she adores you, seen the smile light up her eyes when you come into a room. We have seen how you idolize her, how you laugh when you're with her, how you play with your children now, how you have finally found joy."

Ryder said, "We've seen how much you laugh now, how you hug your children for no good reason at all, how you simply play. Play? Neither Douglas nor I had seen you play since you turned eighteen and decided to become a complete and utterly pious prig."

Douglas said, "Oh, yes, Max sidled up to me when we arrived back here at the vicarage a while ago, and said, his head bowed, his voice all sad and hopeless, that something must have happened, that you were his old papa again. I thought he would start crying. Damn you, Tysen, what the hell is going on with you? Even that first short letter you wrote to Ryder and me was filled with humor and excitement. It was filled with your love for a woman. And then you brought your family to see us. We realized that you finally saw the beauty, not only in life but in the open love for your wife and your children. You finally realized the importance of them to you, and you gloried in it. All of us marveled. We were excited, so pleased that you had finally met a woman who could give you joy, show you her deep love, a woman who could teach you to smile and maybe even kick up your heels."

Ryder said, "Now it's all sucked out of you again. I should have realized it when we first got here yesterday, but neither of us did. We just thought you were preoccupied by a church matter, or perhaps you were even worried about Mary Rose dealing with all of us.

"But it wasn't that, was it? Something had already happened to blight you again. What the hell was it?"

Tysen looked blindly at his brothers.

"I don't want you to be the old you," Ryder said, more gently now, seeing the ravages of pain in his brother's eyes. "I want to see the new you, the new you I met at Chadwyck House, the man I had never before realized I loved quite so much—the father who shows his love to his children, who shares his contentment and happiness with them, who teases them and shouts with laughter when Leo tries a new acrobatic move and falls flat on his face or when Max spouts some new Latin, especially a curse word."

They were his own personal Greek chorus, Tysen thought, taking turns, getting it all out.

It was Douglas's turn, and he said now, "And what about Meggie? She worships you, her little face lights up from within when she sees you, but now the light is gone. Where the hell is that Tysen? What happened to make you bury him away again? What happened to freeze him back up?"

"He does not belong here," Tysen said quietly. "He is not what God wants. That man wasn't a man of God, he was a man of the world, a man swallowed by the temptations of the world, content to wallow in his own indulgences, his own wants and desires—no, not a man of

God." He pushed past his brothers and left by the garden gate, closing it quietly behind him.

They stood there, staring after him. Douglas said slowly, "Something is very wrong here, Ryder. I've never seen a more miserable man. And it has come about so quickly. What the hell happened?"

Ryder said, "Before, when Tysen acted like he did at church—all uncaring and remote and stern—you and I both knew that he truly believed that cold, distant man was who and what he saw himself to be. Nothing more, nothing less, and he was content with that man. We weren't, but we'd finally accepted him as the humorless prig he was. Yes, that man was comfortable being who and what he was, and he was smug in his belief."

Douglas said something very crude and strode back to the vicarage. Ryder remained in the garden, wondering what the hell would happen now. He felt very sorry for Mary Rose and the children. For his brother he felt deep, strangling pain.

Mary Rose sat in front of her dressing table, a small brooch that her mother had given her before she'd left Scotland held loose in her hand. Her dressing table had been moved back in here, along with her brushes, her clothes, her shoes.

While she'd been sitting in church listening to that grim stranger speak, everything of hers that had been in Tysen's bedchamber had been brought into Melinda Beatrice's. Dear God, it was a dreadful room, and now Tysen had sent her here.

It was so dreadful a room that she hadn't even considering placing any of their guests, even the children, in here.

It was late afternoon. Mary Rose went looking for her husband. She found him in the graveyard, sitting on a bench, his hands clasped between his knees, just staring at a very old grave. She walked up to him, and stood there, watching him, saying nothing.

"Is there a problem?" he said finally, not looking at her.

"Yes, I believe there is," she said. "You have never spoken to me so coldly before, Tysen. Won't you please tell me what is wrong? Did something happen?"

"No, nothing happened. Please go attend to our guests. I have an appointment very shortly." Even as he spoke, he rose. He looked at her briefly, then turned on his heel and made his way through the graves to the far cemetery gate.

She stood there, looking after him until he was gone from her sight. She returned to the vicarage and asked Mrs. Priddie to have all her things moved from Melinda Beatrice's bedchamber back to Tysen's.

Mrs. Priddie said, "I don't know if we should do that, ma'am. The vicar didn't say anything to me about moving you back into the big room."

"I am the mistress here, Mrs. Priddie. I shall do as I please. Is there anything else you would like to say?"

"Would you like any of your guests moved in here? All the boys are crammed into one room."

"Oh, no, it would give them nightmares, particularly the children. Can you imagine the tales Grayson could make up with this room as his ambiance? No, we will just close the room up again. Now, excuse me, Mrs. Priddie. I must find my husband."

But she didn't find him. He was doing a fine job of avoiding her.

He didn't return to the vicarage until very late that night. When he came into his bedchamber, he cradled the single candle. He didn't want to disturb Meggie. But Meggie wasn't there. Mary Rose was, and she was sleeping right in the middle of his bed.

He made no noise, he was sure of it, but she sat up in bed, looking toward him. "Hello, Tysen."

"Mary Rose. What are you doing here?"

"We are husband and wife. This is also my bedchamber. I will not be sent like an outcast to Melinda Beatrice's room."

"Nonetheless, I would prefer it if you slept in the other room."

"No, I won't be banished to that dreadful room. If you cannot bear to have me near you, then you will just have to move in there yourself."

Tysen set the candle down on the bedside table. He began automatically to take off his clothes, realized what he was doing, and stopped cold. He stood there, his hands at his sides, looking blankly at the bed that had his wife sitting in the middle of it.

"It is enough, Tysen," Mary Rose said. She hugged her knees to her chest. "I'm glad you came back. No, I won't ask you where you have been hiding. I was praying you would come back, and finally you have. Your brothers tried very hard to make things appear normal, but of course, nothing was normal. Even the children were quiet. They don't know what's happening, but they know something is very wrong."

"Nothing is wrong," Tysen said. "Everything is as it should be again."

She digested that, then said slowly, "I spoke to Samuel Pritchert this afternoon, when I gave up trying to find you. He agrees with you. He said to me that everything is as it should be again. He told me how all your flock would just as soon see the back of me, that they wanted you to become again the way you were before you came to Scotland, before you met and married me."

He said nothing at all, just stood there, his hands at his

sides. He looked very tired. No, he looked beyond tired. He looked deadened.

She didn't know whose pain was greater in that moment, hers or his. "Do you want me to leave, Tysen?"

"You can't leave. You're my wife."

"Do you really want to be that man I saw in church this morning who spoke of sin and corruption and moral laxity? The man who stood aloof from everyone, the man who looked so cold, so withdrawn that he could have been forged from stone?"

"That man is the man I was, the man I must be again. It is God's will."

"I don't know that God," she said slowly. "My God is loving, forgiving. My God wants us to laugh, to see the beauty of the world He created." She shook herself. It didn't matter. She said then, "I should have told you this before, Tysen. Perhaps now isn't a good time, but I think I owe it to myself that you know the truth."

Still, he said nothing.

"I love you."

He flinched as if she'd struck him, hard. Then, slowly, he shook his head. "No, Mary Rose. Please, don't."

"You cannot even bear to hear me say that to you?"

"No."

"I see," she said. "Well, that does make a difference." Without another word, Mary Rose left the bed. She grabbed her dressing gown, pulled two blankets off the top of the bed, and without another word, without another look at her husband, she left the bedchamber. Meggie was sleeping in the small sewing room at the end of the corridor. Mary Rose curled up next to her and finally, after a very long time, she fell asleep.

"It's all over," Max said the next morning. He was sitting against the wall, his arms dangling between his bent knees, two books open on the floor beside him. He looked defeated.

Leo said, "Papa is as he used to be again." Leo wasn't turning cartwheels or even standing on his head. He was stretched out on his stomach, his chin on his fists, and he looked ready to burst into tears.

"No," Meggie said, from her perch on Max's bed, "Papa is now even more than he used to be. Before, he wasn't so distant, so set apart from us. He loved us and we knew it. Now he is so far away he can't even see us."

"That's right," Leo said. "Before, he would laugh, every once in a while. He hugged us once in a while. He even frowned when we irritated him. But now there's nothing. It's like he's afraid to say or do anything that could be seen as not utterly serious."

Mary Rose couldn't bear it. She'd come in a few minutes before and listened to them. Now, she said, "Where are all your cousins?"

"They're in the graveyard," Max said. "Grayson likes the graveyard. He makes up stories about all the dead people. Even though it's cold out there today, no one wants to miss one of Grayson's stories."

"Except the three of you."

"Everything is scary enough," Max said. "We don't need Grayson's stories."

"All right, then. You three are coming with me. We're going riding."

They didn't want to, but when Meggie looked closely at Mary Rose, saw her pallor, saw her determination, she nodded slowly. "You're right, Mary Rose. It will put things at a distance for a while. Come on, Max, Leo. I don't want to have to hurt either of you. Move, now."

There were enough horses, if Mary Rose rode Garth, Douglas's huge stallion. "I'll sing to him, a different ditty this time, since he obviously didn't like the one I sang to him last time." Garth was seventeen hands high, a huge black beast, with mean eyes. Mary Rose sang one ditty after the other as she saddled him.

He let her mount him. "He is very big," she said, her heart thumping a bit faster as she looked over at her three stepchildren atop their own horses.

"You will be all right, Mary Rose?" Leo said.

"I'm a good rider. We won't have any races, all right?"

They rode single file until they were in the countryside. It was cloudy and cold, and Mary Rose felt the chill to her crooked toe. "Is everyone warm enough?"

"Poor old Ricketts is cold," Leo said, patting the gelding's neck. "I hope he lasts through the winter. He's nearly twenty now, you know."

Mary Rose hoped he lasted too. Actually, she hoped she lasted as well.

After they'd ridden through Grapple Thorpe, a small village very close to the Channel, Mary Rose said, "Who would like to go down to the beach?"

"I think we should go back to that inn in Grapple Thorpe and have some chocolate," Meggie said. "I'm cold, Mary Rose."

They would have made it back to Grapple Thorpe had it not been for the mail coach coming at breakneck speed around a corner of the country road.

Mary Rose saw that coach flying toward them, saw poor old Ricketts falter, rear back in panic, then stumble. She watched Leo fly over his head and land in a ditch beside the road.

"Meggie, Max, get out of the way, go! I'll see to Leo!"

She couldn't do a thing until the mail coach passed them, whipping up thick winds of dust in its wake.

Mary Rose slid off Garth's back and ran to Leo. He was pulling himself upright, shaking his head. She didn't touch him, just came down on her knees beside him. Meggie and Max were right behind her. "Are you all right, Leo?"

"My brains are scrambled," Leo said, panting a bit. "My ribs feel like they're broken into little sticks, my stomach is jumping into my neck—" He looked up and gave her a blazing smile. "Don't worry, Mary Rose, I'm all right."

"Oh, Leo," she said and gently pulled him into her arms. "Just sit very still a moment."

There was a sharp hitch to his breath, then he eased against her. Mary Rose said to Max and Meggie, "Let's just stay here a moment until Leo gets his brains unscrambled."

Leo laughed.

Slowly, Mary Rose leaned away from him. She studied his pale face. "How do you feel? Tell me the truth now, Leo."

"Just a bit dizzy."

"No wonder. I want you to lie down a minute. There's no rush, we can stay here as long as you need to. Max, tie the horses so they don't run back to the vicarage stables along with old Ricketts."

Leo was indeed dizzy, and so he didn't argue. Mary Rose touched each of his ribs lightly. None were broken, thank God. She looked up when she heard Max trying to calm Garth. "He will be all right," she said, and knew even as she spoke that she was praying it was true. He could be injured internally. "Leo, does this hurt?"

She touched him here and there, ending finally by lightly pressing on his belly. No pain, thank God.

"Do you want to vomit?"

"No, even the dizziness isn't so bad now."

"Good. Now, how would you like to ride Garth with me back to Grapple Thorpe? Chocolate for everyone. Oh, dear, did anyone bring any money?"

"Meggie always has money," Leo said.

"She wins it off us," Max said. "I wish she'd cheat, then we could complain to Papa about it."

Leo said, "Just yesterday, Papa would have laughed if we'd said that. But not today. Not ever again."

Mary Rose didn't know what to say, and so she concentrated on helping Leo to rise. He was a bit shaky on his feet, but he was upright and walking, and then, finally, he smiled. "I'm all right, Mary Rose. Poor old Ricketts, when the fellow blew that silly horn, Ricketts must have thought it was Saint Peter calling him to the horse pearly gates in heaven."

Meggie laughed. "Oh, Leo, if you ever let anything happen to you, I will kill you."

Fifteen minutes later, they sat on a long, scarred old oak bench in the taproom at the Golden Goose Inn in the middle of Grapple Thorpe village, right across from a lovely green that boasted a pond and at least half a dozen ducks.

And that was where Mr. Dimplegate found them, that lovely young woman, all windblown, shepherding three children. He was the town bully, drank too much, and believed himself to be God's special treasure to womankind. When he spotted Mary Rose, he knew this day would work out to be just dandy for him. All jocular, grinning widely, just a dash of ale froth on his upper lip, he walked to their table, hands on hips, and leaned down close to Mary Rose. "Eh, ye a governess, little gal? Ye sure are purty as a picture, ye are."

Mary Rose looked up at the man, who was surely large, looked strong, and was young enough and drunk enough to be a problem. He was also standing much too close.

"No, I am their mother, sir," she said and turned away from him. When he didn't move, she said over her shoulder, "Good day, sir."

It degenerated from there, beginning with a roar from Mr. Dimplegate. "Ye ain't bloody well their mother, girl! What are ye, then? A maid seeing them back to their home?"

"Go away," Mary Rose said.

"No female turns her back on Dimplegate," he yelled and grabbed her arm. "Me, I'm a grand lover, a man o' yer dreams."

"You, sir, are more in the nature of a nightmare." Mary Rose threw her chocolate in his face. Too bad it had cooled a bit.

Max yelled, "Get away from our mother, sir!"

"Shut yer trap, little sprat!"

Leo jumped up on the end of the table, turned a backward flip and landed on his feet, right in Mr. Dimplegate's face. Leo shoved him hard, but Mr. Dimplegate had grabbed Mary Rose's other arm. As he fell over backward, he jerked her up from the bench. They went down together.

The children were on their feet, yelling at him, hitting him. The owner was wringing his hands, having had too many run-ins with Dimplegate to come close. "See yerself home now, Danny," he yelled. "Hey, you let the lady alone. She didn't do nothin'. Let her go!" But his voice was swallowed by all the racket.

Mary Rose scrambled off Mr. Dimplegate and backed away from him. But he was fast. He grabbed her hand and held on to her like a lifeline as he came to his feet. "I'm going to wallop that little codshead," he said, then yelled over his shoulder, "Ye get yer butt here, boy!"

It was Meggie who grabbed up a thick log from beside the fireplace, climbed up on a chair, and bashed Mr. Dimplegate on his large head. He whirled around, blinked up at the little girl who was now his height standing on that chair, and yelled not six inches from her face, "Why'd ye do that fer, little gal? This one, she ain't nothing, jest a maid or a governess, or a nanny, and she needs a man."

He poked his finger against his chest. "Ye see? All she needs is me. Now I'll jest take her out o' here for a bit and make her all 'appy."

"She's my mother, you idiot!" And Meggie hit him again with that log, really hard.

Mr. Dimplegate dropped Mary Rose's hand, swayed where he stood, and collapsed finally against Meggie's chair. The chair rocked a bit, then went flying. Mary Rose managed to break Meggie's fall, which could have been nasty, since she would have landed too close to the stone fireplace. It was Mary Rose who landed against the fireplace, carrying Meggie's weight, slamming against the hearthstone.

Leo was on his knees beside them in an instant. Meggie was blinking hard, getting herself together. "Mary Rose, are you all right? Oh, God, Max, do something!"

Leo was patting her face, even as Meggie was on her knees now beside her, frantically rubbing her hand.

"Oh, dear, oh, dear," said Mr. Randall, the owner, still wringing his hands.

"Sir," Max said, "we need you to get us a wagon. We must get our mother home. We live in Glenclose-on-Rowan. Our father is Reverend Sherbrooke, the vicar there. Please, sir, hurry!"

"Yes, yes," Meggie said, crying now, "Papa will know what to do."

29

CLOSE TO AN hour later, an ancient wagon belonging to Farmer Biggs, quickly emptied of moldering hay, and pulled by a gray gelding that was even older than Ricketts, lumbered to a stop in front of the vicarage gate.

Both Leo and Max were yelling even before the wagon pulled to a halt.

Mary Rose was awake, had awakened before Mr. Randall had carried her to the wagon and carefully laid her on a pile of smelly blankets. All three children had hovered over her on the bumpy ride back to Glenclose-on-Rowan.

She'd been content not to move, to let everything settle, she told the children. She smiled now up at Meggie. "I just feel a bit strange, Meggie, nothing bad, I'm sure of it."

"You're awfully pale, Mary Rose."

"Well, I landed against the brick hearth. It was very hard and unforgiving. But I'll be fine. I just feel a bit dull, heavy."

"If you're all right, then why do you look like you want to cry?"

Shouting voices poured out of the vicarage.

"I won't cry. Please, love, don't make a fuss. We don't want to worry your father."

But Meggie just shook her head.

Tysen was beside that old doddering wagon in an instant. He saw Mary Rose lying there, covered with blankets, so pale and listless that he knew she was dying. He'd never been so afraid in his life.

He climbed up beside her, studying her face closely before he said, "Mary Rose, are you all right?"

His beloved face was above her. He was worried. She wanted to weep. "It was an accident, a very silly accident, Tysen. I am quite all right, I just landed against a brick hearth at the inn in Grapple Thorpe, that's all, and—" Suddenly she grabbed her stomach and cried out.

The pain lessened. "I don't understand," she said, and then the pain slashed through her again. This time it didn't stop, just kept on and on, tearing at her insides, making her cry and whimper, making her twist, trying desperately to get away from it. She heard Tysen say, his voice hoarse with shock, "Oh, my God, she's bleeding." He'd been about to lift her out of the wagon and he lifted his hand. It was covered with blood.

"A miscarriage."

Was that Sophie who had said that? The pain tore through her again, harder this time, deeper, and she wanted, quite simply, to die.

What was that Sophie had said? A miscarriage? Mary Rose was pregnant? She was losing her babe?

"Tysen," she said and grabbed at his hand.

"It will be all right, Mary Rose, I swear it to you." Then she was in his arms, and the pain was twisting and tearing her insides apart.

"A babe? Tysen, am I losing our babe?"

"Hush, Mary Rose. Please, it will be all right." Tysen carried her to their bedchamber, aware that Sophie and Alex were running ahead of him, yelling out orders to Mrs. Priddie. Sophie was spreading towels on the bed.

He laid his wife down, only to have her clasp his hands so tightly she hurt him. "It's all right," he said over and over. She was lost to him for several moments. He felt the dreadful pain in her. He knew the exact moment when her body expelled the babe. Blood, so much blood, on his hands, his arms, covering her gown, weighing it down, stark red against the white towels.

She was crying, and he was holding her tightly against him, rocking her, talking nonsense, really, but he just couldn't stop himself.

He heard Alex yell, "Fetch the doctor, Douglas, quickly! She's bleeding too much!"

Tysen simply pulled away from her. "Hold still," he said, his voice harsh enough to get through to her. Then he was between her legs, jerking away the bloody gown, tearing away her petticoats and chemise. So much blood, and it was nearly black now, that blood, and it was not only her blood but also the bloody waste that had been their babe.

"Mary Rose, listen to me."

She forced herself outward at that hard voice, saw Tysen between her legs at the foot of the bed. "Stay with me," he said, then pressed a towel wrapped around his fist as hard as he could against her. "I mean it, Mary Rose, you will stay with me, look at me. Damn you, don't leave me. Open your eyes. That's right."

He knew little about childbirth, even less than that about miscarriage. He'd prayed with many women who had lost their babes, but he'd never seen it happen. He'd consoled men who'd lost their wives to childbirth. Oh, Jesus. He was the father of three children, yet he'd never been in the same room when Melinda Beatrice had given birth. He remembered her yelling. And now he shuddered.

So much blood, covering his hands. He pulled away the towel and took another one from Sophie and pressed it against her again.

"It will be all right, Mary Rose." It was his litany, he thought. Oh, dear God, what else should he do?

It seemed a lifetime had passed and another begun before Dr. Clowder ran into the bedchamber, took in the situation at a glance, and very gently pushed Tysen away.

Tysen realized that his brothers and their wives were in the bedchamber. At least they'd kept the children outside. But he knew that they had heard her screaming, that they knew what had happened.

Tysen gathered Mary Rose against him and held her while Dr. Clowder plied his instruments. He felt her shock, her pain, her deadening sorrow. He felt it all deep inside himself.

He just held her, his bloody hands pressed against her, his face pressed against her tangled hair. She was still wearing her riding hat. He gently pulled it off and flung it to the floor. He saw Alex slowly pick it up and lay it on a table. Anything, he thought, anything anyone could do to keep all this pain at bay.

"I didn't know," she said, her voice hoarse from her yelling. "I didn't even know I was pregnant."

"I didn't either," he said. "It's all right, Mary Rose. Please, my love, it will be all right."

She stilled, utterly. And he realized then what he had said, and it filled him with quiet joy. At that exact moment, he knew that if he didn't have her, he wouldn't have anything at all. In those minutes, feeling her blood dry on his hands, feeling her tears wet his linen shirt, prickle against his neck, he knew to his very soul that without this woman, his life was meaningless.

No, not that, never that, but that his life would have no more importance to him. And if he was of no importance to himself, then how could he possibly serve God?

In that instant, holding this precious human being

against him, realizing that he could so easily have lost her, still could lose her, he finally understood. Everything fell into place. All the confusion, all the chaos and uncertainty, it was gone as if it had never existed in the first place. He felt peace flow through him, fill him, and he knew it was all right now, all of it.

He smiled as he kissed her forehead, her nose, and finally her mouth. "We are together," he said against her dry lips. "I love you, Mary Rose. I love you with all my heart, I will love you all my life and beyond, and together we will bring joy to this damned town and to ourselves and to our children. Please tell me that I haven't lost you. If I lost you, it would be all over for me. And for my children, too, I suspect."

Mary Rose looked at his dearly loved face through the tears that blurred her sight. "Tysen," she said, "I'm so glad you came back to me. I love you so very much. I don't want to ever leave you."

Then she simply closed her eyes. She was unconscious, that or asleep. He touched his forehead to hers, not moving.

"The bleeding has nearly stopped, Reverend Sherbrooke. Your wife will be all right. You did well."

Tysen realized he was praying again, and it was a prayer filled with hope and endless gratitude, a prayer of promise and soul-deep joy.

Tysen stepped to his pulpit. Brilliant sunlight poured through the stained-glass windows. He felt the warmth of it on his face. He paused a moment, looking out over the many faces he'd known for eight years, all of them focused now on him, wondering at his silence, starting to get nervous because they didn't understand.

Tysen looked at his brothers and their families, then at his own family—his boys, Meggie, and Mary Rose, who was still too pale, too thin, but she'd insisted she was well enough to come. And she was smiling at him, the most beautiful smile he'd ever seen in his life.

He felt a smile tugging at his own mouth. He wondered if he would ever stop smiling. He leaned forward, clasped his hands atop the pulpit, and said, "I have been here for eight years. I was a very young man when I came to Glenclose-on-Rowan, given this living by my brother, the earl of Northcliffe. You have, all of you, seen me grow to my full manhood amongst you. You have held me and my children close to you. I know each of you and I cherish what you are, what you doubtless will come to be.

"As you all know, I am now Lord Barthwick of Kildrummy Castle in Scotland. I went there solely out of duty, but God must have been directing my steps, for what I found was a very special woman who has shown me the absolute wonder of life, the glory of being a man who is beloved not only by God, but by a woman that He fashioned just for me.

"Through her, my dearest wife, Mary Rose Sherbrooke, I finally realized how very lucky I am. I finally saw what was right in front of me. I finally saw my children as the precious beings they are. I found that life could be filled with joy—endless joy. All I had to do was embrace it. I did.

"Now, however, I see that many of you wish that I would return to being that very devout and sober man you were used to, that very serious young man you had nurtured and watched grow in his faith and his self-belief. Since you had never seen him as a man filled with contentment and laughter and so much love he threatened to burst with it, you did not know that person, and thus he made you uncomfortable, and thus you did not want him,

"He was a stranger to you. He made you uncertain because where he once was stern in his admonishments to you as God's creatures, once told you in no uncertain terms that a sin would blight your soul, he now wanted you to see the simple pleasure of just being alive, to feel the sun on your face and to smile under its warmth, to hear the sound of your children's voices, knowing that they are yours and you will love them into eternity. This man now wants you to believe with all your hearts that God loves you, wishes you to be devout and loyal and honest, to worship Him with all the joy in your hearts, to be grateful to Him and to each other for the happiness we find here, on His magnificent earth.

"Our Lord created us, all the men and women who are sitting here today. And what he gave us, what he placed deep within each of us, is the capacity to love and honor and know in our hearts that there is meaning in our lives, meaning that allows for us to come together and give each other boundless happiness.

"I stand before you this morning a man who has been given one of our dear God's greatest gifts. God has blessed me, opened my heart to know more pleasure than a simple man deserves.

"All of you know that I returned from Scotland with a wife. Her name, as you well know now, is Mary Rose Sherbrooke. She and I and our three children are a family, and we will remain a family who loves God and each other, a family that rejoices that we are together, that we care endlessly for each other.

"This will be my last service as your vicar. Mr. Samuel Pritchert, a man you all admire and respect, will be here to advise you and assist you in any spiritual matters. I do not know who will come to Glenclose-on-Rowan as your vicar, but I know that the earl of Northcliffe will give it serious and careful thought.

"I thank you again for my eight years as your vicar. I will think well of all of you for the rest of my days."

And he smiled again, at everyone, and stepped back from the pulpit.

The silence was deafening.

Meggie said, her voice delighted and spontaneous, reaching to every pew in the church, "Oh, my, Mary Rose, just imagine. We're all together. You can have babies and I can teach them what's what, just as I have Max and Leo."

"I will teach them how to tell ghost stories," Grayson Sherbrooke said.

Ryder Sherbrooke shouted with laughter.

Epilogue

Bleaker's Bluff
Kildrummy Castle
September 15, 1816

THE SUN WAS a ball of fire, warming the land as it slowly rose to fill the sky and turn the sea red.

"It is the most beautiful sight in the world," Mary Rose said as she leaned closer to her husband. She was sitting against him, cradled between his arms and legs, and he tightened his arms around her, pulling his cloak closer around her, just in case, since it was still early morning.

"It is one of them," he said, and kissed her ear. His fingers splayed over her swollen belly. "Our babe does well this morning? He is not kicking you?"

"He is fine. Mayhap he is resting after performing Leo's acrobatics all night."

"We must leave next week, love. I don't wish to, but I don't want you too far along in your pregnancy before we go back to Glenclose-on-Rowan. Also, Dr. Clowder has threatened me to ask that you be there for him to deliver our child."

"Dr. Clowder told me that since Max and Leo and Meggie are such marvelous children, if we don't want this one, he will be delighted to adopt him or her."

Tysen laughed, then said more soberly, "Well, the poor man had two sons, both of them rotters. One got sent to Botany Bay for beating two men and stealing their purses; the other was killed in a duel for sleeping with a man's wife."

"We can give him very liberal visitation rights," Mary Rose said.

"Did you enjoy your mother's birthday last evening?"

"Oh, yes, everyone was in such high spirits. Isn't it grand, Tysen? She's so very happy with Miles. All those years playing a madwoman, and now all she does is sing and laugh, just like we do."

Tysen wasn't sure what he felt about Mary Rose's mother. He supposed he wished her well now. He was kissing Mary Rose's ear when she said, "Isn't it odd that Donnatella was married to Erickson for three months and his mother just up and died so suddenly, in her sleep? At least that's what my mother told me."

Tysen thought of Donnatella. It didn't take long for him to say, "No. I don't find that particularly odd. Donnatella, I think, was born knowing how to land on her feet."

"You don't really think that she—"

"I think it best not to visit that notion. Oh, yes, love, I got a letter from Samuel Pritchert."

"Oh, my, I don't like the way you said that. All right, Tysen. I'm ready. What did Samuel write to you?"

"Actually, he's pleading with me to come home. He said that Mr. Gaither, as the congregation's representative, came to see him. It seems that everyone is despondent, nearly miserable. We have been gone for three months, much too long a time, it seems. A great cloud of melancholia has descended over the town, and all because they were so used to leaving the church smiling, perhaps even grinning a bit at something the vicar had said during his sermon, feeling warm that the vicar told them they were worthy of God's love. Yes, they were used to discussing their problems and their neighbors' problems with a vicar who made them see that silver linings abounded, and not just misery and bad feelings. He wrote that they want me back so I may bring optimism into their lives again."

"Was Samuel truly pathetic?"

"Very."

"Well, then. Perhaps after we spend some time with Sinjun and Colin at Vere Castle, we can return. At the first frost?"

"Probably before that. I believe that Oliver can't wait to see the back of me. Bless his heart, he finds himself in a bind. He loves the children so much, they follow him everywhere, and yet he much enjoys being the master here. If he could get away with it, he'd have me go back to England and keep the rest of you here."

She turned a bit in his arms to look up at him. "I'm glad that Douglas and Alex were here so they could see how very well Oliver is doing. I've never seen such a proud man as your brother, striding along beside while Oliver showed him everything." She snuggled against him, breathing in the scent of him, and then his fingers moved lightly over her belly, and she knew such a burst of love, such overflowing gratitude, that she wanted to shout with it. Instead, she said, "It was just a year ago that I met you. Remember, Tysen? I was stuck in one of those dratted sheep killers and you hauled me out."

"The luckiest day of my life," he said.

She was silent a moment, the sun filling the sky now, the warmth on her face. She closed her eyes for a moment, her head on his shoulder, and said against his throat, "And mine as well."